BINGO KING

A Murder Mystery

ROBERT ROEHL

© 2017 Robert Roehl
All rights reserved.

ISBN: 1545482594
ISBN 13: 9781545482599

Bingo King is a work of fiction. Although *inspired by* various rumors, hearsay and fake news accounts about certain people *allegedly* behaving badly throughout the late 80s and early 90s, the events, names, characters, businesses and incidents described herein are products of the author's imagination and used in a creative and fictitious manner. Any resemblance to actual persons, living or dead, or actual events is entirely and completely coincidental.

For my mother,

Liliana Anita Brini

Acknowledgements

I would like to thank Charles Stirum and William Hobbs without whose contributions…seriously. I am also grateful for the artistic eye of Lisa McGuire… And to Bob Nevans whose early encouragement… and Karen Roehl whose support… Also, Mike and Pat Shields who were there when… And special thanks to William Jordan and, especially, Barbara Wright who inspired me to…

Chapter 1

"**B**-15!" the caller sang. "Be-e-e-e...fif-te-e-e-n-n-n."

Saturday night and I found myself leaning against the pickle bar at Clancy's Bingo City mulling over the meaning of life, or lack thereof. I wondered about time, the ebb and flow, its intractability, the excruciating minutiae of its passage. Standing here amid the game in full swing, change was barely detectable, marked only by the recurrent drone of random numbers called.

"N-37!" the man intoned. "E-e-e-n-n-n-n...thirty-seven-n-n."

The congregation in front of me did nothing to inspire my thoughts from the absurd. Under dull florescent glow, the players slumped in rows along the end-to-end tables, heads bowed, shoulders hunched forward, hands hovering over their playing cards. Mostly white but quite a few Hispanics, fewer blacks and Asians, a low-rent version of the American pie. Every one my eyes lit upon was too fat or too thin and there wasn't a fashionable piece of clothing in the place. They came to play, dressed for comfort, some looking like they only just made it out of their Lay-Z-Boys to get here.

A large number of older folks peppered the room but not so many as you might think, and women outnumbered the men, by about four to one. Most wore no makeup but the few that did had slathered on enough for everyone. Of the many variations on the family theme, the man of the family was absent from most of them and children under ten were scarce and knew to keep quiet during a game.

And then there were the hardcore players, compulsives on the cheap, sitting alone, marking their territory with three sheets fanned out in front of them. That's eighteen games simultaneously. Their Day-Glo daubers dangled from crooked hands, pecking at their cards like a buzzard's beaks to road-kill, their faces intense yet flaccid, their eyes glazed over like someone who'd watched every minute of a Jerry Lewis Telethon. I wouldn't put it past them.

"I-18!" the caller said. "I-i-i-e-e-e...eight-e-e-e-n-n."

Plumes of smoke rose and swayed and thinned out along the strip lighting overhead. The incessant hum of ceiling-mounted blowers did little to dispel the haze. From where I stood, the simmering nachos cheese-food and the oily heat from the popcorn maker dampened the reek of second-hand smoke, creating a viscous mixture of aromas that, over time, coated my tongue and throat and tied my stomach into a knot. Maybe that's all that was bothering me. I wouldn't be the first armchair philosopher to mistake indigestion for *angst*.

Undercover for a month now, the job was looking as trite and farcical as it had sounded the first time my former boss at the DA's office proposed it to me. But the severance they had packed me off with several months before had dwindled down to nothing and I wasn't making dick as a private dick. It seems you *had* to do divorces if you wanted work and it didn't take long for me to figure out why those haughty heroes in Raymond Chandler's world disdained to take it on.

I came in early six days a week, hit the lights and pushed a broom, then loitered with the moonlighting cops that pretended to do security and pretended to do it for free. They get paid in cash and don't report it and that's about all I'd seen in the way of crime. As doorman, would-be bouncer and part-time go-fer, I wasn't seeing anything that justified a fraud investigation by the Denver district attorney.

Still... The bingo industry: $300 million a year in reported revenues in Colorado alone, $5 billion nationally and I hear it's big in Europe.

Regulated here by the secretary of state and undertaken for the sole purpose of raising funds for non-profit organizations. Supposedly. Church raffles, Boy Scout troops, the B.P.O.E. and Loyal Order of the Moose, and every other Catholic school that had a pep club or soccer team in need of uniforms. So what if the operators skimmed some off the top? So what if the most recently elected secretary of state was soft on enforcement? The crime, if there was one, was as slow and boring and small-time as the game itself.

"G-52!" the man called out. "Ge-e-e-e-e-e...fifty...*two!*" He was getting into it.

In spite of my mood, I had to admit that the crowd I looked down on was neither as bored nor as boring as me. And it was precisely in that moment of commiseration, of self-loathing, of wishing for something to happen, that headlight beams swept across the bank of full-length windows at the front of the building. The players, in the full stupor of the game, didn't even cock an ear.

A late-model Caddy pulled up across the handicap spaces and then just sat there. Wide white-wall tires and a pastel paint job with the faux-leather top. Brand-new money or a pimp-mobile, not all that suspicious in itself. Could be someone's ride or a curious cruise-by looking for action. The occupants remained shrouded behind lights reflecting on tinted glass.

The hall manager, a slick and wiry Caucasian named Eddie Lyons, rested one butt cheek on the hot-food counter and leaned toward the underage Girl Scout volunteer on the other side, talking low, making time. I thought about strolling over there, bringing the Caddy to Eddie's attention. The girl smiled shyly then dropped her head with muffled laughter. I decided not to bother.

That was my first mistake. Just beyond them, the Caddy's doors swung open and I saw, to my astonishment, the short barrel and fat butt of a sawed-off shotgun profiled above the car's roofline. A jolt of adrenaline riveted me in place as I watched two men in black climb out, wool hats with eye-holes coming down over their faces. A third man—tall and gaunt, heavily inked skinny arms—circled around the driver's side, sunglasses and a fake beard his disguise, a ZZ Top knock-off. As they came through the entrance, I slid out of sight down the hallway. My back against the wall, I thought about the gun in my car, and waited for something to happen.

"B-1! *Be* one, be *one*," the caller joked. "Be-e-e-e-e-e-e…one."

So quiet, I thought I might have dreamt it. Peeking around the corner, I watched Eddie being led by the collar, a good-sized handgun shoved into his ear. They made straight for the office. Eddie's eyes bulged and his lips moved but no sound came out. The other two took up posts by the door, the ZZ Top look-alike dancing in place, striking Rambo stances, fending off imaginary attackers. The players, facing away from him, didn't know to be impressed. The petrified Girl Scout finally squeaked out a puppy-yelp. Heads came up, eyes pulled reluctantly away from their numbered sheets. Behind the podium, his vision blinded by the spotlight on his face, the caller droned on oblivious.

"O-65!" he said. "O-o-o-o-o-o-o… sixty-five."

"Oh my God!" a woman blurted and that finally got things going.

"Everybody *fucking* sit tight," ZZ Top yelled, his voice high-pitched and edgy. "No one gets hurt."

Finding that hard to believe, the crowd went into a kind of subdued hysteria. Whispers grew in volume, mothers beckoned to their kids, chairs scooted sideways along the floor. A few folks raised their hands reflexively, ready to surrender.

Even through the adrenaline, the scene struck me as comical. Three guys with guns and a hundred and fifty hostages? Who holds up a bingo hall? What were they thinking? What would they do if the crowd panicked? Which gave me the idea. It seemed a little rash but I'm not one to stand by for bad theatrics. Besides, what could happen? I backed down to the end of the hallway and, in the furnace room, flipped open the fuse-box. I tripped the main breaker.

Darkness blanketed the entire hall and that's when the real noise started. Screams and shouts filled the air, furniture clattered to the floor, and a terrible crash of glass exploded at the back end of the room.

I broke into a jog along the wall with an idea—not fully thought out—to outflank these amateur holdup boys on their way out the entrance. Rounding the corner with abandon, I slammed full-length into a body crossing my path. Long hair engulfed my face as we went down in a heap. The woman absorbed much of the fall but my head whip-lashed above her, hitting the floor with a thump. I saw stars as I turned my gaze towards the front of the room. Gray backlight cast the two men with guns in silhouette. The bearded one stepped forward and took aim at the ceiling. His shotgun went off with a tremendous blast. Flames creased the darkness at an upward angle like short-range fireworks, illuminating for an instant, the chaos of tangled human figures swimming drunkenly. The shrieking hit a wild crescendo. Pieces of ceiling tile rained down upon us. I huddled over the body stirring beneath me.

"C'mon!" yelled the high-pitched gunman. "Let's get outta here!"

Two more shots sounded off from where the office was—pops from a smaller caliber gun. Then the third man appeared and bounded towards the exit.

Still dazed, I rolled away and struggled to disentangle myself.

"Ouch, goddammit," the woman cried and clubbed me hard to head. I half rolled, half fell sideways as she kicked at me and pulled away.

"Jesus Christ. Take it easy."

"Henry? Is that you?"

"Claire?"

A second shotgun blast cut short the exchange, exploding through the transom window and taking out the Bingo City purple neon above the doors. Glass shards tinkled along the linolcum as I again huddled over Claire. The cacophony of human noises rose and united into one frightened outcry. Then the room went strangely quiet.

I heard the deep groan of the Caddy's engine as the car pulled away.

Someone moaned in the darkness. Disembodied voices began to speak.

"Peter? Where are you?"

"Is that you, mom?"

"Martha? You all right?"

Rolling away from Claire, this time without getting kicked, I craned my neck around a fallen table to see the taillights of the Caddy fifty yards gone and turning out of sight.

"What's happened?" Claire asked, sniffling loudly.

"It's all right. They're gone. You okay?"

She sniffled again. "I think you broke my nose."

"Someone get the lights!" an invisible man demanded from a distance.

"Wait here," I told Claire, then made my way down the hall. Still light-headed, it took a few tries to find the right door and the breaker box inside. When I flipped it on, a unified groan stirred and gathered force. Someone began to cry. Then children joined in as if on cue.

A man's deep voice drawled, "Holy *shit*!" And as I came back into the room, I saw what he meant. Tables overturned or shoved out of line, chairs tossed and scattered, people strewn along the floor amongst the rubble. They moved slowly or not at all, exchanging wide-eyed stares, looks of surprised self-awareness. One of the floor-to-ceiling panes of glass that enclosed the non-smokers had shattered into a thousand pieces of costume jewelry. A beefy man in his fifties sat in the middle of the gleaming shards holding bloody hands in front of his face in disbelief.

The girl who had been flirting with Eddie sat scrunched against the counter, curled up in a ball, her forehead against her knees. A woman went there to comfort her, but the girl pointed towards the office, whining indecipherably. The woman's eyes widened at what she saw and she moved that way. Something was wrong up there. But I couldn't leave Claire bleeding at my feet.

"Aren't you going to help a lady out?" she said.

Leaning back, she held one hand over her nose. Droplets of blood streaked the front of her white shirt. I pulled her hand away. It might not be broken, but it was already swelling.

"Let's get you to the bathroom," I said, bringing her to her feet.

A woman's voice cut through the commotion behind me. "It's Eddie! He's shot!"

The desperate tone made Claire jerk from my grip and dash towards the office.

Eddie lay sprawled and slack-looking in the open doorway. A pool of blood formed beneath his dark-stained pant-legs.

"Eddie!" Claire moaned, shoving her way past two people crouched at his side. Kneeling down, she cradled his head. "Don't you die, goddammit. Don't you die."

Eddie's head lolled in her hands and his eyes rolled a bit. But then I caught a sidelong smile widening his lips as he looked up and focused on Claire's worried features. He groaned and said, "I think I been shot."

A man ripped open one of his pant-legs and I tended to the other. One bullet had entered his left thigh dead center. Blood oozed steadily from beneath it. We rolled him over and I applied pressure above the wound.

"Somebody call an ambulance," I said.

"Better get the cops, too," said a voice from behind me.

Yeah. Better get the cops

Chapter 2

Up until a few months ago, I worked for Luis Sanchez at the Office of the Denver District Attorney as an aide—to the assistant—of the deputy—DA. It was a pretty low rung on the ladder, but it paid the bills. And it got me working with a lot of cops. Even though this was Aurora and it wasn't likely that anyone from their PD would know my face, I didn't want to risk some local cruiser jockey blowing my cover in front of all my new-found bingo buddies. So when the first patrol cars arrived—sirens blaring, lights full on—a few minutes after the ambulance, as I went to rinse out my handkerchief for Claire, I perused the room for routes of escape. No path seemed clear.

One of the cops parted the throng gathered around Eddie. Leaning over the EMTs who had beat them to the scene, he squinted down at the gruesome details. "How bad is it?"

"Gunshot wounds in both legs. One of them is opened up pretty bad. We gotta send him."

"He's not gonna die, is he?" The cop sounded perturbed.

The paramedic took pause to give him a look, his blue-gloved hands still pressing above the wound. "It's not a homicide, if that's what you mean. As long as we get him out of here."

"Where you taking him?"

"Aurora General."

The cop nodded, frowned, and turned to the nervously chattering assembly. "What a mess," he said in passing.

I dampened my handkerchief and went back over to Claire. She leaned against me, shaking as I wiped the blood from her face. When the EMTs put Eddie on a stretcher and cut their way through the chaos, I guided Claire along their wake, grimacing like a concerned family member. We made it out to the ambulance, no questions asked.

"You'll be all right, Eddie," Claire half-shouted as they loaded him in. Eddie didn't respond.

The paramedic turned to Claire. He gently pulled her hand away from her face. "That your husband?"

"Yeah…no. He's my ex."

"He'll be all right. As for you, I'd say your nose is broken. Can you get yourself to the emergency room?"

"I'll take her," I said.

She was one of the few full-timers working the hall, younger than the other paid employees and cut from a different cloth. I had noticed her early on and found her easy to talk to and nice to look at, had spent some time thinking about ways to get to know her. Breaking her nose was not an approach I had considered.

I led her in a wide arch through the parking lot and around the side of the building to my car. As I opened her door, inquisitive eyes took me in from above the handkerchief.

"Are you in trouble with the cops, Henry?"

"I just don't like dealing with them."

We drove fast down the wide empty lanes. Claire gazed ahead, unconcerned. Passing streetlights cast a silvery pallor over the texture of her hair.

"You know they're going to want to know who turned out the lights."

"Not sure *that* was a good idea."

"You kidding? You'll probably be a hero." I thought I detected a note of sarcasm but it dropped away when she added, "Running full-speed through the darkness though…not so bright."

"Yeah, no, I'm really sorry, Claire." She sniffled in silence. I groped for a change of subject. "At least your daughter wasn't there."

"Thank God. She's with her grandparents. Maybe I should think twice about bringing her in anymore." A short silence lingered that she apparently found awkward. "I had this hot date for the weekend," she said, sounding strangely enthused. "We were going to drive up to the mountains, see the aspens turning." She laughed then sniffled and grimaced with pain. "The jerk called this morning to cancel. Eventually, I figured out his wife didn't like the idea."

I didn't have anything to say about that.

"I guess I'm just feeling sorry for myself."

"I don't blame you. I feel that way every time someone pops me in the face."

She started to laugh then stopped abruptly.

"Don't say anything funny."

"Not usually my problem."

She laughed again then snorted and cringed.

"I'm sorry. I'll shut up now.

Just through the swinging doors of the emergency room, a green-clad nurse met us and led Claire away amid a flurry of kindly but quick questions. I sauntered further down the corridor, peeking through doorways and between parted curtains. I found Eddie laid out in his boxers with tubes attached to his arms and two doctor-types working on his legs. I waited until they moved on then I went in to see him, drawing the curtains fully closed.

Eddie's eyes were closed but his breathing was heavy and when I touched him he moved his head and pried open one eye. He was already flying high on a morphine drip. He blinked at the sight of me, as if to dispel the possibility of hallucinations. Even through the antiseptic odor of the room I could smell his sweat.

"Henry?"

"How you doin' there, Eddie?"

"Sons a' bitches…shot me," he said between breaths.

"Yeah, I can see that."

"What you doin' here?"

"I brought Claire in."

"Claire? She here to see me?" An insipid smile blossomed on his face.

"Well, actually, she got hurt."

"What happened? She all right?"

"Yeah, nothing serious. She got hit when the lights went out. I think her nose is broken."

"I'll get those sons a' bitches," he slurred.

I thought it best not to explain further. "Do you know who they were, Eddie?"

"Nah, they had masks." As if I hadn't been there. "He knew my name though, Henry. The one that shot me? He said, 'Let's go, Eddie,' when he was pushin' me to the office."

"He say anything else?"

"He told me to open the safe…he knew where the drop box was, behind the desk. Shoved me over there. That's when the lights went out." He smiled as if pleased by the memory. His eyelids began to sag. The painkillers were coming on.

"Eddie," I said, speaking sharply, "did you recognize the voice? Was it someone we know?"

"Yeah, yeah, I was just thinkin'… can't really…place it…"

"Eddie?"

No response. His breathing had slowed into a deep heavy rhythm. I figured he was out but when I turned to go he came back to life. "Henry," he stammered. "Tell Frank, will ya? Tell Frank what happened." He tilted his head and eyed me forlornly. "Tell him I didn' lay down for them sons a' bitches."

"I'll do that, Eddie. You did all right."

His eyes closed, his head rolled back, a sloppy wet grin dragging down one side of his mouth.

Chapter 3

On the drive away from there, Claire started in on how she felt about Eddie some years back. She was twenty, a single mom, and not particularly happy about it. He was an older man by her standards, nice clothes, a nice car, lots of friends, everybody seemed to like him. Plus he was part of the family, she said.

"What family is that?"

"The bingo family," she snipped, "Frank Coyne and all them. As it turned out his social circle didn't extend much beyond it but I didn't care at the time. I guess I didn't know any better. Honestly, I needed help. When Eddie came along, I thought my problems were solved."

"So he's not Shanie's father?"

"Heck no," surprised I would ask. "He really liked Shanie though, at first, anyway. We got married…I don't know, it wasn't exactly a marriage of convenience but…I was so *young*. Immature is probably a better word. I don't know what I was thinking."

I figured that wasn't the whole story but I had no reason to press.

"Shanie was a handful. I wasn't a great mom maybe but eventually I got the hang of it. About that same time Eddie lost interest. He started working more nights. Then he was gone all the time, even the nights he didn't work. I didn't take that too well."

"How is he about Shanie now?"

"He's the only father she's ever known." She stopped talking and it made me look over at her. She was looking away, preoccupied with wherever that particular thought had led her—probably to the father Shanie doesn't know. "Anyway, that isn't much lately. He hardly sees her outside of Clancy's. That's one reason why I bring her in." After a moment she added, "Maybe not so much anymore..."

She directed me off the freeway and through a curved layout of streets lined with fifties-style tract homes looking too small for their yards. Claire's was a red brick bungalow with a pyramid roof, situated on a well-tended corner lot. White shutters bordered the windows and the porch light was on, a glaring yellow bulb harassing the insects.

I walked her to the door.

"I'd invite you in but under the circumstances..." She smiled a pathetic, crooked smile. She had taken the cotton swabs out of her nostrils but her features remained swollen and the discoloring had deepened towards Day-Glo purple.

"Maybe another time."

"You mean it?" She turned away to unlock the door then pushed it open with what could have been an inviting sweep of her arm.

"Sure," I said, much too late. "We could do that."

"Yeah, sure," she said, sounding miffed. "Anyway, thanks for the black eye."

"Listen, Claire. I'm really sorry. You have to let me make it up."

"I'm just teasing you, Henry. I should be thanking you for...what the hell was that, anyway? Men with masks and guns in the middle of a game? It's like something you'd see in the movies." A visible shiver ran through her and she gripped the edge of the doorjamb.

I reached out. Her eyes met mine with a look of fear. "Why'd they shoot Eddie?"

She leaned into me, her hair smelling of sweet shampoo and something else, something tangy and stirring, like the fumes from cognac. I had drifted into savoring it when she turned her face upward, looking for a response.

"Maybe he resisted," I said. "Trying to be a hero."

"He'd just hand it over, if I know Eddie."

"Then I'd say Frank Coyne has some mean competition."

"C'mon. It's just bingo."

"You know it's more than that to them. There's some out-of-staters moving in on Frank's turf. I would imagine he's made them feel less than welcome." Just like that, I was working her.

Frank Coyne was Eddie's boss. Mine too, for that matter, though I'd only met him briefly. His family held enough licenses to corner the market on bingo and raffles in most of the metro area. He sat on the board of several bingo-financed charitable organizations and he owned a piece of the only bingo supply house in the mountain states. The gossip that he also owned a few cops was probably hyperbole but he did sponsor the annual Policeman's Charity Ball, sidling around with that crowd as well as entry-level local politicians, school board members, city council members. And everyone said that he bought the election for Secretary of State Marcia Herrera. When it came to bingo in Colorado, Frank Coyne was the man. After tonight, I was beginning to think that was no joke.

"Are you saying this was some kind of gang-war Mafia thing?" Claire asked. "C'mon Henry, this is a Catholic fund-raiser. I get tuition for Shanie at St. Mary's as a trade-out."

"That's illegal, you know," I said, giving her my clever smile. "And I bet that's not all you get, considering the hours you put in."

Her eyebrows arched. "And what do *you* get?"

"I get paid cash. Good money. Under the table."

She stared at me bright-eyed and brassy, like she'd unmasked me. "I gotta go to the bathroom," she said and turned and disappeared down a hallway. I was left standing there—half in, half out.

I stepped into the small, uncluttered living room, made smaller by the richness of the rust-colored walls. There was a lamp glowing low in the corner where two comfortable-looking stuffed chairs flanked an oak end table. The chairs almost faced each other, as if arranged for a leisurely game of chess or rummy or, more likely, 'go fish' considering Shanie's age. An archway beyond opened into the cramped dinette/kitchen. Schoolbooks spilled out of a pink backpack on the table. It was a real home, warm and cozy and safe. Closing the front door behind me, I felt like a snake slithering under it.

Claire returned wearing a clean white top that followed the contours of her breasts and waistline and black jeans that left no room for miscalculation. Her dark hair, brushed back, fell in thick waves to the shoulders. She made for the kitchen, pretending not to notice the male gaze she had elicited.

"Want some coffee? I've got decaf."

"Coffee sounds good."

Claire cleared the table then turned away, busy at the kitchen counter. "So you're the hired muscle from out of state?" I laughed and she kept right on. "Big strong guy like you. Come in to shore-up Frank's army? Horse's head between the sheets? That sort of thing?"

A cynical sense of humor is so much more charming in a woman.

"I just help run the games. Did this sort of thing up in Seattle. My family's from here. I came back to get out of the rain."

"Did you know Milo Finnes?"

A red flag. One of the names Luis Sanchez told me to listen for. What Milo Finnes left behind in Seattle, after they ran him out of town, was part of my cover. A well-planted police informant still working that scene for a Washington State organized crime task-force supplied us with history and some names to drop, as well as Milo Finnes as a strong lead. The clock was ticking on that operation, so I'd been told. When they moved to indict, my cover would be blown. I would be forewarned. Supposedly.

"Does he work for Frank now?" I asked, although I knew he didn't.

"Used to. He's from the Northwest too. I was around when he moved here."

"I didn't know him back then, but I worked with some of his people."

"I never liked the guy," she said.

"Okay, me neither."

She brought my coffee and sat across from me and eyed me above an ice-packed washcloth she held to her face.

"He's supposed to be moving in on them."

"So it's not news to you."

Claire shrugged. "My brother's in on all this stuff."

"Your brother?"

"Mickey. Gilmore. You know him, don't you?"

Another flag. One of Frank Coyne's lieutenants of long standing.

"Yeah, I met him. Stocky guy, blonde hair. Doesn't look much like you, though."

She dropped her eyes and smiled minutely, like I had paid her a rash compliment.

"So *he* says they're moving in on Frank?"

She nodded vaguely, dropping her gaze. "He doesn't say much. Doesn't want me getting involved."

"You think this Milo Finnes was behind tonight's fiasco?" I asked, trying to make it sound farfetched.

"*I* don't know. The whole thing sounds insane to me. You're the one who got me started. Couldn't it just be a hold-up? That's happened before."

"It happens that someone head-knocks the manager after closing and grabs the cash bag. These games at churches or rented halls where the take is moved off-site at the end of the night. Easy enough target. But this was something else. This was in front of a hundred and fifty people. Three guys with masks and shotguns? Definitely done to intimidate. And shooting Eddie in the legs? You don't aim for the legs if you're stopping someone with a gun."

"How do you know that?"

"The movies," I said. "And even then, you don't see it unless it's convenient for the plot. Not since John Wayne shot the six-gun out of the bad guy's hand on a regular basis."

"Jeez, I didn't think you were that old."

"I'm not *that old*."

Smiling, she reached over and squeezed my hand. "You're an easy target too."

"You give all your prospective dates this hard a time."

"Yes I do," she said, offering a lingering look and the slightest blush in her neck and cheeks. It looked a little goofy within the purple-ish bruises and the swelling. But that didn't stop the air from thickening between us for a few seconds before she withdrew her hand.

"Anyway, time for bed." She stood up. "Thanks for coming in. I needed to wind down from all that. Talking helped."

"You think we figured out who did it?"

"I think we could if we tried."

I thought so too but didn't say it.

"Anyway, that's Frank's problem, not mine, and he can have it. You hang around bingo parlors long enough, you start to like it. Next thing you know you've become your mother."

"My mother would never forgive me," I said.

We didn't kiss goodnight, given the condition of her face. But that was all that held me back. I liked the way she spoke, open and unabashed, and I liked the way she smelled. Part of me was hoping for another sample in the doorway but she saw me off with a wave of fingers and a final distorted grin.

Thinking back, I remembered watching her at Clancy's like I watched everyone there. But she was different. She stood out from the frumpy housewives and nerdy teenagers who usually staffed the games. On the other hand, she did what it took to fit in. And her brother, Mickey, belonged to the inner circle. I wondered how involved she might be. And what she got out of it. And I wondered what kind of jam I'd get into if I pursued her.

Chapter 4

Luis Sanchez called even before my dog woke me for his early morning constitutional. No one staffs the DA's office on Sundays so it surprised me that Luis got wind of what went down. He should have been on his way to church with Consuela and the kids. That's what I told him.

"Too busy doing God's work in the field," he said and I couldn't quite tell if he was jibing me or meant it. "You all right?"

"Yeah, fine." Sitting up on the edge of the bed, I drummed my fingers on the soft spot where my head had met the floor. "The hall manager, Eddie Lyons, caught two bullets in the thighs. Looked like a…"

"I got those files you asked for," he said, cutting me off. "How 'bout I drop them by. You gonna be home for a while."

"Yeah, sure. C'mon over."

I barely had coffee made by the time he knocked on the door. I opened it to find Luis' stocky frame bent over the dog, scratching his brownish mane. He wore his standard attire; navy blue sport coat, white shirt, and gray slacks, but without the red necktie for a change. And he had no files with him.

"You still got this dog, huh? What's his name?"

"Pimpy," I said, expecting the usual comment.

"Yeah, I remember that. Kinda weird."

He stepped in and looked the apartment over as if scanning for probable cause. The place was messy, maybe—what comes from living by myself, or with a dog for a roommate. Luis seemed assured by the shabbiness. His thick Latino features relaxed with a sigh, as if relieved not to find eight-foot marijuana plants lined up against the sliding glass doors.

"Sorry about the phone call," he said. "I wouldn't have called at all but I wanted to make sure it wasn't you who got shot." He smiled as though he'd said something funny. "That coffee I smell?"

Sitting at the kitchen table, Luis' slow brown eyes settled on the thick manila folder that he *had* delivered a month ago. It still had the thick rubber band around it, holding it together. Which, in my mind, didn't prove a thing.

"So it was Eddie Lyons who caught the slugs, huh. Anybody else get hurt?"

"I don't think so. I kind of got the hell out when the cops showed up."

I gave him my version of the events. Without mentioning her name, I told him what I had learned from Claire, including her suspicions about Milo Finnes. "You didn't tell me they'd be shooting up the place. Maybe I should be getting hazard pay for this."

"You're lucky to be getting paid at all from the office," he said, nudging the manila folder, then eyeing me. "Anyway, I did tell you about those other holdups."

"This was something else altogether though. Three masked men, brazen, violent, heavily armed. They were putting on a show, making a point."

"What would that be?" he asked, typically obtuse.

"Hell, Luis, it's your investigation. You tell me."

Luis didn't respond. Pimpy appeared through a half-opened door with a mouth full of dirty sock. He gave me a tail-wag and that, 'let's do something' look he uses on me all the time. I kneaded his furry scalp, calming myself as I soothed him.

"You think Milo Finnes was behind it?" Luis asked eventually. "What kind of proof can you offer? Did you get the plate number from the Caddy?"

"I was too busy dodging buckshot."

That slowed him but he stayed with his point. "I don't see what Finnes would have to gain."

"He could be trying to scare off Frank Coyne's clientele, get them to change their habits, start coming to his clubs instead."

"Doesn't sound like good business." Luis' calm, almost languid demeanor was legion among his cohorts. On the witness stand, he sat unmoved and unperturbed for as long as the defense attorneys cared to take to ramble through their speculations. And in the interrogation room, his deliberate, plodding style and those steady brown eyes wore away at the most complex alibis like Chinese water torture. Criminals, as a rule, are not a patient lot. Given time, Luis gets to most of them. Unfortunately, he gets to me too.

"You got another theory or you just want me back down there turning out the lights every time thugs drop by to shoot up the place?"

"I'm not so sure that was a good idea."

"What?"

"Turning out the lights."

"*What?*"

"You're not in there to stop robberies, Henry."

"I had to do something."

"Why?" he snapped. "What *are* you there for?"

I wanted to say I'd been asking myself that same question. But that wouldn't go. He wouldn't understand my predicament. Or he understood it all too well. Either way, I had nothing to say.

"There's no place here for wild heroics, Henry. Draws too much attention. You've got to be subtle. Like I told you before, win their confidence, commit to their operation. It takes time to infiltrate a group like this. Anyway, it's steady work, isn't it?"

"It's boring work, Luis."

"Yeah, but you're good at this. Besides, what else you gonna do? Sit around here and contemplate your private dick…business?" He pretended to hold back a smile.

"This what you came by to tell me?"

"No," he said and waited until our eyes met. "There was another shooting, Henry. I want you to tell you to be careful."

"What other shooting?"

"It was some time ago, '89. A guy got grabbed up from a bingo hall. They walked out into a field northeast of the old airport. He took a bullet in the back of the head. Kneeling position, hands taped behind his back."

"Execution style."

"Clearly meant to look that way."

"Who was it?"

"Another operator from Milo's old turf, name of Harvey Cline. He left Seattle a couple years previous, apparently to avoid a similar fate. But that was before the current investigation up there got underway, so they don't have much on him. Rumors were he skimmed the house take a little too deep. So they made an example."

"These guys from Seattle took him out?"

"No, they just rode him out of town."

"Then you don't know who killed him."

"Oh yeah, we got a pretty good idea." He said it like he wanted me to guess. "Your predecessor has been a little slow to divulge everything."

"You mean *your* investigator for the secretary of state?"

"Former investigator, the one who got fired. He gave us this file." He gestured to the folder on the table. "Did you look at it?"

"I didn't see any mention of a professional execution," I said, thinking it was a safe guess.

"'Cause it's not in there. But what *is* in there—the stuff he found out about the increased revenues—that's what got him fired when Herrera took over as secretary of state. Now he's suing her for unlawful dismissal. So he's lawyered up about that. But I finally got to him last week off the record. He couldn't say any more about this," he said, tapping the folder, "but the Cline killing wasn't part of it. I guess the secretary of state isn't particularly interested in murder. He brought it up when I told him I had a man in the field. The suspects in that are still workin' this bingo scene."

"So who, Luis?"

Luis smiled and shook his head, as if disappointed. "This Harvey Cline was thick with Mickey Gilmore. Came into the organization with all kinds of ideas about expanding the operation. Apparently, Frank Coyne didn't take to it, so Cline and Gilmore went out on their own, opened a hall. Gilmore bankrolled the scheme. But something went sour."

"So Mickey Gilmore took him out?" I said, wondering if this was why her brother didn't want Claire getting in too deep.

"That's the word," Luis said. "The grapevine was livid at the time. Everyone in the bingo world seemed to know what happened and why."

The bingo world. Another planet all together.

"What's with all these thugs from the Northwest?" I said. "Not exactly a hot-bed of organized crime."

"Lots of bingo up there, apparently. Maybe the rain drives them indoors. They figured upwards of $60 million a year going unreported back when, so they tightened the laws. This was eight, nine years ago. And they gave enforcement over to the state attorney general, like they ought to do here. Lots of operators got squeezed out. Started looking for softer terrain. When Herrera got elected here, word got out. Sort of an all-clear signal when she fired her entire investigative staff—which was only two guys anyway. They've been moving in ever since."

I shook my head, trying to picture thousands of people, millions maybe, across the nation hunkered over their playing cards.

"Jesus, Luis, why don't we just let them have their fun? I mean, so what if they're skimming a little? They'd just be making book or rigging slots in Central City instead, wouldn't they? Why don't we go after Herrera?"

Luis waited a few ticks to see if I was finished. Then he said, "We are."

"The secretary of state?"

"And a few of her girl-friends. You remember Rhonda Schomberg?"

"Sure. Big deal Republican lobbyist back in the '80's. Headed up that movement to keep the Olympics out, didn't she?"

"That was '85, when she was mayor of Wellshire Village. It was some time after that she became a lobbyist."

"I didn't know she carried much weight anymore."

Luis filled me in on a decade of hard times for Rhonda Schomberg. I tried to look interested while he worked his way into the current era. Four years ago Schomberg took Marcia Herrera under her wing and lifted her from mid-level clerical worker in the state bureaucracy to viable contender for the Office of Secretary of State. It didn't hurt that she was Latino, female, and willing to be a Republican. Or that the Democratic frontrunner had an outside woman whose head popped up from under his desk for an indelicate selfie just weeks before the election.

"But why?" I asked. "I mean, there's no money in a secretary of state's election."

"Well, Schomberg's driving a new Lincoln Towncar these days. Guess who paid for it?"

"Marcia Herrera?"

Luis smiled. "Frank Coyne."

"Really?"

"And in '96, the year Herrera got elected? Schomberg reported over a hundred K in income. And that's above and beyond some cushy write-offs."

"Where's that coming from?"

"Most of it comes from BACCO."

I looked at him expectantly.

"It's in the file, Henry."

"I must have missed it." I snapped the rubber band off the folder.

"It's an acronym," Luis hinted.

"Let's see," I said, "Bingo Association of Colorado…."

"…Charity Organization. Frank Coyne's main dummy corporation. His sister, Tanya, is also on the board. Tanya Gilmore."

"As in Mickey Gilmore."

"Her husband, strictly speaking, though I gather it's more of a marriage of mutual interests by now."

"So they're paying Schomberg to grease the wheels. But lobbyists aren't bound by campaign law."

"All perfectly legal, as they say. But there's more money than that floating around. Eight hundred thou went from BACCO into the coffers of a PAC called American Community Services. Non-profit, of course, so their records are public. Guess who's on the board."

"Frank Coyne?"

"His father, Willard Coyne. And, of course…Tanya Gilmore."

"This *is* getting rich," I said flipping through the loose pages in the file. "What about campaign contributions?"

"Yeah, Herrera's committee reported over three hundred K for that race. Broke the record by half. A big chunk came from American Community Services but there was other PAC money in there too. The Republicans loved having a female Hispanic on the ticket."

"*Viva las mujeras*," I said, taking a stab at it in his native tongue.

"Very good, Henry. You've been practicing?"

"I'm trying to get on your good side."

"Keep workin' at it," he slurred. "Anyway, that's not your end. What we want you to do is find out where the extra cash is coming from."

"That's obvious, isn't it? These bingo games are cash cows."

"Yeah, but they're *reporting* more now. And I don't think they've had a change of heart about paying taxes. So if they're reporting more, they're hiding more. And attendance isn't up at these halls. So…we need to know where it's coming from. We need documentation. We need their books. And we need informants, people willing to testify. Barnes is waiting on us to bring it to CBI."

William Barnes is the District Attorney, Luis' boss and my ex-boss. Strictly speaking, I was working for him now, apparently on an undefined contract basis—as in, no actual contract. Luis had been sketchy about the details, which was fine by me. My last gig under the auspices of the DA's office had led me on a crusade to uncover the truth about my father's death. Suffice it to say I stomped on quite a few official toes trying to shake things loose. In the end, Barnes was kind enough to drop all charges against me in exchange for my going quietly into the night.

"So this is politically motivated," I said. "Barnes wants to bring Herrera down."

"Everything's politics, Henry." Luis spoke with some juice in his voice. "We *work* for politicians. District Attorney Barnes is an *elected* official."

I, personally, hadn't voted for the guy. But even I knew this wasn't a good time to mention it. "So why didn't you tell me about Herrera and Schomberg before? You have to know that's more up my alley."

"Because I didn't want you barging into the secretary of state's office slinging wild accusations or breaking into Schomberg's house to steal a bunch of supposed 'evidence'. What we need here is *admissible* evidence, Henry. We need a little subtlety for a change, which, frankly, is not why I chose you. I'm going against the grain giving you a second chance. You know that, don't you?"

"I appreciate it, Luis."

"Do you know why?"

I thought about it for a moment but didn't come up with anything else. "Because of my father," I said.

"No, that's not it. I need someone I can trust no matter where the investigation goes. Someone independent and someone with an instinct for the lie. That's why I chose you." He paused for effect, but continued before I had a chance to grovel. "Barnes doesn't know anything about your involvement yet. And I don't want him finding out about it in the papers. I don't want him finding out at all until we have something to show him. The last thing I need is you getting on your high horse and charging the warlord's castle."

"This is not the same, Luis."

"Of course not. Everyone assumes your recent…*transgressions* were due to the personal nature of that so-called investigation. Otherwise, you'd be in County." His brown eyes narrowed into a knowing smile, not soft, not joking. "I know better, Henry. I know *you*."

I tried to laugh it off but Luis just shook his head.

"Okay, Luis. I get it. What do you suggest I do next?"

He took a deep breath. "Chase down these rumors. Start a few of your own. People are going to talk about this holdup. You'll have to separate the wheat from the chaff. When you can give us something solid, I can requisition for surveillance, maybe file for wiretaps, cell phone records. But we've got to have more than rumors. We already had rumors."

"All right, I'll lay low, strictly behind the scenes, snuggle up to the principles. You won't hear from me for six months."

"Very funny," he said, getting up and moving toward the door. "You'll check in twice a week via pager, like we said. But don't use your cell and don't call me at the office. And don't confide in the cops. I'll meet you Thursday at Joe's Mug. Eleven o'clock. Don't be late. That's way past my bedtime."

He stopped in the doorway, turned to look at me. I was expecting a parting shot.

"Henry, be careful. I mean it. You don't know what these people are capable of."

I kept a straight face and gave him a nod. It was enough to get him out the room.

Chapter 5

Nothing was open in the L-shaped strip-mall on a Sunday morning but you couldn't tell that from the gathering of cars in front of Clancy's Bingo City. Frank Coyne's teal-green Jag and three late-model Cadillacs took up the spaces nearest the street looking like the front row of an uptown used car dealership. Their precise alignment had me picturing them in a criminal lineup: "You seen any a' these Caddies before, ma'am?" "Yes, that's the one. Number three." "All right, Charlie, hold the beige one with the wide sidewalls. The rest of 'em can take a drive." Cadillacs are the ride of choice among the bingo bigwigs. I tried not to think about it but I suspected some homage to Elvis. Furry dice hung from the rear view mirrors of two of them. Frank Coyne's Jag had them too.

Nearer the building, a police cruiser and two unmarked cop cars filled all the handicap spaces and further along the curb sat a City of Aurora inspector's vehicle and a red SUV from the fire department. Backed up to the front doors, a monster-truck-sized Ram Charger with **O'Connor Construction** and a wavy American flag stenciled on its door was being loaded with debris.

The buckshot blasted glass above the doors had been replaced with plywood sheeting and the Bingo City sign lay on the sidewalk face down. A tangle of electrical wiring trailed from its split seam like spilled innards. Hardhats in shirtsleeves stood surrounding it casually regarding the jagged hole in its backside. Heads turned as I eased my aging Mercedes by the scene and pulled up at the end of the Caddy lineup.

As I emerged from the car, Mickey Gilmore came out the front door shoulder to shoulder with an overdressed, high-priced looking dame that I guessed to be his wife—and Frank Coyne's sister—Tanya. They were striding along akimbo in a kind of anger-embracing tango, leaning in and grousing low into each other's faces, oblivious to where I stood in their path. They pulled up just short of colliding with me, Mickey looking surprised and Tanya annoyed. He stopped in mid-sentence while she went on to make her point, giving me a glance that put me in my place.

"Where the hell've you been?" Mickey finally managed.

"Well, I…"

Collecting himself, he glanced at his wife, then said, "Tanya, this is Henry Burkhart,"

"You!" she said, as if to some troublesome kid who had finally been caught out. Heavy mascara darkened her wide-set brown eyes and the expensive blond dye-job, done up in a youthful bob, contrasted nicely with her salon-tanned shoulders. She had muscular arms and a sinuous, almost masculine frame. The bare-shouldered dress, a satiny burnt sienna accented with black lace and fake fur trim—and all that makeup—made her look a little butch, like a drag queen decked out for the alt-prom. I wondered what kind of church service she might have just come from.

Mickey's thick features broke into a chummy if disingenuous smile. "Nice work last night, Henry, turning out the lights. Coulda been a nasty situation." Wide-eyed, he held out a hand to be shaken.

"I'm not so sure that was a good idea," his wife commented, echoing Luis verbatim.

"Let us have a minute, Tanya, will ya?" The strength of his after-shave engulfed me as he turned me away with an arm around my shoulders.

"I'm talking to the insurance agent," Tanya tossed out, having the last word.

"Yeah, yeah," Mickey said under his breath. "So. You didn't talk to the cops yet, did ya." There was no inquisitiveness in his lowered tone.

"No, I took Claire to the hospital. Then..."

"Yeah, she told me you took her home. You're gonna have to talk to them today though. Couple of 'em here now. But I don't want you sayin' anything...*interesting*. Know what I mean?" His eyes held mine long and hard to make it clear he wanted my agreement even if I didn't know what he meant.

"I'd just as soon not talk to them at all."

"Yeah, well, that can't be helped. Might as well get it over with. But we'd kinda like to keep this low profile. Don't wanna give the wrong impression about the game, ya know?"

"Yeah, sure."

"You don't have any ideas anyway, right?" he said, abandoning any last trace of discreetness. "I mean, three hold-up men, wearing masks, you kill the lights, shots were fired, and then they bolted. Okay?"

"That's all I need to tell the cops."

He went on staring at me. "Yeah, good. We'll talk later. Frank wants to see you first." His eyes brightened again and he gave me a pat on the back before guiding me past the milling workers at the entrance. "He's impressed with what you did. Hell, we all are. Our folks in Seattle were right about you."

They had checked on me since last night. Apparently, my references were holding up.

Inside, the place looked like a major remodel well underway. Dust motes floated and flickered in the light above two men pushing brooms. They had formed the broken glass into a mound of crystals at the opening to the smoking area. Men on stepladders handed down buckshot-ridden pieces of ceiling tile. On the floor near the office, the blood from Eddie Lyons' wounds had been mopped up but traces remained, the linoleum squares darkly outlined.

Frank Coyne stood just inside the office door speaking to someone I couldn't see. Although over six feet tall, his hunched shoulders and thin frame made him look frail and nondescript. He wore polyester slacks and a white shirt with short sleeves, buttoned at the collar and tied off with a bolo tie. A few wisps of brown hair arched over his baldpate and horn-rimmed glasses sunk down on the bridge of his Roman nose. With big ears, a wide mouth, and nothing much for a chin, he looked like an aging nerd destined to a life of introversion.

Mickey filled the doorway in front of me and nodded back in my direction.

"Give us a minute, will you boys," Frank said. His voice had a nasal quality but still conveyed a sense of authority. Ushering his lackeys past us, he greeted me in the doorway with an extended hand and an unappealing grin. "Henry Burkhart?" He said it like he couldn't remember if we had met. His nearly colorless eyes took me in, protruding abnormally, enlarged by the thick-lensed glasses. "You're the one who doused the lights, right?"

"Claire tell you about that?"

He nodded and guided me into the office with a soft, cool grip.

"She also tell you I broke her nose?"

He gave that a light chuckle and Mickey joined in from behind us as he closed the door.

"I think she'll forgive you for that," Frank assured me, speaking through a propped up smile. "Did you talk to the cops yet?"

"I told him," Mickey said, before I could answer.

Frank's gaze cut to Mickey, then back to me.

"We got anything to hide?" I said, trying on a conspiratorial grin.

Frank's fake smile widened. "Nothing like that. We just don't want this to get blown out of proportion. It's a robbery. Happens all the time. We don't need any added attention from it, is all."

"That's what I figured. Of course, there's a couple hundred eye-witnesses I've gotta stay consistent with."

"You'd be amazed at the range of descriptions," Mickey put in. "But the gist is like I told you."

"Late-model Cadillac, light colored?"

Both men nodded, their eyes locked onto me.

"You talk to Eddie yet?"

"First thing this morning," Mickey said. "The cops were there last night but, apparently, he was pretty out of it. When they follow up, that'll be his story."

Frank Coyne's bulging eyes shifted between Mickey and me, the phony smile lingering all the while. I focused on him and said, "Did he tell you it was friends of yours?"

The smile gave way around the edges and he feigned a look of mild surprise. "Really?"

"Before he went under last night, he told me they knew him. Called him by his name."

Their eyes stayed with me but neither man spoke.

"They knew about the drop box, too. In the floor behind the desk."

Mickey shuffled in place. "I *told* you."

Frank checked Mickey with a look. "All wild speculation as far as we're concerned."

Mickey frowned and turned away, glaring at nothing.

"Yeah, well, certainly no need to complicate things with hearsay," I said. "Just thought *you* might want to know. If it wasn't an inside job, it was someone who used to work for you."

"Wild speculation," Frank repeated, shooting another look at Mickey. They stared each other down until Frank's dour smile turned more so. Mickey dropped his eyes and sighed audibly, rocking back on his heels. Frank returned his attention to me. "How come you're interested, anyway?"

I shrugged. "This kind of thing went down in Seattle a few years back. Rivalries between operators got out of hand. Certain disloyalties came to the surface. You gotta watch out for your own, ya know?"

"Well, that's a point," Frank said, "But I don't think we have to worry about that around here." He gave a nod of finality.

"Good."

"Listen, there's one other thing. You might want to say you work for Star Foods. That's who runs our concessions here, officially. You don't look like the average volunteer." We exchanged knowing grins. "If we need employment records to back you up, I can do that. Okay?"

"No problem. As long as I don't have to pay taxes."

Low chuckles all around.

"I'll take care of that," Frank said. Grinning broadly, he moved to the door and put his hand on the knob. "We're going to get together with the staff tonight. Try to ease their minds. I'd like you to be there. It'll be out at Bingo Palace, the new place on Parker Road."

"I can do that."

Frank opened the door. "Well, you better give these cops what they want," he said, still holding up that grin.

I stepped through the door and Mickey came up behind me and led me towards three men seated around one of the fold-out tables. A uniform cop sat next to a youthful-looking man who wore a white shirt with the collar open and the sleeves rolled up. He had a badge folded over his shirt pocket. Layers of paperwork spread out in front of them. Dull-eyed and with their heads tilted, they seemed to be enduring a long story from the man seated across from them, a heavyset dandy in upscale spa attire. I had seen this man around the halls, hanging with the security cops and the old boy crew. His salt-and-pepper hair was nicely groomed and his broad face sported a thick black mustache, perfectly trimmed, probably dyed. He had the look of new money about him, though not very much. I pegged him for an ex-cop working for Frank Coyne, loosening his scruples to make green in the private sector. As is the case in national politics and big business—and apparently bingo—there's a demand for inside info, knowing exactly what's legal and what's not, what exactly you can get away with.

The youthful man didn't look much like a cop, but he wore that familiar expression of stony patience that detectives adapt when wading through the rambling bullshit of witnesses wanting to sound important. Both cops looked up when Mickey and I approached as if welcoming the intrusion. The well-dressed man stood and smiled expectantly.

"You met Henry yet?" Mickey said.

"Chuck Burrows," the man said. "Pleased to meet you."

"He's the one who turned out the lights," Mickey boasted.

"Well, well," Burrows said, shaking my hand. "Sure put a wrench in their works."

Amid their chuckles, the youthful detective cleared his throat.

Mickey said, "Henry, this is Detective Scott Harris, Aurora PD. He wants to talk to you."

Without getting up, the detective reached out to shake my hand. "Have a seat." He gestured to the chair Chuck Burrows had barely vacated and, without further niceties, he asked me what happened.

I gave it to him the way we had discussed it. He didn't like the lights-out strategy any better than Luis Sanchez and Tanya Gilmore had. Standing just away from the table, Mickey and Chuck listened in, occasionally turning away to speak in whispers and grunts. Harris glanced up at them several times but they pretended not to notice.

When he had the whole story from me, Harris addressed Mickey and Chuck directly. "Can we have a moment?"

"Sure, Scotty," Chuck said, wryly. "Don't mean to be crampin' your style."

Once they strolled out of earshot, Harris started over. For the second time, he asked where I was from and how long I had been in Denver. Because my cover story had me coming from Seattle, I had to explain the Colorado driver's license.

"I was down visiting my parents. I got pulled over, actually, and discovered my Washington license had expired. You boys were kind enough to overlook that for the moment. I had it reissued here."

Harris frowned as if unhappy with this lapse in law enforcement. "So this is where your parents live?"

"Yeah, it was," I said, wondering if this was going to come back on me down the road. "They've moved away since then. I'm staying with a guy I know up in Five Points." I gave him the address and phone number of a friend I knew I could count on.

The detective seemed satisfied with that but he wasn't done being suspicious. "Mickey rehearse you before we talked?"

I laughed. "He just asked me what I saw. I told him the same stuff I'm telling you. What's to hide?"

Harris shrugged. "Got any idea who did it?"

"What's that supposed to mean?"

"Well, you know, you hear a lot of shit around these games. Just wondered what's on the grapevine."

"I'm not really in the loop, detective. Like I said, I've only been around a few weeks."

"What you doin' working for Frank Coyne?"

"It's a job. I work the concessions, get a paycheck, been in the food business for a while. How come you're a cop?"

He didn't like that. The creases of his frown shifted unevenly, as if someone had grabbed his face and twisted. "Okay, Burkhart, that's all for now. I can reach you at this number?" He tapped on the sheet in front of him. I repeated the number and headed towards the door.

Mickey Gilmore intercepted me on the sidewalk and offered me a smoke.

"Everything all right?"

I took a drag and blew it out. "I don't like cops much."

"They can be your friend, ya know."

I looked at him like I didn't get it. "They're never around when you need one if you ask me."

"Unless they're on your payroll," he said, through a rakish grin.

"You mean like Chuck Burrows?"

"What makes you say that?"

I shrugged. "The way he was hamming it up with those two, I guess."

Mickey nodded, still amused. "He's retired. But he's got connections."

Then his face went serious, assessing me with his eyes. "I appreciate you didn't mention what Eddie said." He stopped and nodded and waited for me to nod back. "Don't be sayin' nothin' to anyone else either though, will ya?"

"You mean like, who?"

"Like the crew—the worker bees and volunteers."

I gave him a quizzical look to see what it would get me.

"We got some ideas of our own, as you might've guessed," he said, aiming a conspiratorial twitch of the eyebrows at me. "We just want to explore it on our own, quiet like. Know what I mean?"

"Yeah, I think so."

"I figured I could trust you." His lips pursed with an affirming gesture. "Anyway, I'll see you tonight."

I got three steps away before he called my name. "Hey, listen," he said, catching up to me. "I just wanted to say…thanks for watching over my little sister. Taking her to the hospital and all."

"Christ, don't thank me. If it wasn't for me, she wouldn't have had to go."

"Well, like Frank said, she forgives you for that." His eyes brightened for an instant. "What'd you have in mind, anyway?"

"You mean, when I ran into her?"

He nodded, smiling, and I smiled back.

"Just trying to get to know her better. The shotgun blast kind of ruined the moment."

"Yeah, them shotguns, they have a tendency to discourage a guy. Anyway, thanks again."

I headed for my car, thinking about Claire and feeling like I was on the right track.

Chapter 6

William Randall Jr. is the only son of a small-time but locally notorious career hustler and prognosticator who goes by the sobriquet of Doctor Randy. From the cramped dining room of his rib joint on East 32nd, the doctor had his finger on the pulse and his eye on the Magic 8-Ball of the Five Points District's shadier subculture throughout the '70s and '80s. But when Willie Jr. came of age, Doctor Randy shipped him off to recently desegregated East coast private schools. This was, no doubt, an attempt to give Willie the opportunities that he, Doctor Randy, and most of his generation had been excluded from. Mostly, it didn't take. To Willie Jr., it was a blatant and repressive attempt to cut him off from his roots and steer him towards 'white boy privilege'. Or that's how he went on about it these days.

I met Willie Jr. as a cellmate in the fishbowl—the Plexiglass-encased holding cell at Denver County Jail. The reason for my incarceration was a slight—to me, anyway—misunderstanding between myself and Captain Tom Connally of the Denver Police Department over the whereabouts of a certain female material witness in a homicide investigation. Suffice it to say that my predicament was sorted out the following day while Willie's dragged on for some time. White boy privilege at work.

During the course of my continued inquiries, I discovered a link between Doctor Randy's connections and the prime—to me, anyway—suspect in a police department cover-up. I managed to strike a deal on Willie's behalf, springing him from County in exchange for a well-oiled introduction to the Doctor which, in fact, produced an honest lead. But once involved, Willie Jr. got way more caught up in the investigation than I had ever intended—or anticipated. He got a taste of the hunt and liked it and, for a while, I couldn't get rid of him. When the case finally broke, Willie was instrumental in its denouement. On that basis, he saw himself as a master of detection and, after my firing from the DA's office, urged me to go into business with him. Randall & Burkhart, Private Investigations. Or, okay, Burkhart & Randall.

In either case, I didn't share his enthusiasm. I did manage to get him a paying gig through my friend and former law-school roommate, Duncan Pruett, at the uptown partnership of Rollins, Jeffery, LLC. It was a paid internship for law students and aspiring legal aides. Willie hated it. He called me to say so at least once a week.

"Gotta get out on the *street*, bro," he would tell me, "run some scams, chase down the *ganstas*, I need a *game*, dog!" His ideas of investigative work may have been loosely formed around watching reruns of "Shaft" and "Superfly" while doing his time in County. I had nothing for him. But he was the first person that came to mind when Luis told me he had money for informants. And when Detective Scott Harris asked where I lived, it was Willie's address I gave.

When he wasn't staying with his fiancé, Willie occupied a slightly refurbished coach house on the alley behind his uncle's home just half a block down from the convoluted intersection of streets that gives Five Points its name. His uncle, Leroy Street, is a wily old codger who, judging by his age alone, must have been the first black lawyer to hang a shingle in this town. He and his wife, Martha, hold the middle ground in the on-again off-again frictions between Willie Jr. and his father. They had made their coach house available to Willie whenever Doctor Randy showed him the door.

I pulled my Mercedes into the graveled space next to the house, but Willie's car wasn't there. He drives a beat-up Mustang that has two bullet holes in the trunk and one in the backseat headrest, mementos from our previous collaboration. His fiancée didn't like that. It was her car. And she had been driving. Since then, Maxine has bequeathed the Mustang to Willie and has given in to doubts about his association with me.

Finding no one home and the door unlocked, I made my way into the pantry area Willie called a kitchen and used his phone to call Maxine's. She answered on the first ring.

"How are you, Henry? Staying out of trouble?"

"Absolutely," I said. "How's school?" Maxine was a serious young woman who drove a school bus part-time to pay her way through grad school. She was strong-willed and determined to make it on her own and, like all of Willie's extended family, keenly protective of her man.

"One more year and I'm out of there. I can't wait. What you doing these days? Still playing cops and robbers?"

"No, no. Just doing some research for my old boss."

"The DA? Uh-huh."

Willie's animated voice beckoned from the background. "My man!"

"I suppose you're looking for Willie," Maxine said, in the tone of a harried mother.

"Yeah, I got a little work for him."

"Work, huh?"

I could hear snippets of Willie's continued ebullience. "What' up? What' he doin'? Lemme talk to that dog, woman."

"Hold *on*, Willie," she said, and then to me, "You're not cooking up another *Lethal Weapon* episode, are you, Henry?"

"Yo, Max-*ine!*" Willie howled.

"Nothing like that, Max. Trust me."

"Uh-huh."

I waited for Willie's rant to take effect.

"*Okay*," she said, probably to both of us. "Here's your boy."

"…gotta give a man some *room*," Willie said, coming onto the phone. "Henry. My man. Ain't that some shit?"

"How's it goin'?"

"Crib gettin' *cramped*, bro. Tell you that."

I heard Maxine going off in the background. "...any time you want," she sang, just before a door closed rather distinctly.

"That desk at R & J gettin' too small, too," Willie continued. "Man needs a change of *pace*."

"It's a good job, Willie. You're rubbing shoulders with some of the best legal minds in the state."

"Yeah, they got some twenty-fi' a' those *legal minds* all hittin' on the same barely legal *white chick* has the same job as me. They get in *line* at that water cooler to fill *her* cup. Don't pay me no mind."

"I'd say you're on the wrong side of that minority, Willie."

"Minority, hell. Women is fifty-one point three per-*cent*, yo!" He said it like it just happened yesterday. "And they all outlive us, ya know? Ridin' us to a early grave."

"Can't live without 'em," I offered.

"I can live without that job," Willie shot back.

"You didn't quit, did you?"

"Nah, but I cut back my hours. Told 'em I was taking some classes." His voice trailed off into a low, lingering chuckle.

"Very clever."

"Don't be sayin' nothin' to Maxine, though," he said, suddenly wary. "She don't need to know every little thing. Dog needs some time to hisself."

"Why aren't you over here, then?"

"What you mean?"

"I'm at your place. It doesn't look like you've wrinkled a..."

"What you doin' at my crib? You break in?"

"Take it easy, Willie. It was unlocked. You in some kind of mood today, or what?"

I could picture Willie's youthful face, the expression of indignation frozen in place. It apparently gave way to something softer.

"Yeah, okay, sorry man," the jive tone dropping away. "We just got off on the wrong foot this morning. Me and Maxine, I mean. Seems like every time we bring up the *M*-word, you know, like last night. Jus' sweet-talkin' an' whatever. Then today, she got some kinda hangover about it, don't let me alone about how hard she's workin', how she's gettin' another *degree*, an' all. Goes on about the *fu*-ture." He said it like it was a dirty word. "Anyway, do me some good to get outta here. What you got?"

"School's a good thing," I said, then immediately regretted it.

"Hey, don't *you* be gettin' in on that shit. I *did* my time with higher ed-u-*ca*-tion. All that done is join you up with the wanna-be capitalist con-*soom*-ers. That and improve your diction so's you can pass for *white* on the phone to your stockbroker."

"Okay, Willie, all right. Let's just call it even and get on to something else."

"Even my ass," Willie slurred, but it was only half-hearted. "What you got for me, anyway?" He said it like I owed him.

"I want you to go undercover with me." Saying it this way, I knew, would pique his interest.

"Ain't that some shit. You jivin' me? We goin' after those cops you let off last time, or what? We goin' into the steamy underworld of vice and corruption?" His low chuckle started up again.

"How about bingo?"

"Bingo? You mean like, what? Bingo what?"

"Bingo. Bingo halls, fraternal organizations and charitable fund-raisers, that sort of thing. The bingo industry grosses more than $300 million a year in Colorado alone…" I faded off, drowned out by Willie's deep rolling laughter.

"Man," Willie said, between guffaws, "My *mama* plays bingo. This ain't nothin' gonna get me in trouble with *her*, is it?"

I had to smile. "Look, Willie, let me tell you about last night. I was out at Clancy's Bingo City. Three guys walked in…"

"*Clancy's* Bingo *City*?"

"…Three guys walk in with guns drawn. One guy caps the manager. The other two blow holes in the ceiling with sawed-offs. The crowd of two hundred goes into a panic. Meanwhile, the perps make off with a safe full of money. Over ten thousand dollars."

"Nah, man. You shitin' me."

"I'm kidding about the money. They didn't get it."

"How come?"

"'Cause I turned out the lights."

Willie thought that was funny too. Not for the first time, his sense of humor was beginning to wear on me.

"Look, Willie. I need some help with this. And I can pay you. But if you don't think it's serious enough crime, you can crawl back behind that desk at Rollins, Jeffery."

"No, no, sorry, Henry. It's just that it sounds so, so…"

I waited for one more comment.

"So what you need?"

"First of all, I need your phone as a contact point for some of my principles."

"Principles of what?"

"Principle targets of the investigation. We're going after the operators of some of these halls. Tax fraud, extortion, money laundering. I need a phone contact as part of my cover."

"You want me taking calls you're gonna have to bump my minutes, man. Maxine's already a total data drain."

"I'd rather have this land line with the message machine. Besides you don't want anyone tracing your cell—location, history, data…if they…"

"Ah, c'mon, man. These bingo bangers are tech heavies, too?"

"You never know…"

"Whatever. What about these shooters? We goin' after them?"

"They'll turn up."

"So what you got for me?"

I told Willie I wanted him to play the games, get known around the halls, talk it up with the players and staff. His street smarts and loquacious personality made him a natural for it, though he lacked any formal training in law enforcement. An intuitive sense for the role is no substitute for experience in the field, especially when it comes down to suspects' rights and rules of evidence. I've had trouble with that myself. I found myself giving him the same lecture about patience and discretion that Luis had given me. Willie listened, somewhat amused, but in the end, pretended to take it seriously.

"Where do I start?"

"I'm not sure yet but I'll know tonight. They're probably moving me to another hall. I want you to start there so you'll be in place to back me up."

"An' what is it I'm scoping for, exactly?"

"Just keep your ears open. These folks love to gossip. There'll be talk about the shooting at Clancy's. Frank Coyne runs it and most of these other halls, but he's getting some competition from a guy named Milo Finnes. He could have done this shoot-up. Sort of an intimidation tactic."

"So you want me to find out about this Finnes fool?"

"No, I just want you to listen. Don't be directing any specific questions about anybody."

"Hey, I *know* how to hang, bro. I been *inside* where you don't even know exists."

"I'm sure you have, Willie" I said, rolling my eyes, "but it's not the 'hood. Most of these folks are white or Hispanic, middle-aged or older. They don't do any cruisin', no bangin', they don't 'get down' on anything and believe me, they aren't your brothers."

"Ah, man, ever'body my brother, bro. Even *you*."

"Wait till you see this bunch before committing yourself," I told him.

Chapter 7

Bingo Palace is out there. From central Denver, you drive southeast for the better part of an hour. The town of Parker, a once quiet roadside farm town, is now a sprawling middle-class suburb, a checkerboard grid of patio homes and cookie-cutter split-levels rolling on for miles across the rise and fall of eastern plains. The monotony of this American Dream is barely distinguishable from its bordering bedroom communities, the houses slightly newer, the trees smaller, and the thoroughfares wider and less worn.

You keep driving until you find the widening of Parker Road still under construction and the housing developments thinning out to a few model homes and desolate looking excavation sites, new curbing laid out like skeletal remains uncovered by prairie winds. The streetlights drop away and stars come out and that's when Bel View Shopping Center appears in the near distance, a newly built island of brick and concrete boxes amid a sea of neatly-lined asphalt; smooth, gray, and linear, and well-lit under an eerie halogen glow.

Doing fifty, I swung the Merc through the empty lot in a wide, reckless arc, imagining a sweeping counter brushstroke across the canvas of Warhol's Campbell's soup cans. My own little rage against the machine.

Cars parked in neat rows—the only sign of life—marked the storefront of Bingo Palace. A glossy canvas banner with three-foot high red lettered—"Grand Opening"—hung slightly festooned above its glass-walled entrance. In contrast to the otherwise darkened facades, the bingo hall's gleaming interior was lit up like an over-sized aquarium. As if taking the plunge into a fish-tank full of badly dressed aliens, I took a deep breath and stepped into the glow.

The place smelled of construction glue and fresh paint, somewhat dampened by the ever-present stench of second-hand smoke. About seventy people occupied less than half the available chairs, hunched over in the usual posture of languid stupefaction.

Frank was calling the game himself, something of a celebrity appearance, no doubt, though he was known as a hands-on operator, one of the folks. He sat above the crowd leaning over an elaborate looking control panel. Mounted on the side of the elevated podium, a clear plastic orb contained the lucky numbers—ping pong balls bouncing and floating like popcorn in the making. Frank's habitual grin drew across his face in a thin line of resoluteness. Plucking out a numbered ball from the feeder tube, his high nasal voice penetrated the silence.

"G-57," he called out. "That's…G…fifty…seven."

The game, in full swing. And Frank Coyne did not sing.

A crowd of staffers—more than you usually see—had gathered along the food counter at the back of the room. I recognized a few faces from the other halls. One of them, a gangly young man who worked at Clancy's, broke free from the group and headed over to greet me.

"Is Mickey here tonight?" I asked, keeping my voice low.

"You kidding?" he said with repressed enthusiasm. "They're all here, all the bingo rock stars."

I searched his adolescent features for signs of sarcasm. Not a hint showed.

"All of them, huh. What's the occasion?"

"It's the grand opening. The big party was last night but they're doing another one, I guess because of the shooting. The whole staff from Clancy's is here."

"Bingo!" someone shouted, and low grumbles spread across the room, whispers of close calls and bad luck, sighs of exasperation.

"We have a bingo," Frank announced, his voice rising gradually. "Anyone else?" He paused to survey the crowd. "Any other good bingos?"

The grumbling swelled, the players leaning back to look around as if for the first time. No one else had won. A few people stood, crumpling their sheets, gathering their belongings to leave. One of the floor girls stood by the winner and recited the numbers to Frank.

"I gotta go," the boy said and he went to join the rest of the staff, busy now setting out food and drink. Some of the players circled around to eye the free offerings, but most made their way towards the exits. It was Sunday night, after all.

Mickey Gilmore appeared at the end of the hallway, well-groomed as usual and looking not particularly happy to see me. He motioned me over and led me down the hall to an open doorway. Chuck Burrows stood there to usher us in. As we entered the office, a man sitting behind the desk stood up.

"Henry, this is Dennis Coyne, Frank's brother."

Not quite as tall as Frank but with the same prominent nose and fading chin, he was easily ten years younger and dressed more like the next generation. Unlike Frank, Dennis still had most of his hair, dark brown, styled like a carefully trimmed hedge, but left long at the back as if to compensate for the signs of thinning at the front.

"I hear you're quite the hero." He held out a limp hand and let me work it up and down.

"Just tried to make it difficult for them."

"It was quick thinking," said Burrows, coming up between us. "Plain to see you're a man of action." The compliment felt out of place.

"Not really," I said, wondering where this was going.

"You learn that from your old man?" Burrows asked.

I knew this could happen. Luis and I had rehearsed it. The bingo crowd was littered with ex-cops and it would probably help my credibility, rather than hurt it, if they discovered my father had been with the DPD. Nevertheless, I felt caught in a lie.

"No, no," I strained to smile. "My father always told me not to follow in his footsteps. He used to say 'Nobody likes you unless they're in trouble.'"

Burrows nodded agreement but his eyes continued searching my face.

"'Sides which, the pay's peanuts unless you work both sides."

"Ain't it the truth."

"Your father was a cop?" Dennis Coyne finally caught on. He sat back down to regard me with a critical skew of his features.

"Long time ago." I turned back to Burrows. "When were you on the job?"

"I been retired ten years. Walter, wasn't it? Yeah, Walter Burkhart. I never worked with him, but I remember the name. And I remember what happened. After my time, though."

"Killed in the line of duty," I said, feeling somehow emboldened to be telling the truth. "Eight years ago."

"Some kind of raid gone wrong up in boogie town, wasn't it?"

Boogie town. Long time since I had to let that kind of thing slide. Willie would love this guy. "He was shot during a domestic disturbance call. Some meth-head went wacko. A white guy," I added.

He ignored the pointed distinction. "Yeah, that's a sad thing. Hell of a job. Glad I got out of there. So wha'd you do instead?"

"Went to law school for a while, but didn't much like that either. Those guys are all crooks," I said, knowing I'd get a laugh.

The door opened and Frank Coyne came in. An impish-looking man, late forties, followed close on his heels, as if he were Frank's man-servant, though out of uniform. He wore a brown flannel shirt with the tails hanging out and grimy jeans that fit the contours of his rounded body as if he'd been wearing them for a week.

Dennis shot up from Frank's chair and slunk around the far side.

"Man, I hate those guys," Burrows continued. "Especially the public defenders. Necessary evil though." Turning to Frank, he said, "Lawyers, I mean. Don't you think?"

"If you're makin' any money," Frank put in. Everybody tried to laugh. Eyeing his brother, he took his place behind the desk and stood there. "Listen. Let's do this meeting out front, after it clears out. You two met?" He waved a thin finger between me and Dennis. Dennis nodded. "Henry's the one I told you all about. He's comin' on board out here."

News to me, but I went with the flow.

"Welcome aboard," Dennis said, no warmth in his voice.

"And this is Benny Palmer." He indicated the imp to his right. "He runs our supply house. He's from Seattle too."

Before I had a chance to say anything stupid, Frank sent everyone except me out of the room. "Dennis, check back in when you're ready out there. I wanna go over some stuff with the two of you."

"Sure," Dennis said, not meeting his brother's eyes.

"Sorry about that," Frank said, after the door closed. "I didn't mean to spring anything on you."

"What do you have in mind exactly?"

Frank sat and gestured for me to do the same.

"You're doin' a good job. Chuck says you check out. And Benny knows people that know you from the Northwest." He let that sit there for a moment. I didn't break out in tears. "And with Eddie out of commission, we need someone who knows his way around." He stopped and aimed his grin at me as if waiting for me to grovel.

"What would I be doing?"

"You'd run this hall. Just opened but these first crowds seem pretty good. It'll take a while to build a following. But don't worry, we're spreading the word."

He made it sound like missionary work. When I didn't say anything, he added, "You know, run the games."

"Am I running it for you?"

"It's Dennis' license, technically. First one we've put in his name. He'll be here some of the time but he's got other things going on." He looked at me as if to see if I believed that. "He'll need the help. He's young, ya know?"

"I'd say he was about my age."

Frank gave it a little chuckle. "He's not exactly from the school of hard knocks. Baby brother, an' all. Anyway, me and Tanya, we'll be keeping an eye on him but we can't be here all the time."

"Tanya. Mickey's wife?"

"My sister," he stated, as if correcting me. "She's here tonight. Likes to run these grand openings and such. Sort of our official hostess. She doesn't work the games. More like our PR rep. It's Dennis you'll be working with."

"I guess I can help out. What's the pay?"

"Five nights a week to start and day games Saturday and Sunday. I'll give you two grand a month, tax free and maybe…ten percent of the house bucket."

Frank's usually dull eyes shone with life for a moment. I nodded and pretended to be thinking it over.

The real money from running these halls comes from the sale of pull-tabs, a kind of in-house lottery. The income from their sales is consistently two to three times what straight bingo generates. And that's just what's reported. Plastic five-gallon buckets have replaced the pickle jars of old that the tickets are drawn from, but they still call it the pickle bar. Before and after and between games, the players kill time buying them up and peeling them open in search of a magic match. Some of them pay big—five grand, sometimes more—but there are a lot of tickets in a batch. In order to be legal, the batch must pay out fifty percent, the rest going to expenses and charitable donations. The manufacturers of the tickets are closely audited by the state. Supposedly. But if you buy out of state, if you find a supplier that wants to play along, or if you stake a guy to run your own supply house under his name, you can get unrecorded batches. He'll give you the winning tickets separately to do with what you will. The rest of the batch goes in a special bucket. The house bucket.

"'Bout how much extra would that be? My ten percent, I mean."

Obviously pleased with my complicity, Frank's smile widened. "Hard to say just starting up. Couple, three hundred a month. More after a while."

In this world, it was a choice offer. And it implicated Frank in conspiracy, fraud, tax evasion, and interstate transport of unlicensed goods. Luis would kill me if I didn't take it.

"Thanks, Frank. That's very generous of you." We grinned like honorable thieves. For good measure, I said, "How do you know you can trust me?"

"Like I said, Chuck checked you out. And Benny. Besides, I can tell. You're our kind of folk." His smile turned complacent as he added, "And Claire put in a good word for you too."

The skin crawled on the back of my neck as I felt the hidden boundary between myself and the so-called bingo family melt around the edges. Me with Frank. Claire with Frank and, presumably, me with Claire. Me with everybody. I didn't like the feel of it.

"How's it sound?" Frank asked, with excruciating zeal.

It sounded inane. "Great," I said.

"Let's get Dennis in here to go over a few details."

Opening the door, he found Dennis leaning against the outer wall close enough to eavesdrop.

"Henry's agreed to work with you."

"Good news," Dennis grumbled, making no effort to conceal his misgivings.

"You two can go over the day-to-day later. I just want to say a little something about the books."

He laid it out for us in a bland, business-like monologue that touched on every aspect of the legitimate take: cover charge, pull-tabs, cash drawers, pay outs, even the sale of food and merchandise. He had it down and I got the idea that Dennis had heard it all before. It was being said for me, to put me in my place. Dennis would oversee the cashiers, work the reports and do deposits, report to Frank every day. Any skimming that might be going on wasn't going to get my hands slimy. I'd be doing the grunt work while Dennis parsed the cash then hustled and bustled his way to the bank—less the house cut.

"Okay with me," I said at the end of it. "I hope you'll stay close the first few days until I get the hang of it."

"Yeah, sure," Dennis said. "No worries." He smiled his brother's smile, not quite as smarmy, but irritating enough. Standing up, we shook hands, wily grins all around.

Chapter 8

"I say let's give it right *back* to 'em," Mickey's voice boomed. "We don't— they'll just hit us again. Pretty soon our halls will be empty."

"Take it *easy*, Mickey!" Chuck Burrows, the ex-cop and the closest thing to a voice of reason, spoke almost as loudly. "We don't even know if Milo was behind this."

"Sure we do. Eddie said as much. 'Sides, who else could it be?"

Coming out of the office hallway, the three of us took in the scene at the far end of the cavernous room. Cigarette smoke coiled upwards and dissipated beyond the suspended fluorescents above their heads. The intensity of the debate waned as Frank approached, then took his place at the head of the table. His large hands gripped the chair back and he leaned forward towards Mickey at the opposite end.

"It could be anybody," Burrows offered. "A bunch of thugs staking us out last week. Saw the easy pickings, came back on a Saturday night when they knew the take was good."

"Yeah, sure," Mickey scoffed. "A bunch of thugs who knew Eddie by name."

"Mickey, *please*," Tanya implored, almost hissing. She sat closest to her husband but not next to him, as if distancing herself from any implied alliance by proximity—or marriage. On closer inspection, I saw the likeness. She had Frank's rounded brow and high cheekbones but a much smaller nose, probably the product of plastic surgeons on retainer. Her more pronounced chin—and maybe they can do jaws these days, too—supported fuller broad lips highlighted with maroon gloss in a way that almost seemed sensuous. And without the glasses, her wide-set eyes created a symmetry not altogether unappealing. Those mascara-laden eyes glowered at her husband with unabashed rancor.

Mickey met her stare with a nasty grin. "My guess is, it was Brent Charmichael did the shooting."

Tanya emitted an audible sigh that threatened to become a groan. She shifted her gaze to Frank, pleading with her eyes.

"You don't know that, Mickey," Frank asserted.

"A good guess though, ain't it? He knows how to get to us."

"Milo wouldn't let him. There's more at stake here than this…*personal* shit."

A hard silence settled over the table. Downcast eyes flitted in Tanya's direction, then towards Frank. Tanya sat frozen in place, almost statuesque. Frank's trademark smile was nowhere to be seen.

"Still…that's who Eddie says it was," Mickey added, treading softer now.

"We need to talk with him," Frank offered, easing into his chair and shooting Tanya a glance. "But we can't discount the possibility that this was a random act, a holdup. It wouldn't be the first time." Mickey sat forward and cleared his throat but Frank cut him off. "We can't count on what Eddie said, Mickey. He's delirious, for Christ's sake. Even if they did know his name that doesn't prove anything." He nodded towards Burrows. "Like Chuck said, they could have cased it out earlier, chummed it up with Eddie. We all know what Eddie's like. Wouldn't take much to get him talking big." Leaning on one elbow, jutting out his baby chin, he dared Mickey to disagree. "Let's just keep our options open, okay?"

Mickey's head bowed, his eyes burning a hole in the tabletop. The rest of us waited like yes-men enduring the boss's temper tantrum. I did my best to stay invisible. Not exactly the Secret Council of the Brotherhood, but I figured I wasn't supposed to be hearing this.

Turning to Burrows, Frank asked, "What'd the cops have to say about it?"

"That guy Harris? Not much. I doubt the Aurora cops know anything about Milo's operation."

"Do we want to plant that seed?"

"I don't think so. We do that, it goes beyond their jurisdiction. Any hint of a broader conspiracy could drop it in the lap of CBI. Believe me, those guys would be goin' through our trash"

"What about Marcia Herrera?" Dennis ventured. "Don't we have an in with her though Rhonda Schomberg?" He said it to Tanya but Burrows fielded the question.

"The secretary of state just does regulation. Wouldn't have anything to do with armed robbery. Besides, Milo made some pretty beefy contributions of his own to Herrera's campaign, right? She gets involved in this, she'll be playin' both sides."

"Can't we get the Denver cops in on this?" Frank asked. "Have them put some pressure on Milo?"

"They're not at my bidding, Frank." Burrows sounded testy. "Aurora doesn't have shit on those guys and they wouldn't be sharing it with Denver anyway."

Leaning forward, Mickey tossed in another live one. "So what you're sayin' is, you *do* think Milo's people pulled this, but you don't want to go after them. You want the cops to do it."

"Now listen, Mickey," Frank said. "Drop that shit, okay? You have bad feelings for his boy Charmichael? Work it out on your own. Don't mix it with business."

"He turned coat on *all* of us, Frank," Mickey's voice gaining strength again. "When he went over to Milo's, they were nothin'. Now look at 'em. They got three halls on the West Side. They squeezed us out of that Elks Club deal. And now they're takin' pot shots at our *people*."

"We don't *know* that."

"*I* do, goddammit!"

"Hey! Take it easy. Everyone!" Burrows raised his voice well above the rise in volume of grumblings around the table.

Mickey pushed his chair back, stood, and marched into the dim expanse at the far end of the room. Everyone's eyes followed his progress until he slowed, then stopped, then made a project out of unwrapping a cigar and lighting it. A few hooded eyes slunk in Tanya's direction, furtive, probing, not sympathetic. She did not meet their glances.

"Okay, guys," Burrows said, conveying an air of insolence, "let's consider this another way. Let's just say it was Milo's people." Frank's head came up but Burrows held out a flat hand. "I'm just sayin' hypothetical. Now we can't count on the cops to do anything, right?"

In the distance, Mickey half-turned and cocked an ear.

"So what are our alternatives?"

As he looked us over, no one offered anything. When he came to me, I shrugged and turned toward Dennis, passing it on.

The light reflecting on Frank's glasses obscured the direction of his gaze. When he leaned back and pushed the glasses up the bridge of his nose, he was looking straight at me.

"Wha'd you do up in Seattle, Henry?"

Apparently, everyone finally noted my presence, their expressions curious and questioning but not necessarily malicious. "Whadda you mean?" I said, my brain scrambling for details of my back-story.

"You told me yesterday," Frank continued. "You had some trouble like this up there, right?" Five seconds crawled by while Mickey strolled over.

"I wasn't really involved."

"But you said you knew about it."

"Yeah, but…from a distance."

"Well, wha'd they *do*?" His tone was edged with impatience. I figured I'd better give it a try.

"The stories I heard went back to the '80s. The game was real popular up there. Not just bingo. Electronic slots, poker machines, all the latest toys. For a while there, every bar had one, a lot of folks elbowing for a piece of the action." I eased into my role. "Some kind of rivalry broke out between operators. I don't know, maybe it started with something like this. It escalated to where there were some shootings, some drive-byes on the clubs. Two guys got killed, employees of a bingo hall."

Tanya huffed and gestured wide-eyed at Frank. He acknowledged it with a glance, but returned his attention to me.

"That got local press. The media tied it to the games, made it a sort of bingo world *exposé* kind of thing. Anyway, pretty soon the cops were crawling all over the halls, busting them for every little violation. It wasn't long before the legislature passed those new laws. Things tightened up. They outlawed the machines altogether and put bingo regulation under the State Attorney General. Everything changed after that."

"Like I told you," Burrows said. "We don't want that here."

"So what happened?" Frank asked me.

"It's still going on. I mean, the game's still popular up there, but the operators have to run a tighter ship." Checking the faces, I decided to chance an inside secret. "Not so much cream anymore. The skim is next to nothing."

It went over like a comment on the weather.

"But we can't just sit here," Mickey persisted. "I mean, we do nothing, what's to keep them from hitting us again?"

"*Mic-key*," Tanya groaned.

"Look, Mickey," Frank said, "we have to take into account the consequences." He looked to me, then Burrows for support.

"We don't want to retaliate with violence," Burrows said.

"We can beef up security, right Chuck?"

Burrows leaned back and puffed his half-smoked cigar. "We can do that. Put a uniform in every hall. Like we got on weekends at Five Aces and Bingo Circle."

"What's that going to cost us?" Mickey put in.

"Hundred a night, each. Cops don't come cheap."

Eyes skittered around the table as if furtively sharing the irony of the ex-cop's wording.

"At every game?" Mickey contended. "And every hall?"

A silence followed while everyone present apparently pondered their paltry slush funds. Within that brooding atmosphere, an idea dawned on me, a way to deepen my credibility.

"There was another round of rivalries up there more recently," I said. Several faces turned my way. "I mean, it wasn't as bad. Some guys opened up a new place not far from where one was already operating. Could've been enough business for everybody, I suppose, but the established guy didn't want to share."

Frank's large eyes took me in. "Sooooo…?"

"So…the place burned down. Middle of the night. Nobody hurt."

Mickey gave it a chuckled. Frank took a breath to speak, but I pushed ahead.

"Thing is, when it's arson, the insurance companies don't pay up right away. They want to know who did it. Fire department investigates, then come the insurance dicks. And the most obvious suspect is always the beneficiary. Sort of like, if the husband gets croaked and the wife gets a million bucks, they look at her first."

A few tight smiles met my glance around the table, including Tanya.

"Turned out this particular operator had a checkered past, a few minor run-ins, a record. Looked a little suspicious, I guess, so the insurance company takes a breath. They stalled and whined and finally turned down the claim, making this guy sue for a settlement. He's over-extended, he can't find a decent lawyer. And the insurance shysters are the best, right? So they drag it out some more. Even if the guy wins, a year goes by, maybe two, while his clientele goes down the road. His lawyer gets a huge percentage. Guy gets about half what he needs to rebuild." I shrugged. "Not likely he's comin' back to the neighborhood."

A triumphant grin lit up Mickey Gilmore's features as he sat back down in his chair.

"So what happened," Frank said, "in this particular case?"

"That was about three or four years ago," I said, being careful to place it after the great bingo exodus from Seattle. "Last I heard, there's only the one hall in that part of town."

"But this isn't some amateur operator," Burrows put in, his eyes nudging toward Frank's cool stare. "I mean, we can't go around torching bingo halls."

"Nobody's talking about burning down any halls," Frank said.

I was relieved to hear him veto the idea. But it was plain that I had struck a chord. Tanya seemed suddenly unsettled. When I met her gaze she looked away, batting those sharpened eyelash extensions like she might fly away on the strength it.

"What about that detective, Chuck?" Frank said, sounding thoughtful. "Perkins."

"Joe Perkins. What about him?"

I knew the name but couldn't put a face to it. He was on the job in Denver.

"Didn't you tell me he was interested in getting in?"

Burrows shifted in his seat, scratched at his neck just above the collar. "Yeah, maybe. Wants to line up some security for us. But there's no way he's gonna initiate an investigation. Besides, he's homicide. Nobody's dead yet." He chuckled at his own words, but no one else did.

"Would he be willing to do more if we let him take the cake?"

The way Frank used the cliché made it sound specific—code for something.

"A pickle jackpot?" Burrows said, and that explained it.

Frank nodded slowly. "We're due at Five Aces. Is he hungry enough to go for it?"

"Maybe," Burrows said. "But even a good piece of cake wouldn't get us a police investigation. It's not even his jurisdiction, he's Denver."

"We don't need a full-fledged investigation," Frank said, a trace of his complacent smile finally making its way back onto his slack features. "Like you said, we don't want one."

"So, what then?"

"What if we get him to poke around off-duty? I mean, passing himself off as if he *was* looking into it."

"You mean, question Milo about the holdup? Question Brent Charmichael?"

"Whoever. Maybe drop into their clubs too. Look around. Make these guys feel like the heat *is* on." The full glory of his grin—smug, self-satisfied, huge—stretched across his face. "Maybe that'd get them to back off."

"I could talk to him, I guess. It might work."

"And maybe that would make Mickey feel better. Eh, Mickey?" Still grinning fully, Frank turned to beam down on Mickey's closed expression.

"What would make me feel better is gettin' Charmichael in a field somewhere and puttin' him on his knees."

Tanya let out a sigh that would have blown out candles on her birthday cake. Frank turned away like he'd been slapped. Dennis and Chuck jittered in their seats. Even if I didn't know about Harvey Cline's murder, I could have guessed something like it had happened.

"Anyway," Frank managed, "let's see what Perkins can do for us. Okay Chuck? It would have to be this week."

Burrows nodded without looking up.

"Benny, you and Dennis can handle him taking the cake?"

Benny Palmer sat backed away from the table looking like he knew he didn't belong here. He looked at Dennis who nodded solemnly.

"Yeah, we can do that. Set it up at Five Aces?"

Frank nodded. With his smile jammed back in place, he adjourned the meeting with thank you's all around.

"Mickey, let's have a word."

Tanya shot out of her chair and swung past Mickey slurring words out the side of her bright red lips. "I'll be waiting in the car." It didn't sound like a happy ride home. She strode across the linoleum floor, stiletto heels clacking hard like she was driving their points into someone's chest.

As I drifted towards the door, I saw Frank guide Mickey into a dimly lit corner, one gangly arm curled around Mickey's wide shoulders drawing him close. He spoke in a low, continuous stream directly into Mickey's quiescent face. There was no mistaking the tone.

Dennis Coyne caught up to me just outside.

"So, we're gonna be working together." He made an effort to smile. It wasn't pretty.

"Yeah, I guess so."

"Won't start till next weekend. Why don't you come out to Five Aces on Thursday. I'll show you the ropes."

Five Aces Bingo was Frank's first and oldest hall and the foundation of his bantam empire. I interviewed there six weeks ago and had worked a 'training' week under his and Mickey's distant eyes. The place was depressing, unless you were already depressed. But the chance to see them work this so-called 'take the cake' was reason to endure it.

"I'd be happy to," I told him. "Show me the ropes."

Chapter 9

Under the guise of checking on her condition, I called Claire. Not that I needed a guise, necessarily, but that's what I told myself. My true motives were a nebulous jumble of conflicting emotions that I, for some unexamined reason, felt perfectly comfortable indulging in. We met for lunch at a neighborhood dive called Pagliacci's in what used to be called the Italian quarter, a downtrodden section of town that hasn't really seen many better days. But this place gets 'discovered' every four or five years by the out-on-the-town set. Lately, it's all the rage.

I found Claire seated in a booth by the window, a half-full glass of wine in her hand. She wore a light cotton dress that left her shoulders bare and underscored the sculpted lines of her collarbones. Her hair was done up in a way that I had never seen at Clancy's, richer somehow and hanging longer, it seemed to me, on either side of her face. Sliding in across from her, I smiled politely and took in the intensity of the look she gave me in return. A Band-Aid bridged her slightly swollen nose but if there was any discoloration left, it was concealed beneath expertly applied rouge.

"So you got promoted?" she said, eyes shining mischievously.

"Yeah, I guess so. Is that what you'd call it?"

"Depends on what you want. I could get worried about you though," she added as the waitress came up. We both ordered seafood capellini and she ordered a second glass of wine. I thought I'd better go along with that.

"You mean, because of this so-called promotion?"

"Well, it's not the nice little mom n' pop operation that it looks like, you know." Her lips curled into a simulated frown. "I don't suppose it looks like that to you, does it?"

"No, it doesn't."

The wine came and we toasted to new beginnings. She regarded me steadily, dark eyes prying at the edges of my persona. "What *are* you in it for, anyway?"

My rehearsed reply didn't fit with the intimacy of the moment. I forced it out anyway.

"Well, I…just moved back. I need to do something to get by for a while."

"Until what?"

"Until I decide what to do."

"That's no answer."

"I don't have a better one." I tried to make it sound light. The truth loomed large and ominous, like monsoon storm clouds billowing over the Front Range. *I'm just a cop. My father was a cop and I find myself walking in his shoes. I don't really like it—even* he *didn't like it—but he tried anyway. And I can't see what else I'm good at. There's bad guys out there and maybe I know something about how to make things harder for them. Not every little shell game and pot dealer, just the ones who take advantage, the duplicitous, the greedy, the callously violent, the really bad ones. And I'll be the judge of that, thank you, but it wouldn't include you. I promise.*

I realized it would be better to lie even if I wasn't undercover.

"I'm sort of starting over," I said, trying on a careful bit of candor. "I don't know what I want." The words sounded evasive, even to me. So I was surprised when she responded with feeling.

"I know what you mean. I'd truly like a new beginning too."

I watched her take another swallow of wine. She was going at it with a drinker's thirst.

"You mean, away from bingo? What's wrong with it?" I felt relieved to be back in character.

"They've made a real mess of it, Frank and them. The whole family really."

"I thought you were part of the family."

"The way they run things, you *have* to be. Part of their whole little world. It's gotten so ingrown, so *incestuous*. Nothing changes, nothing happens, the same people all the time. It makes me feel stuck." She paused to drown her sorrows. Her eyes took me in above the rim of the glass. "It'll happen to you too, you know. If you stick around long enough."

Ignoring the implied question, I said, "It's that bad, huh?"

"It just doesn't go anywhere. It's turned into this machine that everybody's plugged into, getting their piece of the pie. We're supposed to be helping people, but half the charities we donate to aren't real. Most of it just goes to one of Frank's or Tanya's little sidelines."

She took another swallow from her glass and set it down nearly empty. The wine was making her garrulous. I found it charming as well as informative. I had a moment's doubt about taking advantage of it. I chose not to dwell on it.

"Plus which it's all generated from the weaknesses of others, you know? I mean the players, the regulars, I see the same people come in three, four times a week. For years now. It bothers me that they're so…small, so small-*time*. Nobody seems to care."

"Nobody's forcing them to play. It's like gamblers in Vegas. Or here, for that matter. It's just been legalized Central City and Blackhawk. That's going to take off."

"I suppose I'm sounding silly. I am a part of it, after all. But it's become a whole different animal."

The food arrived. She drained her glass and ordered another.

"I don't see what's so wrong with it. I mean, our whole consumer economy's based on that sort of thing. Retailers, car dealers, even food stores. They all market their goods to our basic appetites and weaknesses. Look at cigarettes. A whole industry based on addiction."

"That's just what I mean," she said after washing down a mouthful of noodles. "It's an addiction and they're taking advantage of it. It's just not right. Not *healthy*!" Her tone had risen to the level of argument. She must have noticed. We ate in silence for a moment.

"So why don't you get out?"

She gave a self-deprecating laugh, more like sighing through a smile. "The money's good, you know? I can't make anything like this for the hours I put in. Unless I work cocktails or pole dance."

The picture flickered across my mind.

"Plus I get schooling for Shanie that I could never afford, at St. Mary's. Hell, I'm not even Catholic. They take good care of me in other ways too. Frank gave me that car last year. Just gave it to me. And Mickey owns my house. Charges me next to nothing for rent. He pays for it on the books from Bingo Circle. Calls it a storage facility."

I took note of that, somewhat reluctantly. "That doesn't sound so bad."

"It's going to be, though. It can't last."

"What do you mean?"

She took a last bite of food then pushed her plate aside.

"It's getting too big, too much money. They don't know what it means." Her eyes regarded me for a serious few seconds. "That's why that shooting happened the other night, don't you think? Isn't that what you meant about Frank having some mean competition?"

I nodded.

"It's true. Frank and Tanya, they're the original big fish in a small pond. Only the pond is getting bigger and now there's some even bigger fish flapping around, all puffed up and intimidating, driving around in their fat fancy cars trying to impress each other. Frank and them don't know how to handle it. I mean, they're not...*sophisticated*. They're like a little church group who suddenly find themselves making deals with the Mafia."

"I think you're underestimating them."

"I know that family," she said, contentious again. "I've known them for years. They're over their heads. They don't have the backbone, the..."

"Balls?"

"Yeah, that's the way Mickey puts it. I was looking for something more...tactful."

"What about Chuck Burrows? He strikes me as a pretty savvy guy."

She nodded agreement. "He's an ex-cop, you know. I think he's practically hired muscle. Ever since he was brought in the whole thing's turned harder somehow."

"What about Mickey?" I said, trying to make it sound offhand.

Claire seemed taken aback at the mention of her brother. "Mickey's good to me. He has a heart of gold."

I let that go. Couldn't very well ask her if he executed Harvey Cline eight years ago on a quiet prairie landscape.

"Besides, he feels the way I do. He'd change things, if he could."

"I got the impression he and Frank don't always see eye to eye. The other night, they sort of got into it."

"He gets carried away sometimes. I'm like that too. Frank's the opposite. Establishment all the way. Of course, he's king of the hill the way things are, so why change, ya know? That's the friction between them. They probably wouldn't still be together if it wasn't for Tanya."

"Tanya's Frank's sister and Mickey's wife, right? That makes her your sister-in-law."

Claire laughed out loud. "You could say that, but I wish you wouldn't."

I gave her a quizzical look.

"Tanya's a real piece of work. Personal trainer, personal hairdresser, personal manicurist. She has a girl do her makeup for her sometimes, for these social events. She's nearly forty and built like a twenty-something bodybuilder. We call her 'Tanya Faye'. Struts around in these Spandex evening gowns. Belle of the ball at the political fund-raisers."

"She's into politics?"

"Not exactly running for office. But she is best friends with Rhonda Schomberg. Know her?"

"I've heard the name," I said, making sure to keep the interest out of my eyes.

"She's a major lobbyist, state government level. Like this," Claire said, holding two fingers entwined, "with the secretary of state. And in case you didn't know, they're the bingo police."

"Or not, as the case may be," I added, raising an eyebrow.

Claire offered up an eyebrow of her own. "So you're not so… *innocent*, are you?"

"It's like that in Seattle too," I said, pretending I wanted to impress her. "Probably in for some kickback."

"They say Rhonda's in bed with Frank, but I can't stand to picture it."

We laughed.

"And Tanya too? Sounds like a rather tasteless threesome."

"Now you're scaring me. Only a metaphor, please."

"So Tanya's not involved in the day-to-day?"

"Not really. Frank calls her our political liaison. The rest of us call her Queen Bee." Claire rolled her eyes. "She throws a lot of parties for the local heavies, the mayor's crowd, the fraternal order of the police, or whatever they call themselves. Anyway, she calls it public relations, but it's just an excuse to show off her Mc-Mansion in Wellshire Village and prance around in designer dresses."

"So just a figurehead type of thing?"

"Oh no, more than that. She holds about half of Frank's licenses. She gets a big percentage, believe me. Then she pours it into her wardrobe, or her facelifts, or props up her interior decorating shop. 'Tanya's Interiors'…" she said it in a haughty tone. "I don't think she's ever made a dime at that. She just keeps redesigning her showroom with the help of her little faggot friends." Claire laughed at herself and brought one hand up to her eyes then patted the Band-Aid on her nose. "Sorry about that. I didn't mean anything."

Ignoring the false contrition, I said, "And Mickey puts up with that? How come they're still married?"

A bare shouldered shrug. "Pressure from Frank, mainly. And the old man. And there's the money, of course. It's all in the family."

"Who's the old man?"

"You don't know about Willard? He's Frank's and Tanya's father. He's the brains behind the whole thing. Used to be, anyway. I guess he's like, semi-retired."

"I see what you mean by ingrown. And Dennis's father too, then. What about him? He's who I'll be working for."

"Dennis," she said, in a derisive tone. She turned away to rummage through her purse. She brought out a cigarette, lit it, and stared out the window. Her eyes narrowed against the sunlight. "Dennis is a problem."

I had killed off her loquacious mood. I let the silence linger for some time before saying, "Did I stumble onto something personal?"

Claire took me in with a crystal stare. "Did you want to avoid the personal?"

It sounded more like evasion than insult, the kind of thing a woman accuses a man of doing when she's doing it herself. I checked back into my role to find I had not drifted that far off. "I only meant if it's a sore subject, it doesn't have to be any of my business."

Her gaze turned towards the window again, then she occupied herself with the cigarette. I made myself busy paying the tab, figuring I had pushed my luck too far.

"Sorry, Henry."

When I looked up, I found her regarding me openly, an expression that plainly asked if I could be trusted. It made me feel uncomfortable but apparently it didn't show.

"I guess maybe that *is* a rather sore subject."

"None of my business, really."

She took another draw from her cigarette and let the smoke drift between us. "Dennis is a nice enough guy, I guess."

"Then he'll be okay to work for?"

She smiled at my attempt to change directions but she didn't take advantage of it.

"Dennis is sort of the heir apparent for the Coyne dynasty, or whatever you want to call it—although he's a long way from being up to it. He's not serious about it."

"And that bothers you?"

"He's not serious about *anything*. What bothers me is that I'm his designated heiress—princess, partner, whatever. He and Frank and all them just take it for granted ever since they gave up on Eddie and me. Nobody's checking with me about it, least of all Dennis."

"Why don't you just tell him?"

She looked back perturbed. "I *have* told him," she said, then immediately recanted. "I've tried, anyway. It's not that simple. But it's not what I want. *He's* not what I want."

"What do you want?"

Part of me wanted to know, but the job was telling me not to go down this road. Something told her not to either.

"Why's this all about me? Here I've been talking about myself for an hour, given away all the family secrets…I feel like I'm getting interviewed, for God's sake." She smiled, unsuspecting. "And you never gave me a straight answer about what *you* want."

Blushing, I tried to make it seem like an expression of humility. "I don't know. Like I said, I'm not sure what I want. But I don't want to get sucked into this thing forever. There *is* life after bingo, isn't there?"

"And no special girl in your life?"

"I'm kind of getting over someone."

"Well, we all are, aren't we? One way or another."

"I suppose, but this was different. She died suddenly. It was a shock."

That backed her off. "I'm sorry, I didn't mean…"

"It's all right. It was a little over a year ago. We weren't all that close, really. Just beginning but, in a way, that made it worse."

"Losing a loved one can be tough," Claire said, rather blithely. "I had a taste of it with what happened to Eddie. I mean, I don't even *care* about the guy anymore. Not after what he's done. Or *not* done, is more like it. But still, seeing him lying there, bleeding, looking like he was dead, you know? It really hit me. I guess I *do* still care for him. I mean, not…just… aarrgh!" She shook her head to clear the contradictions.

I nodded reassuringly but hoped to convey finality to the subject. I regretted bringing it up. "Listen, sorry to spoil the mood. I gotta go anyway. I got some things…"

"Sure, sure." She pushed away her wineglass. "I have to pick up Shanie soon."

I walked Claire to her car. A Cadillac, of course, but a sporty version, smaller than a boat and not the latest model. A generous gift nevertheless. At least no furry dice hung from the mirror.

She opened the door then turned and looked up at me, radiant in slanting afternoon sunlight. "Thanks for lunch, Henry. Next time it's on me."

"I'll take you up on that."

"I'll be seeing you around the hall, I guess."

"Maybe not. Frank's sending me out to the new place. Bingo Palace."

"I know. I'll be working there too. They always put me in the new locations. I kind of like it, setting it up, doing the openings. It has some life to it, don't you think?"

"Yeah, I guess. It'll be easier anyway with you around," I said, thinking I didn't mean it the way it sounded. But then again, maybe I did.

Claire pursed her lips. "Well, *I'm* looking forward to it." Her eyes sparkled with humor. "Don't worry, it'll be fun."

With my own smile stiffening on my face, I watched her drive away. It was tricky, this undercover work and I began to see I didn't really like it. On the other hand, I was making progress. I told myself I'd sort it out later.

Chapter 10

A call from Willie woke me.
"What up, dog?"
"Not me," I said groggily. "Whadda' you want?"
"Checkin' in, man. You said you'd call."
"What about?"
"About *bingo*, bro. What's with you?"

I looked at the clock. It was almost nine. "Why aren't you at work?" I managed.

"I got the rest of the week off. Plus which, I cleared the weekend with Maxine. So I could work this bingo scene. What we workin', boss-man?"

"Okay, Willie, all right." 'Boss-man'; Willie likes tossing that term around to rub in his perception of subtle subjugation that whites—apparently including me—employ, consciously or otherwise, in perpetuating racial biases. Or, rarely, he says it endearingly, to indicate that he trusts me not to. I read this occasion as the latter, an opportunity not to be passed up. I sat up in bed.

"Here's what we got. Bingo Palace. It's the new place way the hell out on Parker Road. I'll be running games there starting tomorrow. You come out, buy a few cards, get to know the folks, like I told you."

"What about today?"
"What about it?"
"Well, what' *you* doin'? C'mon, bro."

Willie was up for it—more than me.

"Okay, there's a game tonight at this other place, Five Aces. You can come out and get your feet wet."

"My feet wet? What? I gotta *train* to play fuckin' *bingo*?"

"Just be there, okay? And remember, you don't know me."

"Yeah, yeah. There's just one thing."

"What's that?"

"What about the money? You said there was *pay* for this, right?"

"Yeah, sure. You're working for the DA. You'll get paid for good info, just like any informant."

"Informant? I ain' no *snitch*, man. No way."

"It's just a word, Willie. You're working undercover gathering information against these bad guys. What do you want to call it?"

"Ah, how 'bout industrial espionage, like some kinda spy thing, ya know? No, wait, I got it. *Operative*. Undercover *operative*." Willie peeled off a few low chuckles. "How 'bout that?"

"That's fine, Willie. You're an operative."

"Yeah, an' operative get *paid* a higher scale, ya know."

"In that case, you're a snitch."

"C'mon, man. How much I get?"

"Look, Willie, we're not in it for the money."

Willie huffed. "Then what the fuck *are* we in it for?"

I thought about passing on Luis's spiel about small-time scofflaws greasing the wheels, cops on the take, politicians begging to be bribed, but then I realized, given who Willie's father was, I'd be hitting too close to home. I almost told him it was because we needed something to do. Finally, I just said, "Free bingo, Willie. We get to play all the games we want."

"Ohhhh, maaan."

"I'll see you out there," I said and hung up the phone.

Five Aces Bingo occupies a converted new-car showroom, circa 1970, that sits in front of an aging suburban strip mall along West Colfax. It's a freestanding glass box whose floor-to-ceiling windows slant outward in precarious support of the overhanging facade. For all its pseudo-modern lines, the building was dilapidated and out of date. Just right for the bingo crowd.

Dennis put me on the front door with a woman named Ellen that he called, "*the* head cashier". In her early to mid-forties, the helmet hair of brownish-gray curls, the tight little grin, and the squinting eyes behind wire-rimmed bifocals made her seem older. But she gave me the rundown on the game card sales in a clipped and business-like tone that belied her grandmotherly demeanor. Together, we sold sheets at six bucks a whack to less than a hundred customers. You couldn't expect much on a Thursday night, or so Dennis had told me just before retreating to the office at the call of the first number.

"N-35," Pause, and then, "E-e-e-n-n-n-n…thirty-five."

Willie Jr. showed up ten minutes late, nattily dressed and all smiles. At six-foot five and around two-twenty and skin like liquid cinnamon, he stands out incidentally in any crowd. But style-wise he goes the extra mile anyway. Wearing a white shirt with billowy sleeves under a black satin vest and with wraparound mirrored shades covering his eyes and a cell phone hanging from his belt in a studded leather case like a holstered gun, his appearance caused a mild stir in the assembly, like a pimp showing up at Sunday morning mass. Sidestepping through the rows, he nodded and greeted people as if recognizing them from having haunted the same after-hours clubs the night before. He took a seat towards the front between a middle-aged black couple—the only other blacks in the place—and a mother-daughter-granddaughter trio, all three well fed and sporting urban cowgirl attire. When I strolled by, Willie was hamming it up good, grilling the daughter for the numbers he'd missed and asking about the crisscross layout. The mother looked on with some apprehension while her daughter, a pert smile pinching her ample, rosy cheeks, clued Willie in on the subtleties of the game. He looked at me and squeezed off an exaggerated wink that gave nothing away since he was winking and nodding at anyone careless enough to make eye contact.

During the games, Ellen guided me through my paltry duties, checking off the scheduled events with the practiced routine of a lifer. We paid the winners and supplied the floor girls with change. You could do it all twice and still have time to watch your opinion of humanity slipping down the slope. Toward the end of the early session, as people lined up outside for the start of the next one, Ellen beckoned me over to the pickle bar. The pickle bar there was huge. The line of plastic buckets behind the glass spanned the width of the room. The floor girls joined us and Ellen fitted me with a money-apron and instructed me on the fine points of selling pull-tabs.

"You think you can handle it?" she said, only half joking.

There I was, working deep cover, an energetic grandmother smiling up at me and teenaged girls on either side, all of us ready and waiting for the onslaught of losers eager for a chance to win back their cover-charge at odds south of one-hundred-to-one. I smiled back.

"B-13," the caller droned. "Be-e-e-e...thirteen."

As the first session's final game dragged on, the gathering out front grew in size and showed signs of restlessness. We watched through the plate-glass windows as a man stepped forward and brashly pulled open the front door, causing a metallic racket.

"Of all the gall," Ellen huffed and headed off to quash this breach in bingo etiquette. But someone shouted "Bingo!" and that stopped Ellen in her tracks. Dennis appeared at the end of the hallway, as if he'd been watching through the half-drawn blinds of the office window.

"Do we have a winner?" the caller asked in mock amazement. "Anybody else?"

The players shuffled to their feet, some preparing to leave, most heading towards the pickle bar. Ellen went to pay the winner sending Dennis to deal with the rude intrusion out front. The gathering out there was significantly larger than I'd seen before on a weeknight. Lined up along the windows, they milled and talked and put their cupped faces against the glass. Something wasn't right. I tried to keep an eye on Dennis talking in the doorway but the crush of anxious pull-tab buyers pretty much overwhelmed my attention.

A barrel-shaped man with thick features and a closely trimmed flattop pushed his ruddy face into my line of vision. He wore wide red suspenders over a torso-hugging T-shirt and crimped a dead cigar butt between his front teeth.

"I need tickets," he said, waving a twenty.

As I counted them out, he watched carefully, the top of his prickly head extending over the edge of the partition.

"New here, huh?" he snarled, sounding like the caricature of a drill sergeant. I looked up to see if he was joking. His round eyes met mine in all seriousness.

"How can you tell?"

Two fat fingers extracted the wet cigar and he licked his brown stained lips. "If you count any slower I'm gonna miss the next session."

I handed him his tickets with a blatant sneer. He ignored that and began popping open the tabs fervidly, dropping the losers to the floor with casual disregard.

Ellen came up next to me slightly harried but putting on her happy face.

"Everything all right," she said, eyeing me, then the barrel-shaped man.

"Couldn't be better."

"Ohhhh, baby!" the barrel-shaped man yelled. "I got me a winner!" He turned to us with a shit-eating grin. "I got me a winner this time!" Stepping up to the counter, he held out the ticket for Ellen to see. The slot under one tab read $5,000 in bright red italics. I couldn't be more pleased for the guy.

"Five thousand big ones," he bellowed.

Heads turned and whispering broke out and grew in volume as the news spread across the room. Ellen circled around the counter to verify the ticket

"Congratulations," she announced, beaming motherly approval.

Upon hearing the commotion, the caller stepped back behind the podium. "Do we have a pickle winner?" he asked, speaking through the microphone.

"Five thousand dollars," Ellen called back, striking a Vanna White-like pose while holding the ticket in the air. That's when I got a second look. It was not the same kind of ticket. It was not from those I had sold him.

The crowd gushed and grumbled. "Five *thou*-sand *dol*-lars," the caller repeated. "I tell you, that pickle bar. All the big winners here at *Five Aces Bingo!*"

The barrel-shaped man gloated openly. Assessing him more closely, I realized he was dressed for the part but didn't quite cut it. The T-shirt was casual enough, but it was clean, unwrinkled, and he wore it neatly tucked in. And the jeans were pressed and fit snuggly, betraying the red suspenders as a prop. He wore cop shoes—black brogues. He was a shill and he was probably new at it.

Spoiling the moment, Dennis came up in a rush with a look on his face that would make you think he'd paid out the five grand himself. "C'mon. We gotta go." He coaxed Ellen and red-suspenders by their elbows, away from the spotlight.

"Dennis!" Ellen whined, twisting away from him.

"Something's happened," he persisted, his eyes bulging like his brother's. I saw an exchange of concerned looks that confirmed red-suspenders was one of them. The trio headed towards the office, Dennis whispering into Ellen's ear. All eyes followed their hurried progress, slurs and wisecracks flitting throughout the room. I kept mine to myself.

"All right, everybody," the caller beckoned, "next game starts in fifteen minutes. Who'll be the next lucky winner?"

By now, the waiting crowd began to filter in but strangely, most of them remained outside, standing around or huddled in lively conversation. It looked like a tailgate party but no pickup trucks—and no beer—in sight.

Giving up my cash apron to one of the girls, I strolled across the back of the room glancing through the office window as I went. The blinds were closed now and I could hear nothing through the glass. I crossed to the front door and went out into the parking lot.

The crowd was animated, everyone talking at once, earnest and too happy, and the volume grew perceptibly as I stood there. It reminded me of something Orwellian, a colorized version of scenes from *Animal Farm*, a rounded up pack of verbose hogs, casually dressed and socially engaged—and livid with the rumor that slaughter was at hand.

"No shit? I don't *believe* it...Who said *that*?..."I knew it..."

I spotted a regular from Bingo Circle, an older man, sixty-five-ish, with perfect dentures and baggy pants and three loose chins that hung like they had lost some weight themselves. He had an eye condition of some sort that made his eyeballs watery and the skin beneath them sag. With handkerchief in hand, he dabbed under the frame of his readers at errant tears. As he turned away from a smaller circle of talkers, I greeted him with a nod.

"What's going on?"

"Well, there's been a fire. Broadway Bingo." He was plainly pleased to be the bearer of bad news, his perfect smile widening in response to my stunned expression. "These folks just came from there. Quite the brouhaha. The hens'll be cluckin' this one up pretty good," he said, incidentally reinforcing my Orwellian imagery.

"It just happened?" I asked, trying hard not to jump to conclusions of my own culpability.

"No, no, last night, middle of the night. But it didn't make the news yet, ya see. Nobody knew it. They showed up out there for tonight's game and found it all charred and barricaded off." He chuckled, glancing back at the crowd. "'Course, they can't miss their game, ya know. Came out here to catch the late one." Perhaps noticing my apparent paralysis, he said, "Hey, you better get ready, son. You're gonna have a packed house." He patted my shoulder encouragingly. "One man's luck is another's good fortune." He smiled and affected a sloppy wink.

I had a fleeting thought that he had misspoken the aphorism but I knew his reasoning—that Frank Coyne stood to gain from this—would be the juiciest of the hotly rumored tid-bits.

As I reentered the hall, I spotted red-suspenders coming toward the entrance. Turning away, I did my best to blend in, watching him through the heads and shoulders between us. With his head down, he made a beeline through the crowd avoiding people's eyes, a man not wanting to be noticed or remembered. Gone was the gloating winner of the pull-tab jackpot.

I let him get to the first row of cars before I started after him. I don't know what I was thinking. I couldn't stop him, didn't want to. But I couldn't just let him go. When he glanced back and spotted me, his flushed features stiffened. Quickening his steps, he made it to his car twenty paces ahead of me; a Cadillac, naturally, not new, but nice enough to be an indictment in my mind. He jumped in, started it up, and began to pull away.

"What's the hurry, copper," I yelled.

The Caddy's engine lagged and the break-lights came on and red suspenders craned his neck to get a better look. I saw confusion on his face and maybe a little fear.

I gave him a salute as he drove off and noted his license number. But I had no doubt that he was Joe Perkins, Burrows' good buddy inside the DPD. And I had just eye-witnessed him play the shill in a rigged pickle bar jackpot—taking the cake—as they say in the trade.

Returning to the hall, the main room hummed with life. Most of the players stood at the back of the room, many of them eating on their feet and talking with their mouths full. Willie stood in the midst of them, looking enthralled by whatever the hefty cowgirls had to say. The pickle bar was backed up four or five deep, the milling crowd obscuring my view of Ellen and the volunteers. I meandered through the throng, eavesdropping easily enough.

A large man with short-cropped white hair and a white goatee, and a wiry old hag that was obviously his wife were playing off each other to inform and apparently entertain a loose circle of listeners.

"Oh yeah, it was arson all right," I heard the man say. He had a clear, sonorous voice and, evidently, he liked the sound of it. He cast his eyes beyond the circle to see who all might be listening. "You could tell by the way it burnt."

I came up behind an older couple who stood at the man's elbow, clucking and hissing and shaking their heads.

"Place went up like a tinderbox. Couldn't be anything else. Four alarms, they said."

"We saw the fire chief looking the place over," his wife said. Then, catching the frown on her husband's face, she added. "Well, somebody like that. You know, one of those red SUV's with the thingy on the hood."

"Inspectors, likely, gathering evidence."

"They weren't very friendly, if you ask me," the woman asserted, jutting out her already jutting out chin. "Fred went right up to 'em."

Fred pushed out his chest. "They weren't talkin' but you could tell by the look on their faces."

"They told Fred to step behind the tape." She prodded with her chin again. "Not too nice about it either."

"Who did it?" someone asked.

"Like I said," Fred answered, "they weren't talkin'."

There was an empty pause. Fred's wife couldn't stand it. "Had to be someone with a grudge though." She nodded knowingly. "I'd say it was pretty obvious." When everyone's eyes, including her husband's, shifted in her direction, she mumbled out of the side of her mouth. "No love lost between them and Frank Coyne."

"Now that's just gossip, Jesse," Fred interjected in a tone of feigned objectivity. "Coulda been anybody."

"Anybody with a grudge against Milo Finnes," Jesse huffed.

"Well, whoever it was, they did a helluva job."

"Mark my words," Jesse continued, "it'll come out."

I had to agree with her.

"Okay folks," the caller's amplified voiced boomed, "Let's get this game under way."

The crowd responded slowly. The noise level rose momentarily, threatening to swell into another barnyard cacophony. I hurried towards the pickle bar where Ellen and the others were still hustling tickets. The stragglers flicked their last losing pull-tabs as they made their way to the tables. There wasn't an empty chair in the place, standing room only for a Thursday night.

"The first game, on the green card, is Lazy L's," the caller persisted, "Lazy L's, on the green card." He pointed to the electronic boards depicting the winning layout. The chatter died down to whispers and then everyone went quiet with the call of the first number.

"I-18," he said. "I…eight…teen."

I moved the ticket buckets below the pickle bar, then took the money aprons from the volunteers. Ellen and I began sorting bills.

"Did Dennis find you?" she asked.

"No. What's he need?"

"Frank's on his way. He wants to see you."

Chapter 11

Wearing over-sized sunglasses over his hornrims and jutting his face and head forward like a man on a mission, Frank Coyne slipped through the front door and scurried along the back of the room like some ill-tempered celebrity trying to avoid his fervid throng of fans. Which, strangely enough, was true. He disappeared down the hallway without a glance in our direction. Shortly after, Dennis came over to where Ellen and I were still counting cash. We had bundled up about three grand so far, not counting the door.

"Frank wants to meet." He eyed the money. "Bring that with you."

The office was a small, square room made smaller by boxes of bingo supplies stacked along three walls. The fourth wall was the picture window that looked out onto the game room. The slats of the venetian blinds had been pulled fully closed. Frank stood behind the desk, his back to us, parting the blinds with a finger. He turned and scanned the three of us standing there.

"You heard, right?"

Ellen huffed. "I thought you had a talk with him." Frank frowned but didn't respond. Placing the cash box and clipboard on the desk in front of him, Ellen said, "This isn't even done yet. Here's what's been counted." She pointed to an entry on the clipboard, held her finger there until Frank took it in. A downturned smile grew across his lips.

"Just our luck," he said, squinting at her. Ellen glared at him mockingly, then she smiled back. These two were a pair.

"How'd the jackpot go?"

"All right, I guess. All these people started showing up right then. I think he was a little spooked."

"This doesn't have anything to do with him," Frank said.

"That's what I told him. Anyway, everybody saw it. It went good." She shot a quick glance in my direction, but didn't bring me into it. "I've got to get back out there. The girls don't have enough to pay winners."

Taking a money apron, she left the room. Dennis slid down into an orange vinyl chair in the corner. Closing the door behind Ellen, I turned to find Frank's lizard eyes fixed on me. The smile had gone.

"You seen Mickey today?"

I shook my head.

"You heard what happened?"

"Yeah, just now." I nodded vaguely toward the bingo masses.

"So you didn't have anything to do with it."

"Christ, Frank. I'm sorry I brought it up. I didn't mean for anything like this…"

"Oh, hell, it's not your fault if the man's half-crazed." With halting steps, he tried pacing in the narrow area behind the desk. He tugged downward at the corners of his mouth with a thumb and forefinger: I guess you could call it a thoughtful expression. "Call the Circle again," he commanded, eyes cutting toward Dennis. Bingo Circle was Mickey's hall.

"Anybody hurt?" I asked.

Frank looked away, apparently nonplussed. "Doesn't sound like it. Middle of the night."

"Can we find out anything more?"

"I can't find anybody. Chuck's not picking up, Mickey's just *gone*. I can't even find my dad."

Dennis spoke into the phone in low tones.

"What about Milo Finnes," I said. "It's his hall, right?"

Frank didn't question how I knew that. "I left a message."

"How about this guy Charmichael?"

"What about him?" he snapped, suddenly wary.

"Well I just…I heard you guys talking about him the other night. Sounds like you all have a past."

Frank came up with a partial grin and one cocked eyebrow. "You don't miss much do you, Henry?" He made it sound like a reprimand. "Brent Charmichael is going to think Mickey did it, no matter what I say to him. It won't serve any purpose calling him unless I want my ass chewed."

Dennis put the phone down. "He's still not there. They don't know where he is." After a pause, he added, "They heard about it there too. Place is packed."

Frank started pacing again. The air was getting dense and warm, and the conversation thin.

"I'd better go see if Ellen needs help," I said.

"Yeah, fine," he responded distractedly, but then he stopped me. "Listen. We're gonna meet later. If we find Mickey. I want you there."

"Okay."

Frank looked at Dennis. He squirmed against the vinyl. "I can't stay," he said. "I got plans."

Frank sighed and ran his fingers gingerly through the few strands of his comb-over. "What about closing?"

"Ah, c'mon Frank. What's the big deal? You got the pickle money. Ellen already closed the front. These people will be outta here in an hour. Henry can do the rest. Right, Henry?"

"Sure," I said, uncertain whose allegiance I should be fostering.

"C'mon with me," Dennis said, moving toward the door, avoiding his brother's eyes. "I'll walk you through it on the way out."

"That all right with you, Frank?"

With his eyes on Dennis and his lips drawn in, Frank gripped the cash box between his large hands as if readying himself to throw it. But then he dropped his gaze and eased himself down into his chair, pulling the box toward him.

"Sure. whatever. But you *are* gonna be at the Palace tomorrow, *right?*"

"Of course."

"It's your club, ya know. No leaving early."

"I *know* that, Frank. That's why I'm takin' care of business tonight."

"Right," Frank said. "Henry, check back in here later."

As we walked toward the entrance, Dennis rattled off a few instructions and gave me keys to the front door and the office. "I'll need these back," he said. I would make copies first. "If you got any questions, check with Ellen."

"Gotcha, no worries," nodding, trying to convey a sense of camaraderie.

Dennis nodded too, his timing slightly off, like an afterthought. "Frank gets like that. Don't pay him any mind."

"Doesn't bother me."

"Anyway, this'll be your first big test." He smiled his brother's complacent smile.

I smiled back, equally smug. "I'll cover for you, Dennis. No problem."

Halfway through the sixth and final game, I checked back into the office. Frank and Ellen were working side-by-side, counting cash, writing figures in a ledger, and passing bundles of bills back and forth. For half a minute, they ignored me, caught up in their calculations. I took note of the ledger and the loose accounting sheets. Behind Frank, the safe was open. Inside, I could see the butt-end of a handgun resting on the top shelf.

"How's it going out there?" Frank asked without looking up. "We gettin' close?"

"The last bingo is coming up."

Raising his head, Frank took me in. "Gettin' the hang of it?"

"Yeah, I think I can handle it." I strained to repress any trace of sarcasm in my tone. "Dennis and Ellen are seeing me through."

"He'll be fine," Ellen said, looking up and squinting at me with an air of maternal pride. She and Frank exchanged innocuous grins. It struck me that they would make a good match. Then it struck me that Ellen was Mrs. Frank Coyne.

"You may have gathered," Frank said, "that Dennis doesn't quite have his heart in the job." The large round eyes rested on me, waiting for the appropriate response.

I shrugged. "He seems all right."

"He's family, kid brother. What can you do? The old man wants him in, but I tell you, if it was up to me…" He leaned back in his chair and turned toward Ellen who met his look with a supportive firming of the lips. If she and Frank weren't a couple, they were definitely cut from the same class at charm school.

"Anyway, part of your job is keeping an eye on him, ya know? Don't let him do anything stupid. One loose cannon's bad enough."

"Speaking of which," I said, risking an irreverent grin, "any word from Mickey yet?"

Frank's parted lips stretched sideways. "I'm sure he's alibi's up somewhere, waiting for things to cool down. Assuming we can round him up, we'll meet tomorrow at the Palace. Before you open. Say three o'clock? Hopefully, we'll know more by then."

I didn't think there was much more to know, but I said, "Sounds good."

"You better get out there." Frank nodded toward the door. Then, addressing Ellen, he said, "You wanna take him through it, honey?"

Ellen Coyne and I stood at the back of the room when three different people called out "Bingo!" almost simultaneously. The loudest voice came from Willie Jr. What are the odds?

We made the rounds, paying each winner two hundred dollars. We got to Willie last. He was celebrating with the multi-generational cowgirls as if it was all in the family.

While Ellen recited his numbers to the caller, Willie tossed out wisecracks like the bogus victor in a WWF wrestling match. "Tha's right, tha's right. Oh, I got your number. I got *all* a' them numbers." Between banters, Ellen managed to verify the win and I paid him off. "We gonna *break* this bank," Willie persisted. The daughter and her mother smiled on him, slightly abashed but clearly won over by the force of his shtick. The little girl looked up at him from under her straw hat with an expression of awe. Or it could have been trepidation.

"You just keep coming out, young man," I offered. "We can handle it."

"Oh, you *gonna* see a lot a' me," Willie said, wide-eyed and grinning with all of his teeth. "I know a jackpot when I see one comin'."

The daughter giggled as if what he said made sense and was funny to boot.

"Well, congratulations." Ellen smiled stiffly.

I gave Willie a perfunctory nod and cast my eyes toward the door, hoping he'd take the hint.

Ellen returned to the office while I stayed to usher out the stragglers. Willie and his entourage of smiley-faced cowgirls moseyed on out dead last, Willie still shooting from the lip even as I locked the doors.

I checked back in at the office, anxious to get out of there. Frank and Ellen were still at it.

"I think we're done out here. Place looks ready to go."

The owlish eyes came up and once again took me in as if waiting for more. I was getting tired of playing along, so I looked back with a blank stare, hoping he would take it as fatigue. Frank smiled. Clutching a bundle of bills in one hand, he got up from the desk and circled around to face me. "You're doin' okay, Henry." With painstaking slowness, he unwrapped the rubber band from around the bills and counted out five twenties. Fanning them out, he held them up for me to admire. "Here's a little something extra to let you know I appreciate it."

"That's not necessary, Frank."

"Take it. You'll earn it."

I glanced at Ellen. With her tight smile and squinting eyes, she nodded approval as if witnessing a touching moment—Frank bestowing his blessings on my wayward soul in the form of five well-worn twenty-dollar bills. I felt my facade beginning to crack. Smug, nerdy, apathetic, he had the cheek to consider himself exceptional on the basis of a mastery of high school arithmetic and a disregard for misdemeanor tax law. Remembering Claire's depiction of him as a big fish in a small pond, I pictured a puffed-up spiky blowfish, pale-skinned and scaly, his bulging eyes leering, and his pithy smile rigid with the effort of holding in his breath. I wanted to prick that chesty posture, cut him down to size, expose him as the smarmy little egocentric guppy that he was.

I figured I better get away from there. Taking the money, I steeled myself to endure another unctuous grin.

"Well, thanks, Frank. I guess I can use it."

Frank glowered, still smiling, perfectly still, like he could hold that pose forever.

I turned away just in time.

Chapter 12

Joe's Mug is an all-night diner at Sixth and Federal whose chrome-trimmed siding and brightly lit interior are beacons of down-home comfort from days gone by. I had arranged to meet Luis there at eleven. It was past midnight.

When I pulled into the nearly empty lot, I noticed a car follow me in. Just in case, I drove back out onto Federal. The car stayed with me. My mind flashed with paranoia, hatching schemes of escape or confrontation. I came to a stop at the next light eyeing a quick U-turn on red. Then I recognized the car. It was Willie Jr.'s Mustang. Tossing him the finger, I headed back towards Joe's Mug, thinking up more direct ways to get rid of him. But then I decided it might be better to hook him up with Luis—should anything happen to me.

"What the hell you doing here?" I said as Willie parked next to me.

"*Ron-day-voo*, man. This the place? The safe house? Where we meet our contact? Our handler? The *man*!"

"This is the *coffee shop*," I said, irritated that his cliché witticisms were on the mark. "I'm going to have some breakfast."

"Hey, how 'bout that tail-job? Didn't have a clue, did ya? Tell me straight. 'Course, to do it right, ya gotta have at least three cars, radio dispatched, and all that. Secured, ah…frequencies. Yeah, that's it. Secured frequencies, too."

"What're you talking, Willie?"

He dragged out his long low chuckle as he got out of the car. I stand six-foot two and two hundred pounds, few men make me feel small. But standing next to Willie, I became viscerally aware of his actual size and strength resting carelessly within that laid-back mien.

"Jus' jivin' you, man," all smiles. "Let's eat. I got things to tell ya. I got the *dope* on these cons."

"Willie, stop."

"What' up, bro? I *got* somethin'. I got the *motive*."

"Just *stop*, will ya?"

The grin dissolved and he hitched his large hands onto his hips. "Okay, what?"

"Broadway Bingo went up in flames last night, right? One of Milo Finnes' clubs."

"Yeah, an'..."

"...Frank Coyne must've done it. Trying to put Milo out of business. Bad blood between them since Milo moved in on Frank's turf."

"Yeah, okay. What about this Brent dude?" Willie said, easing up. "Works for Milo."

That impressed me, but I didn't let on. "Brent Charmichael used to work for Frank. Jumped ship over to Milo's operation. Sold out all of Frank's secrets to get in."

"Okay, okay." All the affectation had dropped from his speech. "I suppose you already know about Mickey Gilmore, too, huh? And the thing with Tanya..."

"Who do you think I'm working for? Mickey is Frank Coyne's right-hand man. He's married to Tanya, who is Frank's sister and also happens to be on the board of directors of their parent company." I gloated for a few ticks before adding, "It's all hearsay, Willie. It doesn't mean anything."

He looked back at me, his gaze hardening. "And?"

"And what?"

"Brent and Tanya?"

"What about them?"

Willie smiled broadly. "Oh, so ya don't *know* 'bout the Brent an' Tanya thang," he said, cocky again.

"What about them, Willie?"

"This Brent dude's been bonin' Tanya on the side, man. Didn't know about that little piece a' *hearsay*, did ya?"

"You mean, Brent Charmichael and Tanya Gilmore are having an affair?"

"Tha's what I'm sayin', yo! Usta' be, anyway. They got a *history*, is what I heard. Tha's a *clue*, man. Ought to be worth somethin'."

"It's just gossip," I managed. "Everybody knows she sleeps around." But I was already thinking I should have guessed it, how it explained Mickey's outrage and Frank's response at the meeting on Sunday night.

"'Course it's gossip," Willie countered. "That's what you told me to do. Talk it up. Gather info. Tha's what I did." He laughed his slow, rumbling chuckle. "'Course, it don't take no *Einstein* to figure tha's why Mickey torched the joint. Must be Brent's club, right?"

"Okay, Willie, yeah it's good to know. But it's not proof that Mickey set the fire. It's not evidence."

"C'mon, man. What you want—a confession?"

"That would be good. Let's go eat." Turning my back on him, I said, "I got someone who wants to see you."

"Oh, see, I *knew* that! We gonna meet the *man*."

Entering the café, I spotted Luis' stocky frame in his navy blue sport coat, hunkered over a coffee mug in a back booth. As I walked toward him, his dark eyes met mine, and then his head shook slowly back and forth at the sight of Willie Jr.

"I think you two know each other."

"Willie Randall Jr.," Luis said, leaning forward to shake his hand.

"So, *you* the man." Willie smiled winningly.

Luis returned a tolerant grin. They had met during the investigation into my father's death, each contributing in very different ways to its resolution. I assumed a certain bond between them because of it, although neither had ever spoken to me about it.

"How's your old man?" Luis asked.

"He good, he good."

I knew for a fact that Luis had had a finger in a number of investigations in which Doctor Randy had been a 'person of interest', at least peripherally. Willie probably knew it too. It didn't show on their faces.

I slid into the booth opposite Luis and Willie sat next to me.

"I brought Willie in to help work the crowds at these halls," I said, straining to keep the obsequious tone out of my voice. "He's good at that sort of thing, as you probably know."

Luis gave it a cautious nod.

The waitress arrived, coffee mugs hooked in the crooked fingers of one hand and a steaming pot in the other. She was a hardened-looking old girl with a workman-like smile and a thinning dome of yellowish hair. "You guys want coffee?"

We nodded and watched in silence as she poured for us.

"You gonna order anything or you just gonna sit here meditating?"

Willie responded with a laugh. "Yeah, I'll have some ham an' eggs, over-medium, and, what else?"

"Toast? We got white, wheat, or dark rye."

"I'll have white. I's a *white*-bread man."

Willie and the waitress chuckled together.

"Ooo-kaay," she said, shifting her pale eyes to me.

"Nothing for me, thanks."

Luis shook his head without looking up.

She arched her penciled eyebrows, then smiled at Willie before moving away.

"You hear about the fire at Broadway Bingo?" I asked Luis.

"Naturally. Wha'd you hear about it?"

"The prevailing rumors hint at the rivalries between Frank Coyne and Milo Finnes. But nothing tangible yet."

"What about the Brent and Tanya thing?" Willie cut in. "That's tangible, ain' it?"

Luis looked at him, then at me. "What?"

"Brent Charmichael is one of Milo's lieutenants, right?" Luis nodded. "Seems he used to work for Frank. Rumor has it that Charmichael and Tanya Gilmore are having an affair."

"*Were* having," Willie piped in. "It's all in the past."

"It's all rumors," I emphasized, "but there's some indication that Mickey knew about it."

"Can't stand by for *that* shit," Willie proclaimed. "I figure he torched the place, you know, revenge. Like Hamlett."

I watched Luis watch Willie. He kept his expression blank, but I couldn't hold back a chuckle.

"What?" Willie said, smiling now.

"Listen, Willie," Luis drawled, "Why don't you let me and Henry have a private word? That be okay? Just be a few minutes."

Willie pretended to be taken aback, but he took the hint. "You the man," he said, sliding out. He strolled along the counter, sat at the far end.

"Hamlett?" Luis said, holding me with a stare. "This is all very interesting."

"It's his first night on the job. He's…apparently trying to impress you. He's still getting a feel for what's important."

"And you're gonna show him?"

"Look, Luis. You're the one who lectured me about infiltrating this crowd, how it's going to take time, how we have to talk it up with them, sift out the evidence. Willie did all right. He came up with Charmichael by himself, and Tanya Gilmore, and their involvement. I know it's circumstantial, but it does point to motive. Arson's not below us, is it?"

Luis continued to stare. Then he slowly pursed his lips and his features constricted, as if swallowing a bitter pill without benefit of water. "So what've you been doing in the meantime?"

"I earned some brownie points for my heroics," I told him. "Turning out the lights? Breaking up the robbery? Frank and his people liked that more than you did."

Luis rolled his eyes, but there was a hint of amusement in the expression.

"So Coyne wants me to run the new place, Bingo Palace. Technically, it's his brother's gig—Dennis—but he's just the family name. Frank's putting me in to cover the operational details."

His eyebrows rose with interest. "You mean, you'll have access to the tally sheets, cash drawers, that sort of thing?"

"I was counting the take with his wife just a few minutes ago. Ellen is Frank's wife, right?"

Luis nodded. "That would be in your homework."

"The place was jumpin'," I said, by way of deflection. "The crowd that showed up at Broadway Bingo came out here for the late games."

"You need to keep a tally of their sales. We can compare it to their quarterlies, note the discrepancies. I don't suppose you could get copies of their daily reports?"

"I got given keys tonight. But I haven't had a chance to get in there on my own. I don't know that they keep any books on the skim."

"Oh, they keep 'em all right. Reivers gave us samples from a couple years back. But we need current ones for the comparison."

"Wha'd they look like. A ledger of some kind?"

"What we got was loose pages. Eight-column graph paper. Done in pencil with a week's worth on each page. Had double entries for all their gross sales figures."

"What about the amounts? How much are we talkin' here?"

"Well, that's the thing, Henry. There was graft goin' on then too. But the past amounts don't correspond to what they're reporting now. I mentioned this to you before. There's new money coming in, a lot of it. It's not bingo money I'm worried about."

"Another source of income? What would that be?"

"Don't know. But they're set up to move major cash. It's built in to their operation. Maybe someone else thought of that too."

"How long you suspected that?" I asked, letting a little irritation show through.

"Since I carefully studied the file I gave you. How long you suspected it?"

I laughed. Maybe I was caught out. "All right, I'll see what I can find. Once we get going at the Palace, I should be able to get you something."

A dissatisfied frown edged along one side of his lips. "What about this fire? Anything more than rumor?"

"Well, maybe, in a way. We had a powwow Sunday night. All the heavies were there talking up the shooting. Mickey Gilmore was in a rage about Charmichael being good for it. He wanted to strike back. Willie's Hamlett reference might not be that far-fetched." This time Luis gave it a chuckle. "Frank Coyne and Chuck Burrows vetoed it, but it didn't stop there." Not wanting to take the rap for instigating arson, I paused to consider various versions.

"Is that it?"

"Somebody brought up a similar scenario played out in Seattle some time back. Place was torched. Drove a guy out of business. I don't know if there was any truth to it, but Mickey's eyes lit up at the idea. So did several others'."

"Who brought it up?"

"I'm not sure."

Luis regarded me with obvious suspicion but he didn't ask the question. "Who else was there besides Mickey and Frank?"

"Burrows, Dennis Coyne and Tanya Gilmore. And a low-life named Benny Palmer, runs their supply house. You got a line on Burrows, right? He's thick with these boys."

"Oh, yeah, we know him. Took early retirement from the force in '95 in lieu of a deeper investigation into his dealings with the Coyne family. He holds title to several of their clubs now, rents them to Frank and Mickey and kicks back a big cut after expending it. That's the standard scheme, but we don't have anything other than the leases that link him to Frank or Mickey or BACCO. We need evidence of the kickback, records of transactions."

"My guess is nothing like that exists."

"Don't be so sure. These people keep good records. They deal with a lot of red tape. Frank's old man is an accountant."

"Any other ex-cops in on their operation?"

"Have been quite a few, as a matter of fact. They start out doing their security, keep a blind eye, work their way into the scam when they see how green the grass is. DPD has lost a few over the years because of it. Aurora, too, I think." Luis stopped and regarded me carefully. "You got a new name?"

I looked over my shoulder to make sure Willie was out of earshot. He was jawing on his cell phone, gesturing dramatically with his free hand. Maxine, I figured. Beyond him, at a booth by the windows a couple sat smoking over empty plates, avoiding each other's eyes. Turning back to Luis, I said, "If this thing's headed into the cop house, I want no part of it."

"C'mon, Henry. We can't limit it like that. It goes where it goes." When I said nothing, and he took a minute to think it over, he tried a different angle. "It's not our jurisdiction, okay? And they're not our targets. I told you what we're after. But it's likely there's people on the job involved—cops, investigators for the secretary of state, even people in our offices—any of them. That's why we're coming in from outside. That's why *you* have this job."

"I'm not going to testify against cops, Luis. I got friends on the force, people that have done my family right."

"I know that, Henry. You know I do."

I lit a cigarette. Luis sipped his coffee.

Eight years ago, my father got caught up in an investigation that eventually led to his involvement with the wife of the principle scumbag suspect. Yeah, that kind of 'involvement'. It was a no-win situation that predictably blew up when he tried to take down the scumbag without tainting the wife. That led to him getting busted down to street duty and triggered an IAD investigation that spiraled into a department-wide sinkhole. Long story short, he found a way out of it—but it cost him his life. A lot of secrets were buried with him, including exactly how he died. But for all intents and purposes, his death ended the IAD investigation. It also preserved his pension for the wife and son—me— that he left behind.

A few years later, I got a whiff of what went down while working a case for the Denver DA. I followed my nose into everybody's business—everyone who was remotely connected to the investigation at the time. Eventually, I found out what happened and why, and I came to understand that it was best to leave that truth buried. It cost me my job and a large portion of my peace of mind but it gave me a new respect for the kinds of situations cops find themselves in. Luis was there when I found out, as was Willie Jr., and Captain Tom Connally of the Homicide Division. They share the burden of that conspiracy to this day. My mother still doesn't know.

From across the table, Luis said, "If it gets too far into the cop house, we'll turn it over to IAD, the standard procedure, as you know. If it's the usual petty graft, all they'll do is hold it over their heads, talk them into movin' on. You won't have to testify. If it's bigger than that, you can decide for yourself. It's a long shot that it would ever get to open hearings."

"Decide for myself? You know what my decision will be."

Luis nodded, smiling an awkward smile. "That's part of why I chose you for this. I knew you'd be…sensitive." Watching me with sad brown eyes, he took a deep breath, like inhaling smoke from a cigarette. "You know how this goes, Henry. Guys reach out that way, jam themselves up between both sides, anything can happen."

I knew and I didn't see a clean way through it. Any investigation could lead there. Cops are human, like the rest of us, like my father. If they hang around the edge long enough—and the edge is mostly where they work—they can get tempted: tempted to help, tempted to shortcut, tempted to dip into the trickle down. As absurd as it seemed, the bingo world was no exception. It had its points of interest, its enticements, its ambiguities.

"I don't think that's where it's going," Luis continued. "But if it does we want to catch it before it spreads." He paused momentarily before saying, "On the other hand, you wanna bail, that's okay. We can call this off."

I gave him a doubtful frown as I pondered the edges I had already pried up, the players I had fawned and flattered. My mind flashed on Claire and, for a moment, I thought about it. I could do it, I saw it. For an instant there, I was completely free. But then, I wasn't.

"If I get slapped for contempt, you'll vouch for my confidentiality?"

"Yeah, right. How 'bout I'll post your bail…"

I huffed out a chuckle I didn't feel. There was no humor in Luis' eyes either. He regarded me patiently.

"You know a detective named Joe Perkins?"

Luis' response was slow, reluctant. "Yeah, worked with him on some stuff."

I could tell this sword cut both ways. "He's buddies with Chuck Burrows. Frank suggested they reel him in, hit him up for a favor. The idea was to get him to put some heat on Milo's people, make it seem like the cops think they're good for the holdup at Clancy's."

"But he's homicide. That wouldn't fly."

"It's a ruse. He'd be off-duty. Poke around, flash his badge, ask some questions."

"It wouldn't take long for Milo to figure that out."

"If he checks or if he knows Perkins, sure. I thought it was a better idea than burning down bingo halls."

"Ok. That all you got on him?"

I had already decided not to mention the con, taking the cake. But I wanted to plant a seed if it turned out that Perkins was past the point of no return.

"Tonight, some guy was chumming around with Dennis Coyne pretty good. I don't know Perkins by sight. Might be him. I got this plate number off his Caddy. Figured you could check it out."

"They're supposed to log their outside work," Luis said, taking the piece of paper and studying it as if looking for visible clues.

"You gonna talk to Connally?" As captain of homicide, and therefore Perkins' boss, Connally would be a logical source.

"He's your friend, not mine," Luis snapped. "And now that I think about it, I don't want you talkin' to him either." He folded the piece of paper and tucked it into his inside pocket.

"You can't suspect Connally," I said, maneuvering to change the subject.

"'Course not. Tom's the best they come. But he's been a cop for twenty-five years. He knows everybody. Lots of potential conflict of interest there."

I took his point, but he didn't need to make it. Connally was the last guy I would go to. Even though he was a long-time family friend and had once partnered with my father, my relations with him had become strained. The results of my investigation into my father's death—not to mention my breakneck methods—had taken a toll on him too.

"What else?" Luis said. "I gotta get home."

"That's it. But things are heating up. I expect it to escalate."

Luis stood up, tossed two tens on the table. "You mean like Milo torching one of Frank's clubs?"

"I wouldn't be completely surprised."

"Me neither. First the hold-up, now the fire. All this cash floatin' around." He gestured toward Willie with his head. "This thing with Tanya and Brent. Yeah, I'd say we could expect some action." Luis' ruddy face broke into a wry grin. "That make you happy?"

No point in lying. "Keeps me interested, yeah."

"Toe the line, Henry my boy. Being undercover doesn't absolve you from the law. And it's not like you're wearing a vest either."

When I turned toward the door without responding, he gripped my arm and gave me a look. "You follow me on that?"

"Yeah, sure."

"You gotta be careful you don't get caught in the crossfire."

"Speaking metaphorically, I presume."

"You never know."

Luis said goodnight to Willie on the way out. It was a nice touch. I stopped at the register to pay for Willie's breakfast.

"My man," Willie said. "How'd it go with the boss-man. Everything copacetic?"

"Everything's fine."

"Yeah, good. So what I get for that tip on Tanya and Brent?"

"What do you mean, 'what do you get'?"

As we walked out the door, Willie pled his case. "You said we get paid for info, paid by the piece. That was a piece. That was a *good* piece."

"It doesn't work that way, Willie."

"Well, how *does* it work, bro? I mean…"

"Take it easy. You won two hundred bucks tonight, right? How do you think that happened?"

It slowed him, but not for long. "Oh, c'mon, man. You tellin' me you put a fix in on that? No way. Tha's *my* money. I won it free and clear."

"You're ahead. Stop crying about it."

"So how much it worth? Just tell me that."

"You'll have to trust me, okay? It's not big money, I told you that. And I told you we're not in it for the money."

"Yeah, I remember that. Jus' before you hung up on me."

I smiled at Willie's blatant sulk. "You're doing good work, Willie. Even Luis thinks so. It'll come back to you."

"Yeah, well. I gave up a lot for this, ya know."

"Right. So anyway, tomorrow night, Bingo Palace. Get there on time. You disrupt the game coming in late, drawing attention to yourself. Come to think of it, you could stand to tone down your wardrobe a bit. Blend in a little better."

"Blend in?" Willie feigned astonishment. "Man, that the *whole* wrong approach. *I* blend in standing *out*." He smiled his wide, toothy smile. "I be the last dude they think of ratted them out."

I had to admit he was probably right.

Chapter 13

Under the big sky of the eastern plains, Bellevue Shopping Center rose up from behind a low canting plateau like a cluster of futuristic monoliths implanted on the prairie landscape of some otherwise undeveloped planet. As I got closer, a huge canvas banner along the top edge of the largest building—an anchor store of preternatural proportion—betrayed the big-box structures as something more contemporary and mundane. **BSC GRAND OPENING - OCTOBER 1ST.** The big event, seven days away.

Except for a FedEx truck and two service vans parked along the curbing, the vast asphalt expanse was an early-bird shopper's dream come true—a thousand empty spaces to choose from. In a neat row nearest the entrance to Bingo Palace, the same three late-model Cadillacs glistened in the afternoon sunlight. Dennis Coyne's souped-up Firebird was there too, and Frank's Jag. I parked precisely in the middle of nowhere and went in out of the brightness.

One rectangular table had been pulled away from the arranged rows and moved closer to the front windows. Frank and Dennis Coyne, Chuck Burrows, and Benny Palmer sat loosely grouped around one end of the table, all half-facing Mickey Gilmore seated alone at the other end. A chair next to him was vacant, apparently reserved for me. Only Tanya was missing from the Sunday night meeting but judging by the dour facial expressions, I had the feeling her disapproval of Mickey's antics was well represented. Streams of smoke tapered and billowed upward, made more apparent by the shafts of sunlight slanting through the glass storefront. I slunk into the chair next to Mickey without disturbing the spirals of smoke or the litany of excuses he was laying down for the benefit of his peers.

"Of *course* I left the gas cans there. It was *meant* to look like a torch-job. That was the whole point. If it had looked like an accident, they wouldn't know it was us getting even."

"But, we didn't *decide* on getting even, Mickey," Frank intoned. His voice sounded whiney as it struggled to override Mickey's pugnacious timbre.

"No, no, that's not true." Mickey wagged an extended finger. "We were all howling to get back at them one way or another, including *you*. We wanted the cops in on it, but that wouldn't work. We wanted Herrera to pester them or that cop Perkins to wind them up but that wasn't gonna show them we mean business. Now they know we aren't gonna stand by while they shoot up our house."

"But we didn't *decide* that, Mickey. We decided to put Perkins on it and wait and see."

"*You* decided that, Frank. I got my own interests to look out for and I'm not waiting around for them to do a fuckin' drive-by at Bingo Circle."

"Your interests!" Frank barked, leaning forward. "Wha'd you mean 'your interests'? We're in this together, goddammit."

"If we were in this together, you guys'd be pattin' me on the back about now. As it stands, I'm beginning to feel like I'm out on my own."

"You think you can pull this kind of shit without my approval, you can *damn well* go out on your own."

"That's fine with me. About goddamn time."

"But you're not taking the Circle with you, Mickey. And this time there's no coming back. I ain't bailing you out again."

That stopped him for an instant, his face reddening, his neck muscles taut. "I *did* something, dammit." His fist hit the table. "Who else was gonna fuckin' *do* something?"

Frank came up out of his chair.

"Now hold on, fellas," Chuck Burrows roared, standing and extending his arms over the table between them. "Just calm down, both of you. Of course we're in this together."

"Not if I have to stand by and watch those assholes shooting up *my* place."

"Just *hold it*, Mickey, will ya? You have a point and I think you've made it. Are you listening to me?"

Mickey sat back, shrugged, and straightened his jacket. That's when I saw the bulge of his handgun. After a long ten seconds, Frank lowered himself into his chair. Burrows did the same.

"Now *my* point is, what's done is done," Burrows said. "We can't undo anything." He turned his head to look at Frank. "Right, boss? What's done is done."

Frank stared back at him without speaking, his owl eyes bulging grotesquely. Then he lowered his gaze to the black plastic ashtray in front of him and ground out his cigarette with a slow twisting motion, as if tightening down the screws on his upwelling rage.

"What we need to do is examine what happened," Burrows continued, "go over it in detail, make sure we've covered our tracks."

"I didn't leave no tracks, Chuck," Mickey asserted. "I bought gas cans at two different places." He counted out his argument on the fingers of an upward thrusting hand. "Paid cash for everything. Guy runs out of gas in the middle of the night, big deal. I waited for the bars to close before goin' anywhere near the place. I started the fire at the back, trailing gas along the sides. I was in and out of there in ten minutes."

Every man listened intently, reluctantly enthralled by the details, the action, the balls on Mickey Gilmore. Glancing around, he sighed and jutted out his chin, forming his wide mouth into a bulldog frown. He wasn't done.

"You guys don't want to vouch for me? Fine." His eyes cut to Frank again. "I got an alibi. Tanya will say I was home all night." The frown curled into a tight, ironic smile. "Sharin' the same bed for a change. *She* didn't think this was a bad idea."

I was surprised at this and I wasn't alone.

"You told Tanya?" Frank was incredulous.

"I told her we were going to strike back. I told her she didn't want to know the details but I might need an alibi. She said I could count on it." He looked around the table as if expecting to be challenged. When no one did, he dropped his gaze and feigned an unconvincing expression of humility. "There ain't much I can count on from her these days, but she knows which side the bread is buttered on. She knows I'm takin' care a' business." Mickey met Frank's eyes again. "I told her you'd be pissed."

The two men stared down again, their smug expressions deeply entrenched. The others around the table studied their hands, looked out the window, or dragged on their smokes. Chuck Burrows shuffled in his seat, then spoke.

"Just as well then. It's all above board. We're gonna have to stick together."

Frank shifted his eyes from Mickey to Chuck.

"What's done is done," Burrows reiterated. "What we better do now is think about what happens next. First of all, we need to guard against retaliation. I'll line up some additional rent-a-cops. Maybe we oughta think about 24/7 patrols from one of these private firms."

No one appeared to be listening and no one bothered to respond. Frank seemed to retreat into his own musings. He reached for a cigarette, leaned back, lit up with a Bic.

Benny Palmer cleared his throat, then scooted his chair before speaking. "I think we ought to make some kind of overture to Milo. Call a truce. Offer some kind of agreement to work together, maybe."

Mickey coughed out a derisive laugh. "You *would* say that. You lookin' to expand your market, Benny boy?"

"Jesus," Chuck said tossing up his hands.

"You ain't sellin' nobody with talk like that, Mickey," Frank cut in, asserting himself again.

"He's runnin' supplies to Milo, Frank! Aren't ya, Benny."

"It's none of your business what I do," Palmer countered.

"I got a little birdie told me one a' your trucks was unloading at Milo's warehouse."

Palmer's face flushed. "I do business with whoever I want," he said, grinding out the words. "I've been supplying you guys exclusively for eight years. But times are tough. You ain't exactly expanding, right? Man's gotta do what he's gotta *do*." He looked around the table. Only Frank met his eyes. "Am I right?" he demanded, but no one offered any support. Mickey smirked.

"That's not the issue at hand," Frank stated. Then, sounding like a paid-off politician, he added, "Anyway that's nobody's business but Benny's."

"Nobody's *business*! Frank, if he's in bed with Milo, there's no tellin' what kind of fuckin' pillow-talk goes on…"

"I'm not in bed with anybody. Not him and not *you*."

"Let it *go*, Mickey!" Frank commanded.

Mickey huffed and tossed down his half-smoked cigar. Leaning back, he went for the inside pocket of his coat. Heads turned, eyes focused, Benny Palmer froze in place. Mickey's hand came out with a pack of cigarettes. The whole ensemble squirmed in their seats, sitting back, looking off. It made me wonder who else might be packing. And if I should be.

Seemingly oblivious to the stir he had caused, Mickey shook out a cigarette, pinched it between his lips, and lit up. "All right, all right. I don't give a shit what he does on his own time. But the point is, if we're drawin' sides against Milo, we gotta know where he stands."

"No one's drawing sides against Milo," Frank said. "What we gotta know is where *you* stand. Are you with us or are you out?"

Mickey withdrew the cigarette from his parted lips. He stared at Frank as if not comprehending. The rest of us waited in silence. With a deep breath, Mickey lowered his gaze then proceeded to speak with his head bowed. "Ah, hell. I didn't mean it to be this way. I thought you guys'd be *proud*." His eyes cut to Frank but he didn't try to match his stare. "It's just that…well, shit. I took a chance, ya know? I figured someone ought to do something, so I took a chance."

No one said anything. Burrows and Palmer took their turns lighting up. Men smoked and avoided each other's eyes, waiting for Frank to pass judgment. It was some time in coming. Frank sat with one hand drawn up to conceal the absence of his grin. Finally, he dropped it and affected a frown of resignation. "Nothing we can do about it now, I guess." He and Chuck Burrows exchanged a glance. Palmer turned in his seat and looked out the front windows. Mickey kept his eyes cast downward, apparently taking great interest in the ashtray in front of him, cigarette tapping at it continuously.

I had been quiet the whole time and Frank finally noticed. As if for the sake of distraction, he said, "What do you think about all this, Henry? After all, it was your idea."

I caught Mickey's eyes, still hot. Frank's look remained intense as well.

"I didn't mean for anything like this to happen. I mean, I don't have the same things at stake here. It's not my business to…take chances like this."

Mickey fumed in place. Just beyond him, Frank's face contracted into a tight frown. As a newcomer, without the history—the baggage—that these men brought to the table, my opinion, conversely, seemed to carry more weight. Frank knew it and had drawn me out to bolster his position. I had my own tightrope to walk, obviously, but I didn't like being manipulated by this makeshift *mafioso*. What did I care if they fought among themselves until the whole thing went up in smoke?

"Having said that, given the circumstances? It's what I would have done. Something like it anyway." Frank's frown deepened into a scowl and Mickey, sitting back, looked at me with the smallest curl of a grin. "But Chuck made the point. What's done is done. We have to figure how to put it to our advantage."

Burrows didn't miss his cue. "I think Benny was right, if you ask me. Now that we *have* shown them we've got some balls, we want to offer the olive branch. Let's say we're even. Let's call this off before we ruin it for everyone. It won't be easy but it's better than tryin' to burn down *all* their halls."

A few nervous chuckles erupted around the table, including one from Mickey.

Frank said, "Assuming they *are* the ones that pulled that holdup."

"I'm with Mickey on that," Burrows stated, and others tossed in grumbles of assent. "There was no reason to cap Eddie otherwise. That adds ten years to a robbery rap."

"Who the fuck is that?" Palmer broke in.

All eyes turned to him, then followed his gaze toward the front. A midnight-blue Cadillac with a black vinyl roof sat at the curb just beyond the doors. As we watched, it rolled away at just above idle then circled around the row of cars and pulled adjacent the front door again. The sunlight pouring down behind made it impossible to glean the features of two heads framed in the Caddy's window. My mind flashed back to the scene last Saturday night. The adrenaline flowed as I thought again about the gun in my car and waited for black-hooded men to swing open the doors.

"That son of a bitch!" Mickey exclaimed, pushing back his chair. He charged the door, reaching inside his blazer again and this time the hand came out with a gun.

"Mickey, don't," Frank yelled, others yelling too. I went after him.

I saw more clearly the silhouette of heads. Then a movement of arms. Then rapid fire flashes and—pop—pop—pop. I heard a howl of pain. It didn't come from Mickey but it was Mickey who caught the bullets. He hopped in place, then crumbled like a loosely hinged crash-test dummy. Two more shots banged out as I hit the floor.

I heard a man's commanding voice, "Fuck! Dammit!" then, "Drive, drive!" and the Caddy's engine growled. Wheels screaming, the car fishtailed heavily as it sped away. Looking out over Mickey's recumbent body, I watched it careen across the expanse of empty parking spaces.

Mickey lay bent at the torso over obscenely splayed legs. Dark stains spread on the back of his jacket. I knew he was dying. I rolled him back to see the wound. His face and hair were a mass of blood. One bullet had gone into his forehead, the others through his chest. I turned away. The air smelled of cordite and Mickey's aftershave.

"My God," Frank said, groping over me at Mickey's shoulders. "Mickey! Mickey!"

I looked up to see the dark blue Caddy in the distance turning onto Parker Road. Then, from the side of the building, another Cadillac appeared, heading out after them. It was beige and white, with white-walled tires, and it cut across the grid of parking spaces like a speedboat over placid waters. I knew that car. I grabbed up Mickey's unfired weapon and sprinted towards my Mercedes. What could happen?

As I brought the Merc up to speed, I caught sight of the beige Caddy poking its way through backed up traffic at a red light on Parker. I was a good hundred yards behind them when they cleared the intersection. Striking a wide arc past the traffic median, I carved a turn that took up all three lanes. Cars braked hard and jammed on their horns. The Caddy pulled away in the stretch as my Mercedes labored towards higher revs.

In the straightaway, I checked to make sure Mickey's gun was loaded. It was a blue steel .357 with a big-hand rubber grip. All six chambers were loaded. I unlocked the safety without a thought.

A half a mile further on, a group of cars waited in rows at the intersection with C-470. The Caddy's brake lights flashed as it maneuvered left. Then the light turned green, forcing the Caddy to cut back in. I was coming down fast by the time it started passing cars on the shoulder. Right up on its bumper, I managed to read the first letters on its plates—NAR—before my windshield shattered and chunks of glass sprayed onto the seat next to me. I hit hard on the brakes and ducked below the dash, steering blind and skidding to a stop. A second blast went off and I felt it hit the Merc's front grill. Steam hissed from the radiator. Assuming two barrels from a shotgun, they'd have to reload. I dragged myself across the broken glass, popped up into the hole in the windshield, and fired off four rounds at the first thing I saw. It was the back of the beige Caddy ten feet in front of me and pulling away. I had hit the trunk lid three times which didn't really slow it down. Spewing dust and pebbles, it spun out in front of the stalled traffic before I could fire again.

I bounced back behind the wheel, restarted the car, and headed out after them. Steam poured over my hood and the odor of antifreeze told me the Merc didn't have much left to give. As I cleared the snarled array of cars, I spotted the beige Cadillac two hundred yards out and swooping onto the entrance ramp of C-470. That would carry it smoothly unhindered toward the outskirts of Denver at speeds my old Mercedes didn't even dream about anymore.

Chapter 14

Adrenaline has the effect, among other things, of blanking the mind, wiping the slate clean, leaving open the channels of consciousness for the clarity of instinct and quickness of reflex. As the heart-pounding flow of blood abated somewhat towards the level of run-of-the-mill fear, my thoughts began to crawl back from their banishment, trailing behind them long chains of cause and effect, implication, and consequence. Things were getting out of hand.

I pulled a U-turn and headed back down Parker Road toward the Palace. Steaming brownish antifreeze billowed from under my hood, whipping through the gaping hole in my shot-out windshield. I had to lean out the driver side window in order to see and to breathe. Other drivers slowed to follow my progress as if watching the locomotion of some runaway train.

Imagining the scene at the Palace—a kaleidoscope of cop cars, a swarm of pushy cops and harried paramedics, the strident voices of the bingo bigwigs offering conflicting accounts and wild accusations, all of it revolving around Mickey's torn and lifeless body—the more I thought about it, the less I wanted to go back to face that cacophonic music. The sound of sirens approaching, and then the flashing lights and howling engine of a sheriff's vehicle overtaking me (without a glance at my smoking and shattered vehicle trundling along), instilled my qualms with the strength of well-grounded logic. I decided to ditch the car and make myself scarce.

I spotted a construction site, a future eight-bay gas station in the later stages of construction encircled by a six-foot high chain-link fence. There were no workers visible on the site. A dried mud two-track road circumnavigated the fenced enclosure. I pulled over as another emergency vehicle passed, this one an ambulance going not much above the speed limit. Just as well, I thought. Then I backed up along the shoulder and turned onto the dirt track, following it around to the back of the site. A gigantic roll-off Dumpster sat back there like a river barge run to ground. I parked the Merc behind it, out of site from passing traffic. Grabbing Mickey's gun and removing my own Glock 19 from the glove box, I put a gun in each jacket pocket before stepping my way through the mud ruts back to Parker Road.

Bingo Palace was half a mile away. I crossed the street and jogged in the opposite direction toward a Seven-Eleven. Two more cop cars roared past, sirens blaring. The guns weighing down my sport coat made me feel conspicuous but I made it to a pay phone without being arrested. I called Willie's house and got no answer then tried his cell phone and was relieved to hear him pick up on the first ring.

"I need you to come and get me."

"Man, I ain't ate yet. It's only five o'clock. You said seven."

"You can forget about the game tonight. Mickey Gilmore was shot down in the doorway of the Palace."

"What palace? *Bingo* Palace?"

"One and the same."

"He dead?"

"No doubt."

"When this happen?"

"Fifteen minutes ago. I just left there."

"What do you mean 'just left'? You on the run?"

"Not exactly."

"Oh yeah. You in some trouble now, ain't ya?"

"Willie, I'm stuck out here in fucking Kansas. They shot up the Merc, blew holes in the radiator. I need a ride."

"Man, you tried to run'em down in that piece a' junk?" Willie found it in himself to peel off a short version of his Eddie Murphy chuckle.

"Dammit, Willie, just get out here, will ya?"

"Yeah, sure man. Where you at?"

I gave him directions and rang off. Then I decided to call Claire. I took a moment to consider what to say. Nothing came to me, but I had to make the call. Her daughter answered the phone.

"Hi, Shanie. Is your mother home?"

"Yeah?" she said, suspicious that I knew her name. Then, with practiced politeness, she said, "Who shall I say is calling?"

"This is Henry Burkhart. I work at the…"

"Oh, *Henry*," she said, blithely.

"You remember me?"

"Ah-huh. From Clancy's. And my mommy told me about you."

She dropped the phone calling out, "Mom-my!", leaving me to wonder what exactly her mother had told her. A television blared in the background. Dealin' Doug was slashing prices. Factory overstock. Everything must go.

Claire greeted me cheerfully.

"Did you get a call?" I said, feeling stupid for saying it.

"What do you mean?"

"Claire, I…"

"What's the matter, Henry? Something happened?"

"There was another incident this afternoon. Out at Bingo Palace."

"What do you mean?"

When I didn't say anything for a moment, she went on, her tone dropping with emotion. "Oh, no. Not another robbery. Did anyone get hurt?"

"Not a robbery. A shooting."

"A shooting? Oh God. Who?"

I couldn't say it, so she knew.

"Mickey?" she said, her voice barely a whisper. "Was Mickey hurt?"

"Mickey's dead, Claire."

"Oh, God, no," her voice cracking.

I heard the jumpy music and crazy sound effects of a cartoon episode from the television in the background. "Cwazy wabbit!" said Elmer Fudd.

Claire didn't speak. I felt compelled to fill the void.

"A car drove up. Mickey went to the door. They just started shooting."

"Oh, Jesus." Another silence followed while I pondered second thoughts about having made this call. She cleared her throat, then asked, "When?"

"Maybe twenty minutes ago."

"I have to get out there," she said, suddenly sounding urgent.

"That's not a good idea, Claire. No need for you to get involved."

"He's my *brother!* I *have* to. I need to talk to…"

"Claire, it's too late. There's nothing you can do."

I heard muffled sounds, a restrained groan, then nothing from her for another long moment. Cymbals crashed in the background at the crescendo of wild violins. When their reverberations stopped, Bugs Bunny said, "Ehhh… you don't look so good, Doc." The violins took up the chase again.

After a noisy intake of breath, Claire sniffled and said, "I'm going. I have to. Call me later. *Please.*"

But she didn't hang up the phone. There was nothing I could do to stop her, to comfort her, to make it better. I thought it would be different. I definitely should not have called. "All right. But be careful. These guys got away. Anything could happen."

"Was Frank there?"

"Yes."

"Is he all right?"

"No one else was hurt." I had fifty questions for her but I held back. I couldn't help noticing she didn't ask about Dennis.

"I'm going. I'll have to drop Shanie…" Her voice trailed off. Then, more urgently, she said, "Where *are* you?"

I didn't want to say too much, I hadn't thought it through. "My car broke down."

"Oh, *no*," she lamented, as if this was an even greater tragedy. "Shall I come and get you?"

"No, no. It's all right. I've got someone coming. Don't worry about me."

She was crying now, unrestrained. I heard Shanie's voice in the background. "Mommy what is it?"

Claire sniffled, took a deep breath. "It's all right, sweetie. It's nothing." Then in a more commanding voice, she said to me, "Okay, Henry, now I've really done it. I've got to go. Call me later, okay?"

"Are you sure you're all right to drive? I don't think you should…"

"I'm all right," she said ardently, as if to demonstrate her self-control. "I'll be okay. I have to go."

The line went dead. I stared at the push buttons on the phone, a knot tightening in my chest.

Willie's Mustang rumbled into the convenience store parking lot. In the interim, I had counted four or five emergency vehicles and two news vans headed toward the Palace. These news hounds were good. It was a long way out for them. The ambulance hadn't yet made the return trip.

I tore a page out of the yellow pages and jumped into Willie's car.

"What' up? We goin' after them?" Willie was ready.

"Yeah, we're going after them. Lemme use your phone."

"Man, I'm over my limit."

"Willie, there's no time."

"Ah, *man*." He handed me his cell. "Where we goin'?"

"West side. One of Milo's clubs."

"Which one?"

"That's what I'm calling about. Shut up and drive. Take 470."

While waiting for Willie, I had worked my way through half the list of bingo halls asking for Milo Finnes with no success. To Willie's relief, I found him on the first call I made from the cellphone. Whoever answered told me Milo was there but unavailable. "We're right in the *middle* of a *game*," she hissed. I got directions and hung up.

"Holiday Bingo on Santa Fe Drive. Let's see what this V-8 can do."

That was all the prompting Willie needed. While he drove hard, I told him how the shooting went down and about the chase afterwards and the three bullet holes I put in the back of the second car. "We've got to find that Caddy before they ditch it."

"How do you know it was Milo's people?"

"It was the same Caddy that held up Clancy's. Mickey figured Brent Charmichael was in on that. He's Milo's right hand man."

"You mean Brent who's bonin' Tanya? Man, no wonder these guys gettin' jacked up. All side banging each other's bitches."

Yeah, worth more thinking about that.

Fifteen minutes hurtling down the freeway brought us to Santa Fe Drive. Holiday Bingo was just inside the city limits. The hall took up three or four storefronts in an L-shaped strip mall. Fluorescents, of course, glowed starkly from within. We rolled through the rows of cars, then circled around the building and into the alley. And there it was, the beige and white Caddy—license number NAR 488—backed up tight against the back wall. There was no sign of the blue Cadillac that the shooters drove. I figured that would be harder to find. I hadn't really expected to find this one so easily. They were just that stupid.

I directed Willie to park up the alley from where we could watch both the Caddy and the entrance to the hall.

"Keep an eye on the doors. If anyone comes out heading my way, honk your horn. Then circle around and get me before they do."

"What you gonna do?"

"Check out that Caddy. See if I can find out who owns it."

Fingering the guns in my pockets, I made my way to the Caddy. Its hood was still warm. The doors were locked and inside there was nothing to see except a pair of hanging furry dice. I went to the back of the car and poked at the three indented bullet holes.

I walked around to the front of the building and peered through the windows. A hundred or so people were in there, casually hunkered down, heads bowed, daubers at the ready. There was nothing to do but wait. I rejoined Willie.

"So you think Milo's people took out Mickey 'cause of the fire?"

"That's what it looks like."

"Why two cars?"

"Maybe backup. Maybe to slow down whoever gave chase."

"That doesn't make sense. Shoulda jacked a car for the job, then meet up with the second one, switch and ditch."

That had been my thinking too, at first. "These guys aren't master criminals, you know. They probably don't know how to steal a car."

Willie laughed at that. "Man, I tell you. They don't seem like criminals at all. Bunch a' fuckin' schoolboys pullin' pranks and gettin' mean."

I agreed, though I didn't tell Willie. These were careless and violent crimes for the likes of bingo king wannabes. But there was real money at stake and greed has a way of making stupid people think they can get away with murder. I wondered how stupid Milo was and I knew I would have to worm my way into a position to find out.

Chapter 15

We sat in the car and waited for something to happen. Nothing did. I killed time rehashing the day's events with Willie. Pondering it all as I spoke began to depress me. I drifted into a sulk while Willie fleshed out a few theories of his own, different scenarios of blind rage, uncontrollable jealousy, or calculated revenge. Finally, he settled on one he liked. It was a love triangle, simple as that. Brent Charmichael killed Mickey Gilmore for love, with Tanya in the middle. I had a hard time picturing Tanya's Botox demeanor as the face that launched a thousand Cadillacs—or even two. But I followed Willie's yarn to humor him, partly wishing for things to be that simple. Maybe romantic love inspired the rest of this shit into something worth fighting for.

Like many of us—mostly men, I suppose—I have a soft spot for crimes of passion, a latent sympathy for those driven by love gone wrong. Not that love justifies murder, but there's no shortage of people dying for it one way or another. It's a realm where the state of mind weighs more heavily on the crime, where the distinctions between right and wrong become clouded with personal transcendence, where the frailty of human happiness and the consequences of its fevered pursuit yield only disappointment in the cold light of day. It's no fun tracking these people down. They're usually not that clever, for one thing, and their actions are often predictable. And once you catch up with them, they tend to break down. It's sad really and often just plain embarrassing. We're all suckers for something.

I moved to shake it off. A drive-by shooting, after all, implies timing and a calculated escape. Hardly poetic. Plus there was too much easy money floating around to allow a love affair that everyone knew about to get in the way. Besides it was years ago, I told Willie, all in the past.

"How you know that?"

"That's what *you* said. I figure it was back when Brent worked for Frank."

"That don't mean they ain't still hooking up."

"In the midst of all these rivalries?"

"It happens. *Romeo and Juliet.* How 'bout that?" Willie chuckled.

"I'm impressed you know your Shakespeare."

"Liberal arts," Willie said. "Class of '95. That shit come in handy. Better than your torts and contracts *legalese*, anyway."

I couldn't disagree.

The first session ended, a throng of people came and went, but no one approached the Caddy. A few minutes into the second session, all was quiet when Frank Coyne's Jaguar pulled in off Santa Fe Drive. The car rolled slowly through the lot and around the back just as we had, pausing in front of the beige Cadillac before parking well away from it near the street. Frank got out of the passenger side—tall and slightly stooped, almost willowy. He stood and surveilled the enemy terrain, then bent down to speak to his driver.

"Who's that?"

"The man himself, Willie. Frank Coyne."

"That geek's the *Bingo King?*" He rolled out a low chuckle. "What the hell *he* doin' here?"

"He knows that beige Caddy. He's here to talk to Milo." That was the best case scenario. I didn't take time to tell Willie the worst one. "I'd better go see."

"I'm comin' with you."

"You can't. It'll blow your cover."

"Ah, *man*."

"Look, Willie. You're through if they see you with me. Just sit tight and keep an eye out." I took Mickey's gun from my coat pocket and gave it to him. "You know how to use this?"

"'Course," Willie said, holding it gingerly, eyeing the cold steel like he expected it to come alive in his hand. "What you got in mind?"

"Can I trust you not to use it?"

"Why you givin' it to me, then?"

"I don't want them to find it on me. Also, if things go bad…well, let's put it this way. You shoot somebody, all your daddy's lawyers ain't gonna get you a walk."

"Hell, I'll just let 'em shoot you then."

"Funny."

Frank strolled across the lot, his shoulders hunched and his horn-rimmed gaze focused warily on the entrance to Holiday Bingo.

"I gotta go. Use your best judgment. And, hey, there's only two bullets left in it."

"*Two bullets!*"

Moving across the pavement, I brought myself into Frank's field of vision. I called out just loud enough to be heard over the passing traffic. He took me in with those bulging eyes. Between the lapels of his tweed sport coat, dark blotches of Mickey's blood stained his shirt.

"What're you doing here?"

"I followed the Caddy, more or less."

"Which one?"

"The beige one. It's around back."

"What about the blue one? Any ideas?"

"Nope. You?"

He regarded me thoughtfully. "We were worried as hell about you 'til Claire said you called."

"She show up out there?"

Frank nodded, his wide lips drooping into a fleshy frown.

"How's she doing?"

"Not good. None of us are. Christ."

When I didn't say anything to that, he asked, "How'd you get here? Claire said you were stranded."

"I borrowed a friend's car." I waved vaguely toward the back row. "I was waiting to see who would turn up to claim the Caddy."

"It's Enos Flood's car," Frank said, feigning a knowing air. "He's one of Milo's flunkies. I called Milo an hour ago. They admit to being there."

"You're kidding."

His eyes narrowed. "He said they exchanged shots with some lunatic in a Mercedes."

"Did they tell you they fired first?"

"No, that wasn't in their version. He also claims they had nothing to do with shooting Mickey. Said they lit out after hearing the shots." He paused to see how I would take that. "Says he doesn't know who was in the blue car. Swears it wasn't his people. I'm here to be convinced."

He looked tense, nervous, but he was here, I had to give him that. "So you arranged a meeting?"

"Not exactly. I told him we'd have to talk, but he was pretty steamed. After we hung up, I got to thinking. Figured it might be better to spring it on him before he had a chance to circle the wagons."

"That all you have in mind?"

Frank dragged up a smile, held it long enough to speak. "You think I'm here to get revenge? Shoot my way through Milo's lackeys? Force out a confession?"

"Doesn't sound so bad."

Frank's features slackening. He fumbled around inside his coat for a cigarette. He offered me one and I took it.

"You trust him enough to walk in there?"

Turning away to blow smoke, he looked off toward the building. "Like Mickey said, ya know? Someone has to *do* something." His eyes shifted back to me. "What do you think?"

I decided not to mention that attitude was pretty likely what got Mickey killed. "You goin' in alone?"

"Chuck and them didn't want anything to do with this." He turned away, took two steps, turned again to face me. "We got into it back there, after the cops came. Things were said. It was a bad scene."

"I can imagine."

"Anyway, after all that, no one was in the mood to come along."

I looked towards his Jaguar. "Who's that?"

He huffed. "That's Dennis. I made him drive, but he won't come in to save his life. Little shit."

"I guess it's just you and me then."

His eyes seemed to bulge further in my direction. "I'd appreciate it.

"I hate to say it, but did you think about bringing in the cops?"

"That's what Chuck said. Hell, they're already in on it. No getting around that." He turned to pace again, then stopped. "I was hoping we could sort some of this out in-house—me and Milo, I mean—so we know where we stand."

"Sounds risky."

"You don't have to come." He puffed up his chest. "Like you said, you don't have the same things at stake. I understand that."

"That's not what I meant. These guys were pretty free with their buckshot this afternoon. Put my car out of its misery—before its time, I might add. And that Caddy around back, the beige one. It's the same car that did that so-called holdup at Clancy's. Same car, same shotgun I'd bet. Whether or not they killed Mickey, they're a gun-happy lot. I don't think we should go in there unarmed."

Frank's head dropped and I followed his gaze to the pocket of his coat. He pulled out a small automatic, held it in his palm to show me. Brushed chrome with pearl grips and a two-inch barrel. A girl's gun, a display gun. But it would shoot bullets. I wanted to ask if the safety was off, but decided against it.

"You still got Mickey's gun?"

I patted the pocket on my jacket. "But the last thing I want is a shootout with these guys in the middle of a crowded bingo hall."

"That's just what I wanted to tell *you*," he said. "But it's good to be prepared. Anyway, Milo ain't crazy. It's his club."

I took a deep drag on my cigarette and ground it out on the pavement. "Okay then."

Frank's features seemed to set. He turned toward the entrance and I fell in step with him, feeling the flush of adrenaline.

"How about we stay in the main room," I offered. "Ask them to come out and meet us in full view of all the players."

"Doesn't give us much privacy."

"It's a lot of witnesses, though. We can find a quiet corner."

"All right. We'll try it."

I opened the front door to let Frank go in first. No reason for me to be the point man.

The hall was shabby, cramped and crowded, a large rectangular room with low ceilings and dark paneled walls. Waist-high partitions divided the rows of seated players into three sections for no apparent reason. The caller's podium rose above the middle section.

"B-12," he intoned. "Be-e-e-e…ta-welv-v-ve."

I'd heard that before.

A man with ambiguous Asian features and short stature came up to greet us and tell us that the games had already started, numbers already called. Did we still want to play? Frank told him who he was and that we wanted to see Milo. At the mention of Frank's name, the man shrank away, almost bowing, and mumbled something about how he would see if "Meester Feen-nes" was available. He hurried down a narrow hallway and tapped urgently on a closed door, putting his face right up to the doorframe. It opened a crack, then widened enough to allow him to pass within. A few seconds later, the closed blinds in an adjacent window shifted slightly. Fingers parted the slates at eyeball level, then dropped away.

We waited.

"N-47," the caller said. "E-e-e-n-n-n…forty-seven."

The door opened and out stepped a heavyset almost ape-shaped man, not a lot of fat, who took us in with dark eyes on a slow burn. He had thick black hair combed straight back and thick black eyebrows like hatchet marks on his forehead. His five o'clock shadow looked more like midnight or later. I took this to be Milo Finnes. Adjusting the loosened knot of his tie and tugging at the lapels of his not inexpensive suitcoat, he strode towards us like he'd been beckoned to break up a fight. Two other men, both wearing suits, followed on his heels. The Asian man brought up the rear, glancing fretfully at the crowd seated to our right, none of whom had disturbed their facile concentration to look our way.

"What the hell you doin' here?" Milo growled in a husky whisper. "Ain't you got troubles of your own?" When Frank didn't say anything, Milo nodded his ample chin in my direction. "Who's this? Your henchman?"

Frank turned to me then back to Milo. He seemed suddenly self-possessed.

"I told you we'd have to talk. I thought it best not to come alone."

Frank eyed the two men standing at Milo's elbows. One of them, built like Milo but older, softer, had graying sideburns and didn't look like any kind of muscle. The other was mid-twenties maybe, tall and wiry, with greased-back dirty-blond hair. The suit he wore looked bought off the rack two sizes too big, and the knot of his necktie was overlarge and slightly askew, giving the impression someone else had dressed him. He didn't look powerfully built, but I couldn't tell what was under the padded shoulders and broad panels of the suit. He had speed-freak eyes and a cocky, mannered grin that displayed bad teeth.

"You're a mess, Frank," Milo said, eyeing his bloody shirt. "You here to make a scene? Cause I ain't gonna let that happen."

"I just want to sort this thing out."

"Sort it out?" Milo scrunched eyebrows, as if not comprehending. He glanced at his yes-men, then gestured with his head. "All right. Come on back. Let's sort it out."

"I think we'd be more comfortable out here. Or perhaps, over there." Frank indicated the glass-enclosed game arcade to the left of the entrance.

Milo's features brightened somewhat. "What're you afraid of, Frank?"

"My brother-in-law got murdered today, Milo. My friend and business partner. I'm pretty much afraid of everything."

The grin wilted on Milo's face. They stared at each other. I thought I saw a glimmer of something human in the ape. The rest of us waited stiffly.

"All right. Let's talk outside." Milo gestured toward the door. "Charlie, you stay here," he told the Asian man. ('Charlie'? Really?) The small man nodded and bowed gratefully, fulfilling yet more of the stereotype.

Frank and I led the way into the parking lot and around to the side of the building. The five of us gathered in a loose circle, sizing up each other's pokerfaced stares and tough-guy stances.

"I told you on the phone," Milo started, "I didn't have nothin' to do with that shooting."

"What were you doing there?"

"Like I said, we came to talk. Who torched the Broadway? Tell me *that*."

Frank went for a cigarette. Milo and his men followed the movements of Frank's hands, but nobody flinched. He lit up, blew smoke, looked away.

"All right, look. Mickey was a good man. Always tried to do what was best for me and my organization. He was family, for Christ's sakes."

"That don't give him the right to burn down my hall."

"I agree. And when the idea came up to retaliate for that holdup last week, I vetoed it. We all did. It was a bad idea, bad business for all of us."

"You're sayin' that's why he did it?"

"I ain't sayin' he did it at all. The idea came up. We talked about it. I vetoed it then and there. I don't have say over everything everybody does in my organization. Mickey was a hot-blooded kind of guy. *You* know that. He may have taken matters in his own hands after your boys saw fit to shoot up Clancy's."

"Trouble with that is, we didn't have nothin' to do with that."

I spat out a mocking laugh.

"What's your problem?" Milo glared at me. It was a formidable stare. "Who're you, anyway?"

"This is Henry Burkhart," Frank said. "Our manager out at Bingo Palace."

"I was there," I put in before Frank could say any more about me. I was supposed to be from Seattle, Milo's hometown. I didn't want to get stuck comparing notes again. "I saw the Caddy there. The one out back with the bullet holes in the trunk."

Milo's eyes darted briefly, but he recovered before giving anything away. "You the one who shot at us?"

"I got a clean shot at the car after someone blew the windshield out of my Mercedes."

The speed freak in the new suit coughed out a phony laugh.

"I could've put those bullets through your back window if I wanted," I lied.

The man laughed more boldly. Milo turned to him and glared until the bad-toothed grin shrank from his face.

"That sort of gunplay don't do anyone any good," he said, before turning back to face me. "That wouldn't have happened if I'd had a chance to stop it."

"So you're saying, you can't always control what *your* people do either?"

"My people do what I say."

"Either you're wrong or you're a liar," I said flatly.

Milo took a step back, as if smacked by the insult, and the younger man moved forward one hand reaching inside his coat. This guy was a firecracker dying to get lit. I figured I better douse his fuse, so I charged him. Grabbing the front of his jacket, I pinned his hand—and the gun in it—against his chest and rode him backwards until we landed on the broad hood of a parked car. He swung at me with his free hand, a small fist, ineffectual blows slapping at my ear and the back of my head. I had his feet off the ground and I kept him pinned with the full weight of my body, freeing one arm to fend off his flaying fist.

"Hold up there," someone said, and heavy hands gripped my shoulders.

"Vince!" Milo commanded, and the hands slid away. I figured I had the floor.

"You must be *Enos*," I said, emphasizing his name with a mocking tone. "That your car I shot up today, Enos?"

"Fuck you!" he spat, panting rancid breath.

Squirming beneath me, he swung one leg in an effort to shift his weight. I shoved a knee into his groin just enough to let him know I was close to home. I lifted my weight to pull his hand, still gripping the gun, from inside his coat, then shoved it up under his chin.

"It'd be a shame if this thing went off in the tussle, wouldn't it?"

"Take it easy," Milo ordered, but more of a warning than a command.

"Give me a minute!" I yelled and continued to press my weight. It was easy, right then, to hate this guy. "I saw you, Enos, Saturday night. You were the driver."

"That's bullshit, man. I wasn't there. I can *prove* it."

"You were the one with the shotgun, weren't you, Enos? That stupid beard on your face. And blowing holes in the ceiling."

"I wasn't *there*, I tell ya."

"You like shotguns, don't you, Enos?"

"It wasn't me. You got the wrong man!"

"It was your Caddy, Enos. I saw it."

"There's a million cars like mine."

"I got your plates. NAR 488."

"No way, we covered the…"

He stopped abruptly, leaving a poignant silence, filled only with the sound of our labored breathing.

"You covered the plates. That's right, Enos. I lied about that. You covered the plates, didn't you?"

His eyes cut to the side, searching for the look on his boss's face. I was through with him, but he still had a grip on that gun. And he was having a bad day, I didn't trust his mood.

Hands gripped my shoulders again, but not very hard. "That's enough. Let him go."

"He's still got the gun. I think ol' Enos here's a little miffed. The way it's been, he can't help shooting things up when he gets miffed."

"All right, Enos," Milo said, close behind me. "Let go of the gun."

"Mee-ster Feen-nes," Charlie called from a distance. "Mee-ster Feen-nes, we have a bingo."

The timing was perfect, though I'm not sure the smile made it to my face. Milo swore under his breath and leaned his bulk against my backside.

"Goddammit, Enos, you fucked up," he growled, reaching in to grab a handful of Enos' suit. "Don't make it any worse. Let go of the gun or I'll shoot you myself."

Enos' grip slackened. I took the gun and palmed him in the face as I pushed off. He slid off the hood, planted his feet, and stared at me with murderous eyes. Milo blind-sided him with an open palm hard against his jaw, sending him staggering against the car again. When he straightened up he wasn't looking at me.

"What the fuck's the matter with you?" Milo hissed.

"It wasn't me though...."

Milo swung again. "You lying little shit."

Enos flinched, deflecting the blow with one arm. "Hold on, dammit! Lemme finish."

"Keep your voice down," Milo commanded. He stood back, but remained wound up to pounce.

"I *mean*," Enos slurred, "it wasn't my idea."

"Who, then? Tell it."

Milo shifted his weight to strike again. Enos took up a boxer's stance, arms raised.

Milo stopped in mid-stride, dropping his extended arm, light dawning on his dark features.

"It was Brent?" he said, incredulous. "Didn't you tell me…"

Behind his raised fists, Enos nodded, glancing side to side as if to see who else might be watching him turn over on his pal.

"God-*dammit!*"

Frank's voice cut in, "Where *is* Brent?"

"Mee-ster Feen-nes," Charlie sang out from the front steps.

"Deal with it Charlie!" he yelled over his shoulder. I saw people shuffling toward the entrance. Milo saw them too. "Let's take this somewhere else." Leading Enos by the collar twisted into one big hand, they headed towards the alley.

The other man, Vince, came up behind me and took hold of my wrist above Enos' gun. It was a firm grip. He has some muscles after all.

"Why don't you let me take that."

I read his eyes and let him take the gun. He didn't shoot me. He tucked the gun into his belt and closed his coat over it. Then he extended one arm, almost politely, gesturing for Frank and me to follow. We went around the back of the building.

"Where is Brent?" Frank repeated.

"Vegas," Milo said. "Been out there since the day before yesterday. He doesn't even know about the fire."

"That doesn't mean anything."

"It means he didn't kill Mickey, Frank. He couldn't have. Enos took them to the airport himself." He turned to look at Enos with doubt dawning on his face. "Right?"

"That's right," Enos said. "He's not due back till Sunday."

No one had to point out the holes in that alibi.

"Who else was in on the holdup, Enos?" I asked. "There were three of you."

Enos glared at me in silence.

Milo stepped up to him, ready to strike. "Was it that lowlife brother of yours?"

Sulking now, Enos gave a partial nod. "But it was Brent's idea, I tell ya. He said you'd be impressed. You'd be *happy* about it."

"Oh, I'm happy all right. Pleased as fucking punch. What the fuck you guys thinking?"

A middle-aged mother with preteens in tow came around the corner of the building. They hesitated when they saw us, their chatter dropping off before they loaded into a minivan. Another car's headlights blinded us as it turned into the alley then crawled by, its passengers gawking through the windows.

"Okay, that's it," Milo said, "We gotta go. Frank, we'll talk. I don't know what you want to do about this, but don't forget, we got a burnt down hall." He pointed to the back door of the building. "Go." Enos and Vince sidled between cars and Milo turned to follow.

"I want to talk to Brent, Milo."

"Yeah, Frank, I can see why you would. Me too. But don't jump to conclusions, will ya? There's been enough shooting, don't you think?"

Frank didn't answer. We watched their backs as they filed toward the door. In the doorway, Enos turned to shoot me a dirty look, smoothing out his rumpled suit, then he slunk away when Milo came up the steps behind him. Milo stopped and turned to face us.

"Go home, Frank. Call me when you get there. Meantime, I'll try to get in touch with Brent. Okay?"

Frank gave him a silent nod. Milo turned and closed the door without looking back.

We headed towards the parking lot. Dusk was settling. People milled about, cars rolled towards the exits.

"What next?"

Frank's face had gained some color. "We wait to hear from Brent Charmichael."

"Is he capable of this kind of thing?"

"I wouldn't have thought so. There's been bad blood between him and Mickey for years, off an' on. It's been worse than this actually—I mean, more of it—but just macho competitive shit. Dogs barking through the fence. They never tried to kill each other." He slowed to a stop and turned to me. "But it's plain he was in on the holdup and, ya know… I gotta think it was him that shot Eddie. He knew Eddie from way back. The two of them got into it over Claire."

My throat constricted. "Brent and Claire were an item?" I heard a flutter in my voice.

Frank must have heard it too. "Well, she ain't a virgin, Henry." He watched to see if it got to me.

I managed a simpering grin that got me through the moment.

"Brent had some ideas, maybe, but I think Claire always knew what was what with him. Then when she and Eddie got together, that ended that. Brent felt the snub I'd guess."

I strained to regain my role. "You think that could've had something to do with this?"

"Nah, that was years ago, eight or ten years. 'Sides which, Brent slept with everything that moved." Frank stopped abruptly, as if about to let something slip. He had to know about Brent and Tanya but, in his mind, I wouldn't know.

"You think it was Brent then?"

"Sounds right, don't it? It's his club got burned. No way he didn't hear about it. Wouldn't take anything for him to fly back from Vegas, do the shooting, and get back on a plane. Hell, he might still be in town."

"You know what kind of car he has?"

Frank shook his head. "Probably a Caddy."

Good guess.

"Could be Brent never went to Vegas. And I'd say Enos' brother is a good bet for the driver. You know him?"

"Never heard of him. I'll have to ask Milo about that one."

"You think you'll get a straight answer?"

Deep wrinkles cut around his eyes, magnified by the thick lenses. "I don't know. For all his bluster, nothing like this ever happened before. I mean, between our outfit and theirs. That's why I didn't like Mickey's stunt. And that's why I don't think Milo had anything to do with the holdup." He squinted with tension. "But now I think Milo hears a fox in the hen house. He may want to flush it out."

"Either that or he's a good liar."

"He called off Vince when you had Enos slung over the car."

"I thought that was you."

Frank offered a tired smile, weaker than his usual pose. "He beat me to it." He looked downward to the gray pavement. We started moving toward the car again. "Hell, I'm no good at this tough guy shit. I didn't know what to do. Not gonna shoot him."

"Yeah, not a good idea. Anyway, it worked out."

"Nice piece of work you pulled on that Enos punk, though."

"Yeah, well, I was tired of letting him shoot at me."

"You sound like Mickey," Frank said, with more of a grin. "But if I were you, I'd expect more of the same."

"You mean, if we don't put him away?"

He thought that over, or had already. "I don't see any way of doing that without making things worse. But that doesn't mean I don't want Mickey's killer. I ain't gonna let that slide for anything."

As the king of bingo, there was nothing Frank liked more than the status quo. If it was going to hurt business, I wondered if he would let it come out. Then I remembered his reaction when Mickey fell, the despair in his voice when he called out Mickey's name. There was something there.

As we approached the Jaguar, Dennis opened his door and stepped out.

"I saw the whole thing, Frank. What happened? What'd they say?"

"You shoulda been there. You'd know."

Dennis bore Frank's look for a few seconds.

Frank turned to me. "I want you out to the Palace tomorrow, but before that, you got problems of your own." He cleared his throat and his eyes dropped away evasively, then refocused. "You're gonna have to talk to the cops, Henry. That Aurora cop, Harris, from crimes against persons, or whatever they call it. He was out there at the Palace. He remembers you from last week. We had no choice but to tell him you were there and that you lit out after the Cadillac." He glanced at Dennis. Dennis' gaze skittered off down the road as if watching me chase that Caddy into the distance. "We, ah…didn't have time to get our stories straight. Anyway, they got questions for you. They got more questions for me too, matter a' fact. I'm supposed to be available first thing tomorrow."

"Did you tell them about the gun?" I let some exasperation seep into saying it.

"It couldn't be helped, Henry. Mickey was wearing a shoulder holster. They found that right away but empty, obviously." I thought about that for a moment and apparently Frank did too. "You'll have to come up with that gun for them," he continued. "Maybe you ought to clean it up, put in some fresh shells." Maybe a criminal mastermind after all.

"I could do that. Kind of covers their tracks though," I said, nodding toward the bingo hall.

"You mean, if we wanted to put them there?"

"If they had anything to do with it, we definitely want to put them there."

Frank nodded sedately. "Tell you the truth, I believe Milo about that. I think Brent pulled this one on his own. The more I think about it, the better it fits. Brent Charmichael always was a rowdy SOB. That's mainly why we parted ways." He shrugged, looked off over our heads. "It's not the first time he's done something like this."

"Killed somebody?"

Frank's eyes came back to me, but his expression remained distant. "Gone too far," he said. "This time he's really stepped off the cliff."

"So you'd rather I sent the cops in his direction and leave out Milo?"

Through the thick glasses, behind the blank expression, I thought I saw something, a concession, a debt owed, a shared past anyway. "Makes sense, don't it?" A trace of his complacent smile widened his lips. "But you've gotta clear yourself with them first and that won't be easy. They found a gun on Chuck, too. He's got a permit and all, but it sure got the cops interested in every little thing."

Great, I thought. "I'm surprised they haven't made it out here yet."

"They will. Anyway, you decide how you want to play it. I'm going home." He moved around the car, opened the door, then turned to speak again. "If you have any trouble, call me at the Palace. I'll do what I can."

"You plan on opening?"

"The Palace? Nah. We gotta let this blow over. And we got a memorial service to do. I'll have to talk to Tanya about that."

"How's she doing?" I asked, like an old family friend.

"Don't know. Haven't seen her yet." He looked away. "She was co-hosting some gig with the mayor's wife. I couldn't see calling her in the middle of that and sayin'..." He paused. "Shit. That's gonna be bad." He sunk out of sight into the car.

Standing on the driver's side, Dennis said, "Nice work out there, Henry. You really handled that guy."

"Yeah, well. Frank backed me up. I couldn't have done it without him."

Dennis nodded but his grin turned sour as he eased in next to his brother.

I watched them drive out of sight before starting back to the Mustang.

Chapter 16

When we got to Willie's place, I put him to work on Mickey's gun. I told him I needed it cleaned and reloaded before turning it in to the cops.

"Man, what're you doing that for? Toss your ass in the hole. Plus which, I thought you were on the run."

"I am not on the run. But I will be if I don't go in. They already know I went after the shooters. And Frank's brother told them I took the gun. I'll say my car broke down and I got a lift from a friend."

"*I* ain't the friend, Henry. Not for that. And I ain't goin' to the cops with you, either. They see my black ass they'll spring you and lock *me* up!"

"Okay, Willie, you ain't the friend. I get your point." It's even more than racial profiling for him, what with his father's extensive scofflaw history. But I had my own law enforcement prejudices to deal with. "I'll tell them I borrowed the car. That's what I told Frank anyway."

He frowned and started dismantling the Smith & Wesson. "Sounds like some fairy tale. You think they'll go for that?"

"It's what happened."

"Yeah, 'cept for that little bullet party out there on Parker Road."

"Don't worry about it," I said, with a confidence I didn't feel. "You weren't there for that either."

"*Damn* right," Willie groused, pretending to be occupied with the gun.

I took the phone into the other room and called Claire but I got the machine. I left Willie's number and put in a call to Luis, hoping to get his voice mail, too. No such luck.

"What the hell you calling here for?" He sounded bothered but not asleep.

"Mickey Gilmore was murdered this afternoon. Thought you'd want to know."

After a measured pause, he said, "Yeah, I'd want to know that, Henry."

When he didn't say anything further, I rolled out an account of the scene and what followed, leaving out the 'bullet party' on Parker road—thought I'd save that for when he was in a better mood. I told him we found the beige and white Caddy at Holiday Bingo on a hunch and that we were staking it out when Frank Coyne showed up.

Luis wasn't impressed. "You shoulda stayed with him the whole time."

"Yeah, well…" I bit my tongue. Luis waited. "As it turned out, I managed to be at Frank's side when he confronted Milo Finnes."

"No one got shot, I presume. Wha'd Finnes have to say?"

"He said they had nothing to do with it. He and his boys were there to talk to Mickey. The timing was a coincidence."

"You buy that?"

"Maybe. Frank did. He seems to think there's an unwritten rule against bingo big-wigs shooting each other. It came out, by the way, that Mickey set the fire. He copped to it at the meeting but, apparently, everyone knew it was him before they had the thing put out."

"Including Milo?"

"That's why he was at the Palace. He pretty much said Mickey had it coming for the torch job. But I tend to agree with Frank. He didn't order that drive-by."

"What did Frank say to all that?"

"He accused Milo of doin' the holdup at Clancy's. Milo denied that too, but as it turned out, one of his boys confessed to a little freelance activity. You know an Enos Flood?"

"Yeah, I seem to remember him on our list somewhere. One of Milo's people, right?"

"Yeah, but he did the holdup on his own with his brother and Brent Charmichael. Said it was Charmichael's plan. Pretty sure Milo knew nothing about it."

"What did Charmichael have to say?"

"He wasn't there."

"So Charmichael was the shooter? He was in the blue Caddy?"

"Probably. He's supposed to be in Vegas. We have Enos Flood's word for that."

"Convenient. So wha'd Aurora PD have to say? How much of this did you tell them?"

When I didn't say anything for a couple of ticks, Luis assumed the worst. "You're not calling from the fishbowl are you?"

"I haven't seen them yet."

Luis took a few seconds to piece it together. "You never went back to the scene?"

"The Merc broke down. I had to get Willie to come get me. Then I figured…"

"Save your story for Aurora, Henry. You're gonna need it."

"I thought I'd try it out on you first. See how it landed."

"Like the Hindenburg. You'd better get yourself in there. The longer you wait, the worse it's gonna be. Who was at the scene?"

"A detective named Scott Harris. Same one who questioned me at Clancy's last week. I guess he's working with homicide because he knows all the parties involved. I'll go in first thing tomorrow."

There was another long pause.

"So if I get jammed up, should I have him call you?"

Luis chuckled. I didn't see the humor. "Ya know, you do that, you're pretty much blown. On the other hand, we may have to bring you in regardless. Give 'em what you got."

"I don't have anything."

"You're an eye witness for the shooting, for Christ's sake."

"Me and four other guys. They don't need me. And I'm more likely to make the case on Charmichael from the inside, right?"

Luis thought that over. "We'll have to see how it plays. I'll reach out to them tomorrow. What's this guy's name? Harris?"

"Yeah, crimes against persons. But you ought to wait till Monday."

"Why's that, Henry?"

"How would the Denver DA's investigator hear about this over the weekend? And why would he be interested?"

Luis thought that over too. "So you ain't gonna call me if they hold you?"

"Depends, ya know? I don't want to live there. But why would they hold me?"

Luis didn't respond to that. "What else are you onto, Henry?" He said it with that 'I-*know*-you' tone of voice.

"Nothing new. I just want to hang a little longer while things are in motion. Everybody's talkin', people are upset, out of their usual roles. A lot of things could shake out. And with Mickey gone, there's bound to be a reorganization in Frank's house."

Luis didn't say anything. I could practically hear the wheels turning. Eventually, he said, "So you don't want my help unless you do. Is that it?"

"Look, Luis. Frank and Milo are calmed down after their little *tete-a-tete*. Neither of them wanted this to happen. Most likely, Charmichael is good for the shooting on his own. You have anything on his background?"

"Hell, I haven't run a check on him. He's just one player on a long list. Besides, he's Milo's boy. We're investigating the Coyne operation, remember?" He sounded defensive, like I'd caught him napping at his desk.

"He used to be with Coyne back when. Remember me telling you that?"

"Yeah, I remember you tellin' me that."

"And while you're at it, check the sheet on Enos Flood and his brother. He's a real gunslinger and the brother was along for the ride. And then there's Vince somebody, works close with Milo…"

"Vince Terrelli. Another ex-cop, also from Washington state. You got any more work you want me to do for you?"

"All I'm sayin', it's not likely that Frank and Milo are involved in these shootings. They're hinky all right, but they're not that stupid. Business-wise, they have too much to lose. If we want to help with the murder investigation, we'll do more good leaving me in place."

"Yeah, sure, stay in place. But if they don't collar Charmichael pretty quick, you gotta come in. Meantime, I'm gonna get some sleep. You're wearin' me out. But *you*," he said, pausing for my attention, "you're goin' in tomorrow with your story. Got it?"

"First thing in the morning, I swear."

"Things get sticky with this guy Harris, tell him I'm a family friend. He can check with me for a character reference. I promise not to say anything about your real past."

"That's a joke isn't it? You're getting better at that, Luis."

"Go to bed, Henry. Call me tomorrow, when you get rid of Harris. *If* you do."

When we rang off, I called Claire again, still got no answer. I paced the floor rethinking events, conversations, people's movements, their motives, their lies. I had the feeling I was missing out—things were happening without me. Fifteen minutes of mulling felt like an hour. Finally I had the idea to track down Brent Charmichael. Why not? No reason to believe Enos Flood's alibi for him. I looked him up in the phone book. There he was, living on Quivas Street, just like any average Joe with nothing to hide.

Willie was sitting at the kitchen table with Mickey's partially disassembled Magnum spread out in front of him. When I came into the room, he held up the cylinder and eyed me through it. "How's that for clean?"

"What about the bullets. Can you get some? We need new rounds."

"Yeah, sure, .357's a dime a dozen 'round here. You off the phone?"

"Yeah, but I have to use your car."

"What for?"

"I've gotta go see Claire."

"I'm ready," he said.

"Willie. I'm going up there to comfort her. You wanna sleep on her couch with me?"

"Comfort, huh?" He flashed a mocking grin. "Whatever."

"Don't creep out on me."

"Hey, you the one goin' up there with the tea and sympathy. What am I supposed to do without a car? I can't get this ammo delivered."

"Line it up for the morning. I'll go by on the way to the cop house."

"Man, the brother don't get up before noon. 'Sides, you sure you wanna turn yourself in?"

"I'm not turning myself in." I said it more fervently than I intended. "I'm a witness. They've got no reason to hold me."

"Yeah, right. That's why I'm cleanin' this gun."

"Look, I gotta go. We'll talk about it in the morning. If Claire calls, tell her I'm on my way."

And I was. I just had one quick stop to make.

Chapter 17

Brent Charmichael's address on Quivas was a few blocks west of Santa Fe Drive and, not surprisingly, a five-minute drive from Holiday Bingo. Six square blocks of rundown tract-homes, circa early '50s, were tucked away between the Hampden Avenue Freeway and the warehouse district that ran along West Evans. The abandoned acreage of the defunct Lakewood Drive-in Theater bordered it to the south. Every third side-street ended in a cul-de-sac so it took some time finding my way. I felt harried and anxious as I searched for legible street numbers.

A half-moon hung low in the western sky, over-grown cottonwoods billowing upward into the moonlight. But the neighborhood was otherwise dark, streetlights few and far between. Some of the houses were older than others but none of them had been built in the last decade and mobile homes sat immobile-looking on several lots. Near-new pickup trucks, rusted-out compacts, and vintage autos waiting to be restored littered yards and dirt driveways and lined the narrow, curb less pavement.

At the far end, I found a grouping of new houses—three in a row and one cattycorner—all of them looking like kit-homes recently plopped onto cookie-cutter foundations. They were modest in size but larger than most of their ramshackle neighbors and they stood out by the clean lines of their aluminum siding and the extravagance of pre-fab bay windows. The middle one of the three was Charmichael's. Even before I found the house number, I knew it by the dark blue Cadillac parked in front, perched diagonally on the loose soil of an unfinished driveway like a cast off toy, a tarnished trophy left lying in the dirt.

The houses on either side looked unoccupied, the detritus of construction work littering their bare dirt yards. No other vehicles took up the space where the driveways would be. I parked down the street along a half-acre of well-kept lawn with a children's plastic playground in the middle of it. A carved-wood sign read: Barnes Park, Denver Recreational District. Our tax dollars at work, even here.

There were no lights on inside the house but a porch light glowed brashly under a small overhang. I approached the door with only the vaguest idea about what to do next. It didn't fit the alibi theory that he would be here but the presence of the Caddy had me thinking twice. Gripping the gun in my pocket, I took the three steps up the porch and rang the bell, listening for signs of life. Nothing stirred while the glow from the porch light rained down on me like a searchlight during a prison break. I rang again and stepped off the porch. White noise hissed in the distance from fast moving traffic on Sante Fe Drive. No one came to the door.

Treading softly, I circled around back. Beyond the small backyard the huge blank wall of a warehouse extended out of sight in either direction. The security lights dotted along its length cast a gray hue on the back door of the house. I tried the knob but it was locked. All the windows were dark. Completing the circle around the house, I felt the hood of the Caddy as I went. Not exactly warm to the touch, but the side panels felt distinctly cooler. I returned to the front porch and tried the doorknob. It turned in my hand like my own front door. I stepped in and closed it behind me. What could happen?

Listening hard and taking the gun out of my pocket, I waited for my eyes to adjust. Very little light penetrated the diaphanous curtains. After a few quiet moments, I called out Brent's name in a tentative tone. No one responded. On the balls of my feet, I crossed the bare floor towards gray light sifting through a doorway. There was a narrow kitchen, its countertops uncluttered, and the sink half-full with cups and glasses reflecting light from the window above it. Beyond that was an open area, a dining nook with a small table and two chairs ashen in the faint glow from the warehouse lights beyond.

I found my way back through the living room, past the sparse furnishings, to a carpeted hallway with a bathroom at the end and closed doors on either side. I turned the knob on the door of the front room and pushed it open with the barrel of my gun. The curtains of one window were pulled back and enough light filtered through to illuminate a double bed with the covers loosely in place. A large dresser flanked the near wall and, to my right, a built-in closet stood with its mirrored doors slid open. Not a lot of clothing hung there; maybe a dozen shirts, some pants, two or three suitcoats and a small pile of shoes. Evidence of a pretty barren existence, perhaps what passed for a life to bingo-world second-tier players. Except for the Caddy, nothing like the Coyne family lived—especially his ex-lover Tanya.

Returning to the hallway, I cracked open the opposite door. Heavy, warm air assailed my nostrils with the familiar and unexpected smell of shit. Immediately, I knew: in the darkness in front of me lay a dead man.

Backing out, I closed the door, wiped the knob clean and retraced my steps, wiping down everything I had touched. I did this, I realized, with the same urgency and distractedness—the restrained panic—of the murderer himself. When I reached the front door, I opened it enough to wipe the outside knob. Leaning out, I stopped myself and took a deep breath of cooling air, then another. It did nothing to dispel the tensions in my gut. A few squares of light glowed sedately from houses down the street. Traffic noise droned from far off, assuring me that life went on out there completely unaffected by what lay in that back room. I wanted to rejoin that life, I ached for it, and for an instant I thought I could do it. Then I stepped back in and closed the door.

I moved slowly across the living room trying to make myself think without much success. Down the hallway, I stood holding the knob wrapped in my handkerchief, steeling myself for what was inside; the smell, the body, the evidence. Holding my breath, I opened the door. The room was totally dark, no diaphanous curtains, no faded outline from where the windows might be. I squatted and felt my way along, extending one arm in sweeping motions like a blind man's cane. My hand glanced across something hard, solid and smooth. It was the sole of a man's shoe facing upward from the cool hardwood floor. I grasped the heel, rocked it from side to side. I retracted my hand. Sweat tickled my face and adrenaline coursed through me like the rush from a fat line of coke. I strained to distinguish the body in the black haze in front of me. All was one in darkness. I reached out a shaky hand to find the shoe again, then traced along the leather to the silk of his sock and under the folded cuff of his pant leg. My fingertips found flesh, but it was not warm enough. It had a waxy feel, like a piece of fruit. Or a dead limb. My fingers brushed the hairs on his leg. That's when it got to me—my being there with this cold corpse invisible in the blackness. I pictured him coming to life, jumping up, traceries of arms waving wildly in front of me, claw-like hands poised for strangulation, gaping crooked fangs, glaring eyes, an unstoppable zombie apparition possessed with vengeance, stalking those that defiled him from the other side of the grave.

Yanking my hand away, I fell backwards with a jolt and landed sitting on my butt. A burst of air escaped my lungs, like a drowning man breaking the surface. Scanning the darkness for signs of that monstrous rebirth, it was all I could do to just sit there, holding in check the impulse to flight. There was no sound but my own labored breathing and my heart pounding in my ears. I wiped my face and shook my head, straining to focus. I could do this. I had to get a grip. I had to get some light on the scene.

Just to my right, I could make out the barest outline of the straight-edged corners of a desk. Up on my knees, I felt my way along its surface to the base of a lamp. With my hand covered in the handkerchief, I traced its flexible neck, then twisted the metal shade to face the wall. When I turned it on, the muted light was blinding nevertheless and the scene was expectedly grotesque.

A man lay face-down on the floor with a ragged-edged hole in the middle of his suitcoat between the shoulder blades. No blood flowed from the wound. There were blood smears and droplets on the floor to his left and a heavier stream formed from beneath him, shiny and black, and followed the contours of the floor to pool up smoothly squared in the nearest corner. One arm stretched out above him, the hand bloody. The corner of the desk he seemed to be reaching for was smeared and splattered with blood. There was a lot of blood.

My mind cleared of its ghostly distractions made me realize the chance I was taking. I stepped around him to feel his face and get a better look at his profile. Rigor had not yet set in. He'd been dead maybe an hour, two at the most. He was young—or had been—maybe thirty-five, with a trim mustache and short-cropped black hair. There were scratches and blistering along the side of his face in a kind of exploding pattern, but no entry or exit wound to the head. I rolled him back by the shoulder, just enough to get a look at where the bullet entered his chest. A burnt halo surrounded the damp hole in his shirt, just over his stilled heart. Any powder smudges were lost in the blood.

On the floor—within reach, if he wasn't dead—a 9 MM Colt automatic lay coolly, clean and guilty looking. To the left, a briefcase sat with its lid ajar. I opened it. Loose papers, some manila folders, a soft-cover book. A folder of airline tickets hung forward from the pocket of the lid. I lifted them out in my handkerchief. There were two sets of tickets for two different airlines, made out to Brent Charmichael. One of them showed a departure from Denver to Vegas a few days ago, with a return on Sunday, like Enos had said. The other sleeve held two tickets purchased this morning in Vegas, one for an 8 A.M. flight to Denver, and the other for a departing flight, one-way to San Diego, on the red-eye tonight. Those tickets had cost over nine hundred dollars. A last minute purchase. He had decided to make a run for it. I looked at my watch. He could still make it if he hurried.

There was a suitcase on the floor, flung open, the clothes tossed and left where they had landed. An office chair stood against the far wall as if it had been knocked or pushed out of the way. There was a four-drawer metal filing cabinet against the other wall but I didn't look inside. I had to get out of there.

Scanning the desk as I went for the light switch, I sensed there was something out of place, a certain incongruity. It took me a few seconds, the muted light glaring impatiently. He had all the tech paraphernalia you might expect of a home office: printer, scanner, an oversized monitor and keyboard, and the stuff looked pretty new. But the reason for all of it was missing. The computer was gone, the hard-drive—with all the data. To the right of the printer, three cables came up between the desk and the wall with their jacks gaping like riled snakes' heads ready to strike. Beneath them, a perfect rectangle of dust could be seen faintly outlined on the desktop. I thought of disks, tapes, CD's, the plastic storage cases, and I didn't see any. Looking through the drawers, I found a pack of unused disks, their shrink-wrap unbroken. They were labeled 'CD-RW', rewriteable, ready to use. I also saw another gun in there, an automatic similar to the one lying on the floor. It didn't mean anything. None of this did. I really had to get out of there.

With my fingers on the light switch, I took one last look around, my eyes stopping and—with an effort—dwelling on the body. He was dead, all right, and he wasn't coming back to life. The basic fact of it got through to me. Whoever Brent Charmichael was, whatever he had done—whoever hated him, vied with him, wished him the worst—he was a man, mortal like the rest of us, and proven so beyond any doubt. There had been people in his life, people who would mourn him, suffer the loss, shed tears of heartache maybe, and disbelief. And there was one person, at least, who would not.

I turned out the light. Soft-stepping through the dimness, I made the front door with no trace of the ghouls that had haunted me. Surveying the street, everything looked quiet as I stepped out onto the porch. Bathed in sweat, the chill air felt like cold metal on my skin. I walked to my car with a thousand eyes upon me and drove away pretending I didn't notice.

I went east to Platte River Drive and followed the bends of the river to Evans, then crossed over, feeling like I was out of the woods. Before getting on I-25, I pulled into a gas station with a pair of roadside pay phones. I sat in the car for a while thinking about what to say to the cops.

I had mucked up the crime scene pretty well, wiping away fingerprints to cover my own, treading over footprints in the unseeded yard. And there were scads of evidence I hadn't taken in: the gun in his desk and the gun by the body, the stolen computer and the filing cabinet. Murder aside, Charmichael's files could be important for the DA's investigation—for *my* investigation. The crime scene cops would gather it all up. It would be good to get the right cops in on it.

I thought about Tom Connally. As Captain of DPD Homicide, he would be involved one way or another eventually. But I dreaded getting entangled with him yet again. Luis could handle Connally through the proper channels without bringing me into it. The problem with that was I'd have to tell Luis. He wouldn't like that I was in there, wouldn't like it at all. And he wouldn't like that I left before calling it in.

I decided Luis could wait. I thought about not calling anyone, waiting it out until someone else came looking for Brent Charmichael. Most likely, that wouldn't be until his scheduled return on Sunday, or even later. It would give me a chance to poke around for people's whereabouts on Friday night before they knew they needed an alibi. But I couldn't do it—just leave him lying there. I wouldn't sleep. I also knew if someone did see me, or if the cops could put me there with something I hadn't thought of, I'd be up for more than obstructing an official investigation.

I dialed 911. A woman dispatcher answered the phone.

"What's your emergency?"

"There's a dead man in a house, 3280 South Quivas. Does that qualify?"

"A man is dead? Can I get your name, sir?"

"3280 South Quivas. Did you get that? He's been murdered."

"Are you sure he's dead? How did it happen, sir?" Her voice was even, almost bland, like she dealt with this shit every day. Maybe she did.

"Sorry I can't help any further." I hung up the phone.

The freeway traffic was lively with the closing time bar crowd apparently in a hurry to get home and sober up. I drove slowly, feeling conspicuous, trying to come back to myself, trying to make sense out of too many nasty facts.

Someone had killed Mickey Gilmore, probably Brent Charmichael. And someone had killed Charmichael, probably in retaliation. But, of those who would want to, who could get close enough to shoot him point-blank in his own home? And the gun was left behind, maybe planted to imply suicide. Very likely it would be the same gun that killed Mickey. If it was meant to look like Charmichael killed Mickey, then lost a mean bout with his own conscience, taking the computer was an afterthought, and not a very good one.

I wondered about Charmichael's accomplice, whoever was in the car with him—his blue Caddy—when Mickey got it. That could be Enos Flood's brother. That could be anybody. That could be who killed Brent Charmichael. Not for retaliation then, but to cover tracks. And why did they kill Mickey? Why even shoot Eddie? When it all came back to bingo, I found myself shaking my head.

Chapter 18

I pulled up in front of the quaint little cottage that Mickey once owned and Claire called home. It was nearly two AM and I was wide-awake. Judging by the light in the windows, I was not alone. As I came up the walk, she opened the front door and stood waiting for me, arms crossed snuggly over her chest. She was wrapped in a full-length white terry robe that showed signs of comfortable wear. Her hair was down and wildly disheveled, her eyes puffy and red. Although the bandage was gone, I could see a bump on the bridge of her nose from when I had head-butted her. She looked good, all the same. And yet, she too was one of Brent Charmichael's ex's.

"Hello, Henry," she managed in a hushed tone, barely meeting my eyes. She drew the lapels of her robe closer together.

"How's it goin'?"

She cracked a crooked smile, acknowledging the lameness of the comment. "I can't sleep."

Turning away, she moved to the couch and lowered herself into a curled position at the far end. I stepped inside, closed the door, then felt awkward about where to put myself in the room. Before I could move, Claire shot up to her feet and glided toward the kitchen. "Do you want some tea?" She barely glanced over her shoulder.

When I didn't answer, she stopped and turned to face me. The fine creases at the edges of her mouth dimpled and her eyes widened. Her hands, down at her sides, formed into little fists.

I came up to her and enclosed her in my arms. She leaned against me and we stayed that way, strangely intimate for some minutes. Her breathing was stilted and uneven. I realized how little I knew this woman.

Eventually she spoke. "I don't understand this," she breathed into my neck. "I don't understand at all."

I remained quiet, trying to feel for her, trying to ignore the questions roiling through my mind. Finally, she moved away from me and went for the Kleenex box on the end table. We sat on the couch, side by side, facing forward, as if watching television.

"They're saying it was Brent Charmichael," she said. "Is that true? Did he do it?"

"Who told you that?"

"Everyone there. Dennis, Frank, Chuck Burrows." Again, I'd forgotten that she had gone to Bingo Palace afterwards. "And then Frank called after talking to Milo Finnes. He said you were there too. At Holiday Bingo."

"I followed a car after…"

"Was it Brent's car?"

"No. It belonged to one of Milo's goons. They were there but they didn't do the shooting. There was a second car. A dark blue Caddy."

"Was that Brent's car?" She sounded desperate to find someone to blame. And she didn't like Brent Charmichael. Not anymore. But I didn't tell her about the blue Caddy.

"It could have been. He wasn't with them at the Holiday." I thought of Brent's body lying on that hardwood floor. "He's supposed to be in Vegas but that won't hold up. He's the one who pulled the holdup at Clancy's. He shot Eddie."

Claire looked at me with sad eyes, but there was something else there too: confusion or inquisitiveness. Or some degree of dawning comprehension. "But why?"

I loaded a question: "How well do you know this guy Charmichael."

She blinked away tears, wiped at them with the back of her hand. "He used to be with us. You know, one of Frank's people. He was around a lot in the old days. He was all right, I guess, until he jumped ship. It was a big deal when he went over to Milo. He hurt a lot of people."

"When was that exactly?"

"Seven years ago, maybe eight. After Shanie was born. I was just coming back to work."

"And how did Mickey take it?"

"Mickey?" She sounded surprised—as if her brother had nothing to do with any of this. Then she made her own connections. "Well, he didn't blame him, not at first, anyway. It was partly his fault, so he couldn't say much."

"His fault? How does that work?"

"He and Brent had formed a partnership to break off from Frank. They were going out on their own with that…creep from Seattle."

I wondered if the creep was the deceased Harvey Cline. "What happened with that?"

She sighed heavily, sat forward concealing her face. "I don't know. I was mostly home with Shanie then. I didn't keep up."

Pretty sure that wasn't true, but I didn't want to lose the line of associations. Plus, accusing someone of lying usually ends the interview.

"How come Mickey came back into the fold and Charmichael didn't?"

"Mickey was family. Brent wasn't. Everything has to do with family." She said it in a tone laced with resentment.

"So Brent was forced out? He didn't have a choice?"

She put her elbows on her knees and turned to look at me. "What do you care? Why do you want to know?"

I shrugged. "I'm trying to figure out who did this. If it was Brent Charmichael, why would he?"

We exchanged a long look, nothing soft and warm about it from her side. Then she hung her head and stared at the floor. She was thinking too hard for this to be mere recollection.

"It was a big scandal back then. Brent was something of a lady's man. Couldn't keep his pants zipped, actually. Eventually he slept with the wrong man's wife. That got him in trouble with Frank and he gave him the boot.

So Brent decided to start his own club." She paused and her eyes narrowed with the trace of a smile. "Everyone was surprised that he got Mickey to go in with him. Everyone but me. They had a chance together. That's what I thought, anyway." She paused before adding, "Then this guy turned up dead. That ruined everything."

"What guy?"

"The guy from Seattle. Harvey somebody. He was going to be their partner. Turned out to be a real sleaze. Somebody caught up with him, I guess."

"He was murdered?"

She nodded. "The gossip at the time was that some mobsters he had cheated in Seattle came after him. Friends of yours?"

"Mine?"

"Your home town, isn't it?"

"Denver's my home town. And the people I worked for in Seattle didn't operate that way. Besides, seven or eight years ago was before my time."

She smiled guilefully as if she didn't believe me, as if we didn't believe each other.

"So the partnership fell apart because of that?"

"I don't know." Her eyes drifted away. "Mickey never talked about it. Not to me."

I let that pass too. "And Mickey came back to Frank's operation after that?"

"Mickey and Tanya reconciled, more or less. Brent was out of the picture. I saw Mickey, of course. He'd come over to play with Shanie. Her Uncle Mickey." The color in her face faded and she looked away. She reached for her cigarettes on the table, shook one out then picked up the lighter and stopped. She slumped in place and let her head fall back. Her eyes glistened and rolled upward, searching the ceiling for something else to think about.

"So Tanya was the wrong man's wife?" I tried to sound matter-of-fact about it.

"Very astute of you."

"But then Mickey went in with him?"

Claire let out a feigned laugh. "Mickey was cheating on *her* from the get-go. Everyone knew it, including Tanya. She couldn't have cared less.

And neither did Mickey when Brent got found out. Brent was just that kind of guy. It pissed off Frank more than anyone."

"How long ago was this?"

"Years," she said. "Ten years ago maybe. Tanya's been fooling around with half a dozen boy toys since then. None of that was important. They had an *arrangement*." She affected a sarcastic frown, then finally lit her cigarette. "It was the '80s. Everyone was sleeping with everyone."

After what Frank had said, I assumed she was including herself.

"Well, it still makes the grapevine."

"So you already knew about it?"

"I heard about it out at Five Aces. Some of the players were speculating about the fire. Said there was bad blood between the Coyne family and Milo's people because of it."

"But you said it was the competition. Milo moving in on Frank's turf."

"That doesn't usually make people turn to killing each other."

"What does?" she asked sharply.

"Well, most the time, money. But more than there is in bingo, I would think." I paused to let her object but she didn't. "Or matters of the heart. Passions, jealousies, men scorned. Women too, for that matter."

"That's not how it was between Tanya and Brent. He and Mickey went in together *after* that. If anyone was pissed off, it was Tanya for getting left behind by both of them." When she stopped speaking, her eyes stayed with me, intense and thoughtful. "Cline," she said, suddenly. "Harvey Cline. That was his name."

"The one who partnered up with Mickey and Brent?"

She nodded, wide-eyed, as if we were on to something. "Do you think Brent could have done that too?"

"Killed Cline? Why would he?"

"I don't know. I guess it doesn't make sense. That's why the whole thing fell apart. Their partnership, I mean. They couldn't do it without him."

"Why not?"

She looked away. "I don't know exactly. That's just the impression I got. Mickey never talked about it," she repeated.

A hint of defensiveness in that made me think I was pressing. I let a silence settle. She smoked.

"What time did Frank call?"

"A couple hours ago." Creases of concern disturbed her features. "Why does that mater?"

"I'm just worried about him. When I left him, he was pretty upset."

After a moment, Claire said, "They were close, you know. I mean, we were talking about their differences the other day but that's not the whole story. Mickey first went to work for him when I was a teenager. He used to get me and my friends in to play for free." Her eyes searched the carpet under the coffee table. "That was at the old Bingo Circle before they moved it. I must have been fifteen." She took a drag from her cigarette, then smiled. "That's when I learned to smoke."

I put a hand on her shoulder, rubbed it, feeling awkward. She didn't soften to my touch.

"Are you going to catch him? Is that why all the questions?"

"I'm just trying to find out what happened. I was afraid Frank might have taken matters into his own hands."

Without looking at me, she said, "Would that be so bad?"

It crossed my mind that she could have killed Brent Charmichael. If she left the Palace early enough, she would have had plenty of time to go to Brent's house and confront him. She wouldn't have known that Brent was supposed to be in Vegas. Given the right circumstances—like finding the smoking gun lying around—she could have picked up that gun and took her revenge. It fit well enough, though I had other conclusions to jump to. Just the same, I took my hand away from her shoulder. Apparently she picked up the vibe. She ground out her cigarette then picked up the ashtray as she stood. "Not supposed to smoke in here," she said, going to the kitchen sink. "I think I'll try to sleep now, Henry, if you don't mind." There was an unmistakable distance in her voice, like a sudden wind gusting up in the open field between us.

"I could sack out on the couch if you want some company when you wake up."

Turning, she smiled, not completely disingenuous. "That would give Shanie quite a jolt, wouldn't it? She's not accustomed to finding strange men here in the morning."

"Yeah, sorry. I hadn't thought…" I got up from the couch and strolled to the door. Claire followed at a certain distance.

"You're sure you'll be all right?"

"No, I won't be all right," she said. "But I can handle it."

"Sorry if I, ah…" My words went nowhere, couldn't gain flight, died in the air between us.

Claire looked into my face and gave me a reassuring wan grin. "It's okay, Henry. It's not you." Stepping forward, she came into my arms, hung there briefly, long enough to leave traces of her scent. It made me think again of sweet liquor, or incongruously, of fresh-baked bread, an aroma that appeals to the instincts, maybe subconsciously. It aroused a sense of delicate want—even in the midst of our exchanged mixed messages.

When she moved away, one hand came around to grasp the lapel of my coat, her arms resting against my chest. "Thanks for coming by. When will I see you?"

"I'll check up on you tomorrow," I managed, the sound of my voice bringing me around. "I've got to see the cops first. Explain my part in this." Immediately, I regretted having said that.

Claire didn't take offense. "You're quite the hero-type aren't you?" She smiled minutely, her eyes on my chest. "Going out after those guys."

"Yeah, right. Too little, too late."

Her hand still gripped my lapel and I didn't move away. After a long moment, she turned her face upward and gave me a quick, tender kiss on the neck, pushing me away as she did so.

"See you." Her eyes didn't quite meet mine, her face sad and serious until she closed the door.

I walked to the car and crawled in behind the wheel feeling like a thief exposed and then forgiven. With Claire's scent still lingering, I drove away wishing I hadn't come.

Chapter 19

I woke with a start at the sound of a voice that may have been my own. I was sitting up, breathing hard, drenched in sweat and fear. Scanning the darkness, I found nothing familiar; what was real, what a dream. Shadowy shapes dissolved as I looked at them, mocking my befuddlement. I flung the covers away and swung my legs off the bed, planting my feet, ready to take it on, whatever. The hardwood floor was cool, firm, stable. Nothing else was moving either. I sat, rubbed my face, waited for the dim outlines in front of me to take form—a chair, a doorway, the pale light from a half-curtained window. I knew that window. I was in Willie's house, the spare room upstairs, the room I had fallen asleep in a few hours earlier.

I got up in the dark, made my way to the bathroom, and flicked on the light, finding relief in its blinding lucidity. In the shower, I ran water cold long enough to wash away the lingering realness of the dream. I closed my eyes, and I could see it again, but now without the fear. It was something like a combination of the shootings I had been in: the gunmen, wrapped in black, standing in silhouette; the crowd, panicked, screaming, huddled at their feet; the gunfire strobing the scene; a slumped, dead human. It was a flashback, more than a dream. It's different when you've been shot at, when you hold fresh the sight, the sound of exploding gun barrels, when you're compelled to recall the visceral proximity between the bullet's path and where you stood. Or when you recall perceiving, in some unknown way, the disappearance of life from a human body.

Toweling off, I was buoyed by the lavender radiance coming through the window from the eastern sky. I got dressed and went downstairs to the kitchen and worked on making breakfast, killing time until Willie awoke. He strolled in about seven, his tall frame draped in an ersatz-velvet robe the color of his skin. Sniffing at the smell of bacon, he stood leaning sleepily against the edge of the table. And then, like a character from my nightmare, he pulled Mickey's gun from the pocket of his robe, held it out, and then set it on the table with a clunk.

"All set," he mumbled, "six clean rounds." He spoke with exaggerated casualness, seemingly unaware of my reflexive fear. "I put in hollow point .38's. Same diameter but shorter shells and different slugs. That way they won't match up if they ever get around to recovering slugs from the scene. Or from that Enos dude's trunk. What kinda name is that, anyway? Enos, Venus, penis. I'd say there's a backwoods Kentucky punch-line lurkin' 'round there somewheres, yo." He rolled out a low chuckle, his cockiness and sick humor somehow reassuring to me.

"Where'd you learn that little trick?" I said, trying to sound glib.

"I got a brother knows 'bout things." He bounced his eyebrows. "Hey, you sure you wanna do this?"

"Do what?"

"Turn yourself in. I mean, you ain't a brotha', but I *still* don't like your chances."

I met his enlivened features with a smile. "I don't need you there. But I gotta go in. If I don't, they'll figure I've got something to hide."

"Like you *don't?* How long you think it'll take 'em to connect a gun battle on the boulevard half a mile away with the shooting at the Palace?"

"I think it's deniable. Anyway, I don't have a choice."

"What's all this?" Willie watched as I put out the scrambled eggs, the flapjacks, and the bacon.

"I was hungry. I guess I got carried away."

"I'll say." He eased into a chair. "Looks like the condemned man's last meal."

We laughed at that, allowing me to bury my chagrin.

"Why don't you wait for them to come looking?" Willie asked, between bites.

"That'll put more heat on Frank Coyne. I don't want that yet." Over the rim of my coffee cup, I took Willie in. He kept his eyes on his plate. "Why do I get the feeling you'd rather have me on the run?"

Willie chuckled. "Ah, man, you got me all wrong. I jus' don't want you doin' time in the *whoos-kow*, pad'ner, while the *trail* gets cold." He said this affecting a John Wayne accent that sounded more Kentucky southern than cowboy western.

I tried to laugh with him, not at him. "It won't happen. They don't have a reason to hold me. And if I run into trouble, Duncan will have me out in no time."

"Duncan!" he said, obviously disquieted at the mention of his employer. "Now, see, that's *another* reason why you shouldn't be doin' it. Duncan's a Boy Scout, comes to this. You get him involved, we might as well all plead out."

"Duncan's great for this. You know that. He's gotten me out of more jams than you'll ever get into."

"Ah, man, you don' *know* the trouble I been in."

"Yes I do. I've seen your rap sheet."

"*Rap* sheet? Man, I ain't got no *rap* sheet."

"Willie, I met you in *jail*. I'm the one who got the charges dropped. Duncan helped with *that*."

"They didn't get no conviction. Not on that or any of the other bogus busts they hauled me in on."

"It still goes on your record."

"'Sides which, the worse things *I* done they never *caught* me at."

Sensing Willie's mood going south, I let it drop. I gathered the dishes. "Anyway, I'm goin' in. But I may need to stay here a while, if that's all right."

"What for?"

I was thinking about Brent Charmichael's body. "I don't think my story will hold up forever. When it falls through, I'd rather not be found until I can reach Luis or Duncan."

"So you *are* on the run."

"You afraid of harboring a fugitive?"

"Shit no! We's undercover, bro, right? They'll sort it all out, you know… eventually, right?"

"I'm sure they will," I said with more certainty than I felt. "Also, I'll need your car."

"My *car*. What you need my car for?"

"Well, I can't show up out there in mine with the windshield shot out. They'd definitely make *that* connection. Besides it's not running."

"They shot out your windshield? That's gettin' close, man. You didn't tell me that."

"I didn't want to scare you," I taunted.

"Ah, man, what you ridin' me for?"

"Listen. I need you to get some wheels, though. I want you at Holiday Bingo for the day game. There's bound to be one on a Saturday. Probably starts at one. I expect the jaws to be flapping overtime about this shooting."

"Where am I supposed to get wheels?"

"C'mon Willie. Ask Maxine."

"Maxine won't loan me her car. Not after the *last* time."

"Yeah, well, that wasn't my fault. Anyway, it won't happen here. Why don't you take her along?"

"Take her along?"

"Will you stop doing that?"

"What?"

"Answering me with questions, like what I'm saying is crazy."

"What you talkin' about?"

I stared at him until he cracked a smile.

"Ah, man, you're too easy."

Chapter 20

The Aurora Police Department takes up a capacious three-story rectangle, one of three such buildings that radiate out from beneath a gigantic, over-arching patina dome suspended above—an architectural feature that makes you wonder how they did it. The city jail takes up the largest wing, with courts and administration and the cops occupying the other two. I parked in the visitors' lot and walked between the symmetry of partitioned flowerbeds and rows of carefully pruned crabapple trees in the courtyard under the dome. A few smokers lingered along concrete benches there with that air of ostracism and slight guilt that you see these days among those relegated to the boundaries of 'designated smoking areas'. I couldn't help think they should take up bingo.

Just inside, an information officer wearing a policeman's dark blue shirt hanging out of faded Wranglers directed me to a chest-high counter walled in with double-plated Plexi-glass at the far end of the spacious lobby. In the middle of the window was a circular metal grid. I tried speaking into it.

"I need to see a detective."

A woman, elevated behind the glass and facing away from me, turned to look. "And this is in relation to…?" Her voice was tinny and distant.

"I have some information about the shooting at the Bingo Palace yesterday."

"Okay," she drawled, fixing me with a sharper gaze. "And can I have your name please."

"Henry Burkhart."

"Have a seat and someone will be right with you."

But I didn't take a seat. The only chairs were against a wall 20 yards across the expansive marbled floor. That's why I was standing close enough to hear her page Detective Harris by name on the radio mouthpiece pinned to her shirt. I had hoped to catch the swing shift on a Saturday, some junior dick who filled in for the higher grades on weekends. It bothered me that Harris might actually be there, and it bothered me more that the duty cop on Saturday morning knew off-hand who was the primary on the case. The shooting, apparently, was the hot topic even among the administrative staff. I recalled seeing the ambulance-chasing news vans speed by while I waited for Willie to pick me up out where the Merc died. I imagined the coverage that must have made the 10 o'clock news: 'Gangland killing in broad daylight tarnishes grand opening of Aurora's latest high-fashion mall. More after this.'

I didn't feel any better when Scott Harris in the flesh buzzed his way through the gunmetal gray doors to the right of the duty desk. He was shorter than me, slender but solid, and had an athletic way of holding himself. His eyes were brightly attentive.

"Well, well," he said, holding the door open. "I was wondering about you." He didn't offer to shake my hand. "Come on up."

After being buzzed through the lock of double doors, I followed him through a maze of hallways and up one flight to the Detectives' Bureau. We entered an impressively vast layout of office cubicles then zigzagged through them, pausing at one—apparently his desk—only long enough to pick up a clipboard stuffed with forms. Beyond that, he directed me to an interview room at the far end of the sea of partitions. It was a small room, maybe twelve by twelve, with a metal-topped table bolted to the floor and mirrored-glass centered in one wall. Closing the door, he gestured for me to sit in the single chair opposite the two-way glass. Then he stepped in front of me to turn on the two floor lamps in the corners that shone on my face. They were the halogen type, the ones that emit a palpable amount of heat. There was an eight-foot florescent fixture above us, fully illuminated.

"Are those really necessary?" I indicated the lamps.

"We need it for the cameras," he said, with a polite smile and nodding towards my reflection in the glass.

I took off my coat, hung it along the back of my chair. "We have to tape this?"

"Absolutely. You're part of a homicide investigation."

I knew from our procedures at the DA's office that I had the right to refuse being video-taped, but I also knew we always took that as the first sign of animosity and lack of cooperation, if not downright guilt. I decided to let it ride, even though it might mean my days undercover were numbered—depending on who viewed it.

Harris sat opposite me but to the side, out of the frame. In an officious tone, he asked me my name and occupation—for the record, he said—then asked me where I was previously employed before working for Frank Coyne. I smelled a rat. More like I saw it standing six-feet tall behind the one-way glass.

"Why does that matter?"

"Just asking. Why wouldn't you want to tell me? Why would you lie about it?" His youthful, almost innocent features went blank, cold. So much for appearing cooperative. We stared at each other. I needed the time to think.

"I looked you up, Burkhart, after hearing that you skipped out on the crime scene last night."

"I didn't skip out. I wasn't compelled to stay there by law. I didn't have anything to do with it." My words sounded defensive, even to me.

"You were a witness to a crime. A felony. Now why wouldn't you want to help?"

"That's why I'm here today."

Harris grinned, a bothered, disappointed smile. He flicked pages upward from his clipboard. "Says here, you were arrested about three years ago for obstruction of a police investigation. You do this sort of thing often?"

"I wasn't charged. It was a misunderstanding."

"Yes you were, but the charges were dropped the next day. We both know what that means, don't we."

"It means I wasn't guilty."

"C'mon, Burkhart. Why the belligerence?"

"Did you want to hear my account of the events last night?"

"Yeah, we'll get to that. But first I want to know why you lied to me about your past." His eyes shone with an intelligence I hadn't noted on our previous meeting. Maybe he was rising to the occasion. When I offered nothing in response, he continued. "On your sheet, it says that you worked for the Denver DA at the time of the arrest. Naturally that made me curious. So this morning, I found someone down there, some little gal, a grunt like me, having to work weekends. Hell, she knew you right off. Sounded almost sweet on you."

Bonnie, I thought to myself, one of the two receptionists that, for all practical purposes, ran the investigators' office.

"She said you'd worked there for six or seven years. That's a long time. Hell, I haven't been here that long."

"Yeah, I worked for the DA."

He regarded me for a moment, as if weighing whether to give me second chance. "Why weren't you forthcoming about it? What's all this crap about being from Seattle? New in town, staying with a friend?"

"I went away for a while after leaving the DA's office. To Seattle. I am staying with a friend now. I didn't think my work history was any of your business." I stopped for a moment to make sure he wasn't satisfied with my answer, then I said, "You questioned me in front of Mickey Gilmore. I didn't think my stint with the DA's office would win me any brownie points with Frank Coyne's right-hand man. I don't have to explain the logic behind that, do I?"

He smiled a genuine smile. At least he had a sense of humor.

"Why the hell does a guy like you want to work for Frank Coyne?"

"How much do you make as a detective?"

Harris sat back in his chair and took a breath. "Okay, Burkhart. Let's try some of the harder questions." He flipped through his notes. "Says here, there was a meeting going on, there at the Bingo Palace. Frank Coyne was there, his brother Dennis, Chuck Burrows, Benny Palmer, yourself, and, of course, Mickey Gilmore. What was the meeting about?"

"Bingo," I said, and considered leaving it at that. "We were discussing operation of the new hall. Going over schedules, staffing, stuff like that."

"And this car drives up? What happened next?"

"It was a blue Cadillac with a black vinyl roof. Late model, maybe not new. It pulled up in front of the door, then pulled away, circled around and stopped in front of the door again."

"You saw this car first?"

"No, I think Benny Palmer saw it first. He said something like, 'Who's that?' and we all turned to look."

"And Mickey went to the door. Why did he do that?"

"I don't know. He may have known the car. He said, 'that son of a bitch' or something like that."

"And you don't know whose car it was?"

I shook my head. It wouldn't take long for them to find out on their own.

"What happened next?"

"Mickey got to the doorway, someone in the car opened fire."

"Just like that."

I nodded.

"Did you get a look at them?"

"Not really. I saw silhouettes of two heads, some movement within, then a flash from the gun. I had started after Mickey, but when more shots were fired, I dove to the floor. The next thing I saw was the car driving away."

"Get a look at the plates?"

"They were too far away."

"Two people in the car?"

"That's all I saw. The shooter fired from inside the car. I never saw the gun."

"White? Black? Hispanic? Were they wearing masks?"

"I told you. All I saw were silhouettes. When I had my head down, one of them was swearing and yelling, 'Drive, drive, drive!' Something like that. A man's voice so I'd guess the shooter was a man."

"And the driver?"

"Couldn't really see him."

"You didn't *see* him?"

"He was behind the shooter. I *told* you—*silhouettes*.

He regarded me quietly, sitting very still. "So you lit out after them?"

"No. I went to Mickey. He was pretty obviously gone. Then a second car appeared. Another Cadillac, this one beige and white. It came out from around the side of the building. I thought I'd have a chance to follow it. I picked up Mickey's gun and jumped in my car."

"You picked up Mickey's gun," he said, tapping his clipboard with a pen.

"That's right."

"You took it out of the holster?"

"No. It was laying on the sidewalk just in front of him."

"You bingo boys carry guns as a rule?"

I shrugged. "Mickey did, apparently. I don't know about anyone else."

"Did it surprise you that Mickey had a gun?"

"To tell you the truth, I didn't think about it. It was lying there. We'd just been sprayed with bullets, right? I just picked it up for the pursuit."

"The pursuit," Harris repeated it as if it had a nice ring. "Had he drawn his gun?"

"I'm not sure. I was behind him."

"But you found it on the sidewalk."

"That's right Just outside the doorway."

"So he probably had it out."

"Maybe."

"Do you think that's why they fired on him? The men in the blue Caddy, I mean."

"Mickey didn't get off a shot so…"

He paused for a long moment, looking over his notes. "So you lit out after this Caddy, right? The beige one? Which way did you go?"

"Up Parker Road, towards town."

"The same direction the other Caddy went?"

"I think so, but I didn't see the blue one after it exited the lot."

"What happened next?"

It was going to get sticky here, and I could tell by his face, a tightness of the lips, the bright eyes unblinking, that Harris thought so too. Everything I had said so far was corroboration. Now was my chance to come clean, offer something new to demonstrate my willingness to cooperate. I didn't hesitate.

"Nothing. I chased after them, but I'm afraid that Mustang just wasn't up to the task." I gave it a light chuckle. "Anyway, by the time I got up to the traffic light there was no sign of them. Must have made the green."

Harris's expression didn't change but that didn't feel encouraging. "Where's Mickey's gun now?"

"In the car. I thought it best not to come strolling in here with a concealed weapon."

"All nice and clean, I suppose."

I shrugged. "I don't know. What do you mean?"

"Did you get any shots off?"

"No, I told you I didn't see them after the first stop light."

"What street was that?"

"I'm not familiar with the street names out there."

Harris nodded mock-agreeably. "Do you have a gun of your own?"

"Yeah. It was in the glove box. I have a permit for it from when I worked for the DA."

Harris smiled. "Okay, let's go take a look at them."

"You mean, now?"

"Yeah, now. What's the matter with that?"

Harris got up, opened the door, and led the way quick-paced through a different maze of offices and hallways. We made it out of the building through an employee's exit that was also manned by a security guard. Slowing to walk beside me through a parking lot full of cop cars, Harris's tone lightened unexpectedly. "I need to know what's going on here, Burkhart. I need an inside look."

I turned my head to see him looking back at me with a surprisingly open expression. Squinting into the sunlight, he could have been smiling.

"You know what these investigations are like. You must have some experience, working with the DA. I need to get an idea of what's going on with these bingo people. Now I don't know what part you're playing with them and I don't *necessarily* need to know. But somebody killed Mickey Gilmore and I need to know about that. You understand?"

"Sure."

"Plainly, you're not a suspect, but you seem to be around when the shooting starts. What's that other place?

"Clancy's Bingo City,"

"Right. And I have to think, if you're working with these people, you have some idea why they're getting shot." He stopped at the chain-linked entrance to the lot and waited for me to turn and face him. "No cameras here, no recordings. Off the record, what can you tell me?"

It was likely that he had already gotten something out of the others. Frank wouldn't say much without a lawyer and Burrows would know how to dance around the likes of Harris. But Benny Palmer was a question. And Dennis, I already knew, couldn't keep his mouth shut. If he hadn't spilled already, he would.

"Off the record?" I repeated.

"For the moment. I can't promise you anything about how it will unfold."

"I've got certain loyalties, you know." I strained to sound convincing.

Harris pursed his lips, eyeing me skeptically. "Oka-a-ay."

"If you ask around, you'll probably uncover most of this without me. Know what I mean?"

"Yeah, sure. But this is a murder investigation. It's big news. When it gets down to cuttin' the nut, I can't pussyfoot around about my sources."

"Just put me at the bottom of your list. Testimony is a long ways off."

"I'll do what I can."

I started toward Willie's car in the visitors' parking and Harris fell into step. "There was that fire the other night," I said, "at another bingo hall."

"Broadway Bingo in Denver. Obviously arson."

"One of Milo Finnes' clubs, Frank Coyne's competition."

"Coyne had it torched? And you think this Milo Finnes retaliated by killing Mickey?"

"Hold on. Hear me out. It came up that maybe Finnes' people pulled that hold up last week at Clancy's. There was talk about setting a fire in retaliation. Frank quashed that idea before it got off the ground. He's got way too much to lose."

"So whose idea was it?"

Yeah, again that question. It was beginning to make me feel guilty. "Not sure, really. Mickey was probably more animated than anyone else. But that doesn't mean he did it. But if he did, I think he acted on his own. Like I said, Frank vetoed the idea."

Harris nodded, pursing his lips again.

"I was there the next day when Frank heard about it. He was livid. The point he made was that *whoever* did it, Finnes would *think* it was Mickey. Apparently, there's some bad blood between them goes back a ways."

"So you *do* think Finnes is good for the shooting."

"No, not at all."

He stared at me, plainly piqued.

"Finnes is in the same position as Coyne. Now, I don't know him from Al Capone, but these guys aren't the Mafia. He's not up to it. And I'd have to think it's bad business for him to do something this visible. Like you said, it's already in the news."

He gave me a doubtful frown.

"I mean, it's bingo, for Christ's sakes. We're not exactly talking about Colombian drug cartels. There's not that much money involved."

"You'd be surprised," he said gravely. I didn't tell him otherwise.

"The Caddy I chased, it was probably the same one that did the job at Clancy's. I wouldn't swear to it, but that's my best guess."

"And you don't think it was Finnes."

"Not directly but you could check that out. Maybe some of his flunkies worked it on the side. Anyway, they didn't kill Mickey. They were parked out of site around the corner of the building when the shooting started. They lit out afterwards. I think they were just at the wrong place at the wrong time."

"Quite a coincidence," he said, dubiously.

It definitely was, but I could see why he wouldn't think so. And that gave me an idea. "Actually, it looked to me like they were chasing down that other Caddy."

Harris huffed and smiled at the thought of it.

We arrived at the Mustang. I reached in and popped open the glove box and handed Harris Mickey's revolver. He smelled it, cracked open the cylinder, spun it and snapped it closed again. "Nice and clean," he said, "Fully loaded."

I handed him my semi-automatic. "I keep mine clean too."

He looked it over carefully, then met my eyes. "You don't know anything about a shootout near County Line Road yesterday? Two cars exchanging bullets in the middle of backed up traffic? It happened just after the shooting at the Palace."

"I never made it that far up. But that sounds like…."

"Where'd you go after the chase?"

I cast my eyes downward, as if he had caught me at something. "I drove around for a while looking for the Caddy."

"And then?"

"Then I went over to Milo's place. Holiday Bingo. I thought of Milo too, at first."

He watched me with steady eyes. "Wha'd you have in mind?"

"I figured I might intercept them there, I mean, just to look for these Caddies. I wasn't planning to shoot the place up or anything. My loyalties to Coyne don't run that deep."

"Wha'd you find out?"

I figured it would be better if they found Enos Flood's Caddy for themselves too. "Nothing. Milo was there already, in the middle of a game. I didn't see either car."

Harris' eyes stayed glued to me but I didn't feel like any cracks were showing.

"Coulda been the two Caddies exchanging fire," I said, developing the story for him. "That would fit with the idea that the second Caddy wasn't involved in the killing."

"Yeah, coulda been," he said, not bothering to tell me it didn't fit with what he already knew.

It occurred to me that I had to retrieve my Merc from that construction site. It was a disquieting thought. I had to get it before workers returned to the job on Monday and discovered it stashed behind their roll-off riddled with buckshot.

"Okay," Harris said. "Let's go back upstairs. Finish the interview."

"That's all I know. You said you'd keep it off the record."

"Don't worry about it. I just have to close it out. And I'll have to give you a receipt for these."

"You're keeping *my* gun?"

"I want the lab boys to look it over. It'll go towards clearing you."

"Of what?"

"Of any involvement in that shootout at County Line Road."

I shook my head, as if disappointed at this breach of trust.

Ignoring me, Harris strode off. I followed him back through the staff parking lot and just inside the building, we made our way to the evidence room. Harris ushered me in and made me wait while he filled out some forms and watched the clerk lock the two guns in an evidence bin.

In the stairwell, out of earshot from other cops, he said, "Lemme just get a few other things on record. I won't go into the details of your involvement with Coyne but I have to get something about Milo Finnes on there, toward probable cause, so we can file for a warrant if we need it. That fair enough?"

"Depends on who's gonna see it."

"At this point, no one except me and my partner are working on the bingo angle. There'll probably be a task force set up on Monday. In-house and strictly confidential. It won't go to the press."

"Then you won't need my name."

"I will for the judge, to get the warrant."

"But not for the cops. The task force, I mean. You can leave my name out of it."

We were on the third floor landing. He stopped with his hand on the door handle and gave me a peculiar smile. "Why the hell does that matter?"

I almost said, 'Cops are people too,' or something smart like that but, in the moment, I thought of a better excuse. "Some of your guys out here came over from Denver, right?"

"Yeah. I s'pose."

"I left the DA's office on good terms," I said, realizing that was one of my bigger lies. "I'd rather not tarnish the reputation. Know what I mean?"

It took some effort to keep a convincing straight face. Harris took me seriously.

"Having second thoughts?"

"What d'you mean?"

"Skip it," he said, displeased. "I'll keep you out of it for the time being. But when we move on Finnes—if we do—then we'll have to go official with our findings. By then, maybe we'll have enough from your bingo pals."

I didn't believe him but it hardly mattered.

We went back into the interview room. He started by asking me where I went after chasing and losing the second Cadillac, then asked me why I went there. I repeated what I had said, repeating my best hypothetical guess that it wasn't Finnes who did the shooting, but maybe some of his underlings acting on their own. I was hoping that might bind up Enos Flood long enough to keep him out of my hair. They might even make him for the Clancy's holdup.

My hopes weren't high, though. Once they snooped around Milo's people, they were bound to hear about Brent Charmichael's body and the gun that lay beside him. I figured they would clear Mickey's murder with that and Denver would take up their own investigation into who killed Charmichael. That was my bigger worry. If my name came up in that connection, Captain Connally would notice. And if he brought me in, I wouldn't likely get out without help from Luis. One way or another that would be the end of my cover. I wanted to stay in. I wanted to find Mickey's killer. I even wanted to find Charmichael's killer.

We ended the interview on an up note, Harris thanking me for my cooperation while still on camera, for the benefit of future audiences. Then he escorted me to the front lobby.

"Thanks again for the help," he said, this time extending his hand. "You know, you don't seem like a dumb enough guy to get involved with the likes of Frank Coyne. No offense, but they're just so many organized grifters. Those games are nothing more than a gambling scam and a tax dodge. The legalized gambling in Black Hawk and Central City will pretty much put bingo out of its misery."

I smiled at the word choice. I found myself liking Harris by now—or respecting him, anyway—and it grated to play the part with him. "Everyone's entitled to their opinion," I said lightly, "And everyone has their own little game."

"Maybe, but these guys." He rolled his eyes and grinned. "You know what we call them around here?"

I found his humor affecting. "Okay, let's hear it."

"Raffle robbers," he said, widening his grin. "You know? Like taking money from the church raffles. Just one step up from snagging bills out of the offerings basket as they pass it around."

"You're the cops. Why don't you do something about it?"

"Not our jurisdiction until they start shooting each other. Secretary of State Herrera's supposed to regulate all those games. Raffles too, for that matter. And their little in-house lottery. *You* must know that. There's another bunch of bureaucratic crooks. It's a major loophole and there's no doubt those so-called staff investigators are milkin' it for all kinds of skim." He shrugged. "But nobody cares. It's what's called permissible levels of corruption."

"Yeah, I hear there's a lot of that going around on the local level."

"Not around here buddy. Nobody ever shows *us* the money."

Chapter 21

I went by my apartment to pack some clothes and check on the arrangements for Pimpy. I found a message on my machine from Luis asking me to call him at home. He had heard about Brent Charmichael's murder, it couldn't be anything else. Thinking about how that conversation was going to go, I decided to take the dog for a walk.

Retrieving Pimpy from Mrs. Parker downstairs, we sniffed and peed our way to a place on South Broadway that sold pizza by the slice. I bought two pieces and gave Pimpy the crusts. Looking at his eager, untroubled face, I decided to take him with me. We should all have ears like that.

When I got to Willie's, I put Pimpy in the yard and went in to call Luis. There was a message on the machine from Claire.

"Hello, Henry. I hope I have the right number. Who's Willie Junior? Anyway, I wanted to apologize for the way I acted last night. I guess I was upset. Well, of course I was. I want you to know that I appreciate your concern and...and *I* want to find out who did this too. I don't think I'll rest easy until...well, you know what I mean? Like you said, bring them to justice, *whoever* it was. Jeez, I hope you get this message. I don't want to freak somebody out. Anyway, Shanie and me are going up to Evergreen to be with my folks. I waited to call them until this morning. They're pretty broken up. Tanya has set a memorial service for Monday. I think we'll stay up there until then. But *call* me."

She left a number and signed off saying, "Hope to see you soon." Those words, and the softness of her tone, stirred my ambivalence. But I dismissed it to consider the rest of the message. I hadn't thought of her parents—Mickey's parents too—and I wondered what they might know about their son's occupation. And there was Tanya, as well. She was family, after all, the grieving widow. Even a sham marriage with a two-timing husband will take on new meaning when the guy turns up dead. Unless she killed him, of course. I wondered what she stood to inherit, though it sounded like she had money and standing of her own. I'd have to get closer to her. The thought made me feel qualmish.

I re-recorded the answering message on Willie's machine to include both of our names. Then I called Luis, gearing myself to face the music. He was close to the phone and, predictably, ready to jump me.

"You heard about Brent Charmichael." Not a question.

I took a deep breath and considered hanging up. "Where'd you hear about it?" I asked, in a feeble attempt at obfuscation.

Luis paused, and the silence was like an accusing stare. "I called records at DPD first thing this morning to run a check on those names you gave me. I mentioned Charmichael and the cop on the line got all jacked up. She had all kinds of questions for *me*." He paused again, as if to let me speak. I couldn't think of a feasible diversion. He came up with the inevitable question. "So let's hear how *you* know about it?"

"Well, I sort of found out on my own," I said, and waited for him to put two and two together. It didn't take long.

"*You* were the caller? Jesus, Henry."

I could picture Luis squinting, wiping his hand across his face, taking a breath. He needed a moment.

"Why didn't you identify yourself?" he demanded. "You can't come onto a murder scene and just tiptoe away."

"I'm supposed to be undercover. I figured it wouldn't stay that way for long if I had to explain myself to a bunch of homicide dicks. You're the one who said not to talk to the cops."

"No way, Henry my boy. You can't hide behind me on this. I also told you to toe the line. Nothing illegal. Now I can't help you if this comes out, but you can sure as hell drag me down."

"It won't come to that."

"Yeah, sure. Listen, you gotta come in. You gotta give 'em what you have."

"I don't have anything, Luis. I mean, nothing they won't get on their own. I didn't touch anything. I just looked around, found the body, got the hell out of there. He'd been dead for a couple of hours. I wiped down doorknobs on the way out."

"Yeah, and you cleaned up after the killer too."

"C'mon, Luis. Someone offed Charmichael and *they* didn't clean up?" He started to speak, but I cut him off. "They took his computer, Luis. Took it off his desk. They took all the disks, anything with memory, right? But they didn't wipe their prints?"

"They took his computer," he said, a trace of thoughtfulness in his voice.

"Left the other equipment, printer, keyboard. Just unplugged the box and left all the wires hanging. I looked for disks. No CD's, no storage, nothing."

"Anything else missing?"

"It wasn't a burglary, if that's what you mean. Somebody was covering tracks. And it was somebody that knew him. He was shot at close range. Burns around the entrance wound."

"You touched the body?"

"Gimme a break, Luis. I've been on crime scenes before, right?"

"Yeah, I know you've been on crime scenes before. I remember the last time you found a dead one. You ended up in lockup for a couple of days while Connally squeezed everyone in your address book. I got bothered just for knowin' you."

"That was a whole different thing."

"Yeah, sure." He coughed out a laugh. "Connally's not that far away on this one. He hasn't called yet, but he will when he hears I was asking about Charmichael."

"You don't have to involve me."

"Of course I will, Henry. I'm not bluffing Connally. Plus Aurora already has your name from the Gilmore shooting. How long do you think you can dodge them?"

"I went in," I said calmly, unable to resist a supercilious tone.

Luis was quiet for a beat. I thought I had him going, but he's nothing if not careful.

"You went in."

"Like I said I would, first thing this morning."

"After discovering Charmichael's body. You just went in."

"Yes."

"But you didn't bother to mention the dead body you found?"

"It didn't come up," I said, smiling to myself, and glad he couldn't see it.

Luis didn't laugh. "And you don't think they'll make the connection?"

"Not for a while. And not with *you*, Luis. Nothing connects me with you, right? All this cloak and dagger wasn't for nothing, was it?"

"It wasn't to cover up tampering with evidence."

"I didn't *tamper*, for Christ's sake. I was in and out in ten minutes. Nobody saw me."

After a long few seconds, Luis said, "What else did you find?"

"The probable murder weapon. A 9 MM Colt, nickel plated. It was left on the floor within reach of the body. I'm guessing it was left there to tell us Charmichael offed himself. Not very convincing, really, but there it is."

"Maybe it *was* his gun, defending himself."

"*His* gun was in the desk drawer."

"And you didn't touch anything?"

"Like I said, I looked around for the disks. I opened a few drawers. I was paying attention, Luis. It didn't take much effort. My guess is it's the same gun that killed Mickey Gilmore. That's why they left it. I'd bet my salary on it."

"Yeah, your salary," Luis drawled. "You mean the salary you'd get from the DA's office if I admitted you were working for me."

I had a snappy comeback for that, but decided not to push it. "It fits, Luis. Charmichael had the obvious motive—Mickey setting the fire at Broadway Bingo. He also had two sets of airline tickets in his briefcase. One was to and from Vegas, like he told Milo. He left on Wednesday. But the second ticket brought him back to Denver on Friday morning, and the return was a flight to San Diego that night."

"You're thinking he was ready to skip?"

"I don't think he was counting on his alibi holding up."

"Somebody turned on him?"

"Yeah, an accomplice, like the driver, maybe, when he shot Mickey. Brent tells him he's high-tailing it. The accomplice didn't like being left holding the bag."

"So a confrontation of some kind."

"Or else Brent sensed he was being set up. Whoever it was wanted the trail to end with Brent, hence the suicide scenario."

"What about taking the computer?"

"Must have been an afterthought. It could be Brent's killing was spur of the moment, the confrontation gone bad. Then the killer improvised, saw how to sew it up. Or at least end one trail of evidence. Like evidence of money laundering."

"Lots of speculation."

"Which is why I need to stay inside."

"Who is this supposed accomplice?"

"At this point, could be anybody in this bingo crowd since Brent was on the outs. We could narrow the field with an accurate time of death. And I got an idea where we could start looking."

Luis said nothing. I figured that was the best response I could expect.

"The room I found him in was a home office setup. There was a filing cabinet in there. I didn't take time to look through it, but I bet there will be stuff to do with Milo Finnes' operation in there. It might even go back to when he worked for Coyne. You could get access to it through the homicide investigation."

"Thank you for pointing that out. And I suppose you have an idea what I should tell Connally about why I'm interested."

I didn't have an answer for that.

Luis sighed into the phone. "Wha'd you tell Harris?"

"As little as possible. I told him the shooting at the Palace points to Milo's people, but probably not Milo. Like you said, he'll make the connection when he hears about Charmichael."

"Any sign of that blue Caddy?"

"It was Charmichael's car. Parked in front of his house. The lab techs can put it at the Palace. They burnt rubber peeling out of there."

"What else?" Luis sounded impatient, or maybe just annoyed.

"That's about it," I said, but Luis' silence worked on me. "I may have left some tracks around the house."

"You left tracks?"

"I circled around before I went in. It's a construction site. They hadn't put in the sod yet."

Luis sighed noticeably again.

"Which gives me another idea," I said, pressing forward. "It's a new house and there's a couple others on either side and one across the street, still being built. But Charmichael's address was in the phone book, so he's lived there for some time. I was thinking he scraped his old house and had a new one built on the lot. And then he bought the lots next door and he's building the others on spec. They're kit-homes, practically the same designs."

"Where would he get the money for that?"

"That's why I'm curious."

"Yeah, that's a reasonable lead, Henry," Luis said, feigning an affable air. "And after you come in, you can help me track it down."

"We can't do that. Things are shaking loose. In terms of our investigation, I couldn't be in a better position."

"It's too risky," he quipped. "Too much shooting. Too much shooting from the hip."

"Luis, the next few days are crucial. Let me play it out. If I get snagged, I'll wait it out without your help. I can handle Connally."

"Yeah, right."

"I've done it before."

"I don't think you can say two days in the can was 'handling it'."

"I didn't call you that time, did I?"

"You didn't have my blessings that time. You were working on you own—way out of bounds, if I remember right—which is just what it feels like now."

"Okay, let me play it that way—on my own. If the shit comes down, I won't bring you in. I won't have to. I'm confident of that."

Luis huffed a quiet laugh. "You're confident."

"I won't bring you down, Luis. I owe you that."

Luis was quiet for a long minute. I bit my tongue to keep from getting smarmy. Finally he said, "I checked up on your Flood brothers. They're a nasty pair. You should be careful."

"Wha'd you find?" I said, noting his tacit acquiescence.

"Their sheets go back ten years, all the way to juvie. A whole list of petty stuff, most of it pled down. But Enos did time for assault and grand theft. Then he and his brother, Alois, got busted in connection with a meth lab about three years ago. Looks like the brother took the rap for that. He got two-to-ten for manufacturing with intent to sell, but he's been sprung recently on a reversed decision."

"How'd that come about?"

"I don't know the details. They filed an appeal, got a hearing. He's out on a PR bond. Sounds like the kind of thing that rolls over on technicalities. What stands out about it is that he got Cater and Holmes to represent him. You know them, right?"

"Who doesn't? All those headline cases. Got the Congressman's son off on that statutory rape charge last year. Where'd these boys get the money for a golden mouthpiece like that?"

"Maybe Milo put it up."

"I doubt it. I didn't see a lot of sweet talk goin' on between him and Enos. And Milo called his brother down in front of him. I got a feeling the Flood brothers are Charmichael's boys more than Milo's. The three of them did the holdup at Clancy's without Milo knowing about it. If Charmichael was deep in the money flow, maybe he paid for Cater and Holmes so he'd have the Flood brothers for muscle."

"You should give *that* to the Aurora cops."

"What?"

"The holdup at Clancy's."

"I don't have anything conclusive. They were wearing masks."

"You said Enos copped to it."

"Yeah, well, not in a way that would be admissible. I sort of had to massage it out of him. Any legal aid could get him a walk on the evidence we have, let alone Cater and Holmes."

Luis said, "You think they could have done Brent?"

"It doesn't fit all that well. Enos is definitely not the brains. I doubt he'd think to take the computer. And as far as that goes, I don't think he had the time. I found his car at Milo's shortly after the shooting at the Palace. That's why Brent's time of death is crucial. Maybe you could nail that down from your end. We could eliminate several suspects if he died before eleven o'clock."

"Including yourself," Luis said, chuckling. I suffered that in silence. "What about the brother? He wasn't there, right?"

"Yeah, he could be good for it. Could have been Brent's driver, too. Could have been worried about taking the rap for whacking Mickey if Brent split. But I don't think it's that simple. What's his name? Aloysius?"

"Alois."

"Where'd these guys come from with names like that?"

"Kentucky," Luis said. "They got an AKA, looks like the original family name got chopped. Something like Floudorel. German? Polish?"

Luis fell silent, allowing me to flirt with the implications of the Flood brothers' ethnic backdrop. I'd have to tell Willie.

"I checked up on Vince Terrelli," Luis continued. "No criminal record. Took early retirement from the Tacoma PD in '91. When he moved here, he did two years with the Jeffco Sheriff's Department. Left in '93. I haven't found out why yet, but he now owns two of Milo's bingo halls. Public records say so, anyway."

"Same arrangement as Frank and his cronies. Who owns the rest of them?"

In a light-hearted tone, Luis said, "The principle owner of Broadway Bingo—recently burned down—and two other clubs run by Milo Finnes? None other than your fresh stiff, Brent Charmichael."

"I guess that's no surprise. I wonder who inherits."

"Good question. I should be able to get that from the case team eventually."

I paused to let the implication from his words settle in. "So-o-o? That mean you want to play it out on the sly?"

"On the *sly*, huh?"

It was a delicate moment. I managed to remain silent, giving him room to consider it on his own—along the lines of giving him enough rope.

"You know, Henry, I've gotten rather fond of you over the years, watching your antics, watching you get in and out of jams." This was an understatement. He had saved my life once. I figured he had that in mind as he spoke. "Now that our investigation is all jammed up with killings and repeat offenders and who knows how much money, I'm afraid for you. I'm afraid of where it's going and that I won't be there when things get tight."

"I'll be careful, Luis."

"Yeah, you being careful. I just don't know if that's gonna be good enough."

I waited for him to continue, thinking about what I could and couldn't do without his help. I was fooling myself pretty well when he interrupted my train of thought.

"No more breaking and entering, Henry. Okay?"

"I can do that."

"And stay away from those Flood brothers. You're investigating the Coyne family. We'll get to Milo's people later."

"All right," I said, but I was weighing Charmichael as the common thread to both operations. "Anything else?"

Luis paused for effect. "*Toe the line,* Henry. I *mean* it."

"Okay."

"Call me Monday from a pay phone. Use the pager number. I'll talk to you then. And Henry, burn your shoes. The ones you were wearing at Charmichael's. It's a double homicide now. It's in two different venues and it's making headlines. And that's gonna make everybody real thorough. Burn those shoes. Got me?"

We hung up, and I actually thought about doing it.

Chapter 22

By the time I reached Bellevue Shopping Center the afternoon clouds had rolled off the front-range, billowing into the big sky overhead, muted sunlight casting a cool, uniform grayness over the big-box structures. Near the broad-arched entrance to the mall, a rent-a-cop sat in his pale green Ford. As I traversed the expanse of empty parking spaces, I saw a second car the same shade of green come around the southern-most corner and pull up next to the first one. They were out in force considering nothing was open for business.

Two Caddies and Frank Coyne's Jaguar lined the first row of spaces opposite Bingo Palace. As I parked next to the Jag, a Sunday driver with a car full of kids made a pass in front of the hall, slowing at the entrance, gawking out their windows, getting a peek at the scene of the crime. There wasn't much to see. A cardboard sign overlapped the front door explaining, in hand drawn lettering, that Bingo Palace was closed until further notice. A small poster next to it identified the site as the scene of an official police investigation. There was no blood, no chalk outline, no bullet holes or broken glass. The disappointed voyeurs rolled away, following the serpentine lane that wound along the blank storefronts.

I found Frank and Dennis Coyne, and Benny Palmer cloistered in the back office, well out of sight of curious passersby—and out of range of drive-by assassins. Somber looks greeted my entrance into the small smoke-filled room. Frank nodded hello and, with an air of getting rid of him, instructed Dennis to head out to Five Aces. Sidling past me, Dennis kept his eyes to the ground. I sat in the chair that he had vacated and tried to ignore the oppressive atmosphere.

"Where you been?" Frank asked, sounding a little miffed.

"I just got done with Detective Harris. That dragged out for a while." I rolled my eyes, affecting exasperation.

"You hear the news?"

"They find something out?"

Frank stared at me blankly. "They found Brent Charmichael," he said.

"Not in Vegas, right?"

Frank shook his head, keeping his eyes riveted to mine. "Where'd you go last night, after we left Holiday Bingo?"

"I went up to Claire's," I said, trying to sound sheepish. "You know, just to see how she was doing."

The two men continued to stare, apparently nonplussed.

"Something the matter with that?"

"You went straight there?"

"I went home first. Changed clothes. I tried calling her but got no answer. What's the matter? You think that was out of line?" I felt like I should be on the short list for a daytime Emmy.

Frank sighed through a frown and dropped his eyes to the desk. He picked up a paper clip and began bending it open. "Brent Charmichael is dead. They found him last night in his house, over near the Holiday. He was shot in the chest. Right through the heart."

"Jeez." I let an appropriate moment pass for the shock of the news to settle in. "They know who did it?"

Frank shook his head. "Nothing conclusive, but they've connected it to what happened here. They found a gun. They think it was the same one used to shoot Mickey."

I wondered who the 'they' was—how anyone besides me and the crime scene cops would be in a position to make that guess. "That make it a suicide?"

"Not convincingly. The cops aren't buying it, and neither am I." Frank leveled his gaze at me. "So you didn't have anything to do with this, did ya?"

"Me?" I coughed out a laugh of incredulity. "Why would I?"

He smiled blandly, shrugged his shoulders. "You're a man of action, you get things done, not afraid of a confrontation. I watched you take on that flunky at Milo's last night. And there's rumors you're sweet on Claire, right? You say you were up there last night. Maybe she's upset. Talks you into something." He shrugged again.

"Hey, c'mon Frank. I like Claire all right, but I'm not crazy in love! And I'm no killer."

Frank looked to Palmer whose bulbous features sagged in a hangdog expression as his eyes met mine.

"I made some calls, Henry," Palmer said. "Calls to Seattle. You know the Ripken family up there, right?"

A fist tightened in my chest and a tingling sensation spread upward on my neck and face. "Yeah, sure." I fumbled for a cigarette while trying to recall what I knew from Luis' notes.

"Never had much use for them myself, frankly," Palmer continued, an awkward grin pinching up one side of his face. "They had their own supply setup. Kinda pressured me out. That and the new legislation is what brought me here in the first place."

"Yeah, me too," I said, relaxing a little.

Frank cleared his throat and Palmer glanced at him, then back to me. "I know a guy up there, knows a guy, says he knows you."

"Who's that?"

"Fella named Gallach? Something like that?"

"Gurlach. Yeah, Richie Gurlach." He was the mole in place in Seattle. He was my reference, arranged by Luis through the Washington AG. Supposedly.

"Yeah, that's him. I finally got to talk to him first hand. I been tryin' for a while."

"How's he doing?" I asked.

"We didn't get too friendly. He didn't seem that friendly about you either, for that matter."

"We didn't work all that much together," I said, feeling cracks in the ice I had stepped out onto.

"I asked him about that torch job. The one you told us about?"

I tried to look humbled. It wasn't that hard.

"He says it sounded like the kind of thing you might have done. Said he wouldn't put it past you."

I smiled. I couldn't help myself. But it went over like I was being cocky. Palmer gave me a sarcastic frown. Frank studied me evenly.

"He said he thought you got into some trouble workin' for the Ripkens. Said he thought they might've run you out of town."

"That's not true," I said, feigning belligerence.

"What did happen?" Frank interjected.

"It was just a parting of the ways, is all. I mean, they weren't sad to see me go, maybe, but there's nothing else to it. And I didn't do that fire."

"But you knew about it? You knew who did?"

"Well, that depends on who's asking, Frank. And why they'd want to know."

Frank held his stare, owl-like in its unwavering focus. But then he looked away and went for a cigarette. When he spoke again, his tone had shifted, deepened. "I don't go in for killing. I'm a businessman. I'm not some kind of hood. I'm not a crook." You couldn't miss the Nixon reference but apparently Frank did. I think I managed a straight face. "I run a legal enterprise and I don't want anyone workin' for me who thinks they can skirt the law." I nodded agreeably. It took some effort. "That's just the kind of thing that's going to bring Milo down. And I don't want anything to do with it." He leaned forward and glared at me. The hand holding the cigarette folded up and two fingers pointed at me in the shape of a gun. "I don't want any of my people acting on their own either. You get my point? You want to go your own way? Do it now. Otherwise you toe the line."

Luis' exact words. It made me wonder—even in character—what I do that makes people worry so much.

"I'm sorry about Mickey," I said. "I shouldn't have said anything." Feeling there was some truth to it, I added, "I feel like it was partly my fault."

Frank watched me for a moment, then spit out a huff of hot air. "That was nobody's fault but Mickey's. That's just what I'm getting at." He took a deep drag on his cigarette then turned away to blow the smoke. "Stupid SOB." He stared off, then bowed his head.

"So they tried to make it look like a suicide?" I offered.

"That's what the cops say, yeah."

"How'd you find out about that?" I asked, playing it a little reckless. "Is Joe Perkins on it?"

"How'd you know that?"

"You mentioned him the other night. You said he was a homicide cop. I know how those guys work from my time at the DA's. They don't usually chat up investigations to just anybody."

Frank ground out his cigarette and blew smoke through a sigh. "He said Brent was shot at close range like he held the gun up to his chest. But the gun looked planted or something. And there were signs of things missing. A strictly amateur cover-up. Those were his words."

"They got any idea who did it?"

"No, but since they've already connected it to Mickey's death, that puts all of us on their list." He shook his head again. "Things are really gonna get gummed up around here."

"Milo know about it?"

Frank nodded, still frowning. "He called. In a tantrum. He said it was that hotheaded new bodyguard of mine. Meaning *you*, I suppose."

I ignored the chiding tone. "What about those two brothers? His henchmen. They were both in with Brent on the holdup at Clancy's. If Brent did kill Mickey, could be the other brother was driving. Something goes wrong between them." I exaggerated a shrug. "There's no honor among thieves," I said, then, given the present company, immediately wished I hadn't.

Fortunately, Frank didn't pick up on it. "Yeah, I hit him with that. Didn't do any good. He just went on ranting. Accused me of not keeping reign on *my* people. I threw *that* back at him." He nodded defiantly. "Anyway, he said this shit would have to stop. We agreed on that much."

We fell into a brooding silence, mulling over what was said and what had been left unspoken. I had more questions, but held back, feeling like I'd pushed my act far enough for now.

"I need some coffee," Frank said eventually. "Those damn tourists still parading by out there?" Without waiting for an answer, he got up and headed towards the door. Benny and I followed.

At the end of the hallway, he came to a stop and scanned the front windows. He turned to catch my eye, then nodded toward the parking lot. There was a police cruiser, a Douglas County Sheriff's vehicle, parked next to Willie's Mustang. In the hazy afternoon light, we could see the two officers sitting inside.

"That your car, Henry?" Frank asked.

"That's what I'm driving. It belongs to a friend."

"Your friend in any kind of trouble?" He turned on his cocky grin. It was the first time today.

"Not that I know of."

After a few seconds, Frank said, "Probably just keeping an eye on the crime scene. There were a bunch of them out here this morning. Press too. And by the way, I don't want anyone talkin' to those people. Bunch a' fuckin' vultures."

Frank and Benny moved toward the concession counter and we gathered around the coffee maker. Just to say something, I said, "You talked to Burrows about that? About the press, I mean?"

"Yeah. He's laying low. He's got all kinds of friends on the force. That makes it pretty sticky for him to be involved in a murder investigation."

"I can imagine."

Out of the corner of my eye, I caught the motion of another vehicle, this one an Aurora Police cruiser, moving diagonally across the lot. Frank noticed it too. When it pulled up next to the Sheriff's car, he said, "What the hell they up to now?"

"Maybe we ought to go see," suggested Palmer.

"Hell, no. The less we deal with them, the better."

But when a third police car approached, cutting hard and fast across the lot, it began to look like something we couldn't avoid. The third car was unmarked, bronze in color, no bells and whistles, concealed lights and low-profile antennas. It pulled up hard along the curb and the four cops in the other two cars were up and out before it came to a full stop. We watched through the glass as Detective Scott Harris got out of the unmarked car and formed a loose huddle with the other cops. Not exactly a no-knock raid. As they moved toward the door, I saw hands going to hips to unbutton their holster straps. This was no friendly check-in, no follow-up questioning, no take a second look. They were here to collar someone and I had a bad feeling about that.

"Now what?" Frank said, clearly agitated. Sensing something of their purpose, he turned to me, as if expecting an answer. I shrugged and grinned guiltily.

Opening the door, Harris led the slow charge across the expanse of floor-space, the uniforms spreading out behind him. No one drew their gun, but there was purpose in their strides and tension on their faces. Frank stepped forward to meet them halfway.

"What's up, Scotty? I thought you guys were done here."

"We got a new development," Harris said, slowing to a stop a few steps away from Frank. The other cops fanned out on either side, a good defensive line. There was little doubt they were keying on me. Palmer read it and drifted casually to one side, out of the line of fire.

Harris jutted his chin in my direction. "You carrying a gun?"

"I gave it to you," I said, as if appalled.

Harris stepped past Frank to face me, then, with a quick jerking motion, he reached out to pat down my waist and torso. "Turn around," he commanded, twisting me with a firm grasp.

"What's this about?"

"Cuffs," he said to someone and I heard a rustle of movement. As I began to turn to face him, strong hands gripped me, kept me in place.

"What's going on?" I asked as they clipped the bracelets on.

"We got some builders workin' time-and-a-half on weekends at a site not far from here. Seems there was a broken down Mercedes parked in the way of their refuse bin." As he spoke, he turned me around and surprised me by shoving his hands deep into my front pants pockets. His face close to mine, his breathe warm, our eyes locked—it could have been an intimate moment. It almost made me smile. Roughly, he pulled my keys out, some loose bills, a lighter, stuff, and passed it to an officer behind him with plastic evidence bags at the ready. "When the tow-truck jockey took a look at it, he wouldn't touch it. Said he thought the car was shot up with bullet holes. That's when they called us."

I felt the blood drain from my face as I thought about who to call and why I didn't want to. Over Harris' shoulder, I saw Frank standing perfectly still, like an animal tracking a passing threat, blending into the background.

"Seems the car is registered in your name, Burkhart," Harris continued. "You remember that now? You remember me asking you about the running shootout about a mile from here, and not three blocks from where we found your car? It fits the descriptions to a tee."

"So you're arresting me?" I don't know why I said that—like it was written in the script.

Harris laughed out loud. It was a healthy, spontaneous laugh. "Discharge of firearms within the city limits, reckless endangerment, obstruction of an official investigation. We'll start there and build on it." Still smiling, he said, "I don't like being lied to. So you can count on me making this as difficult as possible for you."

He jerked me toward the door, letting me feel the chaffing of the cuffs. One of the uniforms grabbed my other arm and jerked me his way for good measure.

"Where you taking him?" Frank asked tentatively.

"Now why would you care?" Harris snapped. "If I were you, I'd be distancing myself as far as possible from this wise guy."

Frank didn't say anything more. I felt like he could have tried a little harder.

Two uniforms loaded me into the back of their patrol car and left me there to sulk. Harris stood near the entrance giving instructions. He pointed at Willie's car and one of the officers walked toward it, speaking into his radio. They were calling in a tow-truck. Willie wasn't going to like that. Harris sent the two Aurora cops in my direction. Before we drove off, I saw Harris walk back into the hall to speak with Frank Coyne and Benny Palmer. They didn't look too happy.

Chapter 23

The Aurora Detention Center—supporting the same patina dome I had walked under that morning—was built to house upwards of three hundred inmates, designed to meet the latest standards of humane incarceration and high-tech security. Construction was completed five years ago, along with the rest of the new government complex, but the jail wasn't put to use for another two or three years. Not enough criminals to make it worth paying the light bill. But it's open for business now and, compared to Denver County Jail, it's a nice place to visit.

Although I didn't get to stroll through the well-pruned courtyard this time, I got the VIP treatment in the rear. They chauffeured me through the drive-in sally port and unloaded me not fifteen feet from the pre-booking station entrance. Two cops escorted me through sliding doors and then into a secured (as in barred) waiting area and clipped my cuffs to a hook at the back of a screwed-down metal chair, leaving me there without a single word of abuse. I busied myself perusing the posters mounted on the opposite wall—bail bondsmen open twenty-four/seven for my convenience: EZ Pay Bonds; Stan the 'Bail Bonds' Man; All Mighty Bonds. Yeah, that last one, I liked the sound of it. I memorized the number just in case.

After a while another cop—this one a woman, rather attractive considering the uniform—took the seat at the computer next to me and proceeded to ask me my relevant vital stats. The nameplate on her lapel read 'P. Haines'. She had dark brown hair pinned back above her ears but flowing beyond her nape, and light-brown eyes that seemed rather small without the highlighting of makeup. The planes of her face were peppered with faint freckles but she didn't see the sun much—a full-time a jailer. With her hair down and a different wardrobe selection—and given her rather slender body-type—you wouldn't make her for a cop. As if to compensate for this, she adapted a stiff, officious air when speaking, working hard to keep some prissy version of a scowl on her face when her eyes met mine. I thought about chiding her for it, flirting a little just to see how it would take. But my heart wasn't in it. The situation worked against me.

"What am I being charged with?"

"You'll have to wait for the arresting officer. He'll explain all that."

"Is that Scott Harris?"

She nodded. She motioned for me to lean forward, then reached behind to unhook me from the chair. I could smell a trace of perfume. She must drive them crazy in here. "C'mon. I'll take you to booking."

She led me through a glassed-in chute, pausing at the second door to speak to invisible controllers through the mic on her shoulder. That door didn't open until the first one buzzed shut behind us. The place smelled of urinal blocks, floor wax, and air-conditioning.

Stepping through the door, I found myself surveilling a large room, the ceiling two stories high and the floor area irregularly divided by waist-high partitions. The diffuse lighting allowed for few shadows and everything sparkled with cleanliness. I could see no prisoners in the adjacent holding cells and only three cops were visible, none of them looking very busy. The space was strangely quiet.

An arrangement of metal desks were equipped with an array of computer and photography equipment, apparently state-of-the-art. Beyond them and elevated slightly, smoked-glass walls encased the control room. I could see no movement in there, no human presence, only the dull glow of TV monitors and neat rows of illuminated indicator lights, red and green. A wide hallway to the right led to the metal doors of individual cells, each with a six-inch wide vertical slot of wire-mesh glass. Partially framed in the first one, a black man, quite young, wearing the orange coveralls, leaned with his face mashed up against the narrow window. His walleyed stare made him look doped up or retarded. The knot in my gut tightened, transforming vague flutters of anxiety into tangible fear.

"Evenin' Pat," Officer Haines said to the silver-haired jailer smiling politely behind the first desk. His nameplate read 'O'Malley' and he had an Irish lilt when he spoke. I'd seen this in a movie somewhere.

"Hello, Missy, who you got there for me?" He looked up at me and smiled wider, as if waiting for an introduction. A four-inch scar, long ago healed over, made the deep-set crow's feet take unnatural lines along one side of his face. His smile was crooked too but his humor seemed almost genuine. His blue eyes shone on me like I was shopping for his best deal on a good used F-150.

"Prints and pictures," Haines said, light-hearted herself now in response to O'Malley's cheerful tone. She stepped behind me and unlocked my cuffs.

"You can't book me without charging me, right?" I said, just to make my presence felt.

"Don't you worry about the details," O'Malley said, encouragingly. "Someone'll be down here shortly to take care of all that."

Haines handed him my paperwork and the jailer led me around his desk and positioned me to stand in a square outlined on the floor.

"Now you just stand still and let me take your picture."

"There's been some kind of mix up," I stammered, realizing as I spoke that he must've heard that a thousand times.

"Well, don't worry about it then. We'll sort it out. Now hold still." He worked the mouse on his desk and suddenly, my face came up on his screen, full color and larger than life. I frowned and watched as the frown formed on my video image, then froze. The perfect mug shot—not Nick Nolte, but with a similarly shamed air.

I thought about telling them, just blurting it out. I was one of them, working undercover, working for the Denver DA. Call Luis Sanchez. Don't go any further until you make that call. And then I caught Officer Haines' expression, her sharp features creased with a condescending grin, smirking like she'd seen it all before, seen that fear on those tough guys' faces, and still she found it amusing.

It's hard to be in law enforcement and not look down on your charges, not judge them automatically for being stupid, being caught, being caught-up in their fate at the low point of an already low life. It was the flush of power that I saw on her face, the sense of superiority, easing into the temptation to disregard, to gloat. I knew where that went. And it pissed me off.

I decided to wait it out, as long as it would take to get on equal ground. Maybe even get one leg up.

"Okay," O'Malley said, "Turn to the right."

I turned, facing Haines more directly. She wasn't smiling any more, but she watched me with a steady gaze that looked like prurient interest.

"There's nothing funny about it," I said evenly, and her eyes widened slightly and stayed with mine for longer than she wanted. "It can happen to anybody, even you."

"Okay now, sir," O'Malley said, standing up, sensing the spark of anger. Firmly gripping my arm, he turned me away. "Let's just step over to the ten printer and we'll do your fingerprints. No ink or nothin' anymore. Just put your hand right here and hold it steady."

I spread my hand on the glass plate and waited for him to finish. When I turned again, Officer Haines had moved away. She faced the reinforced glass door through which we had entered and spoke into her mic. The door slid open with a buzz and a clank and, without looking back, she stepped towards the outside.

O'Malley gave me a cursory pat down then asked me about my personal belongings.

"Detective Harris has them."

One eyebrow raised significantly. "All right, then," he said, as if that was standard procedure. He led me to the doors of the holding cell across from his desks. "You're gonna have to wait in here until Detective Harris comes down." Putting his hand to his radio, he said, "D-D-2," and the door slid open before us. I stepped in without protest and headed for the bank of pay phones along the back wall.

I called Duncan Pruett, my constant friend and occasional—perhaps too occasional—legal counsel. When he didn't pick up his cell, I called his home number. His wife, Sara, said he was playing racquetball with his boss—who is the senior partner at Rollins, Jeffery & Associates. Right away, she knew something was up. Duncan and I have a history. It went back to well before he and Sara met and, petty jealousies aside, she knew that history was punctuated with tight spots and blind alleys, none of them her husband's fault. I couldn't blame her for the attitude but I cut it short, not wanting to waste time on their family politics. Anyway, he was playing racquetball.

I thought about calling Luis but not for long. It would mean the end of my cover and, by now, I was paying dearly for it, which made it feel all the more valuable.

I called Willie Junior.

"You *what*!" Willie said, several times, as I described my predicament. His low rolling laughter let me know how much he enjoyed being right about this. But when I told him they had impounded the Mustang, the laughter stopped flat.

"What you mean 'impounded'? They got my *car*?"

"Your car's in the slammer, Willie. And they're gonna have to clear me to release it. Now, I need you to find Duncan. He's not home, but I know where you can find him. He's got a weekly game with his boss. They're at the Denver Athletic Club. You know where that is?"

"The DAC? Ah, man, I ain't goin' in there. That place so white even *you* couldn't get in."

"Willie, it hasn't been segregated for decades."

"Yeah, after they passed a *law* against it. Only niggers in that place *payin'* to be white. Know what I'm sayin'? Ain't no brothas in there."

"Willie, I don't have time for this. You have to get word to Duncan. Tell them you're with Rollins, Jeffery. Hell, ask for Mr. Rollins himself, if you want to. That's who he plays with."

"Oh, yeah, that should be good. You *tryin'* to get me fired?"

"I *got* you that job, dammit…" I stopped and took a breath. "Look, Willie, I need some action here. The right kind of pressure up front might keep Harris from filing charges, keep me out of the system. Otherwise, I'll be in here till Monday and it'll take months to sort out."

"How 'bout Uncle Leroy? I know he's home. He *likes* you. I could drive him out."

"Leroy? Does he even practice anymore?"

"Yeah, sure. He's *my* lawyer."

"That why you spent thirty days inside before *I* sprung you?"

"Ah'ight, ah'ight, I'll find Duncan. But you owe me for this. Man! I can't *believe* you let them take my car."

"*Willie!*"

"Yeah, okay. I'm goin'. I'm gone."

Two hours ticked by like two days. The jailhouse came to life. I was joined in the holding cell by two black youths who pretended they didn't know each other. Eventually, they took up leaning space along the back wall, jiving in undertones, likely getting their stories straight. They wanted nothing to do with me.

More people came into the booking area. More cops and more prisoners. I saw Haines once, escorting a female ward into the far wing. She didn't stop to chat.

Eventually, Harris appeared from an inner hallway carrying my personal belongings in a plastic bag. He gave them to O'Malley and they talked for some time. I stood by the cell doorway, waiting for my turn to speak and be spoken to. Harris lobbed me a one-eyed glance before moving toward the exit.

"Harris," I hollered, almost involuntarily, my tone betraying my anxieties.

He stopped and turned but didn't approach.

"You gonna tell me what's going on?"

He took two steps in my direction, looked past me into the cell, then around the room as if taking it all in. His bright eyes met mine and he gave me a perfunctory smile. "You know the drill," he said. "I'm doing the five forms now. I'll be filing charges shortly. You'll see a judge—tomorrow maybe. No later than Monday."

"C'mon, Harris. It doesn't have to be like this."

He smiled again and this time the expression carried a little more feeling. "You would know, I guess." He turned and walked off and buzzed his way out of the booking area.

One of my cellmates let out a contemptuous chuckle. He took me in with hooded eyes. "Man, that dude ain't no friend a' yours." He smiled a complicit smile.

"Tell me about it." I said, grateful for any small sympathy.

The jailhouse hustle and bustle gained momentum for another long hour before any of it had to do with me. I heard my name spoken and looked over to see a uniformed cop standing at O'Malley's desk. O'Malley pointed at me and together they stared. They approached the cell door and O'Malley spoke into his mouthpiece. When the door slid open the cop motioned to me, turned me around and cuffed me. Standing there facing the inner hallway, I felt suddenly hopeful. They wouldn't cuff me just to move me to another cell.

O'Malley spoke over the middle partition to a female cop and then I heard the crackle of the intercom and a page for Officer Haines. She appeared from around a corner.

"Go with Kazinski here to escort Mr. Burkhart upstairs. Interview three-ten, up in detective's."

Keeping her eyes averted, Haines stepped in front of me and led the way further into the complex. Passing by the single-bed cells, we entered into the inner cellblocks, then continued through a single door at the far end and finally through a double-locked chute. Kazinski kept a grip on my arm the whole time. When we exited the security chute, the next set of doors were finished in wood veneer and unsecured. My hopes bounded. We passed into a wide, carpeted hallway with subdued lighting and pastel-colored walls and followed it to the elevators.

Unloading on the third floor, I looked, with a sigh of relief, at the by now familiar sign of the Detectives' Bureau hanging from the ceiling. Kazinski and Haines escorted me around the front counter, and along the line of office cubicles, most of them unoccupied, towards a brightly lit conference room one door down from the room where I had previously been interviewed. It was much larger, nicer chairs, two fake plants in the corners, and without the one-way mirrored glass. Something gave way in my chest when I saw Duncan through the glass doors sitting across from Harris at one end of a long table. Another man, unknown to me, sat next to him. Haines knocked, then opened the door, and held it for me to pass through.

The three men in the room watched quietly as Kazinski unlocked my cuffs, then backed out of the room, closing the door. Looking over my shoulder, I saw Haines and Kazinski taking up the edge of a desk. Haines still avoided eye contact. I turned to my saviors.

For a change, Duncan didn't look like a lawyer. He wore khaki shorts and tennis shoes and his pin-striped shirt was open at the front, exposing sweat stains on a faded blue T-shirt. His closely trimmed hair was uncombed and darkened with sweat. He smiled through a frown and shook his head, an apparent attempt to express the mix of feelings he had about my being here. I had seen that expression before. I felt better, nevertheless.

The other man, rising out of his chair, stood six feet tall and carried an ample girth. Although suited up for an appearance in court, he had the bearing of an ex-athlete, an aging football player or former pro-wrestler, more or less gone to seed. His freshly knotted tie bound up the starched white collar that strained with the pressure from his second chin. As he leaned forward leading with an outstretched hand, he gave me a fleshy grin that was probably meant to be reassuring.

"I'm Stanley Riggs. Frank Coyne sent me." His voice had a gravelly quality and his thick lower lip curved outward when the smile died, leaving his mouth slack and partly open.

I shook his hand, glad to find out I was still in Frank's good graces, but unhappy with the prospect of pussyfooting around this guy to talk with Duncan. He was the one person I could be straight with and the only one I wanted to listen to. I needed his perspective. I needed to hear the precautions and counter arguments that I knew he would fastidiously extend. I also needed his cut-through-the-crap legal agility. He sat quietly, seemingly relaxed, waiting for Riggs to say his piece.

"I see no reason why you should be held against your will as a material witness. I've got a call in now to Judge Goldberg..." Riggs faded off, glancing in Harris's direction.

Harris sighed. "Sit down, Burkhart."

When I was seated, Harris addressed Riggs across the table. "I told you, he's more than a material witness. He was involved in a shootout Friday night on Parker Road in the middle of rush hour."

"You can't expect to keep my client locked up on circumstantial evidence. There's nothing that puts him in that car or at that location at the time in question. We're not talking about some gun-happy hoodlum, Detective. Mr. Burkhart is an upstanding citizen of this community. I want the duty judge notified immediately."

"We haven't even filed charges yet. Hell, I haven't even finished the arrest report."

"I don't think Judge Goldberg is going to look favorably at you dragging your feet," Riggs countered, building steam. "As you know, he's not sympathetic to the inadequacies of the police department."

"Inadequacies?" Harris gaped, stared. "Look, I haven't even questioned the guy yet. I'm not dragging my feet. You want to call in a judge—Goldberg or anybody—fine. Stick your neck out there. Mr. Burkhart is not going anywhere until I interview him."

"You have no right to question my client without his attorney present. And you have no right to keep him here."

"He's a suspect in a shooting, for Christ's sake. I can hold him for seventy-two hours. You know that."

"Those are only the *outside* limits of due process. In this case, it constitutes harassment. You keep him here overnight and I assure you, I'll have a judge's order by morning and the press will be filling up the courtyard."

Harris chuckled then tried to suppress it. He was taking some punches but it didn't look like any of the blows were hitting home. "Hell," he slurred, "I haven't even asked him if he wants an attorney and he's got two of 'em present. How's that for due process."

Duncan smiled and dropped his head, then looked up at me questioningly, as if to ask if I wanted him to join the fray. I gave him a faint shake of my head.

"All I want," Harris said, cutting off Riggs' next verbal feint, "is to ask Mr. Burkhart a few questions to ascertain his involvement. I can't finish my report without that. It would be done by now if you jokers hadn't shown up to toss your weight around."

Riggs readily took exception. "I'm not going to stand by for your snide aspersions. Knowing the judge personally, I'm sure he would frown on such character attacks."

"Character attacks? What?"

"Comments about my weight won't go over well with Judge Goldberg either."

I gathered the judge was a man of healthy corpulence as well.

Harris stared back with amazement, repressing a smile. "Look. I just want to talk to him."

"And I want my client released. You can't force him to answer questions. You have no right to hold him."

"He's a material witness in the…."

"You just said he wasn't."

"Christ. Then I'll file the charges. That make you happy?"

"Fine. Get a DA in here. Let's go before the judge. And don't try to tell me there's no DA available. We'll roust one from home before you keep my client incarcerated overnight."

"Hold on now," Duncan interrupted. "Are we talking about an arraignment? It's Saturday night."

"There's a duty judge on call," Riggs persisted, "and there better be a DA available."

"I hardly think the circumstances call for…"

"*I'm* the principle counsel here…"

"Gentlemen, please," I said, and everyone looked my way. Harris, smiling ironically, shook his head. "Mr. Riggs, I thank you for your efforts on my behalf. But if it would facilitate the, ah…goings-on here, I'd be happy to talk with the detective."

Harris' eyes narrowed some.

"I wouldn't advise that, Mr. Burkhart," Riggs said. "Mr. Coyne has informed me how the police have been harassing his people since the event of this unfortunate incident…"

"I understand, believe me," I said, unsure which 'event' he was referring to. "But if you would be willing to stand by for a few minutes…If I get into any trouble, I could just call you in." Shaking his head, Riggs opened his mouth to speak, but I didn't give him the chance. "And perhaps, Mr. Pruett would be willing to do the same. Would that be all right with you, Duncan?"

Duncan got the hint. "Yeah, sure. I think we would be amenable to that, provided Detective Harris will let us consult with you afterwards." He stood up and gestured past Riggs towards the door. "Let's put our heads together out here for a minute."

"Well, that's damned nice of you," Harris said, putting on his crooked frown.

"I'm not sure that's wise," Riggs said, his voice climbing up the musical scale.

"That's okay, Mr. Riggs," I told him. "Just stay close."

"I'll put in another call to the judge," he offered, huffing as he stood.

Moving behind him, Duncan rolled his eyes upward and smiled. "You all right?"

"Yeah, so far."

Watching them file out, I noticed Officer Kazinski still waiting, but Haines had gone. I was somehow disappointed.

"Can you believe that guy?" Harris said, circling around the table to look through the window. We could see Riggs mouthing to Duncan. Harris seemed amused, if also obviously frustrated. I had to give him points for attitude. Stuck here on a Saturday night, no partner in sight, lawyers arguing bullshit and bluster for a guy he knew he had by the balls. He was one patient cop.

"Who's the other guy?" he asked, referring to Duncan.

"He's my lawyer. Rollins, Jeffery & Associates."

"Yeah, I *know* he's your lawyer. Ya know, we could *both* be cooperative. Or not."

We exchanged a look.

"He's an old friend, too. We went to law school together."

"I take it you didn't graduate. Or is that another part of your secret past?"

I let that go. "What'd you want to ask me? I don't think Mr. Riggs is gonna wait long."

"You want a lawyer present? Take your pick."

"Not for the time being."

"Okay." Harris drew in a deep breath. "You want to tell me what's going on? Why are you jerking me around, anyway?"

Again, I was tempted to tell all. But Luis had warned me about the likelihood of cops being part of our investigation. And I remembered Harris being on a first name basis with Mickey and Frank.

"I'm not jerking you around. I'm just trying to find out who killed Mickey Gilmore. I might be in a better position to find that out than you are. Did you think of that possibility?"

"I thought of the possibility that you might've already found out. I thought of the possibility that you might've already retaliated."

"I didn't kill Brent Charmichael, if that's what you mean."

"How'd you even know about that?"

"Frank Coyne told me. He's got an in with Denver homicide. Maybe he's got one here too."

He let that go by with nothing more than a blank stare. "Where were you last night?"

"Like I told you this morning, I was out at Holiday Bingo. I was with Frank Coyne when Charmichael got killed."

"Well, there you go. The perfect alibi."

"It gets better. We were talking with Milo Finnes and a couple of his... associates. They'll vouch for us, too, if you press it. But you'll have to press it. Those guys aren't pals. Dennis Coyne was there, as well, if you want to eliminate likely suspects."

Harris nodded but he stuck to the point. "What were you doing there?"

I paused, as if deciding to confide in him. "I told you I was looking for the Caddy. Frank and Dennis showed up there too, for the same reason. We confronted Milo about the shooting. We got them to admit they were at the Palace when the thing went down. But they didn't do it. Like I said, their car pulled out from around the side of the building after the shots were fired. The blue Cadillac, the one that did the shooting? It was long gone by the time I got to my car."

"Your Mercedes?"

I nodded.

"You went after the beige Caddy?"

I nodded.

"You take a shot at them?"

I feigned a sigh of resignation. "I caught up to them about a mile down the road at a stop light."

"County Line Road?"

"Maybe. I was trying to get the license number. They opened up on me with a shotgun. I put a few slugs in their trunk. They fired first," I said, pointedly. "The beige Caddy belongs to one of Milo's flunkies. Guy named Enos Flood. We found it at the Holiday."

"Why didn't you tell me that this morning?"

I smiled. "I figured you'd hassle me about it. Arrest me, maybe. Put me in jail."

Harris smiled back. "And you don't think they had anything to do with it?"

"I know they didn't. I was there, I saw it."

"You don't think them being there involves them?"

"Not after talking with them."

"You sticking up for them too?"

"I'm not sticking up for anybody. Except maybe Mickey Gilmore."

Harris looked away, annoyed.

"I think you'll find this guy Flood is good for the holdup at Clancy's last week," I told him. "It was the same car."

"And we have your word for that?"

I shrugged. "It's a start, if you're interested."

"I'm more interested in this blue Cadillac. Got any ideas who was in it?"

"Only speculation."

Harris smiled again. "Let's hear it."

"Brent Charmichael and a driver."

"And Charmichael is dead. Who might the driver be?"

"Enos Flood has a brother, Alois, a con fresh out of Cañon City. He and Brent and Enos did the job at Clancy's together. But Enos was driving the Caddy—the beige one—last night and he was at Milo's afterwards. So that leaves the brother."

"You talk to him too?"

I shook my head. "Never met him."

"Then how do you know about him?"

I hesitated for an instant, but I didn't think he noticed. "It came out when we were talking to Enos Flood at Milo's place."

"That he was a con?"

"Milo spilled it when he was chewing out Enos for taking part in the job at Clancy's. Apparently, Milo didn't have anything to do with that either."

Harris mulled, seemed to savor it, maybe smelling something off about it. But when he spoke, he was moving on.

"You think this guy—Alois Flood?—might have killed Charmichael?"

"Like I said, I'm just speculating…on more likely suspects than me."

There was a commotion in the office area, voices muffled by the glass. Harris ignored it. "Why would Charmichael kill Mickey Gilmore?"

"Mickey set that fire, Broadway Bingo. And apparently, they have a… complicated past. If you've been around bingo for a while…you know more about it than I do. Charmichael used to work for Frank Coyne, right?"

Harris pursed his lips, trying not to react.

There was a kind of tapping on the wall and the muffled voices gained in pitch. He turned to look through the window. When I followed his gaze, I spotted Leroy Street, Willie's uncle and erstwhile lawyer. He was nudging his way forward, gray-haired head bowed like some feckless battering ram, through the knot of people just beyond the glass. Willie leaned in closely behind him, possibly propping him up with one arm while gesticulated wildly with the other at Kazinski—and Haines, again—who stood in Leroy's path. By the motion of his extended arm, I could tell that Leroy was sweeping his cane, like a blind man feeling for the curbs and potholes. Leroy is not blind, by any means, though he takes on the role with practiced ease, sometimes to garner sympathy, more often as an excuse for righteous indignation. This was, apparently, one of the latter instances.

Just beyond Willie, Duncan stood aside, smiling apologetically, no stranger to Leroy's antics. Behind the two cops who blocked Leroy's way, Stanley Riggs stood with his mouth hanging open, gaping in disbelief.

"What the hell?" Harris mumbled, moving towards the door. When it opened, the cacophony of voices flooded in like the imperious cries of my liberators.

"What's going on here?" Harris bellowed.

"Don't you be raising your voice at me, young man," Leroy Street exalted. "I've fought my way through the white ruling class for longer than you been wearin' britches. It don't take good eyes to hear *that* tone of voice."

Harris turned red, completely taken aback.

"Now I demand you let that boy go," Leroy continued. "You have no right to hold him. Get your hands off me, woman."

Haines, who had been restraining Leroy with a gentle hand on his extended forearm, released her grip and turned in place, keeping herself between Leroy and Detective Harris. "Sir, this gentlemen claims to be legal counsel for the suspect."

"*I'm* Mr. Burkhart's legal counsel," Riggs declared, "and he's *not* a suspect."

"The hell you are, sir!" Leroy countered. "I can tell a carpetbagger when I see one."

"Carpetbagger?" Riggs said, bewildered. And no one took exception to the blind man selectively 'seeing' Riggs' apparent airs.

"Sir," Haines said, raising her voice. "Mr. Street turned up downstairs wanting to speak to his client." She shot me a quick glance. "Apparently he's been waiting with his assistant for some time." She turned to indicate Willie. "There was a little commotion down there. I thought it best to bring them up." Her eyes suddenly widened and she whirled to face Leroy. "Mr. *Street*. I'm an officer of the law. Please do *not* touch me with that thing."

"I've a right to see my client, but you'd see fit to put hands on me. If I was *white* I expect you'd *all* be standin' aside."

"Mr. Street, I'm merely trying to tell you you'll have to wait…"

"We *been* waitin' lady," Willie piped in from over Leroy's shoulder, contorting his lips to disguise his incorrigible grin.

"Okay, now *hold on! Everyone!*" Harris roared, with a surprisingly deep tone of authority. The din of voices faded momentarily. Assessing the situation, Harris addressed Leroy directly. "Mr. Street, I'm sorry about the delay. If you'll come with me I'll bring you to see your client."

"Damn right," Leroy grumbled.

"He's *my* client," Riggs asserted.

"Shut up, Riggs," Harris slurred. "Kazinski, Haines, get them out… out, out to the waiting area." Raising his arms in the air, he got Willie and Duncan and Riggs all moving backwards. "Out behind the counter. Authorized personnel only back here."

"What about *me*?" Willie demanded. "I'm Mr. Street's *assistant*. He's a sick man. Needs my help to get around."

"I don't need no one's help gettin' 'round," Leroy proclaimed, apparently forgetting Willie's part in the play. Willie's features froze with amazement.

"Just wait out behind the counter, sir," Harris said, guiding Leroy forward. "I'll help Mr. Street. Just go with the officers here."

"C'mon, Willie," Duncan said. Looking through the glass, he flashed me a beguiling grin as he took Willie by the arm.

Still grumbling, Leroy allowed Harris to guide him into the interview room. "Your *other* lawyer is here, Mr. Burkhart," Harris quipped, extending an open palm by way of introduction. "Why don't you take a few minutes." He closed the door behind him. I smiled at Leroy.

"Hello, Henry." He raised his chin to fix me with a stare and sneak a sideways grin. The thickness of the wire-rimmed lenses made his coal-black eyes seem small, but there was nothing vague about their focus.

Wearing a dark suit that looked two sizes too big, Leroy stood barely five feet tall and had the spindly frame of an undernourished adolescent. He once told me he was pushing eighty, but his wife, Martha, says he lies about his age. I never asked in which direction. But I had seen him in action before and when he wants to, he gets things done—in a roundabout sort of fashion.

Helping him into a chair, I felt his gnarly bones under the slack material of his suit. "Glad to see you, Leroy."

"I expect you would be. You're more trouble than Willie Junior these days."

"Yeah, well. Thanks for coming down but I think things are working out. This Detective Harris is okay for a cop, if you know what I mean."

"You mean he's on the fix? You can't trust 'em, Henry, if they're on the fix. You ought to know that."

"No, that's not it," I said, but I knew why he had made that jump. "I'm just thinking he's gonna give me a break. Besides, I didn't do anything wrong. Not illegal, anyway."

"Don't have to be illegal to get in trouble with the *po*-lice." He eyed me skeptically. "You workin' with the rat squad, Henry? That's tricky business."

"No, no, nothing like that." I tried to imagine what Willie had told him. "I'm just doing some snooping for the Denver DA. Kind of outside official channels."

Leroy regarded me. "So if you're covered, why they got you in here?"

"Well, Aurora doesn't know about it and that's the way Denver wants to keep it. But if push comes to shove, I'm not in any real trouble."

Leroy nodded slowly, as if losing interest. Or taking his time to digest it. "Why the hell Willie brought me all the way out here then? I don't much like it out in the 'burbs. Don't know who lives here, ya know?"

"I don't much like it either. But don't worry about me. I'll be out of here in no time."

"Yeah, well, we *do* worry about you some," he said. "Me and the Doctor. After what you did for Willie an' all. And that other stuff that come down about your papa." He stopped and gave me a steady look that ended with a nod of finality.

"How *is* Doctor Randy?"

"All right, I guess." Leaning forward, he planted his cane to stand. "He's got more lawyers than you can shake a…a *cane* at these days. Don't need the likes of me anymore."

Taking his arm, I guided him out of the room. I asked after Martha, his wife of forty-odd years who also acts as his secretary, nurse, and bodyguard as the needs arise.

"She's fine, she's fine." We approached Harris and Haines waiting at the front counter. "Still keeps after me though. Know what I mean?" He gave me that one-sided grin.

"Yeah, I think I do, Leroy."

"Where's my nephew at?" he demanded, looking from one cop to the other. "Bringin' me out here for no good reason."

The two cops looked back at him as if he were ranting.

"Willie Randall," I offered. "His assistant."

"Oh, yes." Officer Haines solicitous tone reappeared. "He's downstairs waiting for you, Mr. Street. I'll be glad to show you the way."

Looking up at her, Leroy smiled roguishly, apparently forgetting their previous altercation. "You s'pose I can trust her, Henry?" he asked, keeping his eyes on her.

Haines blushed slightly and looked from Leroy's face to mine.

"She's young," I said, "a bit inexperienced. You'd better watch out for your own self."

Haines eyelids fluttered as she tried not to react.

"Can't be too young for me," Leroy quipped. He shuffled two steps, then stopped and turned to face the detective. "What's your name again?"

"Harris. Detective Scott Harris."

"You take good care of my boy here, Detective Harris, you understand? His old man was a cop. Damn good one, too."

"Well, I didn't know that," Harris said, giving me a piercing look. "I'll keep that in mind."

Leroy stepped along the hallway feeling his way with his cane. Officer Haines accompanying him, kept one hand tucked under his arm.

"Another old friend of yours?" Harris asked.

"I didn't go to law school with him, if that's what you mean."

Harris gave it a tired frown. He gestured toward the conference room. "C'mon you'll have to wait in here."

"For what?"

"For the officers to clear the lobby. I sent everyone home. Then they'll come up to take you back downstairs."

He ignored the stunned look on my face. "What do you mean 'downstairs'?"

"To the cell block."

"Listen, I've told you everything I know. I thought we had an understanding."

"Yeah, *I* have an understanding. You discharged a firearm within city limits, endangering the lives of innocent bystanders. You withheld information pertinent to an official investigation. You and your battery of slipshod lawyers don't have a chance in hell of getting a judge and an ADA down here this time of night. So I'm holding you until I can check your story. Once I get corroboration, assuming I do, we'll see what else you forgot to tell me and then we'll decide whether or not to file charges. Now wait in there and shut up or I'll have to cuff you. You have an understanding now too?"

"Yeah. I think I do."

Haines and Kazinski showed up ten minutes later, cuffed me, and led me out of the room. There was no sign of Harris as we went along the hall and no sign of my 'battery' of lawyers.

Standing in the elevator, Haines slid a glance in my direction. When I turned to look, her eyes were relaxed, if not warm, and she kept them on me long enough to let me know she thought I might be human after all. It didn't seem to matter anymore.

"That old man a friend of yours?" she asked. "I mean, besides being your lawyer."

I thought about her snide grin when I was first brought in. "He took a shining to me a few years back when I helped get his nephew out of jail. The arrest was bogus, the charges dropped."

She started to speak but her eyes went to Kazinski on the other side of me, and she turned to face forward.

Back in booking, Haines unlocked my handcuffs and said, "Good luck," before disappearing into the other side. Kazinski led me over to O'Malley's desk. Business had picked up. There were more people around, more cops and more perps. Both holding cells were crowded with drunks and black teenagers and gangbanger wannabes. There were only two white guys in sight. Except for the drunks, they all looked slightly startled, alert, most of them on their feet. When O'Malley got to me, I was relieved to be escorted away from there. We stopped at one of the smaller cells and he said, "T-3," into the mic on his lapel. The door buzzed and slid open and I stepped into the cell. O'Malley handed me a plastic bag with plastic toiletries and said, "Stand clear from the door." He spoke to the control room again and gave me his crooked smile as the door slid shut.

I turned and looked for a mint on the pillow. There was no pillow. The narrow metal bench that passed for a bed was lined with a plastic-coated mattress, three inches thick, with folded sheets and a woolen blanket at its foot. In the opposite corner, mounted on the wall, an angular stainless steel sculpture incorporated a small hand sink and a toilet bowl with no seat. It wasn't the Ritz, it wasn't even Motel 6, but it was a far cry from four bunks to a cell in County.

Mounted on the enamel-tiled wall, a sconce-shaped light fixture glowed dull yellow. It went off when I flipped the switch, leaving only the slant of light coming through the door.

I kicked off my shoes and stretched out on the mattress and found myself staring at the ceiling—not just a cliché movie scene anymore. It's what you do.

Things could be worse, I told myself, and deep inside I believed it. I was going to have to wait. That's how they worked it. I had seen it before—had *done* it from the other side. They tell you all they've got on you and make you think it's only half, and then they leave you for a while with your story and your lies and your jones if you have one, and let it work on you from inside. You polish the story, rework the lies, tinker with rationale and excuses, and wait for your next chance to pitch it. Then you tell them what you hope they want to hear—everything but a confession—and you think you did yourself some good. That's when they turn it back on you with what you didn't know they knew. They start hanging out the legal consequences with cruel over-confidence and, if they're any good, they convince you that your worst case scenario is your best. But they can help. But they're busy just now so they let you think it over some more, let you ponder your dismal existential future. It's a waiting game and it's hard to beat because they own the clock and there's nothing else to do but play.

I felt like I could handle it. My hopes for tomorrow were alive. Duncan wouldn't leave me here, even on a Sunday. And this guy Riggs didn't seem to know when to quit. If Frank retained him to come down here, he'd soon come back for more billable hours. I had nothing to worry about and nothing to do but wait. Yeah, sure.

Chapter 24

By lunchtime the next day, my equanimity had apparently eroded from within. A qualmishness had settled in, a stagnant sensation in my gut that might have been the result of eating breakfast too fast, or eating it at all. Scrambled yellowish globules served in their own watery juices, warmed over hash browns, dirt-colored toast that looked like a dish sponge too long in use, and coffee that looked like the dishwater the toast-sponge had come out of. To stay on the safe side, I passed on lunch and asked again to use the phones. This meant moving me back into the holding area and queuing me up with the ongoing shuffle of prisoners to and from the communal housing pods, the booking area, and the visitors' stations.

Sunday morning in a jailhouse is a solemn yet spirited assembly, not wholly unlike Sunday morning gatherings in other institutions devoted to a Higher Authority. The multitude of Saturday night sinners hungover, humbled and contrite, gird themselves to face their sorry fates, ask forgiveness, and accept their penance, offering themselves up to the gray-metal altars of the booking stations or the wire-meshed glass of the visitors' confessionals. It's not an entirely reverent congregation, but those who recognize their transgressions seem passably sincere in proclaiming their venial guilt and expressing their gratitude for a second chance to walk the straight and narrow. Absolution usually comes by way of a reduction of charges, or making bail, or getting off with time served. But for a chosen few, total vindication is at hand, granted through the greater graces of that most revered of guardian angels, the well-connected lawyer for the defense. Born again, so to speak. With my own conscience a clean slate, and with a host of legal archangels pleading my case, I was opting for complete redemption.

But time, that great equalizer, was wearing down my faith. And the tinny, inhuman voices on the answering machines of all of those who could serve as my personal savior did nothing to bolster the strength of my convictions. By the time they took me back to my cell, I was siding with the likes of Beelzebub. I wanted a cigarette, goddammit, and I wanted to talk to detective Harris *now*. I told the guard as much, as he escorted me back to my cell. "Yeah, sure," he said, guiding me firmly. "I'm meeting Scott for a smoke break in the courtyard in about fifteen minutes. Why don't you join us there?"

A couple hours later, a jailer and a uniformed cop wearing a DPD shield showed up at my cell door and commanded it open. The presence of the Denver cop put a knot in my already queasy stomach and sent my thoughts spiraling again towards full disclosure. As they cuffed me and led into the booking area, I said nothing, helplessly feigning stoic resolve.

O'Malley was sitting at his desk, apparently just coming back on duty.

"Didn't expect to see you still here," he said, through his scarred grin. "All that help you were gettin' last night." His eyes shone with the turnkey humor.

"These things are complicated," I said, trying to keep up my side of the banter.

"'Parently so." He nodded to the forms in front of him, then held the top sheet in the air as if to demonstrate. "This one's getting' complicated-er and complicated-er." His eyes danced and he smiled at me like he had a surprise and wanted me to guess which hand it was in.

"What?" I strained to read the print on the page he held forth.

"You're on your way to Denver, son. 'Parently they want a crack at you too."

I turned to the uniformed cop standing beside me. Stone-faced and chest puffed out, he stared mutely, disinclined to go along with O'Malley's playful shtick.

"I'm going to Denver?" The stomach knot tightened and turned a few degrees.

"That's what I been told," the cop said, without bothering to meet my eyes. "We all set here?"

"Ready to go," O'Malley said, ever cheerful. "Good luck to ya, son."

Even from the caged back seat of a police cruiser, the sky seemed bluer than I remembered and the sun shone brighter. Breezy gusts coming through the cracked-open window tickled my face and rearranged my hair. The air smelled different somehow, substantial and nourishing—in contrast, anyway, to that canned stuffiness they apparently reserve for use in penal institutions.

We drove in silence through the Sunday afternoon quiet. There was a Broncos home game going on, had to be. The absence of traffic—and possibly my uplifting mood—had me reminiscing about Denver in my youth, when lanes stretched open and lights were mostly green, and we buzzed around in Duncan's MGB, sharing the road with about three hundred thousand fewer out-of-staters in SUV's. My anxieties didn't resurface until we descended out of the sunlight into the subterranean parking garage beneath the Denver Police complex.

I tugged at my metal bracelets.

"You guys got any idea what this is about?" I said to the two cops now shrouded in dimness in the front seat.

They looked at each other, squinted their eyes in unison as if listening for some vague sound in the distance, then turned their heads forward without responding. But I was offered some relief when they pulled up to the entrance of the administration building instead of driving through to the jailhouse sally port. With a cop on each arm, I was escorted through two sets of security double-doors into an elevator in the basement lobby. One of them hit the button for the third floor. Crimes Against Persons, Homicide Division. Captain Connally's realm.

After disembarking, one cop disappeared towards the detectives' wing while the other took me into an interview room, only minimally secured, but the door latch clicked solidly behind him. And he left without taking off the cuffs. I crossed the room and stood looking out the window and contemplated my rights. I didn't get very far with that before the door opened behind me. Luis Sanchez poked his dark face around the edge, grinned, and huffed out a mocking chuckle.

"There you are, Henry my boy. How's it…?"

"Luis, for Christ's sakes…" I said, then cut it short when Captain Connally appeared behind him, followed him in, and closed the door with another solid click.

Connally is a large man with an imposing presence, well fed but still athletically sound, with still thick hair, prematurely white, and a sanguine complexion that makes you wonder about the stresses of his job. His rounded facial features can be warm, almost jolly, when he's on his own time, but a twitch of his contrasting solid-black eyebrows, a crease on his brow, a cant of his posture can make the whole effect turn mean. At that moment, his demeanor seemed to hover in some ambiguous middle ground, as if poised to see which mood the situation called for. He took me in with an objectifying air, then drew a quick breath like a man overworked and anxious to get on with it.

"Hello, Henry. Up to your old tricks?" He cracked a not completely derisive grin, then took note of the handcuffs. His brows drew together with concern. "They got you in the bracelets?" he said, unable to conceal an undertone of ironic appreciation.

I tried on an expression of rueful complaisance. It came pretty easily. Connally stepped to the door, opened it, and called out imperiously to someone named Walker. One of the cops who had picked me up appeared from down the hall.

"Why'd you put him in cuffs?" Connally asked.

"That's the way he came," the cop said, exchanging a long look with Connally before advancing to unlock them. Luis sat at the end of the table, shot me a glance, and bounced his eyebrows furtively.

It was pretty convincing, but I knew Connally well enough to guess the scene was staged. He had a penchant for trying to teach me lessons, an avuncular trait that had cropped up at various intervals since my father's death. It often took the form of long harangues that loosely paralleled the story of the tortoise and the hare. Not so long ago I would argue with him about it. But lately I had taken a different tack, playing the role of a slow learner. I wasn't sure he was buying it.

He remained standing until the cop left the room, then he motioned for me to sit and took the chair directly across from me. His large shoulders and upper arms bulged at the seams of the tweed blazer as he leaned across the table. But before he could start in, Luis spoke up.

"Ya' know, Henry, you deserve what you get for not telling me about this shootout. What the hell's that about?"

"Well, I…"

"That's the way he always plays it," Connally put in, "close to the vest, out on his own, no patience for legal procedure. Right, Henry?"

"I'm working undercover, for Christ's sakes." I appealed to Luis with my eyes.

"You're working for *me*, Henry." Luis' look conveyed no sympathy. "You have to follow departmental guidelines. I *told* you that."

I settled in. Clearly they needed to vent.

"Any shooting," Luis continued, "has to be reported to your supervising senior officer—that's me—and from there it goes to the incident review board. That involves a shoot team and an automatic suspension from active duty. As you well know. It's done for your sake as much as anyone's. Otherwise you're up for charges like anybody would be. Which you are. Not to mention the publicity jam it puts our department in."

"If anyone knew I was with the department," I said.

"Anyone does, Henry. *I* know and pretty soon anybody who reads a paper will know."

"That's why I didn't tell you, Luis."

"That's not a reason, goddammit. If I let that go, I gotta let *you* go."

Luis had a right to be angry but there was an air of exaggeration about it, a vehemence that he didn't usually waste on me. It made me think he was putting it on for Connally and insinuating, by example, that I should do the same. I sulked openly.

"You got any idea what kind of trouble I'll have to go through to get you out?"

The question hung in the air like a threat. An appropriate response was called for, something along the lines of complete acquiescence. And I wanted to say it, but I couldn't quite, and not because I wasn't afraid. It was just…too easy. It wouldn't fool these two anyway. And if I wanted to stay undercover, I was going stay under arrest. But I couldn't quite bring myself to suggest that either. I continued brooding.

Connally seemed to read my thoughts. "You don't know when to quit, do you Henry?" A knowing grin appeared and he leaned back and folded his arms. "Ya' know, I was gonna say, you have no idea how many times I had this conversation with your father. Back in the day when we were on the job, on the street together." His eyes took me in dispassionately. "But, of course, you *do* know. You know all about that."

"For all of that, you've told me he was a good cop."

Connally nodded. "He was the best. He taught me a lot. But that didn't keep him from getting jammed up on his own. On the contrary."

We took that in in silence. I looked at Luis. He arched his brows and his eyes bulged in a caricature of impatience.

"I'll do whatever you want," I managed. "If you want me out, I'm out. I realize the position I put you in, Luis, and I'm sorry."

The two of them watched me, cool yet also attentive, as if—maybe—concealing their interest in what I'd found out while running renegade. Luis' lips curled into a frown. Connally unfolded his arms and looked to Luis. Luis shrugged as if to say this might be the best they could expect.

It would have to do. I was only just holding back from telling them what I thought about getting thrown in jail while working for them and then being chewed out for it afterwards.

"What can you tell me about Brent Charmichael's death?" Connally asked, leaning forward again.

Not knowing what Luis had told him, I wanted to glance his way for a sign—a nod or a look askance—but Connally's eyes held mine, watching for it.

"I was there," I said, "not long after it happened. He was shot in the chest at close range and bled out without much movement. The bleeding had stopped by the time I got there. He was pale but there was no lividity, as far as I could tell. It was maybe an hour after it happened. My guess."

Connally didn't blink. "Forensics puts it between nine-thirty and eleven P.M. No later."

"I was there just about midnight."

"What were you doing there?"

"Following the obvious hunch. Everything pointed to him for the Mickey Gilmore shooting." I waited to see if Connally knew what I was talking about.

"You were there for that one too, huh?" A trace of derision returned.

"I was there as part of our undercover operation. I was sitting in on a meeting with some of the principles of the…bingo…" I faltered, stuck again on trying to make bingo crimes sound important. I guess dead bodies helped in that regard.

"And you saw what happened?"

"I was ten feet behind Mickey when he got it." I paused to allow for the appropriate expressions of concern and sympathy, but his stolid gaze told me it was going to be a while. I gave him the abridged version, figuring Luis had filled him in on most of it. When I started in on what followed, what I hadn't told Luis—the car chase, the exchange of fire with Enos Flood's Caddy, I expected more disapprobation, but I guess they'd had their fill. Luis gave it a little cough and shake of the head, Connally shared a wise-guy grin with him. I realized they already knew most of it from Harris. They were cross-checking my account.

"How'd you know where to look for the car?"

"Brent Charmichael was good for it from the start. He's…"

"How so?"

"He used to work with Mickey. Both of them started out with Frank Coyne." I waited for him to ask who Frank was, but that didn't happen either. Connally was fully briefed. I looked to Luis. His face was a stone worn smooth by years of spin and harangue flowing over him like a gentle mountain stream, as he sat through hundreds of interviews not unlike this one. "After a while Mickey and Brent went out on their own with a guy from Seattle. A guy named Harvey Cline."

That got a rise out of Luis. "Mickey and *Brent* went out on their own? Where'd you get that?"

"From Mickey's sister. It was Mickey and Brent and Harvey Cline. But something went wrong and Cline turned up dead. Mickey's reputation took a boost. You know about that, I suppose?"

Connally nodded shortly. "How does Charmichael fit in to that?"

"I don't know that he does explicitly. Rumor had it Mickey did the deed. After that partnership was dissolved, so to speak, Mickey went back to Frank Coyne and Charmichael signed on with Milo Finnes. It was Charmichael's club that got torched the other night, the night before Mickey was killed. I went over to Milo's looking for Charmichael or either of the two Caddies. The beige one was there with my bullet holes in it. I waited around to see who would claim it."

"And Frank Coyne showed up?"

"With his brother Dennis, apparently following the same logic. We went in together to confront Milo and Brent. That was Frank's idea," I added, knowing what Connally would think of it. "Milo told us Charmichael was in Vegas."

"But you didn't buy it?"

"Not really. Milo didn't seem too convinced either, though he didn't act concerned. I decided to check it out. When I got there the front door was unlocked. So I…"

"Did you take anything from the scene?"

I gave him a miffed look. He just stared back at me. "All I did was raise the body to check the wound. It was a contact wound just above the heart. I left the gun where it lay."

Their tandem doubtful looks told me they knew what was missing. "The computer was gone already. I didn't take it. Why would I?"

Connally ignored my defensiveness. "You wiped your prints?"

"Yeah. I cleaned the doorknobs on the way out. I didn't want to get involved in the murder investigation."

"Involved?" Connally gave that a condescending chuckle but he stayed on point. "What else did you find?"

"A briefcase with plane tickets in it. You must know about that."

"Tell it."

"There were round trip tickets to Vegas that corresponded to what Milo told us, but there was another set as well, different airline. Charmichael was planning to split."

"You didn't find any money?"

"There was no money that I saw. There was a suitcase in the room. Looked like someone had already gone through it."

"No disks or tapes?"

I smiled at Connally's astuteness. "I gave it a quick look after realizing the computer was missing. Anything with data on it was gone."

Connally thought that over for a minute before continuing. "You wearin' the same shoes you had on that night?"

"No." I didn't see how that could matter now, unless Connally wanted to make me for the killing which, I felt *fairly* safe in assuming, was not the case. I sneaked a guilty glance at Luis. Humor creased the edges of his slow brown eyes.

"So you were at Milo's hall, the one on Santa Fe Drive. What's it called?" He reached into an inner pocket to withdraw a small notebook.

"Holiday Bingo."

"You were there from when to when?"

"Got there about seven, seven-thirty. Left about eleven."

"Right." Flicking open his notebook, he read from it. "Milo Finnes was there, Vince Terrelli, Enos Flood, and you and the Coyne brothers. When did they show up again?"

"About nine fifteen, just after the second session."

"Session?"

"Bingo session. They run the games in sessions, about two hours long. Usually six games per session. The second one probably started at nine."

"Bingo," Connally slurred, dropping his eyes to his notebook. "Frank and Dennis Coyne showed up and the three of you went in to speak with Milo Finnes."

"No. Dennis Coyne stayed in the car."

"Anybody else in the car? Chuck Burrows?" He said it without looking at his notes. Luis could have mentioned him, of course, but I got the feeling Connally knew him from when Burrows was DPD. And maybe knew of him since then.

"There was no one else there. I walked with Frank to the car afterwards. I saw Dennis. That was it."

Connally's tone had become casual, the edge taken off. This was no longer a grilling. More like a case meeting, a pooling of information. Sensing this, I offered up a bright idea. "The other Flood brother wasn't there. Aloysius, or something. He's a con pretty recently out of Cañon. Works for Milo on occasion…."

"Alois Flood," Connally interrupted, looking at his notes this time. "He's alibied up pretty well. A work-release program out at Lowry. He was scheduled for the swing shift. But we'll verify that."

I looked from Connally to Luis and arched my eyebrows questioningly. Luis crossed his arms and stared back like he had no idea what the question was. They were way ahead of me.

I had assumed that Luis had heard of my arrest and contacted Connally, but now, maybe not. Connally could have made the connection between Charmichael's death and Mickey's and reached out to Harris on his own. If so, it was Connally, not Luis, who had me transferred from Aurora. Maybe that meant we were all on the same side. I decided to poke my nose in.

"Did *you* make Charmichael for shooting Mickey?"

Connally eyed me for a few seconds, then deigned to answer. "He was killed with the same caliber bullet as the one that did Charmichael. We don't have the complete work-up, but that's what it looks like. Assuming he started with a full clip, there were six shots fired. That fits with the count on the two preliminary reports."

"Six?" I said. "I count five. Four at the Palace and the one that killed Charmichael."

"There were two shots fired at Charmichael's place. One slug went through him and landed on the floor, and the other one ended up in the wall above the desk."

"So there was a struggle?"

"That's one possible scenario. Either Charmichael did Gilmore and his partner—whoever that was—turned on him, or the same person killed them both and tried to make it *look* like Charmichael did Gilmore, then lost a bout with his conscience."

"Any chance it was suicide? Residue on his hands?"

"Crime scene tech did find some smudges. Said they thought it was a put-up job, though. The killer may have put the gun in his hand after he was shot and fired off the second round to get the residue on him. The hole in the wall above the desk could work for that. Ballistics will tell, but I don't think it was suicide. Not likely from what I know of him."

"How *do* you know him? How come you're taking an interest?"

"It's a homicide, Henry," Connally growled. "Isn't that enough?"

I kept my mouth shut.

Connally sighed. "We were looking at Charmichael for Cline's murder, back in '92."

"You mean currently?"

Connally nodded.

I tried not to smile. "I thought Mickey was good for that."

"Yeah, we heard that too, but Charmichael was his alibi, among others. We were riding Charmichael about that but then *he* started sweating. Nevertheless, they had their stories straight. But things have changed, as you say."

He stopped to let me take this in.

"So why the sudden interest in a nine-year-old case?"

"Eight," Connally corrected and stared back at me.

I waited.

Connally glanced at Luis. Whatever passed between them was invisible to me, but it seemed to make a difference.

"We got some dope on him recently from the AG's office," Connally said. "They've been running an investigation into Milo Finnes' operation. Out-of-state transfer of goods, evading the Use Tax, the freight taxes, part of this whole bingo scam. They were goin' at Charmichael from that angle, tryin' to get the goods on Milo, when he offered up info on the Cline murder." He and Luis exchanged another look. "That's when they called us in. But the way Charmichael unwrapped it made it sound like he was in on it from the start. We were workin' him like we liked Mickey for the killing, figuring he'd lose track of his story line eventually. As it turns out, he must have smelled a rat."

It was news to me that the Attorney General was investigating bingo and from the look on Luis' face, still blank but maybe some smolder in those eyes, it was news to him as well.

"So where does that leave the AG's investigation?"

"Hell, I don't know," Connally said. "They got what they got. They weren't done with him, I know that. Guess they are now." After a pause, he asked, "Who do you like for killing Charmichael?"

I shrugged. "I thought this Alois Flood guy. He and his brother were in on the hold-up with Charmichael at Clancy's last week. I figured he was probably Brent's driver. But if his alibi's solid…it could be any of Frank's people, if we're talking retaliation."

Connally nodded. "Soooo?"

"If Milo got wind of the AG's investigation, it could be someone from his side of the fence wanting to shut Charmichael up. Seems like you'd have a better line on that than me. Or the AG would."

"Why couldn't it be someone from Frank's side wanting to shut him up?"

"I thought they were investigating Milo. Besides, how would they know he was talking?"

"Hell, these people can't keep their mouths shut. Charmichael would talk to us, then call Mickey to tell him about it. We'd go see Mickey and he'd say Charmichael was lying, long before he should've known what was said."

"You talked to Mickey?" I asked, but Connally didn't bite.

"For a while there, it looked like they were playin' off each other. But then it just started sounding silly. I think they were makin' shit up."

Noting Connally's frustration, I thought I saw a way out—for myself.

"Mickey rubbed his own people raw with his antics, especially Frank. He wanted to move out on his own again. It's possible one of Frank's people put Charmichael up to it, gave themselves an alibi, then killed Charmichael when he wouldn't take the fall."

"Which one?"

The payoff question and I was ready for it. "I'm in good with these people," I said, trying to sound humble. "I've managed to work my way into Frank's confidences—standing up for him at Milo's and taking the rap with Harris." Connally nodded impatiently and spun a finger in the air. "Give me some time to work them. Get me out without blowing my cover and I might be in a position find something, hear something."

Connally smiled a complacent smile. He stood up, walked over to the windows, and cracked open one panel, then pulled out a cigarette from his shirt pocket, lit it, and blew smoke toward the opening.

I turned to Luis. "I'm closing in on some stuff for our investigation, as well. It won't take long."

Luis' face held a humorless grin of affirmation. He looked over at Connally and nodded. It came to me they had this in mind all along. I thought about calling them on it but I managed to hold back. The thought of their complicity didn't make me feel better, but it might land me in the driver's seat.

"What do you know about Joe Perkins?" Connally asked, pretty much out of the blue.

"What I told Luis. I haven't met him. He's offered to line up uniforms to do security for Coyne's halls. Maybe he's working up to something more. He was the ringer on a pickle jackpot the other night."

Connally squinted as if I had spoken Chinese, then looked to Luis.

"Yeah, it's an in-house scam they run. Kick back some prize money." He shook his head. "You're not interested at this point."

"But Frank has a line on Perkins through Burrows," I added, then paused before pressing my point. "You know Burrows personally?"

"He was all right back when," Connally said, eyes drifting towards the window. "But he got in with Coyne somewhere along the line and saw greener grasses. He took early retirement the last time we cleaned house."

"Well, he's still connected somehow. Frank knew about Charmichael's death before you did, I'd say. That had to come from Perkins. Is he working the case?"

When Connally looked at me his expression turned severe, his eyes hard and still. "He asked for it. And he wasn't up."

We fell into silence, pondering the implications. They weren't clear enough for me.

"Is he dirty?"

Connally frowned and looked out the window again. "These damn bingo people are a fuckin' pain. They jump a few hoops for the secretary of state, pay her off for all I know, butter up the legislature, and they end up with their own set of rules. If it was up to me, the DA would regulate the lot of them," he nodded towards Luis, "and we'd be all over it. The way it is, our people get involved with them on the side and all that loose cash gets flashed around. I don't blame 'em for workin' OT. God knows they don't make as much as the bad guys half the time. But I don't care how smeared the line gets out there, if they cross it, if they get found out, it's too late. I got no use for them."

Turning towards the room, Connally looked from me to Luis. It was a harsh statement of a reality we shared considering my father's past—and we all three knew some exceptions to that rule.

In a sedate tone, Luis said, "I explained to Tom that the police department was not our target. But if it goes in that direction, he wants to be in on it."

"And then we take it to IAB," Connally added. "I'm sure you know what that means for you. For all of us."

I nodded.

"That's one reason why we have to proceed with caution here, cross our t's and dot our i's. Not exactly your strong suit, Henry."

"I get your point."

We exchanged looks, the three of us, but the tension seemed to slacken. We were entering delicate ground, a minefield of cross-purposes and imperfectly charted legalities. It's not the kind of thing cops are comfortable with. They have loyalties at stake, and careers, and ethical questions that they usually leave to habit. When it comes time to challenge the honesty and integrity of one of their own, it's best left to someone outside the ranks, or someone willing to leave those ranks behind and sign on with Internal Affairs, the purgatory of law enforcement. When I realized it was me they were looking at for the job, I wanted to tell them to shove it. Given our past, they had to know that.

Then again, we couldn't just let it go. And if they were putting it out there for me, it was going to be my show. I convinced myself I could control it, control my own involvement and quit whenever I wanted. I would find Mickey's killer and then I would be gone. What would they do? Fire me again?Looking at their faces, I decided the point was made tacitly. Or speaking about it would open the can of worms that would end this now.

Connally broke up our reveries. "What would you do next?"

"Assuming I get out?"

Connally cracked half a grin and nodded.

I had an idea but I knew to bide my time. Better if they came up with it themselves. "I'd cozy up with Frank and his boys some more, see who talks it up. This whole thing with the shootings has everyone stirring."

"You don't want to be in an active position, ya know. Right? Otherwise, you might get maneuvered into breaking some laws."

I put a hand up. "I know, I know."

"On the other hand," Luis said, "we're running out of time." He turned to Connally. "We used a plant in a Seattle investigation, through the DA up there, to give Henry his creds. Guy named Richie Gurlach. He's shouldered up with this Rifkin crime family that used to work with Benny Palmer."

"Who's Palmer again?" Connally asked.

"He's Coyne's supplier. Bingo supplies. He works out of Wyoming to avoid the state regulators here. Before that he worked the same racket in the Northwest, till they tightened up the laws. Anyway, that Seattle sting is coming to a close. They're set to shut it down next week. Gurlach's cover is gonna be blown when he doesn't go down with the rest of them. Word should get to Palmer pretty fast. I don't want Henry in the field when it does."

I wanted to argue the point, but I knew what it would sound like. Besides, a week might be enough. "Time is of the essence," I said. "How do you guys get me out of here?" I smiled large and looked at them. They responded with droll grimaces.

"That's a good question," Connally offered. "Best way would be to give you back to Harris and let Coyne's guy spring you after arraignment. What's his name?"

My stupid grin deflated. "Wait a minute. You mean, going back to Aurora?"

Connally acted bewildered. "We can't just let you go. How would that look to Coyne? Besides, Harris would have my head on a platter, and rightfully so. He still wants a piece of you for playin' cowboys and Indians out there on Parker Road. The Douglas County Sheriff is watching too. Brother, I had to talk to get you over here."

"What did you tell them?"

"That we liked you for Charmichael's murder." He said it like it was a stroke of genius. "I had to swear a writ to change the venue. And that only worked because Harris didn't want to come in on Sunday to argue it. Since he hadn't filed charges yet, they had no choice. But he still wants you. I told him charges here were imminent. Wha'd you do to piss him off?"

"You're going to charge me with murder?" I asked, incredulous. "How's that going to work? I mean, Jesus, we got an ADA that would play along with that?"

Connally and I looked to Luis. He shook his head.

"A murder charge would attract too much scrutiny. And a judge might not grant bail if the ADA put up a fight. Which I couldn't guarantee against."

They looked at each other blankly, like it was good enough for them.

"What about the breaking and entering." I said. "Felony level. That should satisfy Harris and afterwards it could be dropped to a 'menor pretty easily"

"You mean Charmichael's house?" Connally asked.

"That would justify my connection to the murder for Harris, wouldn't it?"

Connally's eyes narrowed with interest. "Who'd you tell about that?"

"No one so far except Luis."

"How would you explain it to Frank Coyne?"

I shrugged. "We were over at Milo's together, looking for Charmichael. I could tell him I had an idea."

"Have you seen him since then?"

"Yeah, I went out to the Palace yesterday afternoon. That's when he told me about Charmichael's murder. I didn't tell him I was in there. I wouldn't, would I?"

"Why not? I mean what would you say to *him* about not telling him?"

I had already been recalling that conversation. "If they're gonna know I was in there, maybe I didn't say anything because I found something. Something incriminating."

Luis smiled very slightly. Connally's gaze shifted suspiciously. "Like what?"

"Like something that implicated one of his circle."

"Assuming they did it?"

"I thought that was your best guess."

"Hell, I don't have a best guess. Too much fuckin' subterfuge. Too many of these smarmy little *operators* on the take. Who knows what they're hiding from each other?" He glared at me, as if I had the answer.

"How about the missing disks?"

"What do you know about that?"

"Nothing. And neither does anyone else except whoever took them."

Connally's mind burned the finer fuel. "You're gonna say *you* took them?"

"I could say I found one that the killer overlooked."

"Then they'd come after you," Luis said.

"If the right person hears about it."

Luis shook his head from side to side, smiling almost pleasantly. "No, I don't like that. We'd just have another dead body to deal with."

"But I'd be ready for them."

"It's too big a chance," Connally stated. "We can't cover you in a situation like that."

I knew to let it drop. "Okay, we could play it another way. I'll tell Frank I suspected *him*. He was pretty much looking for blood when I left him that night. If I didn't know the time of death—which I didn't at the time—he'd be a likely suspect. He can't blame me for thinking that."

Both men eyed me with obvious aplomb. I pretended not to notice.

"You think you can pull that off?" Connally asked.

"It's just mean enough to sound true. I'll tell him my suspicions fell through when you told me a more exact time of death. That's what clears me too, right?"

Connally nodded and looked to Luis. I sat very still until Luis nodded too. Connally leaned back and looked at his watch. "Well, we'd better do something if you don't want another sleepover." Speaking to Luis, he said, "There's a duty judge on till five. Can you get an ADA down there to file?"

"George Kirby is on call."

"Kirby? C'mon Luis, I used to work with him."

"Hell, Henry, you worked with all those guys. I'm not gonna find anyone else today." Luis couldn't keep himself from smiling at my predicament. Or, anyway, he didn't.

"It's not gonna do much for my reputation."

"I wouldn't worry about that," Connally slurred, eyes bright with humor. "You wanna do it or are you goin' back to Aurora?"

"Some choice," I said, pretending doubt, knowing I could stay in place. "All right, I'm willing. But I want your support when the time comes."

Still stifling grins, both men nodded their assurances—something of an understatement, I thought.

"What's this guy's name? Coyne's shyster?"

"Stanley Riggs. His card is in the bag there." I pointed to my pocket contents in the plastic bag on the table.

"Okay. Let's do it. I'll have to take you down to lockup."

The two men exchanged a glance.

"Can't you just take me straight into court? I'm not enjoying this as much as you guys are."

Luis looked at Connally. It was his game.

"All right," Connally said. "I'll take you down myself. I'll call Riggs and give him the scoop. He can meet you in court." He turned to Luis. "You sure you can get Kirby to go along?"

"He'll do it," Luis said, getting up to leave. "He's got a soft spot for Henry, too."

We three took the elevator together down to street level. Luis slathered on another layer of warnings and cautions as we rode. I was getting tired of it. When he stepped out to unload, he half-turned to regard me, holding the doors open with his hand. I gathered from the dour look on his face that he didn't like what he saw.

"Okay, Henry my boy," he said, sighing heavily. "Do your worst."

I coughed out a half-hearted laugh.

"Page me tomorrow," he added, stepping back. "Or call me at home after six."

The doors slid closed on his doubt-filled expression. Connally and I descended another level.

Chapter 25

Stepping off in the basement, entering into the concrete garage, moving through the chain-link enclosed walkway that leads to the jailhouse sally port, my state of mind sunk towards the Underground Man—for pretty good reasons. Connally, walking beside me, chose that moment to express some doubt.

"You gonna be able to handle this," he chided, "without gettin' into trouble?" His tone challenging now, more familiar and more derogatory than when speaking in front of Luis.

"Tell me again why I'm doing this. If you can explain that, maybe I'll let you tell me *how* I should do it." I was pushing it. I couldn't care less.

He took my arm and stopped me short of the gate, stepping around to face me. His hard eyes focused on mine, but when he spoke he wasn't angry. "Look. Undercover work is different. That's all I'm getting at. I'm not surprised you're good at it."

The backhanded compliment disarmed me somewhat. I paid attention.

"The thing is, there's no backup. And that's what worries me. That's what always worries me about you, your…approach. Even the way you live these days. You're too much on your own."

The comment was professionally out of line. He wasn't just speaking professionally.

"Now in a situation like this, maybe that's to your advantage. To all our advantages if you do it right. But don't let go of the thread. You follow? Frankly, I don't know why you're doin' this. Do you?"

He paused to see if I would respond. I actually didn't know what to say. It made me think of Claire, when she had asked me what I wanted.

"You can just walk away, as far as I'm concerned. Luis too. He was thinkin' you should come in before I brought you over here. I'd say you pretty much talked him out of it. So I'm thinking you're on to something, and it'll probably be good. You've got a nose for it. Like your father. But you miss the forest for the trees. Like this idea about having found some disks. That just puts you in the crosshairs. You don't need to go to those extremes. You come out with a few decent leads—we can track 'em down with good old-fashioned *investigative* police work. You know that. These people aren't smart enough to get away with murder. And as far as your investigation for Luis goes, well, it's not worth endangering yourself. You want to do this? I'm behind you. But you have to tell me you're gonna be careful. You're gonna have to stay in touch."

His voice had dropped in volume as he spoke and the tone turned almost paternal, like the Tom Connally I used to know, the man off-duty, the only man who knew how to share my loss when my father died.

"Okay, Tom." And I meant it.

"There's one other thing I want you to be aware of. I'm gonna leave Joe Perkins on the case for the time being, but he'll be closely watched. He's partnered up with a guy I can trust. McQuitty, Ross McQuitty. You know him?"

"I've heard the name. New guy, right?"

"Came over from LA six months ago. Couldn't stand the murky waters out there. His record is squeaky clean. Probably why he didn't fit. I'm gonna put them on to you, know what I mean? Tell them we cleared you on the murder charge, but you were in there. That comes out with this B and E bullshit anyway. Perkins is gonna want to ask you some questions, I assume. You can tell him everything you've told me about the scene." He paused briefly, then added, "That's everything, right?"

"Absolutely."

"Anyway, I want you to get in touch with me after you've seen him. I want to know everything he says. Every question he asks. Okay?"

"Got it."

"And another thing. Burrows *was* a good cop in his day, good enough to smell out a snitch. You gotta be careful around him. Best thing would be to avoid him altogether."

"That may not be possible."

"I know, I'm just sayin'. Don't go out of your way to rub shoulders with him. He knows his own kind."

There were several ways I could take that.

"Thing is," he said, lowering his voice. "I half expect something else to go down. I mean, Charmichael's death was to keep him quiet, right? And the way these people talk, hell, this killer could have a busy week."

"But the heat's on now. They aren't likely to think they can get away with it again."

Connally exaggerated a frown. "You'd be surprised. So far they think they got away clean. You kill once, it comes easier and for a lot less reason. Like I said, these people aren't that smart. At least you've got that over them."

He wanted a smile from me and I managed it. "All right. I'll be careful. Now let's get this fuckin' jailhouse scene behind me. I can't stand this place."

"I don't blame you for that," he said, sounding almost sympathetic.

We walked on down to the gate. The deputy sheriff behind the glass buzzed us through at Connally's command. He walked me into pre-booking and arranged for my priority appearance in court, doing the paperwork himself. The sheriff's deputies he worked with handled him in a business-like fashion, not devoid of the usual men-in-blue camaraderie, but more respectful than friendly. When he finished, he gave me my belongings and led me into the jail annex courtroom.

Because of overcrowded dockets, court was in session on a Sunday. No rest for the wicked. At the far end of the room, two sheriff's deputies checked us through the security station that led into the public gallery. As we crossed along the back of the room, I caught a glimpse of daylight through the doors on the other side. The sun still shone brightly.

Connally sat me down at the defendants' bench and went to put in the call to Riggs. A few minutes later, he came up behind me and leaned over my shoulder, resting his forearms on the back of the bench. He looked out over the room, taking in the assemblage of common folks in trouble and those assigned to help.

"Your man is on his way."

"You found him?"

"Waitin' by the phone. He's all worked up. Talks like you're the Archbishop and Coyne's the Pope." Connally smiled, almost intimately. "I told him your arraignment was waitin' on him as we spoke. Told him to get with Kirby on the charges, which is probably impossible. He'll have to come down here to find him. That way he can get the story from you. I couldn't remember all the details anyway. Hope *you* can keep it straight."

"I think I got it down."

"You're still not off the hook in Aurora, ya know. Harris has a murder on his hands that he thinks you can help with, which is true enough. I can tell him we charged you, and he doesn't have to know from me that you made bail, but he's gonna find out soon enough. The press is onto this too. It's only a matter of time before they make the bingo connection. That will stoke the fires under Harris. When he gets word that you're on the streets, he'll probably bring you in on that reckless endangerment. I would count on it."

"Can't you head him off on that, Tom?"

"Not without blowin' your cover. Best we can do is stall him."

I saw his point, but I didn't like it. "When the time comes, can I count on you to help me out?" I craned my neck to read his expression.

He held my eyes and let a menacing grin cross his face. "It's not a fuckin' license to kill, Henry. You do any more to get yourself in the shit, I won't lift a finger. The shit you're in now is workable provided we can show Harris something eventually. But you get put in the system out there, the party's pretty much over. Not to mention the strain it'll put on departmental relations."

I didn't speak. He had his own ass to cover. But he must have seen the concern on my face.

"We'll sort it out," he said, looking away. "Just don't get yourself pulled over out there, ya' know? And no more gunplay, dammit." The derisive tone was clear enough, but his voice softened in the next moment. "I gotta go see Kirby, give him this stuff. Warn him about Riggs, too. Good luck." He patted my shoulder before walking away. I watched him go around the metal detectors and past the security guards and through the set of double doors, into the sunlight pouring down on the courtyard.

I spent the next hour looking over my shoulder, watching people come and go at will, tempting myself with the pros and cons of bolting for daylight, sizing up my chances. When Stanley Riggs appeared, I was somewhat appalled to find myself happy to see him.

He chewed my ear for twenty minutes, asking questions, plotting strategies, boring me blind with arguments I knew to be irrelevant. I held him off with nods and grumbles until they got to my name on the docket. When we approached the podium, George Kirby appeared from the back of the room and stepped up to the prosecutor's table. He turned and gave me a long, piercing look, as if beholding Mr. Hyde. At the judge's behest, he read the charges—breaking and entering—and the reasonable suspicions behind the people's case and offered minimal bail.

Riggs was dumbfounded. "What the hell is this?" he hissed into my ear, keeping his gaze fixed on the judge. I gave him a shrug and tried to look surprised. His next question was drowned out by the judge asking to hear from the defense. Red-faced and blustering, Riggs launched into his original line of argument, revising it as he went, countering the charges with the usual doubts, and offering a flowery version of my standings in the community. He then proposed that anything short of a personal recognizance bond would be a grave offense to my rights as a citizen, not to mention my dignity as a human being.

The judge frowned impatiently and shifted his gaze to the prosecutor. Looking slightly stunned, Kirby stared at Riggs, then looked to me, his eyes narrowing with a question.

"Mr. Kirby?" the judge prodded.

"The people have no objection, your honor," he said, dropping his head and gathering up his papers. For a moment I thought his honor smelled a rat. But he let it go with a look and a sigh and granted PR bail, setting a court date six weeks away.

Obviously surprised by the easy win, Riggs was too proud of himself to question it. But he escorted me out of there in some hurry, as if concerned that we might be called back once the mistake was discovered.

Out through those doors, the rays of afternoon sunlight slanted eastward beneath a billow of high cumulus. The air was clean and dry. It was one of those perfect September days, or so it seemed to me, a perfect balance of warmth and freshness and light, with the scent of summer still lingering like the happiest of memories. I was in a mood to appreciate it.

Riggs was in a celebratory mood of his own. As we walked along, he reconstructed the courtroom scene, hard pressed to rationalize the outcome but determined to take credit for it. I let him have his moment.

"What now?" I asked almost cheerfully.

"How about dinner?" he said, and I was about to make excuses when he added, "*And…I think she's got a car for you.*" He smiled big, like a gameshow host about to reveal what's behind door number three.

"She?" I asked, thinking of Claire.

"Tanya, Tanya Gilmore. That's why I'm here."

"Well, I thought Frank…"

"Well, sure, Frank, of course. But *he* couldn't get me down here on a Sunday, no way." He gave me a goofy, schoolboy grin, encouraging me to go along with the bad joke. "Tanya's very grateful for what you've done, you know. She asked me as a personal favor. I think she feels like she owes it to you. *And*…she asked me to bring you to dinner tonight. That is, if I got you out. She'll be very pleased," he added, obviously thinking of himself as the object of her pleasure.

Somewhat relieved, I said, "Who's going to be there?"

"The whole family. Frank and Dennis, their parents, of course, and a few of their inner circle—chief among them, Rhonda Schomberg." Involuntarily, my eyebrows went up at the mention of the lobbyist, but Riggs didn't know to be suspicious. "Pretty much just the family. It's quite an honor." Again I got the feeling he was referring to himself, but I felt lucky too.

"What's this about a car?"

"Frank told her about the car chase, how you tried to chase down Mickey's killer. A real shoot-em-up, sounds like." He gawked at me expectantly, like an adolescent wanting to hear the gory details. I responded with an insipid smile and didn't speak.

"Anyway, she offered to let you use one of her cars until you get yours running. These people take care of their own, you know."

He came to a stop and gestured with an open hand, indicating a two-toned cream and salmon-colored Cadillac parked along the curb. It was an Eldorado, as long and sleek as the rest of them, with wide-brimmed whitewalls and a chrome-spoked spare mounted rakishly on the trunk. For an instant I thought this was the loaner from Tanya. Then Riggs unlocked the passenger-side door and held it open for me, giving me that game-show grin.

"Well, I see what you mean," I said, easing myself onto the velveteen easy chair that passed for the shotgun seat. I stretched my legs along the tawny carpeting and took in the sculpted lines of the Naugahyde dash. Like all of them, he had furry dice. Smiling to myself, I wondered at the irony of their shared values, the banality of their choices for symbols of status and success. When Riggs climbed in next to me I was still smiling, I couldn't help it. But it didn't matter. His own smile met mine, priggish and self-satisfied. He couldn't imagine anyone seeing him differently from the way he saw himself.

"Drive on, Stanley," I joked, sinking back into the cushiony velveteen seat.

Chapter 26

I had Riggs chauffeur me by Willie's place for a shower and a change of clothes. The parking space off the alley was vacant but, with Willie's Mustang in the pound, it didn't mean he wasn't there. Telling Riggs my roommate worked nights and slept days, I asked him to wait in the car. He was happy enough to play with his cell phone, anxious no doubt to spread the word of his recent courtroom triumph.

Entering the house, there was no sign of Willie, but Pimpy was glad to see me, plainly bored and starved for affection. Fending off his puppy-dog antics, I let him out to mark his territory around Leroy Street's side yard.

After a shower, I called Duncan at home.

"Where the hell are you?"

"I'm at Willie's. I just wanted to tell you I got sprung and I wanted to ask you…"

"Sprung from where though?"

"City jail, in Denver."

"Yeah, how'd that happen?"

"Connally worked it."

"Connally? I didn't think you two were speaking."

"I never know from one week to the next. But listen, I can't talk now. I just wanted…"

"How'd you end up in Denver?"

"It's a long story, Duncan."

"So what happened in Aurora?"

"Well, things are still pending out there."

"I figured. 'Pending' how, exactly?"

"Duncan, I really can't talk. I've got Riggs waiting in the car and we're late for dinner with the Coyne family."

"*Coyne's* lawyer? Did *he* spring you?"

"Not really. Like I said, Connally set it up."

"You know what you're doing with these bingo people, Henry?"

I realized I'd hardly told him anything about my investigations. "Don't believe everything Willie tells you, Duncan."

"No danger there. But dinner with the Coyne family? Now *there's* an engaging social circle. Who're you sleeping with, Henry?"

"*Duncan!*"

"What?"

"I told you I can't talk. I'll tell you all about it later."

"All right. Lunch tomorrow. Sounds like you're going to need a *real* lawyer."

"Well, not yet, but I…"

"By the time *you* think you need one, it's too late."

"Okay, we'll have lunch. But I gotta go."

"How about one o'clock. Come by my office. I got a new one, ya know."

"A new one what?"

"A new office. You gotta see it."

"All right, fine, but listen. Can you call Willie for me? Tell him I'm out and I'll be at his place later tonight. And tell him to tell his Uncle Leroy. I don't want him worrying about me."

"Yeah, I remembered that old codger. What the hell was he doing there?"

"Duncan, I gotta go."

"All right, all right. One o'clock tomorrow. Forty-first floor. Just ask the receptionist."

"Your new office. I'll find it. Will you call Willie for me? And Leroy?"

"Yeah. Will do."

From the bag I had packed, I took a clean white shirt and a sport coat and tried to shake the wrinkles out. I threaded a necktie through my collar thinking about Tanya's tendency to overdress. Calling Pimpy in, I filled his bowl and patted him for good luck. Then I joined Riggs in his Caddy. It was a little after seven, the light was fading to yellow and gray in the western sky. Mediocre beauty. I took it in.

"The tie's a good idea," Riggs said, looking me over, speaking in that coaching tone of voice I was beginning to hate him for. He engineered his luxury tank into the narrow alley and out onto the street. "Tanya's a bit of a stickler about protocol. Manners, really. And appearance."

"To tell you the truth, I am feeling a bit out of place. What's this dinner about? I'm not exactly a family friend."

"It's business," he said, then caught himself. "Not to take anything away from the family's grief. But they're concerned about the situation. Very concerned." Cocking one eyebrow, he glanced sideways to let me know it was my turn to speak. When I said nothing, he continued to prod. "I mean, there's two people dead and its beginning to look like the family business is involved."

"Isn't it?" I asked, trenchantly.

"What do you mean by that?"

I mocked him with a low laugh. "C'mon Riggs. I thought we're on the same side."

"Let me make this perfectly clear. Nobody asked you to kill Brent Charmichael. I *talked* to Frank…"

"Is that what he thinks?"

"Well, what the hell is all this about a break-in? I mean, it's Charmichael's address, right? Sounds to me like they're biding their time to make a case." His tone rose anxiously, his words tumbling out. "I told Frank I'm not defending you for a capital offense. I mean, I can do the corporate stuff, tax stuff…and I've *done* courtroom work, but it's not exactly my forte."

The car slowed in inverse proportion to the pace of his rationalizing. We were doing about fifty in the middle lane of the freeway. Other cars rolled by, their drivers gawking and flipping us off. I suppressed a smile.

"Frank is my alibi."

"You can't count on *that*," Riggs countered.

"No, I mean he already has been, apparently. *And* Dennis *and* Milo Finnes and any of Milo's crew that were out at Holiday Bingo on Friday night. We were together when Charmichael got killed. Didn't the cops talk to Frank?"

Riggs seemed dumbstruck as he thought this through. The car had slowed to about forty. Drivers were flashing their lights. "You mean the time of death?"

"I guess. I told them where I was and with whom. They must have checked it out."

A long horn blast from a passing car seemed to bring Riggs around. Glancing in the mirror, he pushed on the gas and brought us up to speed. After a not very long thoughtful moment, he said, "Then what's the break-in charge for?" Still puzzled and still suspicious.

"When I left Frank at Milo's, I went to Charmichael's place. I found him already dead. I called it in. Anonymously. Got out of there."

"You broke in there? What the hell for?"

"I didn't exactly break in. The door was unlocked. I wanted to check on Charmichael's alibi. He was supposed to be in Vegas when Mickey got it, but nobody believed that. Not Frank, anyway, and not me either."

He stared at me long enough to drift out of his lane. A horn blared and he jerked the car back between the lines.

After a minute, with a put-on air of nonchalance, he said, "So what did you find?"

"I told you. Charmichael was dead."

"But you went in there on your own initiative," he said, in a predictably cautious tone.

"Frank didn't have anything to do with it. And that's what I told the cops."

"Why'd you tell them anything?"

"They have a way of putting the pressure on, ya know? When they came at me with a murder charge, I figured it was time to come clean."

After another thoughtful pause, he feigned a chuckle. "You're lucky to be out."

"I suppose so."

Riggs fell silent after that. His bulbous features seemed to gradually constrict into what might have been a look of concentration, his brain working like stripped gears in an over-revved transmission. Several moves I'd made probably didn't fit into the cautionary mindset of a bingo world *consigliere*, if that's what he was. I thought about pressuring him for what he knew but decided he was too skittish and too exactingly paranoid to be all the way into the inner circle.

Chapter 27

Exiting on Hampton Avenue, we drove along the southern edge of Cherry Hills Country Club, its nicely aged lilac hedges, thick and impenetrable, lining the curb like some flowered bulwark against the teaming hordes. Before we reached its end, we turned south into a divided parkway that led to the gated entrance of Crestmoor Heights. A uniformed security guard leaned out of his kiosk and gave us half a wave, half a signal to stop. Riggs announced Tanya Gilmore's name with an air of familiarity. The stone-faced guard showed no sign of recognition but, after checking his clipboard, he waved us through.

Crestmoor Heights is a relatively affluent suburb just inside the Denver city limits that pretends to the status of its autonomous and more blue-blooded neighbors to the south, the big-moneyed enclave of Wellshire Village. That was where Rhonda Schomberg had made a name for herself. With a firm grip on her husband's coattails—a three-term state senator twice her age—Schomberg had ridden a temporary wave of Republican feminist sympathies into the office of mayor of that little berg back in the 80s. For all of its country atmosphere, its whitewashed fencing, and the neatly maintained stables and corrals in the foreground of its ranch- or country-style mansions, Wellshire Village is a legal township, whose pool of wealth and influence pervades Colorado politics.

It should have been no surprise to me that Tanya Gilmore lived in its vicinity, although the Heights—as it was often called, somewhat facetiously—was newer blood and newer money. But new money is as green as old and it usually spends easier. The likes of the Coyne family, the aristocracy of the bingo kingdom, had to live somewhere to flaunt their relative rank, and their special interests would be well served by a proximity to their representatives in state and local government. For all I had seen and heard, that connection went through Rhonda Schomberg to the secretary of state. And Tanya was uncannily appropriate as ambassador in the fight to protect their inalienable rights to skim profits and dodge taxes.

As I mentally fleshed out this perspective, we came to a stop at the wrought iron gates of a private drive tucked between man-made berms lined with Christmas tree-size pines. Beyond the gates, a crescent-shaped flagstone drive swept toward the well-lit foyer of an ultra-modern structure too cold and linear to be the entrance of a private residence. But private it was and, as if he had read my thoughts, Riggs assured me who resided therein as the gates fanned open before us.

"The humble digs of Tanya Gilmore," Riggs said. "And her husband Mickey, now deceased."

I looked at his face but there was no trace of sarcasm. His narrow eyes twinkled with unmistakable, if voyeuristic, pride and a clever smile pinched at his bulbous cheeks. I ventured to guess that, with Mickey out of the picture, Riggs had his own designs on the recently widowed bingo heiress.

Retro-modern lamp posts dotted the plush grounds, punctiliously manicured though still growing in. A low hedge along the drive circumnavigated a four-tiered fountain like those you expect to see in Rome. Or anyway, Vegas. The water trickled peacefully from one textured plastic oyster-shell to the next.

We pulled up at the end of a row of luxury cars, two of which were Cadillacs. There was also a shiny Lexus coupe and a Mercedes two-seater with the top down. Frank's faded green Jaguar looked out of date in the midst of them. Parked length-wise along the semicircular drive was a full-sized Lincoln Continental shining black like a politician's limo, or a funeral car. Frank's gift to Rhonda Schomberg. Claire's car was conspicuously absent. I felt reassured.

Beyond and between two matching stands of immature aspens, the glass-paneled lines of the building rose up thirty feet. From where I stood, I had no real sense of the overall size of the house. Probably it was big. I could put Willie's alley house on the front porch and still have room to walk the dog—though there was little doubt I'd feel compelled to clean up after him.

At the top-most level of semi-circular flagstone tiers, Riggs leaned on a lit button next to the black-lacquered over-sized double doors. The first few bars of something from Brahms chimed out in church-organ tones. I couldn't hold back a smile. Riggs caught it and answered with a grin of his own, smug and conspiratorial.

A manservant, young for the job and looking distinctly out of place, pulled the door aside and looked us over with dark offended eyes. He had neatly trimmed black hair and a small goatee and carried some workout-muscle under his waistcoat.

"Mr. Riggs," he said, "Mrs. Gilmore is expecting you." His eyes flitted in my direction then away, as if it hurt to look at me.

"Thank you, James," Riggs said. (James? *Really?* Why not *Jeeves?*)

"And I'm Mr. Burkhart," I said as I passed, just to let him know I wasn't applying for his job. He nodded and tried to keep his face blank but the dark eyes held mine for an extra second as he turned to close the door.

We stepped into a circle of richly-stained parquet flooring situated like a raft in a frozen sea of white high-pile carpet. You could see footprints in it like tracks in new fallen snow. Thirty feet overhead, a glass-rimmed rotunda opened out like the inside of a crystal parachute and, beneath that, an oak-trimmed stairway circled upward towards the promise of the clouds of heaven. The cavernous space on our right could have been an extra-large living room or a small, uniquely appointed auditorium. It had a cathedral ceiling that rose out of sight and a fireplace at the end about the size of Duncan's mountain cabin. Reflected light shimmered and shone along the far walls from an indoor pool I couldn't see.

Before I could take it all in, James led us off through an elongated loggia with faux-brick vaulted ceilings and plaster Cupids doing somersaults in relief along the velour wainscoting. The only consistent theme I could discern amidst this mélange of interior design gone amuck was that of conspicuous spending. There was ornamental money everywhere. By the time we reached the arched doorway of the dining hall, I was beginning to wonder if there wasn't more to it than bingo. James swung the hand-carved oak doors wide and a lively conversation died off abruptly as he stepped in to announce us.

"Mr. Riggs has arrived, Madame," he said affecting a haughty tone that didn't suit his mid-western drawl. "And a…Mr. Burkhart."

At the near end of an antique cherry wood runway that doubled as a dining table, a group of eight people took up less than half its length. They were clustered together in high-backed chairs, their faces glowing evenly in the muted radiance of three ersatz-crystal chandeliers. Their heads turned to take us in, their expressions stiff, as if poised for more bad news.

Tanya Gilmore, enthroned at the head of the table, turned out of her chair with a sprightly grace, her flawlessly painted face not reflecting the concern I saw on the others. Her eyes passed quickly over Stanley Riggs and came to rest on me with an impassive smile. She seemed happy to see me and perfectly at ease with that illusion. Next to her, Frank and Ellen Coyne sat with their backs to us, leaning around their chair-backs to get a better look. With some effort, Frank shuffled his chair a quarter turn, then stood and approached me. Riggs crossed to greet Tanya, fawning over her "simply *elegant*" shoulder-less black dress. I had to admit, she had some shoulders.

When Frank moved his chair, I noticed an older couple sitting across from him and I recognized the man's features—he must be Willard Coyne. He had Frank's missing jawline and wide lips, with deeper creases and more weathered skin. What little hair was left on the sides of his head was snow white and wispy. He wore glasses thicker than his son's, a more rounded but similar horn-rim style that made his eyes look like dotted cue balls. Next to him was a plump woman with curly brown hair that might have been a wig, the thick curls too healthy for the finely lined face they framed. This was, no doubt, Willard's wife.

Next to her sat Chuck Burrows, impeccably dressed and sitting stiffly, with an air of being on his best behavior. Down from him was another face I recognized, but only from her picture in local news media. Rhonda Schomberg sat gazing at me, staring pointedly through a pair of wire-framed bifocals. She held them delicately just above her nose, like pince-nez, and she gave me a look of slight amusement and unmistakable curiosity before letting the glasses hang from the gold chain around her neck. She was still quite young, probably early forties, with handsome features and richly colored dark hair, cut rather short and combed back in well-placed waves.

"My God, Henry, I can't believe you made it," Frank said through his long-toothed grin, his eyes bulging more emphatically than ever. He gave me a hardy handshake and patted my shoulder several times. His suede Western-cut sport coat emitted the heavy scent of newly tanned leather. "How'd you hold up in there?"

"As well as could be expected, I guess. Not a pleasant place."

"I should say not." His gray eyes held mine appraisingly. "They give you much trouble?"

"Yeah, they did. And I don't think it's over."

"Well," he said, then paused as if giving my words some thought. "Come in, come in. Have something to eat. We'll talk about it."

He took me by the elbow and guided me toward the table and introduced me to his mother and father. The old man gave me a curt nod like he didn't want to be bothered.

Tanya had moved around to frame me between Frank and herself. She was wrapped in a black double-knit dress that pretended to hang from a single string over her sculpted shoulders, leaving her shapely arms bare and touchable. White pearls that looked real enough to me accented her neck and left wrist. She wasn't my type, but I could see how she would seem desirable from a distance. She faced me toward the assembly with a practiced ease, nimble fingers caressing my inner arm.

"And you haven't met Rhonda, have you?" She gestured across the table. "She's a very close friend of the family."

Rhonda gave me a charming, Cheshire cat smile.

"Pleased to meet you."

Tanya guided me toward the chair next to Dennis who was seated down one from Ellen. He looked at me askance, his cheek bulging with a mouthful of food. He was the only one who had kept eating as we made our introductions and the only one who didn't exchange a greeting with me. Nobody seemed to care. Riggs took a seat across from me next to Rhonda and the two of them started in on the small talk like old friends. Or party comrades.

Working around Dennis, Ellen Coyne fawned over me like I was the prodigal son, offering to serve me from the plethora of savory dishes—catered no doubt—surrounding a centerpiece of artificially brightened colored carnations. In her gray tweed suit and white blouse, and her ingratiating manner, she gave the impression she might be affiliated with the Sisters of Mercy Mission. I was famished and gratefully accepted the samplings. Dennis and I were the only ones eating.

"Have you sorted everything out with the police, Henry?" Tanya asked, in a low and silky voice that seemed slightly out of place. There was no trace of the widow's tears in her artfully applied mascara, no redness of the eyes nor puffy cheeks.

"For the time being," I said. "There's some complications, but I'm sure I can get them sorted out with help from Mr. Riggs."

No one responded to that. Riggs looked around as if planning an escape route. I took another mouthful. There were serious expressions around that table, but none of them were sad, none bereaved. The gathering was all business, like Riggs had said, a meeting of the minds, the minds behind the Bingo Empire, such as they were. All except Benny Palmer. I wondered if he was on the outs for doing business with Milo.

"I can't tell you how much we appreciate what you've done for us," Tanya offered. Leaning toward her father and raising her voice slightly, she said, "He's the one who tried to catch the car. He followed them to Milo Finnes' place." The old man took me in again and nodded vaguely. I wasn't sure if he was following or smoothly faking it.

With an officious air, Frank asked Riggs to update everyone present—that's the way he put it—with what had happened in court. Riggs was happy to get the spotlight. I ate while he ran off at the mouth, pausing once to give the Mexican hired help a chance to clear the table and serve dessert. When he got to the part about my appearance in court and the charges of breaking and entering, Frank interrupted with a firm declaration of his authority.

"That's enough, Stanley. I want to hear this from the horse's mouth." He eyed me closely, and spoke through his full-blown humorless grin. "You want to fill us in on what happened Friday night? After we parted company, I mean."

The hands that had been picking at dessert or tipping coffee cups and wineglasses came to rest. Rhonda Schomberg gave me that amused look again, a confident look, like she already knew the story and was curious to hear how I would spin it. Everyone else eyed me expectantly, except Dennis who was working on the remains of Ellen's dessert. And Riggs, sitting across from me, dropped his gaze, as if not wanting to hear anything off the record.

Giving up on the last of my perfectly cooked prime rib, I tried out a nervous chuckle. I was nervous enough. "Well, you know, it was stupid of me. I knew I was in trouble right away." I scanned the listeners. No one shared with me the humor of the situation. "I mean, I didn't expect to find him...dead."

"What did you expect?" Willard Coyne asked, in a particularly strident voice. I was surprised to find him on point. The atmosphere of the room turned ambiguous, as if the glow from the overhead chandeliers had dimmed. I pressed forward, pretending not to notice.

"I got to thinking about it, about Charmichael's alibi." I appealed to Frank with a nod. "Like we had talked about. I figured if he *had* come back from Vegas, he wasn't going to hang around for long, especially if Milo got word to him. So I thought I'd see if I could catch up with him before he skipped."

"My goodness. What would you have done if you had?" Tanya feigned being appalled, yet there was something pointed—interested—in her tone.

"To tell you the truth, I hadn't thought it through. I mean, I was just thinking, if he was there, I could spot him, and that would undermine his alibi. I wasn't going to *do* anything."

The listeners' faces remained politely expressionless, though there were hints of skepticism—squinting, focused eyes and hands covering mouths. Preposterous as it might have sounded, I realized I was telling the truth so far and it was okay with me if they didn't like it.

"I tried the doorbell and got no answer, so I tried the knob. It was unlocked. Even if he wasn't there, I thought I might find something that would indicate he had been." I paused long enough to let everyone know the punch line was at hand. "I found him lying dead in a pool of blood. He had been shot through the heart."

Nervous reactions skittered through the room, chairs creaked and people cleared their throats. "How *aw*ful," the elder Mrs. Coyne said.

In a low, even tone, Frank asked the question that I knew would be bothering him. "Why didn't you tell me? On Saturday, I mean, before Detective Harris picked you up."

I sighed and offered a thoughtful frown and looked to Chuck Burrows, who was rigidly attentive, then back to Frank.

"Well, to tell you the truth, I didn't know who to trust. I mean, I haven't been around you people all that long." (That 'you people' sounded off, even to me. No one seemed to take offense). "I don't know you all that well. You'll have to excuse my saying this, but the obvious motives pointed to *you*." I looked at the brightly flowered centerpiece, avoiding eye contact. "To someone in this circle."

Willard Coyne broke into a low chuckle, and Chuck Burrows smiled demurely. Tanya frowned like she didn't like their responses. Rhonda brought up her bifocals to check with the far end of the table. She seemed to be stifling a grin. No matter how they took it, I could tell they believed me.

"There is *nothing* to indicate," Riggs piped in, "that my clients had anything to do with Brent Charmichael's death. You said yourself the time of death exculpates not only *you*, but Frank and Dennis as well."

"I didn't know that at the time," I said.

"Take it easy, Stanley," Frank said, still holding his superior grin. "I don't think Henry suspects any of us now. Isn't that right, Henry?"

Looking towards Frank's end of the table, I found Willard Coyne smiling serenely. It was a nicer smile than his son's, effortless and more palpable.

"I wouldn't be here if I did. But I didn't know what to think then and I sure as hell didn't want to get mixed up in someone else's murder."

"But there's more to it than the time of death, right?" Frank's tone might have indicated foreknowledge. "What else did you find out from the cops?"

Thinly concealed interest shone from everyone's faces. They all wanted to know why they weren't suspects.

"They found a gun there by the body. I saw it too." I directed my gaze to Tanya. "This Connally guy told me it was the same gun that killed Mickey."

"Connally!" Burrows blurted. "Tom Connally?

I nodded.

"You know him?" Frank asked.

"Yeah, I know him. I worked under him in the third precinct years ago. He's a tough nut, I'll tell ya that. But he's Captain of Homicide now. What's he doin' getting involved?"

"Beats me. He just showed up." Remembering Connally's response when I asked him the same question, I added, "I mean, he's homicide, right?"

"Yeah, but captains don't get involved in individual cases," Burrows said, directing his words to the head of the table. "Not initially, anyway. Not unless they're high profile." He looked at me, as if he expected me to explain it. "Who else questioned you?"

"A detective named Ross McQuitty," I said, wishing I had thought through this line of questioning. "Connally showed up later."

Burrows and Frank Coyne exchanged a furtive look, and Burrows offered a minute shake of his head. Then his eyes came back to me. "How'd they know it was the same gun?" His words were crisp, in the tone of a cross-examination.

"That's just what they said. I mean, I don't think they had it tested yet, but they said it was the same caliber. Anyway, because of that, they figure Charmichael killed Mickey. And his partner—whoever was in the car with him—killed Charmichael."

"I knew it," Tanya said in a harsh whisper, sounding more angry than sad.

The room went quiet, as if everyone was awkwardly reminded of Tanya's loss—and her past involvement with the likely killer. As the silence endured, I had the feeling they were mulling over other theories. They weren't buying this one on impulse.

I broke the silence blithely. "Anyway, that pretty much eliminates… well, everyone here, and everyone who was at the Palace at the time." I figured it would be bad form to point out the discrepancies in my logic.

"So do they have a suspect?" Tanya inquired.

I shrugged. "They didn't tell me straight out, but I'm pretty sure that's half the reason they let me off. You know this Enos Flood character?"

Tanya flashed a puzzled look, then shrugged her naked shoulders. I thought it was a little overdone.

"He's one of Milo's goons," Frank explained. "He's the one Henry roughed up at Holiday Bingo. He admitted to being in on the holdup at Clancy's with Brent."

"He and his brother, Alois," I added. "Some kind of ex-con. I think the cops are looking for them."

"How'd you know about that?" Burrows, the ex-cop, interjected. Throughout my little performance, more than anyone, he had been listening critically, listening for the ring of truth.

"The cops asked me if I knew them, if I'd ever seen them around the halls or had any dealings with them. It's only a guess, but they asked a lot of question, like, more than once." To Frank, I said, "I told them Enos was there—at the Holiday, I mean—but his brother wasn't. They check with you on that?"

Frank nodded. "I told them we were there. I assumed that would help you out. Didn't do much for my standings but…"

"That's hardly the issue at hand, Frank," Tanya scolded. "Besides you had every right…" She stopped herself in mid-sentence. Clearing her throat, she said, "So they think this person killed Brent? This Flood person?"

"I think that's where they're going to look. I told them I thought it was Brent and the Flood brothers that pulled the stickup."

"But you don't think Milo knew about that, right?" Willard Coyne asked. "Why not?"

Wiley old Willard, indeed. "It seemed to me that Milo was genuinely surprised when we got that out of Enos. Right, Frank?"

"So, in fact," Willard continued, without letting Frank speak, "Milo may not be involved in any of this."

"I don't think the cops have established that." I leaned forward to look at Frank. "Do we know that?"

He shrugged and smiled his innocuous smile. I figured he had been in touch with Milo, but he wasn't sharing that with just anybody.

Looking around the table, no one met my eyes. A heavy silence followed, like the slow inevitable rise of floodwaters in the narrow canyons of their thoughts. I got the impression they had what they wanted from me and weren't about to share their conclusions—or their plans. I had to do something to stay in place, to remain in their trust. Fending off Connally's parting words, I decided to go with my original scheme. If he and Luis didn't like it, they didn't have to know about it until later, until it all worked out. What could happen?

"I found something else there too," I said. "At Charmichael's house. Something that may have been of interest to the killer."

All eyes—several keen looks—came around to focus on me but no one asked the question.

"There was computer equipment in there, in the room where I found his body. Actually, the computer itself was missing. The cops noticed that too."

"The killer took the computer?" Frank asked, playing the role of straight man with intentional precision. "Why would he do that?"

I shrugged, pretending to be as naïve as he was pretending to be.

"Memory," Willard Coyne offered. "Bookkeeping, accounting records. And email correspondences maybe."

I couldn't read past Frank's fixed grin but I thought he and Willard exchanged an invisible signal. The old man's eyes were shining behind the Coke bottle lenses. He tossed a glance at Tanya too. And Dennis perked up for the first time. He looked from them to me with a plainly guilty expression. Apparently, he hadn't yet developed the implacable mask that otherwise ran in the family.

"Yeah," I said, "that's what the cops seem to think. They asked me what I knew about it." The entire table was hanging on my words and I felt compelled to elaborate. "They pressed pretty hard on the theory that I took it, that even if I didn't kill him, I knew it had happened, and I went in there afterwards to cover up." I looked into the tinted lenses on Frank's forward tilting face. "To cover up for you."

"Me?" he said. "I haven't had dealings with Brent Charmichael for years."

"That's what I told them. I guess they bought it or I wouldn't be here."

"But you didn't take it?" Willard asked.

"No," I said, and let a few seconds pass. "That is, I didn't take the computer. It was already gone, as were any disks or tapes or whatever that would have been obvious."

After a few seconds of rigid silence, Burrows picked up on the implication. "So?" He sounded like the bad cop in a police interview. "What *did* you take?"

I smiled as if caught in the act. "Well, I found a disk. One that was apparently overlooked. It was an accident really. I didn't know Brent by sight. I had to look for an ID to know for sure it was him. I, ah, knelt down to turn the body over looking for his wallet."

Tanya cringed and the other women frowned and huffed.

"Sorry," I said, "Perhaps this isn't the appropriate time."

"No, no," Tanya insisted with a dismissive flap of her maroon-polished fingernails. "I'm sure we all want to know."

"Go on, Henry," Frank prompted.

"There was this disk in a plastic case taped to the bottom of the desk drawer. The tape had come loose along one edge, so it was hanging down." I thought this a masterful bit of realistic detail, and it inspired me further. "That's actually what made me realize the computer was gone."

"So, what is it, Henry?" Frank persisted. "Don't keep us in suspense."

"Beats me. I'm not really that up on this tech stuff. I have no way of opening it."

"But you took it," Burrows stated flatly.

I nodded. "It was labeled 'full backup August 2000'. Even I know what that means. Whatever tracks the killer was trying cover, I bet a few of them are on that disk."

"And you didn't give it to the cops?" Burrows asked, somewhat incredulous.

"Should I have?"

Burrows checked with Frank across the table and decided not to give the quick answer.

Speaking to Frank, I said, "When they told me about the time of death, I figured you were cleared. But after what they said, well, I wasn't sure if there might not be something incriminating on there."

Frank smiled artificially and his rigid shoulders came up and down as if of a piece. "I appreciate that, Henry, but like I said, I've had nothing to do with him for a long time. I'd say it's more likely to point to Milo. Wouldn't you, Chuck?"

"Absolutely. All the more reason to hand it over to the cops."

"Maybe so, but still…" Willard Coyne was staring off into space, long fingers tracing the vague line of his chin. "Wouldn't you like to get a look at it first?" He smiled a wide, disingenuous smile. I saw now where Frank got it.

His wife, sitting next to him, let out a high pitched giggle, sounding like a mischievous sorority girl in on a prank. Everyone seemed enlivened by the idea, except Tanya who affected a disapproving frown.

"What kind of disk is it?" she asked.

"I'm not sure." I figured I was taking a chance here, but I remembered seeing the blanks in the desk drawer. "It looked like a music CD, but there was no label. Just the piece of masking tape with the handwriting on it."

"You should give it to Tanya," Frank said. "She's something of a computer wiz." He turned to her. "Don't you think? We might find something we can use against him."

Tanya's frown deepened rather pointedly. "Use against him? Why do we even want something to use against him? Isn't it obvious what this silly rivalry has done so far?"

Frank didn't respond. From across the table, his father's gaze came up to take him in.

Burrows spoke up. "I agree wholeheartedly, Tanya. On the other hand, if Brent Charmichael and Milo Finnes were up to something, I don't think we want to get in the way of an investigation. After all, someone in that organization is a murderer."

Willard's head tilted back, his lips pursed in a stiff upward thrusting frown. Frank leaned forward to span the distance with his eyes between himself and Chuck Burrows. Next to him, his wife squirmed in her seat and gave him an anxious look that he ignored. It came to me that no one was smoking. It must be the rule of the house and it was beginning to have an effect on the chain-smoking side of the family.

I knew what Frank was thinking. Regardless of what he said, he had a past with Brent Charmichael. And obviously Tanya, too. No record of Charmichael's dealings was going to go through their hands to the cops. This family had a lot to hide, even if they weren't very good at it. I waited for Frank to speak.

Instead, Tanya said it for him. "Why don't we just destroy it? I don't see what we have to gain by stirring this up any further."

Burrows took a breath as if to speak, but he held up when his eyes met Frank's.

"All kidding aside," Willard said, rather suddenly, "we need to know what's on it before we can make a decision."

Frank took the hint. "I'm not passing it to the cops until I know. If there's anything to do with their books, it would go to the secretary of state's investigators." He stopped and stared at Chuck and held it until Chuck nodded affirmatively. "Once we know that, we can decide what to do with it." With a distinct craning of his neck, he turned toward his sister. "That okay with you, Tanya?"

"Yes, I suppose."

"So I can trust you with it then?" he added lightly.

Tanya huffed out a small laugh. "I guess I'd like to see what's on it, too. But I don't know if I can even get into it. I may not have the right equipment." Looking past Frank to me, she said, "Is it encrypted?"

It was supposed to be a trick question. Not very subtle, really. I shrugged my shoulders. "Beats me. How do you tell?" I was smiling, trying to look stupid, pulling it off pretty well. I was buoyed by the fact that any question of the disk's actual existence had been completely passed over.

"Why don't you give it to Tanya? Maybe she can figure it out."

"Well, there's a problem there," I said, introducing the most carefully thought-out part of my charade. "I don't exactly have it. Not with me, that is, and I can't get to it right away."

"Why the hell not?" Frank demanded.

"I left it in that car I borrowed—the Mustang I drove to the Palace on Saturday. It belongs to a friend of mine. The cops impounded it when they arrested me and it's still in there."

"Christ," Frank uttered. "Nothing's simple." He turned to Tanya. "I gotta have a cigarette. Is their anywhere we can smoke?"

Shifting her chair, Ellen gripped his forearm like she thought he'd never ask. Tanya sighed, got up, and strode the length of the room in purposeful steps. She unlatched the French doors and they swung open with the breeze. Fresh air wafted through the room. Frank and Ellen made their way towards the open doors, lit up, and sucked smoke like it was life-giving oxygen. Dennis joined them. Their brownish exhalations followed the breeze deeper into the room.

"Well, I think we'd better go," Willard said, struggling to push back his chair. "We ain't as young like the rest of you." People started standing and moving and he put up a fuss. "Don't get up. You've got things to discuss. We'll just leave you to it."

"I gotta go too," Dennis said, approaching from the far end of the room. "I gotta check up on Claire."

"She's not back yet, is she?" Frank asked.

"I'll find her," Dennis responded.

I didn't know what that meant but I was glad to hear she was out of touch. I watched as Frank came over and took Dennis aside, moving toward the door and out of earshot from the table.

Willard and his wife exchanged good-byes around the table. "Nice to meet you young man," he said to me in turn. His tone was perfunctory and his magnified eyes gave nothing away. Tanya escorted them out the door. Riggs went with them, shamelessly sucking up to Tanya. Dennis and Frank were nowhere to be seen.

I sat down and Ellen Coyne sank into the seat next to me.

"Did you get enough to eat," she said, almost into my ear.

"Oh, yes, thanks."

"I bet they didn't feed you too good in jail."

"I couldn't eat after the first meal."

"Well, we certainly wouldn't want that to happen again," she said. I looked her in the face. She was smiling innocently enough, but there was something in her tone I didn't get.

Across the table, I caught Rhonda Schomberg watching me, smiling politely, no humor in it. I didn't know what that meant either. But I noted how tactfully she had let the rest of the crowd incriminate themselves while not saying a word. Riggs, too, for that matter, though you'd expect it from him.

Frank reentered the room in full gait and addressed Chuck Burrows from a distance with the force of a public announcement. "Is there anything you can do about this impounded car?"

Burrows shrugged. "I can look into it, sure." Then his gaze turned to me. "Did you ask Harris about it?"

"I haven't had the chance yet. Before I knew what was happening, they transferred me to Denver. I haven't seen Harris since. I didn't even think about it until Mr. Riggs got me out."

Burrows smiled and narrowed his eyes, shaking his head doubtfully. He didn't like that transfer. He looked like he was going to ask about it but Riggs came back into the room.

"I'm sure I can get the car released, Frank," he said, blustering with false confidence. "They have no grounds for keeping it now that Henry's been cleared. Detective Harris and I have established a certain rapport."

"If you don't mind," I said, "I'd like to take a crack at it myself. It's a friend's car. You met him at the Aurora police station. Willie Randolph. It was his uncle that he brought down there to help me out. Supposedly, my lawyer."

"The old man with the cane? That cantankerous old black guy? It's his car?"

"No, no. That's Leroy Street. It's his nephew's car, the younger one that was with him."

"What's this now?" Frank was clearly confused. Tanya returned and closed the door behind her. Rhonda stood up to meet her and the two of them stood at the farthest point in the room away from the wafting smoke. The party was breaking up, but they were still paying attention.

"I borrowed the car from Willie Randolph. I'm staying at his house… temporarily. When they impounded it, I thought I better tell him about it. The next thing I know, he shows up with his uncle, who's a lawyer—from the old school, you might say." I glanced at Riggs, and he gave me a sardonic grin. "They sort of barged their way in to complicate things just when Mr. Riggs was making progress."

Riggs chuckled appreciatively at the positive light I shed on his shortfall with the Aurora Police. "You can call me Stanley," he said.

"And who was the other lawyer?" Frank asked.

Riggs' raised eyebrows gestured towards me.

"Oh, you mean Duncan, Duncan Pruett. He's a friend from back when I was in law school. Since before that, actually. I called him before I knew Stanley was coming down."

Quiet filled the room. It was the third or fourth time the congregation fell into pensive silence at the end of one of my spiels. They were still checking my story. I thought I was fielding the grounders pretty briskly but it was hard to tell with all these wooden faces and mannered grins.

"Anyway, I think he's going to want his uncle to tackle this problem with the car. It's his car, after all. And Leroy Street…" I smiled as I pictured him slashing with his cane at Officer Haines. "He's kind of an eccentric SOB. Cantankerous, as Stanley says. He's going to want a piece of the action now that he sees himself involved."

From the look on his face, Frank wasn't amused, but I had more cards to play. "Besides, since it's his car, Willie can go after it without me, without any reference to me." I paused to let my meaning sink in, then decided they needed it spelled out. "Harris still has charges pending against me, or so I gather, for chasing after that Caddy."

"I thought that was all cleared up," Frank charged, his eyes cutting towards Riggs.

Riggs cleared his throat. "Well I…I haven't spoken with the *Aurora* police yet," he said, letting his words fade off.

"Connally told me I'd have to clear that up with Harris for myself. I guess I got out because he hadn't pressed charges yet. I'd just as soon avoid that whole confrontation for the time being. At least until after we get the car back."

Frank's face was pinched with concentration. "What do you think, Chuck?"

"Yeah, I see his point. I'm surprised he got out at all, frankly." He didn't quite say it like an accusation, but he paused to see how I would take it. I stared back at him like I expected him to continue. Eventually, he did. "Harris can hold that car it if he wants to, charges or no."

"I figure he would for sure if it was me asking about it." I nodded to Riggs. "Or my lawyer."

"This Leroy guy any good?" Frank asked. "I mean, from the sounds of it…he *is* a lawyer, right?"

"Yeah, he's a lawyer. Past his prime, maybe, but I think he can handle it. I'd like to give him a few days, before you send in the big guns." I nodded at Riggs and he took the compliment with predictable conceit.

"Maybe it's just as well this way, Frank," Burrows asserted. "I mean, we don't want to give them any ideas about that car. No reasons for searching it themselves." Turning his face to me, he said, "Where'd you put the disk?"

"In the glove box," I said, without thinking, then wished I had come up with something less accessible.

Frank looked thoughtful but I didn't detect anything to worry about in his expression. "Well, Henry," he said finally. "Get him on it tomorrow. We've got Mickey's memorial service tomorrow anyway," he added, as if it were a business lunch we'd have to work around. No one's feelings were hurt. "If it's not done by Tuesday, we'll put Stanley on it."

Frank moved toward the French doors to light up again and Ellen joined him. Turning back to the other end of the room, I saw Rhonda and Tanya speaking in quiet undertones in the opposite corner. Taking Tanya gently by the arm, Rhonda led her through the swinging doors to the kitchen. Shortly thereafter, the servers showed up to clear the remains of dinner.

From across the table, Chuck Burrows addressed me. "Did you run into Joe Perkins down there? He's supposed to be the primary on the Charmichael investigation."

"I didn't see him, but Connally mentioned him, told me he would probably want to question me. I guess he's on it with this guy McQuitty."

"Yeah, McQuitty I don't know, but Joe Perkins is a friend. A close friend. Know what I mean?" He gave me a long look, man-to-man.

"So he's going to be able to help?"

"Well, he can't buy you a walk, but you can count on him to do what he can."

"That's good to know."

"Just play along, ya know? He'll guide you the right way." His eyes glistened with self-importance.

I nodded but it didn't feel convincing. I was feeling the strain.

Frank and Ellen came back from the open air to stand near the end of the table.

"We're going home. It's late."

Burrows pushed back his chair and I followed suit.

"Where's Tanya?" Frank asked.

Standing just outside the kitchen doors looking like an anxiously loyal dog, Riggs indicated with a thumb over his shoulder. Frank went over and pushed open the swinging door. Tanya and Rhonda Schomberg stood just inside.

"We're leaving," Frank said. "The service is at four, right? Shall we meet here first?"

"Yes, let's," Tanya said, reentering the room. "We can all go over together. I think three o'clock would be appropriate." She spoke in an accommodating tone, the cheerfulness of a good hostess. I intercepted Stanley Riggs in the line that loosely formed in the loggia, waiting to pay respects to Tanya.

"Can I get a ride with you?"

"Oh, that's right. Let me ask Tanya about the car."

"That's all right," I said, but he brushed me off with an arm gesture. We positioned ourselves behind Burrows who was walking slowly with Tanya, holding her hand and talking in undertones. Tanya held a stiff smile. She didn't like him much. As we made our way into the entryway and people shuffled past James and out the doors, Riggs spoke to Tanya.

"This is a horrible business, but we'll make the best of it. Don't worry about a thing."

Tanya smiled something like her brother's smile. It wasn't her best feature.

"About that car you mentioned. Is that still available for Henry's use or…"

Riggs trailed off, grinning anxiously. Tanya looked momentarily puzzled.

"Oh, that's right," she said, looking to me and putting some charm back into it. "I was going to loan you the Lexus, wasn't I. Would that help?"

"Yes, of course. It would make it easier to work on getting my car back."

"You mean, your friend's car?"

"Yeah, well, that and my car too. The police have both of them."

"Why don't you just keep it as long as you need it," she said, giving me a steady look that probably was meant to make a point. I nodded vaguely. She said, "Wait here, I'll get the keys."

She went off toward the kitchen leaving Riggs and me standing at the open door opposite Rhonda Schomberg.

"You look familiar somehow," I said to her.

She smiled. "You know, I was thinking the same thing about you. Have you ever worked around the Capitol?"

"The State Capitol? Here in Denver? Can't say that I have. You work there?"

"I'm a lobbyist," she said with predictable haughtiness. "I've been in and around that dome for years. You get local press coverage pretty regularly around there. That's probably where you recognize me from."

I nodded assuredly. "You wouldn't be the same Schomberg as in the Schomberg Amendment, would you?"

She gave me a complacent grin. "One and the same. It's been haunting me for decades now."

"Quite the celebrity," Riggs put in, obviously proud to be rubbing shoulders with it. I did my best to go along. Tanya showed up before it got unbearable.

"It's the silver Lexus in the circle drive. I'm selling it anyway, but don't be chasing any gangsters in it, okay?" Her face stretched into a look of admonishment that softened into a grin. She held out the keys and when I reached for them she took my hand in both of hers and placed the keys and her calling card in my palm. "And be careful for your own sake, too," she added, closing my fingers and giving my fist a slow squeeze.

I thanked her and said that I would be careful—like I had been telling everybody.

"And good luck with that other car," she added, giving me another lingering glare, eyes bright, maybe flirtatious, maybe just pressing the point. "You'll call me first when you get this disk, okay?"

I nodded, eye to eye. A coy smile crease one side of her lips and her eyes definitely softened when she said, "We'll find a time to get together…"

I'm pretty sure 'just the two of us' hung in the air, but she held back for the sake of discretion.

She turned to Riggs who looked a little ruffled, as if he too had picked up on the innuendo. He took his turn to hold her hand and say good-bye. I took another step and met Rhonda's watchful eyes. "Nice meeting you, young man," she said shaking my hand in a pointedly business-like manner. "I hope we see more of you."

Me too, lady, I thought to myself.

Riggs and I walked out together, two cocks of the walk. Riggs seemed perfectly at home with it. He launched into a stream of advice and procedures for how I—or Leroy Street—should go about getting the Mustang released. I listened politely, anxious now to get away from him.

"Let me know if you have any problems. I'm sure I can help."

Climbing into the Lexus, I told him I would and I pulled the door closed, clipping off the end of his farewell.

I drove away thinking I had played it pretty well. I had set the trap and was poised for their next move. It was a fleeting sense of accomplishment but I did what I could to drag out the moment. The soft leather seats and the muted dashboard lighting and the inner hum of the engine, steady and unconcerned, added to my illusion of well-being.

Driving past the security guard at his post, I nodded purposefully, like I owned that car and the place it had come from. As I took it through the gears, the faint smell of leather seemed to give forth directly from the smooth purr of the engine. Along the edge of the golf course, on the unbroken stretch of the boulevard, I made a hundred in about ten seconds. Compared to this, my Mercedes belonged on the junk heap even before it got shot up. And Willie's Mustang was nothing more than a beat-up go-cart with horsy emblems.

Then I remembered why Willie's car was important. My daydreams faded as I considered how to talk him into letting me use it for bait. Like Connally and Luis, he wasn't going to like it—although for different reasons. I would have to win him over. Without support from Luis and Connally on this scheme, Willie Jr. was my only backup. That gave me pause.

I decided to go by my place on the way back to Willie's, pick up a few more clothes and a heavier coat, and snag my other gun from the top drawer. It was Beretta Model 90. It was smaller than the Glock, an eight-shot with a custom shoulder holster. It would fit snuggly under my black leather jacket. The nights were getting chilly, after all, and I was beginning to feel naked without it.

Chapter 28

By the time I rolled that Lexus onto the graveled driveway behind Willie's house, I was feeling the effects of my overnight in jail. The sight of Pimpy in the headlights perked me up. With his front paws hooked over the crosspiece of the sagging picket fence, he stood on his hind legs, his head cocked questioningly, his nose pinching the air for familiar scents. When I climbed out of the car, his ears flattened and perked and his head dipped from side to side and he did a little two-step along that fence looking for a way to get at me. The fluffy curve of his tail—long white and black tangles going to dread-locks—waved like a pompom. As I squeezed through the gate, he pawed my clean pant legs and growled willfully, letting me know he was ready for some quality time with his pet human. I sent him running after the mangled remains of a tennis shoe that he had apparently converted into a dog toy. He tracked it down and pranced back shaking it viciously, jerking and gnawing the last bits of imaginary fight out of the thing. Then he dropped it at my feet and looked up at me like we had an understanding. I don't know what it is about this dog that makes me feel like a nice guy.

A few of these romps, interspersed with my usual puppy-dog endearments, roused Willie from the house. He came out onto the small square of loose planking that serve as the front porch.

"Man, where you been?" he said, not asking to be answered. Pimpy brought the shoe to Willie. "Shit, man." He wrangled it from the dog's mouth and regarded it with mock distress. "This was a perfectly good

CrossFit yesterday." He held out the pulpy mass of torn leather and frayed string for display. Pimpy lunged at it, couldn't get a grip as Willie reacted. "You! Dog! Not your shoe." He raised it high above the dog's head, smiling as Pimpy's eyes followed his every move. "Fuck it", he said, then tossed it the length of the yard. "That dog's gonna be shittin' Reebok emblems tomorrow, ya know."

I gave that a laugh and Willie joined in with that low, slow chuckle.

"Yeah, he's some watchdog too," Willie added. "Doesn't even bark at the mailman."

"Yeah, but he sure knows how to keep your feet warm."

"Hogs the bed, if you ask me."

We watched the dog romp through the darkened yard, jaws and Reebok held high in triumph.

"So what up, bro? Word is, you got sprung by *Cap-tain* Connally *hisself*. We workin' for him now or what?"

He didn't like the prospect. "Duncan talked to you?"

"Told me to wait and see. Couldn't tell me nothin' about my car, neither. Connally spring that too?"

"Not exactly." I moved toward the door. "C'mon inside. We'll talk about it."

"*Talk* about it? Man, I don't like the sound of that. You didn't *wreck* it did ya?"

"No, no, the cops still have it. It's in the pound."

"The pound, huh. That where your *dog's* gonna be if you don't get me my car back."

I turned and gave him a scowl but he was grinning victoriously. "How'd you get here, anyway?"

"Check it out." I nodded toward the door as I made my way to the bathroom.

Before I came out, I heard Willie reenter the house moaning hyperboles about those bad-ass wheels. "We gonna *chop* that mothafucka inta somethin' with some *class*."

"Ah, no."

"It's a loaner, right? You lined it up for me till you get mine back."

"It's Tanya Gilmore's car. You remember her, right?"

"Yeah. Brent what's-his-name's outside squeeze. Oh, *I* see," he said, his features lighting up. "You steppin' in as the new boy *love* muscle. You workin' fast, Henry."

"Not quite. It's a token of her appreciation until I get *my* car back."

"What about *my* car, bro?"

I gave him a devilish grin. "Your car is part of my master plan, Willie."

"*Master plan!* Oh man, I seen your master plans before. No way, you puttin' *my* ride in the middle a' that. That car's a *classic*."

"It's a hand-me-down from Maxine."

"Jus' cuz she don' know the value of it. '75 Mustang *is* a classic. Will be, anyway."

"Then you'll be glad to know my plan involves keeping a close eye on it the whole time it's impounded."

"Why don't we jus' get it out of the pound? Keep a close eye on it *here*."

"Then my plan wouldn't work."

Willie sighed. "Okay. You better tell me 'bout this *master plan* of yours."

All he had was beer so we settled over two cold ones in his cramped living room. I filled him in on Tanya's dinner party while I slowly loosened my party attire, hoping to unwrap the layers of my playacting façade at the same time. He was somewhat taken aback, like everyone else, to hear that I had broken into Charmichael's house and found him dead, but his response stemmed from a different point of view.

"Man, I shoulda been there, keepin' a lookout. I thought we were in this *together*."

"Well, you're in on the next one. We're gonna stake out your car tomorrow night. Someone's going to move on it."

"*Move* on it? What the hell for?"

I told him about the backup disk that I had fabricated for the sake of the Coyne family's paranoia. "That's where I said I stashed it. In your glove box. My bet is someone will try to break in to get it."

"Break into the pound? That sounds crazy. What kinda security they got out there? Dogs?"

"I don't know. We'll have to check it out in the morning."

Willie mulled that over. "I don't know, man. Could be a long wait. I need my car."

"We'll give it one night. If it doesn't happen, we'll get the car out and plant the seed with Milo's people instead. Then we'll see who shows up to deal. That make you feel better?"

"Why tell Milo's people?"

"Because it could have been one of Milo's thugs that killed Charmichael. If nobody bites from the Coyne side, I'll give Milo a call, lay down a little blackmail."

"Man, you one cagey sum' bitch, bro'. I always thought so."

"That's what you like about me, isn't it?"

"Damn right," Willie said, newly animated. "You ace cool, man, and we a *team*. Where we gonna set that up?"

I had Willie's house in mind for that, but I didn't think now was the time to say so. And I was hoping for a better idea. Actually, I was hoping it would never happen. "We'll cross that bridge when we come to it," I said. "Right now, I gotta get some sleep."

The next morning, I was on the phone to Aurora PD by eight A.M. I told them I had paid the fines on my car but I had forgotten where to pick it up. The information officer was sleepy enough to give me an address for K & K Impound without any further whoop-jumping.

Willie came into the kitchen carrying a *Rocky Mountain News*. Wide-eyed and grinning excitedly, he set it down over my coffee cup and tapped on the bold-printed sub-heading along the bottom of the front page.

"We in the *news,* bro. We makin' *headlines.*"

It was the lead story in the local section. Not bad.

BINGO WORLD ROCKED BY MURDERS

The story took up two half-page columns and several smaller ones wrapped around a file photo of Frank Coyne. He was sitting on a stool, legs akimbo with his elbows resting on his thighs, in the middle of some kind of public gathering—had to be a bingo hall. Wearing the standard shit-eating grin and his thick-rimmed glasses, he stared directly into the camera. Two smaller photos next to his looked like mug shots of Mickey Gilmore and Brent Charmichael.

The first few paragraphs offered a minimalist account of the drive-by shooting of Mickey Gilmore and the discovery of Brent Charmichael's body—gleaned from an anonymous source, of course—all in the same day. They made the connection between them clear, lionizing both men with the label of 'high-ranking movers and shakers in the bingo industry'. A police spokesman was quoted as saying they had no suspects at this time.

Despite the prominence of his photo, Frank Coyne wasn't mentioned all that often, except to label him as the 'Bingo King' of the Rocky Mountain region and as the licensee of the club where Mickey was killed. Charmichael was identified as one of Milo Finnes' 'associates' and Milo's criminal record apparently made the best copy. With an air of underworld intrigue, the article chronicled his past run-ins with law enforcement in Washington state—investigations into 'financial irregularities' and potential violations of gaming regs and tax liabilities. As far as I could surmise, all of it resulted in fines and revoked licenses rather than incarceration. But the spin implied that he was driven out of state, which was accurate enough if he wanted to run bingo scams. The 'unnamed sources' that alleged competitive frictions and underhanded techniques Milo used to move in on Frank Coyne's terrain made me wonder who talked. As the founder of BACCO, whose charitable works were well known in the Denver metro area, Frank came off as a local hero threatened by the evil out-of-stater. The reporter made it sound like it was safe to assume Milo was somehow behind the killings, or anyway, everyone in 'the bingo world' assumed so.

Charmichael had a record too, according to the article, having been arrested in Commerce City in connection with a methamphetamine ring. That was news to me and it hooked up rather neatly with what Luis had told me about the Flood brothers. Alois Flood, recently released, had gone up for a meth related rap. And from what I had seen, his brother Enos fit the tweeker profile to a tee—gaunt and underweight, bad teeth, bad breath, and an inordinate penchant for the use of firearms in awkward social situations. It figured, if Charmichael was cozy with them, that he'd be using too, which might go a ways toward explaining why the tensions between him and Mickey escalated into violence. It gave me the idea that we (Luis, anyway) should be cross-checking our suspects—especially those in Milo's crowd—with DEA. And I thought to ask Willie who he knew in that particular lunatic fringe.

"Nah, man. That a *cracker* high. White-trash gangstas', brawlers, wife-beaters. Mostly we don't mix with them freaks. Them pipeheads are...different."

'We' who, I wondered, and what could be a meaningful distinction between two classes of strung-out low-life rock-smoking addicts prone to violent crime? I decided to let the implied color-of-skin discrimination slide. Probably, I shared that particular bias.

Over a quick breakfast and too much coffee, Willie made light of the newspaper account, tossing off derisive comments as if we were above all that. I was disinclined to join in, preoccupied with a tightness in my gut as I recalled how close I had been in place and time to the two dead men in the article. It moved me to action.

"Let's head out to the pound. See what we can do about your car."

The address I had been given was way the hell out on East Colfax where it turns into a country highway. Willie was all up for getting behind the wheel of the Lexus, an idea I resisted at first. But in the hope of cutting short his garrulous mood, I decided to let him drive. It didn't work.

"Man, this some *smooth* ride," Willie slurred, elongating the words. "I knew this ace brah, had *two* a' these rides. Lex-*eye*, he'd call them. 'Bring around the Lex-*eye*.'" Willie gave himself an appreciative chuckle. "Identical paint jobs, gold trim, spoke-mags, these lights, like *underneath*. *All* nigged up. Worked the 'hood 'round City Park. Used to, anyway, a few summers ago. Had a system worked out where he'd have his boys park the one Lex-eye on the curb making contact, and the other cruising slow, holding the stash, sorta' trollin' down along 26th across from the park. Like a moving target for the narcos and the neighborhood watch groups. Callin' his street dealers in on pagers when the coast was clear. Didn't have cells yet, or just one of those bricks with the antenna. He'd stroll from one car to the other, stockin' up the dealers or havin' his bitches run it down for him. He'd send these girls, these headhunters, into the park with a rock and a kit, meet up with those white boys from the burbs. Most times, for a bonus and a blast from the pipe, the bitches would do the guy in the bushes 'fore he got hisself off. Man, he had them lined up out there most nights, just crawlin' 'round the block."

When I didn't say anything, Willie asked, "Don't you want to know what happened?"

I turned from staring out the window, kind of wondering how he knew so many details. "What happened?"

"Man, you're in a mood, huh?"

I turned to look out the window again.

"Anyways, sometimes he'd sell too, I heard, just for the action. One of those times, he's strollin' between cars with a package and his wheelmen took off. Both Lex-eye, *and* the bitches, *and* the main stash. Meanwhile, the dude gets grabbed holding by a *convenient* patrol car. Word was one'a his homies narc'd him out from a payphone when the pager went off, left him hangin'."

"How long did they get away with that?"

Willie laid down his low chuckle. "One of those SUV's got all shot up the next day. Brand new, all shiny black. Looked like they took a AK to it. I heard the cops found the other one up in Park Hill. Confiscated the thing forever. The homies behind the wheel, well, they disappeared one way or the other."

"And the dealer?"

"He's doin' hard time, like, down at Big Max."

"Nice system."

"Had a few bugs."

We took the Tower Road exit off I-70, just past the turnoff to the airport. Unbroken plains of cut grass and dry dirt stretched out on either side of the highway, farm acreage quietly waiting for the next growing season or the next creeping subdivision. When we got near Colfax, two lanes widened into four and civilization crept back up along the roadsides like tarnished crystal formations along an asphalt gash. An aging Sinclair service station stood cattycorner from an equally old barn-shaped structure that probably was once a barn. It was home now to Joe Bob's Western Wear. One last development of '70s-style cracker-box homes ran parallel to Colfax, set back a ways from the avenue. We kept driving until the cracker-boxes fell away and the curbing disappeared and the places of business sat some distances apart with more barren fields in between.

We came upon an overgrown thicket of willows that obscured a line of wood-slat fencing that ran for several hundred feet. The tangled and dead branches gave way to a more carefully managed hedge above which I could see the irregular roofline of an aluminum-sided building running lengthwise along the highway, set back behind a row of parking spaces. It had been built in at least four sections, different structural designs apparently glommed on in stages to the half-barrel dome of the original garage. Mounted below the apex of one of its gabled arches, a sign read: K & K AUTOMOTIVE STORAGE & RECONDITIONING. I was impressed with the wording. It seemed to include some hint at what would happen if you left your car there too long.

"This must be the place," Willie said, sounding tentative, as we turned into the lot.

Another sign, hand-painted and mounted only a few feet off the ground, called the place K & K Paint & Body. In smaller lettering along the bottom, it said, IMPOUND LOT IN REAR, with an arrow pointing the way. More hand-painted signs hung along the roller-mounted chain-link gate at the back of the building. One located the office with an arrow pointing to a doorway. Another told us not to enter the yard without checking in. A third warned of attack dogs on the premises and advised against trespassing, as if one could get that far unawares.

I indicated to Willie to drive along the front of the building. Through some of the small windows we saw well-lit work areas. At the end of the lot, we drove off the pavement, following tire tracks that paralleled the wood-slat fencing. More private property and attack dog warning signs hung at intervals along its length. Rolling along, we could see through the gaps between slats. The rows of cars were laid out at least fifty deep, their chrome and glass trimmings glistening under the late morning sun. There were a lot of cars in there.

"Let's see who runs this dump," I said.

Willie chuckled. "Literally, right?"

We returned to park near the office and, following my gesture, Willie led the way toward the grease-smudged gray-metal door.

"It's your car," I said to him. "Just find out what they need to get it released. Don't make a big deal out of it."

"Yeah, whatever," he slurred, pushing open the door.

A white-man in black—faded black jeans and a faded black sleeveless T-shirt, steel-toed black boots and a three-inch wide black belt with a protruding silver buckle—stood leaning against a chest-high Formica counter. A heavy-duty chromed chain looped from the belt to a jagged lump of keys bulging through the pocket of his pants. Of course he had greasy black hair, slicked back in sculpted, flattened waves. He was a big man, maybe two inches shorter than Willie but much heavier, not as young and not in very good shape. With his elbows jutting backwards along the countertop as if to keep himself propped up, his rounded gut protruded a good deal further than his broad chest. His tanned upper arms were thick, shapeless cylinders, two slabs of ham with indistinct tattoos that could have been stamps of approval from the USFDA. He regarded us blankly from behind mirrored teardrop sunglasses—definitely a *Cool Hand Luke* daydream—chewing a good-sized wad with slow circular motions of his jaw.

Behind the counter, a middle-aged woman with the complexion of someone who had lived her twenties too hard and too fast leaned forward across the countertop, as if she had been whispering to the man in black before we came in. She was chewing too, accentuating the loose skin of her jowls. She sported a ratted crinkle of straw-colored hair that puffed up into the shape of a helmet. A swath of it swept across her forehead in a shelf, as if to give the effect of girlish bangs. It might have worked from a hundred yards out. She had nervous pale-blue eyes that flitted all around the room.

"Can I help you?" the woman squeaked, her eyes resting on me rather than Willie for all of two seconds before taking flight again. She raised an arm as if to salute then nudged at the edge of her Brillo pad bangs with an extended forefinger. The sheaf of hair moved up and back, all of a piece.

"Came here to see about my car," Willie said, affecting his deepest angry black man's drawl.

The woman's eyes bulged like she had been insulted. Keeping her eyes askance and her face forward, she reached under the counter and fumbled around noisily, then huffed and bent down to disappear behind the counter. I glanced toward the man in black. His face was expressionless behind the glasses. Other than the chewing cud, he didn't move a muscle. The woman popped up holding a clipboard with a tablet of forms on it. She slid it across the countertop towards Willie.

Willie looked at it like he couldn't read. "I jus' wanna see if it's here. Don't even know that for sure. Is this the Aurora city pound or what?"

The woman's eyes strained towards the man in black. He turned his head. "We contract with the city, yeah," he said, his low voice carrying an unfriendly nonchalance.

"You work here?" Willie countered, smiling with disbelief.

The man paused as if considering whether to take offense. "What kinda car is it?"

"A '75 Mustang. Dark green with gray base paint in spots. I been fixin' it up. It's a classic."

I buried a smile. The man's leathery face wrinkled up out of his permanent scowl. "A classic, huh?" He turned away to amble around the end of the counter. "We got about a half dozen a' those *classics* back in the yard." He unhooked another clipboard hanging from a post, propped up the mirrored glasses onto his forehead, and ran a dirty finger down the handwritten list. "Yeah, we got one a' those, came in over the weekend. You got registration?"

Willie fished out the card from his wallet. The man pretended to look it over carefully, his jaws working at the wad of gum. I was checking the window glass and the doorways for burglar alarm wiring. There was tape on the windows and a contact switch on the doorframe but nothing to indicate that the wiring went outside.

"You really have attack dogs in the yard?" I asked, jocularly.

"Only one way to find out," the man said, without looking up. "According to this," he tapped the clipboard, "we got a hold on it from Aurora PD. You'll hafta speak with them first."

"What's it gonna cost me?"

"Ninety-five for the tow job, twenty-five a day for storage. No credit cards, no personal checks. An' we don't give change. An' ya gotta pay the violations first, whatever they are."

Willie nodded and scowled for no apparent reason. I thought he was overacting a bit. "Ah'ight," he grumbled, "We'll be back tomorrow."

As we turned to leave the man spoke to our backs. "I unloaded that one myself," he said. "Had a couple a' bullet holes in it, looked like. I bet those violations'll run you pretty steep."

Turning to face him, Willie sighed, and hitched up his pants, stretching to the full height of his frame. "Don't you have to worry 'bout the vio-*la*-tions. You just take care of it till we get back."

The man half-smiled and started to chew again. His eyes, mocking yet cheerful, closed intentionally before he lowered the sunglasses over them. His expression reminded me of Frank Coyne's smile in an ugly-mug sort of way—cocky, gloating yet rigidly held in place, stuck on too long to be convincing.

I touched Willie's arm and pulled open the door and we filed out of there.

"Friendly folks," I said, walking back to the Lexus.

"Dude's got a nasty attitude, if you ask me."

"Not usually the cream of the crop running junkyards. Anyway, don't worry about it. I'm meeting Duncan for lunch. I'll put him on this first thing in the morning. And tonight, we'll come back out here and keep an eye on it ourselves."

"Damn right we'll keep an eye on it," Willie pouted. "Better not be any scratches on it, either," he added, as if he could have picked out new ones from the array of scrapes and dents—and bullet holes—that already covered it.

Chapter 29

Rollins, Jeffery, & Associates is one of a plethora of up-scale law firms that occupy the upper floors of 17th Street office buildings. They're a dime a dozen if you're a multi-millionaire doing any kind of business and there seem to be a lot of those around these days. From the looks of his new digs, Duncan was exchanging legal repartee with a good number of them. It wasn't a corner office, but one floor-to-ceiling glass wall offered a view of the Rocky Mountains that money just can't buy. On a clear day like today—and you can't buy those either—you can see from Pike's Peak to Long's Peak and every ragged crest in between. The solid cherry-wood desk was not quite long enough for shuffleboard but the high-backed leather chair, burnished lamb-skin with padded arms, could easily work as a kinky loveseat for the high-powered attorney and his spunky little executive sec, if Duncan was the type. Which he's not. He was settled into it all by himself when I walked in, leaning back, grinning dryly, feeding some smooth palaver to someone on speaker who apparently had a great deal of confidence in him.

He'd come a long ways since we shared a one-bedroom apartment in law school a thousand years ago, where he studied for the bar while I was off drinking in one. Looking back to those days and looking around Duncan's plush surroundings didn't do much for my esteem.

"How do you like it?" Duncan asked after disconnecting the caller, a mischievous grin creasing his clean-shaven, youthful features. He gripped the arms of his chair like he expected it to levitate. I wouldn't have been completely surprised.

"Looks like you're selling out for the top dollar these days," I said, trying to sound jovial about it.

"Yeah, I knew you'd say that. I'm up for associate partner too, if you remember what that means."

"It probably means you don't have time for my little problems."

"Aren't we feeling sorry for ourselves today."

"I get that way whenever I spend a night in jail. C'mon. Let's get out of here. Go someplace where talk is cheap. I can't afford to sneeze in here."

I walked over to the window while Duncan went for his coat. He came up behind me and put an arm around my shoulders. "All of this could be yours, my son," he intoned dramatically, gesturing with a sweep of his arm, "if only you'd bow down and renounce your errant ways."

"At the risk of abandoning the last of my holier-than-thou attitude, I'm tempted to take you up on it."

"I don't think there's any real danger of that," he said, chuckling roguishly. "C'mon, I'll take you to lunch."

"No way. I'm buying."

As we made our way through the polished marble corridors, people nodded to Duncan, smiling well-paid smiles. The hustle and bustle was muted, almost relaxed. Everyone was so well dressed and perfectly groomed, I couldn't tell the hired help from the bigwigs, all of them seemingly content with their station. Shiny happy people, as the song goes. I couldn't picture any of them spending a night in jail wondering if their life choices and professional goals were worth reconsidering. Just then, for obviously different reasons, it didn't seem like much of a question to me either.

On the ride down to the parking garage, we continued to banter about where to go to lunch. Duncan acquiesced when I ushered him up to the passenger side of the Lexus LS.

"Well, well. I see you've already sold your soul to a higher bidder."

"It's not really me, is it?" I said, gloating momentarily.

"You mean, it's not really *yours*. Not unless you've taken the blood oath with your bingo brotherhood. You haven't, have you?"

"Jesus, Duncan, how long have you known me?"

"Long enough to feel your frustrations, Henry. And long enough to know your open-mindedness is often accompanied by a certain… gullibility."

To counter his point, I started the car and revved the engine aggressively. The smooth muted hum didn't really create the effect I was looking for. "Couldn't we call it romanticism?" I said.

"When there's a woman involved."

I laughed that off and preoccupied myself with maneuvering out of the garage.

"*Is* there a woman involved?"

"Is that what Willie said?"

"Willie," Duncan huffed, shaking his head. "He doesn't have the story straight, whatever it is. First he told me you were working for Luis Sanchez—you *and* him. Then he said you were working for Frank Coyne. Then he said, not *for* him, exactly, but more like *with* him. When I called him on that, he obfuscated by saying it was all hush-hush, need-to-know, undercover. I gather the bingo crowd has attained nuclear capabilities and the CIA brought you two in to save the world."

"Pretty close."

"Well, that's not what Luis said."

I looked at him. "You talked to Luis?"

Duncan nodded. "He told me to talk to you before I said or did anything. So here I am."

"I'll tell you over lunch."

I took him to a Fifties-era fast food walk-up called Jay-Jay's, just off Five Points. The older black couple who own the place, and their crew, think 'fast' means ten to fifteen minutes. They cook burgers to order on a flattop grill and make French fries from raw potatoes. Lunch for two cost me fifteen bucks. We sat outside at a weather-beaten picnic table, every square inch of its wooden surface carved with gang signs, lover's initials, or grade school graffiti. It was situated on a cement slab about ten feet from the fairly steady through-traffic on Downing Street.

Duncan admitted the burgers were good. "I can't say much for the atmosphere." He eyed the passing cars.

"With a budget like mine, *al fresco* takes on a whole new meaning."

A few bites in, Duncan started prodding. "So about this bingo thing, Henry. Frankly, I don't see it as quite your style."

"Why not?"

"Too simple for one thing. You're nothing if not complicated." He smiled before taking another bite, then spoke around a mouthful of food. "Luis wouldn't tell me much, but I can't believe it's busting the scam on these non-profits. That's the secretary of state's turf, right?"

"But they aren't doing it. You know how much money's involved?"

"I got an idea, matter of fact. I worked on a case with some Korean immigrants who had a couple halls in Northglenn. The family patriarch wanted to set up a non-profit trust for his grandchildren—through a legal assistance grant, of all things—in order to avoid estate taxes. They were raking it in under the table and couldn't figure out how to launder it into a bank account."

"Did you set it up for him?"

Duncan shook his head. "We declined when we ran into trouble communicating the concept of paying taxes—like income tax—*before* he died. That sort of thing."

"A cultural gap, maybe."

"Maybe. So Luis hired you on a contract basis?"

"Something like that. He's paying me through the DA's office but I'm supposed to stay clear of Barnes."

"Given your recent 'successes' with him, I'm not surprised. How did Connally get involved?"

"A couple of principles of the investigation killed each other, more or less. It made the local section this morning. Connally gets involved when they make the news."

"Yeah, I saw that. Looked for your name, glad I didn't see it. But after yesterday, I figured you were in the middle of it. Dead guys make it more interesting for you, huh?"

"Funny."

"You looking at the cops too?"

"Why do you say that?"

Duncan shrugged. "It's that kind of thing. Off-duty cops help out around those clubs. Or after retirement they do security 'consulting', so to say. That's part of the reason regulation is so tricky. Lot of investigators turning a blind eye to the outside interests of their brothers in blue."

I concentrated on my burger.

"That must be awkward for you," he said, fishing for my feelings.

When I still didn't comment, Duncan took the hint.

"So, how'd you end up in jail in Aurora? They think you killed those guys?"

"I was there when Mickey Gilmore got shot. He was one of our principal targets."

"Out at that new shopping center in Parker?"

I nodded. "Bingo Palace. I chased out after one of the shooter's cars."

"Guns blazing? High-speed chase? That sort of thing, right?"

"You heard about it then."

"I got that much from Harris yesterday. I'd say that's more your style," he said, smiling.

"They shot the hell out of my Mercedes."

"Put it out of its misery, if you ask me."

"Easy for you to say."

"So that's how you got the Lexus, then."

"It belongs to Mickey Gilmore's widow. She loaned it to me—out of gratitude, I guess. She also happens to be Frank Coyne's sister."

"The bingo king."

"You've heard of him?"

"It's what they called him in the article. He's made the news before though. I remember something around the last election. Basically bought Herrera's office for her, didn't he? You investigating that?"

"Strictly bingo," I said, not surprised that Duncan was up on it. "He runs a dozen or so halls around the city, and a supply house, and a few dummy corporations that they use to launder their take. He's our principle target."

"So what about these jokers that shot up your car? The cops find them?"

"Turned out they weren't the killers, but they *are* involved in a rival bingo operation. Guy named Milo Finnes heads it. He was in the article too."

Duncan nodded.

"The second victim was one of his lieutenants. Could be some of Coyne's people were involved in that one."

"And you're undercover in the midst of them?"

"Yeah, more or less. I'm supposed to be focusing on the Coyne family, but, as you say, murder makes it more…interesting."

"What's Willie Jr. have to do with it? You're not putting him in the line of fire, are you?"

"Nothing like that. He wanted to help out," I said, stretching the truth. "Said he was bored stiff working for you. I just dropped him off actually."

"He called in sick today," he said, bouncing his eyebrows. "But that's okay, as long as he doesn't go off the deep end."

"He won't go far from his steady paycheck. There's no money to speak of for him. He just wants a change of pace, you know? We can't all be happy sitting behind a desk juggling other people's money."

He looked at me with an exaggerated frown, but his eyes sparkled with humor. "Should I start taking that personally?"

"Oh, hell no," I said, guiltily. "Everyone has to follow their own muse. Mine just happens to be out on the street most of the time. Willie's too, maybe."

"Yeah, maybe so."

I decided I had better get to the point. "I was thinking you might want to get out of the office yourself for a bit. It would help Willie out, actually, or maybe it's more accurate to say it would help me out."

"You mean this thing about his car? He whined about it to me yesterday."

"The cops confiscated it when they picked me up. This guy Harris has it out for me."

"Probably doesn't like those rolling shootouts in his jurisdiction."

"Right?" We shared an eye-rolling grin. "They haven't pressed charges, but I'm in no position to ask for favors."

"So you want me to go in as your lawyer…"

"Willie's lawyer," I corrected.

"As Willie's lawyer and try to get the car released?"

"That's it. But not until tomorrow."

He gave me a puzzled look. "Why wait?"

"It fits in with something I'm working on. You don't want to know about it."

He laughed at that. "All right, I'll look into it. Maybe I'll go out there with you to pick it up. Get out of the office, as you say. Prowl the streets with you and Willie."

"Like the good old days," I said, waggishly. "Remember that little excursion the three of us took up to Central City? Shook down that casino that Sheriff Quigley had a piece of?"

"Shook down? More like breaking and entering and inciting to riot." He scowled at me, but his lips formed into a restrained grin. "Of course I remember it. You had me flirting with accessory to a felony. Damn lucky we got away with that."

I did what I could to laugh that off. "This is nothing like that," I assured him. "No fast cars, no confrontations, all perfectly legal. You can see to it yourself."

He gave me an appraising look. "I never know with you on board."

"C'mon, Duncan. Broad daylight. You can drive, for Christ's sake. Should be safe enough, even for you."

I meant it when I said it. And if everything went as planned, it would have been true.

Chapter 30

After dropping Duncan off, I went by my apartment for a change of clothes, something appropriate to mourn in. I thought about getting a second gun for Willie, for tonight's little escapade, but I decided against it. He'd probably shoot that junkyard jockey on sight. Smiling to myself, I called his house to check the machine for messages. Willie picked up the phone on the second ring. When I told him Duncan was on for tomorrow, he was pleased. He told me Claire had called. Also, Frank Coyne was looking for me and had left information about the where and when of the memorial service. He wanted to be sure I was going to be there. Tanya had called too, or someone from her household, and left the same message.

I called Claire. When she answered, her voice was subdued.

"How are you doing? Not so well, huh?"

"No, not so well. My parents are here. We just got in this morning. We're all moping around, getting on each other's nerves." She gave that a faint laugh. I thought it was a good sign. "Are you coming to the service?"

"Yes, of course."

"That's good. I want to see you."

I was suddenly aware of my heartbeat and an urge to say something stupid, but she continued before I could get my foot anywhere near my mouth.

"I want to talk to you about…this. Are you still trying to find out who did it?"

"Yes, I am. Can you help?"

"I don't know. What do you mean?"

I was going too fast. If she knew something about Mickey, something incriminating, the day of his funeral was not the time to press. I had mixed feelings about involving her anyway, but I figured she had more helpful info than she knew. And if she did open up, I thought she'd be straight with me. "I just wondered what you wanted to talk about," I said.

"It's nothing, really. I just want to know I've done everything I can."

"Yeah, sure. We can talk later."

We sat there on the phone.

"I'm sorry, Henry," she said, finally. "It's just that this is all too hard to believe."

"I understand. I mean, I understand what it means to lose someone." My words sounded trite. I wanted to clarify but I held back.

"There was this man," Claire said, in an almost lofty tone. "Mickey talked about him. His name was Spence. He had initials for his first name. You know, something like B.J. or R.J. or R.D. I can't remember. I don't know who he is. I mean, I never met him."

An unmistakable stress vibrated in her voice. Shifting the phone to my other ear, I went to my desk/kitchen table to write down the name. "Could he be involved?"

"He had something to do with Brent Charmichael. I think he was Brent's new partner. Or was going to be."

"Mickey said this?"

"Not exactly. He talked about him, just once, really. It was after a big blowup he had with Frank. He said he couldn't handle working with him anymore. It wasn't the first time I heard that, but this was different. This time I think he was going to do it."

"Do what?"

"Go out on his own. He said he'd had it with the whole family. Frank and Tanya, old man Willard. He said he was going to get a divorce. I mean, he said it like he meant it. He told me he'd disown me if I married Dennis." She let out a nervous chuckle that recoiled into a stifled moan. Then she said, "I mean in a joking way, you know? Along the lines of brotherly advice, I guess. I told him not to worry about *that*."

I tried out a mild clarification. "You think Mickey was planning to take up with Brent again?"

"Yes," she said, as if startled by the accuracy of my guess. "Or anyway, he said he wanted to until this came up—I mean, Brent's involvement with this guy Spence. I asked him who Spence was and he said, 'Brent's new boyfriend. New kid on the block.'"

"Was Brent gay?" I asked, just to hear her reaction.

She laughed it off, giving nothing away. "'Fraid not. It's just the way Mickey put it. Anyway, I didn't know what he was getting at. I think we got interrupted. I was going to ask him about it, but, well, I never did."

"You think Frank or Tanya knew about this? Knew Spence?"

She was slow to respond. "Why does that matter?"

I didn't know what to say. "I was just thinking…"

"…That Frank and Tanya would try to squeeze out their competition?" she said in a rush. "'Cause that's what I was thinking, Henry. And if that competition was Brent, or Brent and Spence, they might've retaliated, right? And maybe Mickey got caught in the middle of that."

She stopped as suddenly as she had started and then, in a cooler tone, she said, "But I didn't know if I should tell it to *you* that way."

I didn't say anything for fifteen seconds and that's all that Claire could stand.

"So whose side *are* you on, Henry?"

"My loyalties don't cover murder. I told you I wanted to find Mickey's killers and I do."

"And what if it *is* Frank? What if he had it *done*?"

"With your help, maybe we can bring him down. Is that what you want?"

"Yes," she said, without hesitation. "It is."

We shared a silence as if to mark what had been said. I heard Claire take a long drag from a cigarette.

"So they know about this Spence guy? Frank and Tanya, I mean?"

"I never heard anything from them, but I got the impression from Mickey that they knew of him. He said Frank wouldn't stand still for that kind of shit from Brent."

"Meaning his involvement with Spence?"

"I guess."

"What else could it mean?"

There was a pause before she answered. "I don't know. Drugs, maybe. Brent's had a problem with drugs. That's why we were… I mean that's *one* reason why he was on the outs with us…with *them* years ago. Mickey called him a doper. I don't know if he meant *still*, or back then, or what."

I heard Shanie's voice in the background. "Mommy?"

"Yes, honey, I'm almost ready. Where's Gram?"

Shanie went into an indecipherable, high-pitched beckoning for her grandmother and Claire's voice moved away from the phone. It gave me a moment to ponder the 'us/them' slip. She broke it off with Brent because of his habit? And/or his drug dealings were an added liability to the family enterprises? Or an added criminal enterprise they were at odds with? Or *weren't* at odds with, except for Mickey? I really, *really* wanted to ask her some questions. Like, maybe, under oath. Would not be good for our relationship.

When Claire came back, her tone was hurried and louder.

"I have to go, Henry. We're late. Can we talk after the service?"

"That would be fine," I said, exercising restraint. Then another part of me stuck my neck out and worked my lips. "I'd like to spend some time with you. I mean, when that's appropriate."

"Okay, Henry," Claire said, in the same hurried voice, as if she hadn't gotten my drift. "I'll look for you there. I'll see you."

I put down the phone and sat picturing Claire at the memorial service surrounded by the extended family, the bingo circle. I imagined them going through the motions, all dressed in black, scrambling at details, taking their places, hurrying in order to stand around together and look like they feel bad at the appointed time. Most of them probably pondering how to avoid a similar fate, or calculating how to take advantage of Mickey's. It was sad and absurd. And it was a depressingly sensitive arena for me to be mucking around in, looking for dope on the recently deceased even before he was underground. It made me feel like slag on the grounds of the family picnic. The last thing I wanted to do was go to the funeral and scour those phony faces for hidden motives and traces of guilt. I decided to reach out to Luis for moral support. If you could call it that.

I entered my number in his pager, then went to get dressed. He called back within fifteen minutes.

"I told you after six," he said, crossly. "And call me at home."

"It can't wait. I got a lead you're gonna want to track down."

"Uh-huh."

Not going as I had hoped. "Listen, Luis, I'm looking for some help here. Are you backing me up or what?"

"Yeah, yeah, I'm trying but I got other things to do. Why can't you stick to the procedures we established?"

"You said yourself we're running out of time. How much you think we'll get done before my cover is blown if I have to wait a day to call you?"

"Quit chewing on me, will ya? I don't have time for this either."

"Tell me again why I'm doing this," I said, not bothering to conceal my anger.

"Because you wanted to?" Luis said, without missing a beat.

I took a breath and waited for the tightening in my chest to dissipate.

"So what do you have?" Luis asked, like nothing had been said.

"I have a name," I said, picking up my notes. "Somebody who had taken up with Charmichael recently, somebody Mickey Gilmore didn't like. The name is Spence. B.J. Spence or R.J. Spence, some initials for a first name that she wasn't sure about."

"She who?"

I could have kicked myself. "Ah, Mickey's sister. She works the bingo halls—just the day-to-day stuff—has been for a while. She said Mickey was upset about this Spence person taking up with Charmichael."

"Taking up how?"

"Obviously, bingo," I said, realizing as I spoke that it wasn't so obvious. "They were going out on their own. It would have been a threat to the Coyne operation. Milo too, for that matter. I think Mickey found out about it first. It may have been the catalyst for him setting the fire. I want… that is, I was hoping you could run the name through records, and maybe NCIC. See if he's got a sheet. Or DEA. There's a drug connection running through this crowd that I think we should delve into. Did you see the article this morning in the *Rocky*?"

"You bet I saw it. Barnes did too. He called me in on the mat this morning. Asked me if I wasn't making things worse."

"So that's what's bothering you."

"What's bothering me is that you can't stick to procedures. What you've done so far is enough to get me busted down if Barnes finds out. And he's gonna find out. I'm supposed to be reporting everything to him."

"Does he know I'm working for you?"

"And for *him*, Henry. And if he did know it, that article would be the end of it."

So I was still on the case. I felt surprisingly buoyed by the ass-backward validation. I decided to give up on the idea of moral support and get down to business.

"The article mentioned that Charmichael had been arrested in connection with a meth operation a few years back. That's the second reference to meth among the… rather *lower* lowlifes in this crowd." When Luis didn't say anything, I thought to refresh his memory. "The one Flood brother, Alois, or whatever. He was doing time for a meth bust, right? Maybe that's how they got the money to pay for Cator and Holmes to represent him."

"From where, exactly?"

"From a meth operation, Luis. You've heard about the war on drugs?"

"Fuck off, Henry."

"Well, Jesus, Luis, you waitin' for approval from the Governor? This is a good lead. Rumors from my end say Brent Charmichael was a long-term user. That means he was connected, right? We need to look into it."

Luis sighed. "This Spence person is involved in dealing drugs?"

"That's what it looks like," I said, realizing it was a stretch. "I think it's worth running his name. Maybe that was the connection to Charmichael that Mickey didn't like. Could be Milo was in on it too. Hell, I'd crosscheck the whole crowd if I were you."

"Yeah, maybe if I had an *assistant*, I'd have him do that," he said, referring to my old job. "I don't have all the time in the world, you know."

Luis was a rock, a man who could stay grounded in the midst of all kinds of pressures. I relied upon him for it. If it was getting to him, Barnes must have worked him over pretty hard.

"I know you've got other things at stake, Luis. I know you stuck your neck out even giving me this job. But still…you knew what you were getting when you did it, right?"

"Yeah, well…"

"The way I see it is we go forward full bore. I'm not doin' this to spruce up my résumé."

Luis chuckled at that, but without much heart.

"It's your call, Luis. What do you want to do?"

He sighed again. "I'll look into it, see what I can find. But I'm not gonna spend the day on it." He paused for a reaction. I managed not to give him one. "What're you doing in the mean time?"

"I'm going to the funeral—Mickey Gilmore's. It's not all fun and games out here either." He huffed at that. "I'll call you tonight after six. According to our established procedures. That sound all right?"

"You do that, Henry," Luis said in a dismissive tone. "But, listen. From here on out, you gotta stay low, stay in the background, you understand? I don't know if I can undo what's been done already. Anything else happens, it's all gonna be comin' back on me."

It was true. And I felt badly about it. But there it was.

Chapter 31

The beige exterior walls and unadorned front entrance—and the lack of a steeple or cross—of the Hilltop Congregational Chapel gave it the look of a low-rent mausoleum, or maybe a 70's era local government building. Architecturally speaking, it didn't want to talk about what it was up to. Despite this, the interior was surprisingly warm. Earthy vermilion carpet rolled down the center aisle as if demarcating the straight and narrow road to salvation. At its end, above the sanctuary, the ceiling vaulted dramatically, something of a 'mystery'—structurally anyway—given I didn't see it from outside. An isosceles triangle of slivered mosaic glass steepled upward and glowed warmly in crimson and saffron hues; a marvel of creative backlighting, modernistic yet ethereal, and pointedly non-denominational. For me, it evoked something more like the Emerald Palace from *The Wizard of Oz* than the stairway to heaven.

The mourners sat shoulder-to-shoulder, filling the wooden pews, and a few men lined the side aisles. Standing room only, on a Monday afternoon. Mickey would be proud. Organ music, heavy laden—possibly a Bach fugue knock-off—overflowed from above and poured down on us like seeping hypnotic gas. Nobody was crying yet, as far as I could tell, but the music made you want to.

A group of shirt-sleeved young professionals, looking bored and not trying to hide it, took up the standing room along the back aisle. I figured them for newshounds without their gear. Probably the camera crews weren't allowed. Wanting to disassociate myself from them, I made my way to the front of the line along the side wall. From there, I could see Claire with Shanie in the front row, sitting next to an older couple that I took to be her—and Mickey's—parents. The Coyne family occupied the pew just behind them, everyone from the dinner the night before except Chuck Burrows—but including Rhonda Schomberg, sitting at Tanya's side.

The trickle of attendees coming in dwindled to nothing, yet the organ droned on, the congregation staring blankly at the massive display of tinted flowers arranged where an altar would have been if this was any kind of actual church. Finally, the music built toward a high-range crescendo, then dropped off abruptly and unresolved—like an intro to the End of Days. People stirred at the shock of it, heads coming to, eyes scanning the room for signs of the Rapture. No such luck.

A distinguished-looking gent with a color-coordinated satin shawl draped over a worsted suit rose up from behind the flowers and mounted the pulpit with two fearless steps, then started in on why we were all gathered here. He affected a trace of Southern accent, which didn't do much for his credibility, and it went downhill from there.

He offered the usual prattle: to know him was to know a *good* man…always upbeat…willing to give a helping hand….generous to a fault… To hear him say it, Mickey was a modern-day Martin Luther, a martyred layman who made the ultimate sacrifice on the front lines of the mission, spreading the Word through the simple joy of family entertainment in that pagan and hard-scrabble land of bingo. It was some pretty solid balderdash up until the hitch in his voice when he stumbled over Mickey's name: "Mick…*Michael* Lewis Gilmore…"

Then he invited anyone amongst us to come forward with our own testimonials. I put some thought into what I might say, but it was a tough room for that. Several less inhibited acquaintances took their turns, offering up appropriately laudatory pictures. Some of it, I have to say, was spoken from the heart. But, by my watch, it was too much, too late.

When it seemed like everyone had said their piece and most of the eyes of the assembly had had a chance to dry, Frank made his move. He mounted the pulpit steps in one long stride and scanned the crowd unabashedly, as if counting heads from his Bingo Palace clientele. He wore a black tuxedo coat with satin lapels that seemed rather flossy for the occasion, but the bolo tie let us know he was just regular folk. Leaning over the edge of the pulpit, his bulging eyes glistened behind the thick-lenses and the endcaps of his tie swung like weight-chains on a coo-coo clock. The wide, fleshy lips formed into a frown of disapprobation, as if he didn't like the shabby state of grace he saw reflected in the faces looking up to him.

He launched into a history of his longstanding friendship with Mickey, going back to before they became brothers-in-law. The trademark insipid grin clawed its way across his face as he offered up touching anecdotes from the good old days when they had started Five Aces Bingo. He spoke of the hard times they endured, the challenges they had faced together, and the prosperity that followed as just reward for all the sacrifices they had made.

Frank had missed his calling. He spun this like a seasoned politician with one eye on the office vacated by the dead man. Between properly restrained sporadic chuckles, the adoring masses started dabbing anew with their hankies. Mickey Gilmore was a good human being, Frank told us, and we could all take comfort in the fact that he was now in a better place. It was, I allowed, a better place than the County lockup he would be occupying if he had stayed with us. There was, of course, no mention of his felonious arson at Broadway Bingo, though I had the feeling Frank would have liked to bring it up—a warning to those perfidious few who might be inclined to wander from the true path of Coyne Family bingo. Nor was there any mention of the murder of Harvey Cline in 1993, of course, though I assumed that was one of the 'challenges' that he and Mickey had faced together.

In spite of these salient omissions, the fact of the man's death was not lost on me. You can't be human and sit through a funeral without reflecting on mortality. It may be the only time we spend pondering the inevitability of death. Death and taxes, so they say, and in this crowd, taxes are a matter of serious debate. But death, when it came to one of their own, had to make even the numbest of them wonder what they were doing with their lives. That's how it worked on me, anyway.

When Frank stepped down, the surrogate priest regained the pulpit and joined us all in a moment of silent prayer. It was, I thought, a rather short moment, followed by an invitation for one and all to join the family in the adjacent banquet room for refreshments.

"Just through these doors…"

Taking their cue, the press contingency moved first, hustling towards the front, only to be stifled by a phalanx of usher/body guard types. Most of the family sidled behind them, disappearing through double doors. The rest of the congregation shuffled awkwardly, some pausing to greet each other with handshakes or hugs. I joined the throng in mid-flow, imagining the family members lined up at the other end, dutifully accepting condolences from each and every mourner. I pictured Frank with his counterfeit grin held barely in reserve, shaking hands and mumbling commiseration. And Tanya glibly poised behind that painted face, greeting the mourners as if in a reception line at one of her society gigs. And then I thought of Claire.

I remembered her saying she had never lost anyone close to her, that her ex, Eddie Lyons, getting wounded had brought that home to her. But this was something else again. Mickey was blood, her only sibling. A part of her had died with him. Her life had changed irrevocably, not dissimilar from how mine had changed when my father died. A surprising surge of emotions welled up in me. I felt compelled to comfort her, to share with her the truth of that experience, how it becomes a part of life, not just bearable but enriching, clarifying, true. I felt like I could touch her with it, help her get through. Then I realized I couldn't.

Passing judgment on the insincerity of others has a way of splashing back in your face. In Claire's life, I was an illusion, a web of fabrications, a spy in the house of the bereaved. I realized this with a sense of awakened conscience and it swept over me, rather unexpectedly, like a wave of the wand of forgiveness, relieving me from some unconscious burden, absolving me from my falsehood. Absolving me because I knew I would have to trust her. I would have to tell her the truth.

With a fuzzy resolve forming in my chest, I joined the last of the dwindling crowd as they funneled through the doors. I felt like I was using them for cover. I felt like Judas, silver coins in the dirt, crawling back for yet one more chance. I felt like I had to get the hell out of that church.

By the time I made it through the doorway, the reception line, if there ever was one, had dispersed. The family members were mixing with the dark-suited crowd overfilling the low-ceilinged room. The hubbub of small talk was muted and restrained but it had the feel of a cocktail party not quite off the ground, threatening to bubble over once everyone got into their champagne.

There was no sign of Claire. I decided to make my way out of there to find her.

A lay-minister type—not the one from the pulpit—was guiding the media people toward the daylight at the far end of the room. Touching elbows and nodding his head, he backed up his directions with the body language of two young bouncer-types standing at his elbows. I figured them for rookie cops, doing a gig for their newfound bingo friends. Shifting their weight from side to side, they nudged shoulders and jutted their chins, slowly herding the reporters out the open doors. As I approached trying to get past them, a hard hand landed on my shoulder. I turned to find Frank Coyne's wall-eyed stare taking me in from inches away.

"Glad you could make it," he said, somewhat warily.

Like the perfect fit of hand to glove, I slipped back into my role. "Well, I wanted to pay my respects," I said, "but I don't much like these sorts of gatherings."

Frank nodded with an affirming frown, as if I was the one who needed support. "I know what you mean, believe me." His eyes danced over the crowd. I thought to comment on his soliloquy but couldn't bring myself to it. I stood there avoiding his eyes.

"I need a smoke," Frank said, craning his neck toward the doors. "And we need to talk."

Guiding me toward the doorway, he came to a stop just behind the two bouncers who now had the knot of media hounds standing outside on the veranda. One of them turned slightly and he and Frank exchanged a knowing nod as we stepped past them.

"These fucking reporters," Frank said, offering me a cigarette. We stood and smoked and watched the camera crews setting up their equipment, positioning for an exit by newsworthy interviewees. Frank spoke close to my ear. There was no mistaking his train of thought. "Have any luck getting that car out?"

"Not yet," I said. "We checked into it, but it sounds like we're gonna need a lawyer after all. Willie's gonna talk to his uncle this afternoon."

He watched me intently. "Ya know, the more I thought about it, the more I want to see what's on that disk. I mean, Tanya's concerns aside, I think it *is* in our best interest to put the screws to Milo if we can. Know what I mean?"

He was nodding affirmation before I had a chance to.

"Yeah, I think I do."

"So it's important to keep *your* name out of it. Like you said, right? Think you can make that clear to your friend? What's his name? Willie something?"

"Willie Randolph. Yeah, he definitely sees it that way too. He's got no love for the cops."

He paused briefly as if weighing my words. I thought I might have overdone it.

"If it doesn't work out, call me. We'll get Riggs on it tomorrow. I think Chuck can grease the wheels a bit too." He gave me a wink and a nod and one side of his mouth hitched up into that unctuous grin.

I dropped my eyes to his chest, to the strands of his bolo tie, and briefly considered grabbing hold of the ends and garroting him. The impulse subsided. "Okay," I managed, "I'll do that."

Partly to make conversation, and because I wanted to know, I asked him if he knew where Claire was. Immediately, I had a sense that I had given something away.

Frank's grin turned mischievous. "You missed her, Henry. She didn't want to stay for all this. Can't say I blame her," he added, but it was obvious he didn't mean it. His eyes gleamed with interest and recognition.

"Maybe she just wants to be alone."

"Yeah, that's what she said," he mumbled, plainly distracted now. "She declined to have dinner with us tonight."

"Well, maybe I'll give her a call at home."

He didn't hear me. A distinguished-looking older couple approached, the woman repeating Frank's name several times in a hushed tone. He turned and greeted them like old friends at a class reunion. The woman was clearly pleased by his attention.

I turned away, planning my escape when I heard my name, a woman's voice, authoritative yet almost cheerful. I turned to see Rhonda Schomberg breaking from the pack.

As she shouldered her way through the knot of people in the doorway, she moved in a boyish fashion, agile and surefooted. She wore a two-piece charcoal business suit that left everything to the imagination except nicely shaped legs, smoothly encased in net stockings. Her handsome features held a friendly, practiced smile spoiled somewhat by the frameless bifocals perched on her nose. Only when she was quite close did she let the glasses drop to the length of the gold chain. She extended her hand to be shaken. The gesture struck me as inappropriate, but I took the hand—warm and bony—and noted the grip was unexpectedly firm.

"I was hoping I'd run into you."

"Actually, I was just leaving," I said, trying not to sound rude, but hoping she'd take the hint.

"I can understand that. I mean, you want to pay your respects but... well, these things can get a little somber." Tilting her head, she arched her eyebrows, looking up at me with wily smiling eyes. "I'm staying for Tanya's sake. She needs all the support she can get, don't you think?" Clearly a rhetorical question, but it kept me there showing *my* support. "I'm sure it's more awkward for you. You don't know the family that well, do you?" Her smile broadened, letting me know she meant no offense.

"No, not really. I've only been working with Frank for a few months. It feels longer than that, with all that's happened."

"Yes, I'm sure. It has been a trying time, hasn't it? Especially for the family. First it was the police, then the press, now this." She shook her head pityingly but continued with the smile. It was a better-looking smile than the Coyne family trademark but it wore thin almost as quickly. "They haven't had any time to themselves, really, to absorb it. Don't you think?"

I smiled back and nodded. I was beginning to think, as perhaps I was meant to, that she needed a friend—or anyway, a vote. Rhonda Schomberg, political prodigy, career lobbyist, one of the best known names in the local inner circles, seeking me out to share her thoughts. I felt important just standing there.

"Anyway, we're hoping all this blows over pretty soon. That would be the best thing."

"Yes, it would," I said, giving her a perfunctory nod that I hoped she would read as perfunctory. It didn't faze her.

"I'm so glad you see it that way. I was afraid…well, never mind, really. It was just a thought." She reached out and squeezed my forearm and then let go of it, as if in a departing gesture, but she continued to stand there beaming at me.

I had little choice: "What was it you were thinking?"

"Well, you know how these things can sound when a person doesn't know the facts. The news bites, the rumors, the insinuations. God knows these people love to gossip. I just hope it doesn't go too far. Tanya's having a difficult enough time with it. Frank too, for that matter. They were very close."

The official family spin. I went along. "They've been together for a long time."

"Yes, and they're private people. I mean, they're not public figures in any real sense of the word. It's so hard to keep one's matters private when everything is sensationalized like this. The press, you know, can be *so* intrusive."

"Not enough real news to go around, I guess."

"That's just what I think. I was afraid you might not understand." She smiled reassuringly. "I mean, you've been so *zealous* about getting to the bottom of this." Her eyes shone with intensity.

"Well, I…"

"Oh, I know Frank and Tanya appreciate it. But I just wouldn't want their private matters to get laundered in public. I mean, we all have our own lives to live. It's so hard when it gets put under a microscope. So distorted."

"I understand," I said, and finally I knew what she was getting at. "It's nobody's business."

It wasn't enough. "They *trust* you, you know. Very much so. And they're not people who trust easily."

"Well, I appreciate that. And you can rest assured I respect their trust." It was surprisingly difficult to say. It was my big lie, succinct and clearly stated, and the exact opposite of what I had felt ten minutes earlier. I looked at Rhonda to see if she sensed my ambivalence, wondering if her intention had been to suss it out.

There was no sign of such clairvoyance. Just the well-polished mask of the perennial vote-getter called upon to express more cheer than any normal person could possibly be expected to believe. Her smiling lips folded inward in an expression of heartfelt confidence. She grasped my arm again. "I knew you would understand. You're a sensitive man. I could tell that right away."

"Yes, well…thanks."

"Are you joining us for dinner tonight?"

"No. That is, I thought I would look in on Claire. See how she was doing."

She feigned an expression of mild surprise. It was clear that she found this news encouraging.

"She's taking it badly, isn't she?" The sad look formed around her eyes again, around the sympathetic smile. "Such bad timing really, on top of everything else."

"Bad timing?" I said, before I could stop myself.

"Well, I mean, not that there's a *good* time to lose your brother. I don't mean *that*." She was almost blushing. "It's just that I know they had made plans, she and Mickey. I think she wanted to start her own business. Mickey was going to help her out financially. It just makes it worse for her, don't you think?"

"Yeah, I suppose." The words came automatically while my thoughts took off with new calculations.

"Anyway, she's a good girl. She'll get through." With narrowed, gleaming eyes, Rhonda added, "She could use a friend like you. Someone to take care of her."

"Yes, well, I…"

"Don't worry, Henry," she said, leaning towards me, "I'm not trying to rush anything. Just be a friend. That's all she needs." Squinting with the effort to emphasize one last cheery grin, she patted my arm supportively. "Give my best to Claire."

Her bright expression endured as she turned away. She was good. She was better than Frank—and probably equally duplicitous. I didn't like her for it, but that didn't make what she said untrue. I turned and pushed through the outer doors feeling like I had trampled roughly through the well-kept flowerbeds of Tanya Gilmore's perfectly manicured estate. And it struck me that, for all of her contrived cheerfulness, Rhonda Schomberg had intended to leave me feeling this way.

Chapter 32

Driving across town, I crawled through the rush hour logjam and through my jumbled thoughts at about the same slow-and-go pace. My intentions to come clean with Claire had been broadsided by Rhonda Schomberg's casual confidences. Claire had more to lose than I had known. That didn't mean she killed anybody, but she had vested interests—potentially, anyway—with the entire slew of murder suspects. She was part of my investigation and I chided myself for forgetting it. I needed to find out more about where, exactly, she stood. But my intention had been to level with her first and that no longer seemed simple—or even possible. And I remembered what else that would cost me. Tom Connally and Luis Sanchez weren't the least of my worries in that regard. I owed them more than a job and I didn't completely disagree with what I knew would be their take on my intentions. If I was wrong about Claire—or even if I was right—telling her would compromise me. It would blow up the investigation.

The line of cars in front of me started and stalled, then came to a full stop. I changed lanes with little regard, taking some twisted solace in the honking horns. That lane stopped too. There was no reason for it. Time moved ahead of me.

I took the exit on 38th telling myself it would all fall into place when we could talk face to face. But when I pulled up in front of Claire's house, I saw that it wasn't going to be that easy.

There was an older gentleman, probably shy of sixty, standing on the front step holding the screen door with his shoulder. He watched me as I parked then turned into the house mouthing words I couldn't make out. When he turned again, I recognized him from the church: Claire's father. I got out of the car trying to imagine how my timing could have been made worse. A cloudburst? A couple Cadillac's rolling by? Some gunplay, maybe?

As I strolled up the walk, Shanie came bouncing out the open doorway, skipping past her grandfather, trailing a light pink sweater, one sleeve dragging along the ground. Upon seeing me, she slowed to a walk and looked at me shyly, but making eye contact and holding it, as younger children often do. I crouched down to her height.

"Hey, Shanie. How're you doin'?"

"Fi-i-n-ne," she said, absently, then turned to her approaching grandfather as if for a cue. He took her gently by the shoulders and steered her around me like I was some stray dog, unknown and likely to bite.

"C'mon sweetie. We don't want to be late. Watch out, you're getting your sweater dirty."

"'Bye, 'bye," Shanie sang.

When he had loaded her into the back seat and closed the door, the man turned and took two steps toward me then adopted a hard stance, hands on hips. Mickey's face with deeper wrinkles and looser skin took me in with angry, dark-blue eyes. Maybe he had Mickey's hot temper too.

"You one of Frank's cronies?" he asked challengingly.

"Ah, yeah...that is, I'm a friend of Claire's."

I moved towards him intending to shake his hand.

"You're no friend of Claire's if you work for that man. Friends like that, who needs enemies."

"My name is Henry Burkhart. I'm sorry about what happened to Mickey."

"Sorry?" the man said. "How could you be sorry? Running those cheap rackets, taking advantage of all those… You don't think I know what's happening here." His chin quivered as he spoke. "Bunch of smalltime *hoods,* if you ask me."

I felt stuck in place. I heard women chattering from the doorway behind me. Then Claire's clear voice cut through the air between her father and me.

"Dad?" she said, her footsteps hurrying along the walk.

"I just hope the rest of you come to grief as well," he added.

"Dad, *please.*" She took hold of my arm and positioned herself next to me, fixing her father with a piercing glare. "This is my friend, Henry. I told you about him."

"I don't know what kind of friend he can be if he's working for Frank Coyne."

"Oh, *Dad.* Don't make this worse. It's not the time."

"Now, Cullen." Another woman's voice approached from behind us, her heels clicking purposefully. She stepped around us emitting a small sigh of impatience. "Let's go now, Cull. I think we all need a little break, don't you?"

"He works for Frank, honey."

"Well, that's no reason to be rude. C'mon. Let's just get going here."

The man continued to grumble as his wife led him to the driver's side of the car. She countered in a high but forceful trill, sounding almost cheerful as she admonished him. When he got in behind the wheel, she circled back to the passenger side and forced a smile, giving me a quick glance.

"We'll be back in a few hours," she said, addressing Claire.

"Not too late, okay? She's got school tomorrow. I think it's best if she goes."

"Oh, I agree, but don't worry about it if she doesn't want to. We could stay down if you like. I could, anyway. I think your father wants to go to work. *I* want him to, anyway." She spoke spiritedly, but her features were drawn, tired. "We'll talk about it later." She looked back and forth between us fleetingly, then turned and got into the car.

Shanie leaned upward from the depths of the child's seat in back, her pixie features framed in the window. She met her mother's gaze with a still, serious expression that seemed very un-childlike, as if she knew just what was going on and mildly disapproved. Her grandfather revved the engine, then pulled away from the curb with a growl from the engine that could have come from his throat. Shanie waved tentatively, we waved back.

Claire's hands came up to cover her mouth. She sighed and said, "She'll be all right."

"Of course she will. Your father's just upset."

She turned to look at me, eyes moist. She coughed out a nervous, low-pitched laugh. "I'm so sorry. He's never... I mean, he's just upset, like you said. Not really a good time to meet the parents, is it?"

"'Suppose not. Maybe I shouldn't have come."

She took my arm again and gripped it firmly and she led me toward the house. "I knew you would," she said. "That is, I was hoping you would. I really needed a break. I mean, I *love* my family, but it's been a little...*heavy* the last few days. Thank God for my mother. She was babysitting the whole lot of us all weekend. My father was...like *that*," she tossed her head, "pretty much the whole time."

I got the idea she needed to talk. "Were they close?" I asked, as we entered the living room. "Mickey and your father, I mean."

"Well, that's the weird part. Maybe not so weird when you think about it." She made a beeline into the kitchen tugging loose her white blouse from the waistband of her skirt. I followed her and watched her rummage around in cabinets. Her hand came out with a bottle of vodka. "They were very close when we were growing up. I mean, he was the only son. They did all the father-son things, including the typical rebellion when Mickey hit adolescence." She broke open a tray of ice with a crack. "I guess it was typical, anyway. But then they had a real blowup when Mickey was, I don't know, maybe twenty-two. He was going to Metro State. He decided to drop out and go to work full-time for Frank. Dad didn't like that and he didn't let go of it." She poured herself a definite stiff one over a couple of ice cubes. "Mickey moved out after that. It's like, twelve years later and I don't think Dad ever accepted it." She swirled her drink and took a good, thirst-quenching gulp. Close-lipped, she strained to swallow. Then she almost laughed: "I'm sorry. Do you want something to drink?"

"Sure," I said, "but maybe with a little tonic?"

She coughed guiltily. "Sorry. I just need to take the edge off."

"I can understand that."

While she worked on mixing my drink, I dug deep for the proper nonchalance for what I wanted to say. It didn't get me very far, but I came up with blaming her dad as an opening. Seemed a little hard-hearted, maybe, but I went with it. "So how'd he feel about *your* involvement? With Frank, I mean?"

She gave me a sharp look, then batted her eyes and turned back to her mixing. "Oh, I don't know. He gave me the same lectures. I did a better job pretending to listen, maybe. Besides, it wasn't the same by then." She handed me the drink, then said, "Shall we go outside? I'm dying for a cigarette. I don't smoke indoors, Shanie and all."

I followed her out to a picnic table at the edge of a flagstone patio. She set her drink down and turned to me and reached out both hands to take hold of the lapels of my coat and pulled herself close to me. I started to move to put down my drink but she held me firmly. She gazed up into my eyes, long enough for me to see the emotion there.

"Kiss me, Henry."

I was caught off guard, but the feel of her lips against mine and the warmth of her breath and that smell that reminded me of cognac created a surge of passions that brought me up to speed in an instant. The kiss was long and alcohol-laced and took some time to ripen, but we had all the time in the world for a few seconds there. Her arms snaked around my waist inside my coat, her fingers cutting a trail of tingling sensation along my ribs. I pulled her closer with my one free arm, feeling the heat and texture of her breasts and the movement of her hips against mine.

Our lips parted and her eyes opened partway, transfixed, serene, still smoldering. She pushed me gently away, slowly, but nearly to arm's length. Then she blinked and dropped her hands and turned to straddle the bench of the picnic table.

I didn't move for a few beats, my knees lacking the confidence to function properly. I stood there holding the glass in my hand like an expectant waiter. It looked cool and refreshing. No one else wanted it, so I took a sip. It hit the spot.

I swung a foot over the bench, bumping my shin before landing roughly on the plank next to her. Claire didn't seem to notice. She was staring off into the yard as if already a long ways away from that kiss. I took out my flattened pack of cigarettes and shook one loose for her. Holding it to her lips, she turned towards me for a light with a different look in her eyes.

She took a deep drag, then exhaled and said, "God that feels good. I've been sneaking outside all weekend for these like some kind of criminal."

"You holding up all right?"

"I guess. I don't know." She ventured a glance and offered a perfunctory smile. "It's funny in a way. In some ways I feel good. I mean, not *good*, not about Mickey, of course, but…suddenly, it seems so important to be *alive*. Sort of like, this sense of the importance of carrying on…*gives* me strength. You know what I mean?"

"Yeah, maybe. It *is* important. Shanie…"

"*Especially* for Shanie," she went on, "I mean, I couldn't say anything about it in front of mom and dad. This was hard for them, especially dad. There were some things between them, things *now* left unsaid. But I got this feeling that we shouldn't dwell on it. It's a fact, it can't be undone. I didn't want Shanie to get too depressed about it. She has to *feel* it, of course. I mean… *God,* he's *dead.*" She stopped, closed her eyes, and drew in her lips. Then she took a deep breathe, took another sip of the vodka, took a drag on her smoke. "I don't know. I just didn't want to make it worse than it is. Life and death. They go hand in hand, don't they?"

She said it so evenly, I almost missed it. "Yes, they do." Feeling awkward, I groped for a serious response, but went to safer ground instead. "Was Shanie close to Mickey?"

"Yeah, they were, mostly. I mean, he and Tanya didn't have any kids, so Shanie kind of got the brunt of his paternal instincts. He was good to her, very protective. She has Eddie too, of course, but sometimes I think Mickey knew her better."

"Is her real father still in the picture?" I asked, wondering, not for the first time, who he was, what part he played.

It was the wrong thing to say. Her eyes hardened and turned downward. "No," she said, "Definitely not in the picture."

Somewhat puzzlingly, it was that moment when she burst into sobs. I put an arm around her shoulders but she didn't yield to the direction of my touch. She tensed up, seemingly against the rolling impulses to let the tears flow. After a moment, one deep sigh marked her effort to get past it. She took a long drag off her cigarette, working it like it was a pain-soothing infusion.

I let a silence take up some time watching her out of the corner of my eye. She exhaled another drag, then seemed to settle into herself. Only then did she lean against me. It was a strangely peaceful moment. The fading light of dusk bathed the well-tended back yard in a wash of pastel, shadowless hues. Her smell lingered in the still air.

A squirrel appeared at the top of the fence, took us in indifferently, then hopped down and across the yard with the lightness of a furry insect. Coming home from a hard day's work, no doubt. Effortlessly, he taloned his way up the trunk of the aging apple tree in the corner of the yard. So shopping, maybe. He looked back at us with the coolness of a reclusive neighbor going about his business. Then he disappeared among the thicker foliage above. You don't want to encourage too much chit-chat with your neighbors. Next thing you know, they'll be over here borrowing fruits and nuts.

"What are you doing here, Henry?"

Claire startled me out of my nature reverie, all the more so by the ambiguity of her meaning.

"What's that?"

"What are you doing here? Really." She straightened up to look at me full-faced, shifting her shoulders so that my arm slid away. Her eyes were cool now, steady with concentration. Even then I noticed the beauty in her face, the fine, even features, the distinct brows darker than her sun-lightened hair, the deep blue eyes, unique. But there was no denying the change in the air between us, like a cold draft wafting at the gaps where bare skin is exposed to the elements.

"What's this about?" she persisted.

For a moment, I considered the romantic interpretation, but I knew it wouldn't fly. It would only belittle the kiss, which left little equivocation about our desire for each other. But something in her tone made me think she also sensed the lie. "I'm not sure what you mean?"

She looked away into the yard, her eyes narrowing as if searching out that lackadaisical rodent. "Frank told me about your adventures over the weekend. You got thrown in jail, right?"

"I got into a little trouble. Nothing to worry about in the long run. It was all a big misunderstanding."

"And that's why they let you out?" She sounded incredulous.

"They didn't have any reason to hold me after Charmichael's time of death was established."

A tree branch vibrated amongst the still leaves, then another further up, shaken by the invisible progress of our busy furry neighbor. A ripe apple thumped to the ground, landing like a stone thrown from afar.

"Frank told me about that. He told me you went to Brent's house Friday night. You were the one that found his body."

She said this evenly but I could detect the quiver of restraint in her voice. I wondered when she had talked to Frank.

"Yeah, that's right. But they cleared me of any suspicion. It was…"

"Henry! That was just before you came to see me. It *had* to be."

"Yes, it was."

"Why didn't you tell me?"

"I just didn't want to worry you. I didn't want to get you involved."

"I was already involved, Henry. They *killed* my *brother*."

"I mean involved in the investigation. The cops, and all that. The media attention."

"But *you're* involved, right?"

I felt a certain panic, seeing the moment pass, wishing I had told her something true when I had the chance. "I am now," I said.

"I mean, that's why you're here. It's no accident, is it?"

She watched me closely, prying at the edges of my facade.

"No," I said. "No accident."

She looked away again and some time passed before she spoke. "It's funny, you know. Part of me was happy that you weren't one of them, one of Frank's good ol' boys. Even when I figured out that you must be part of something else, something....*sneaky*, something threatening to them, isn't it?" She stopped, as if to let me respond but then continued before I could unstick my thoughts. "Anyway, I was glad you weren't just another small-time bingo operator. On the other hand, you *are* going after them, aren't you?"

"I'm not going after anybody in particular," I said, feeling desperate right then to keep all my options—my roles—open.

"Frank doesn't trust you either," she said, and I heard that word 'either' as if she had emphasized it. "He told me to be careful, to be careful about what I felt for you." She offered a dry chuckle. "Of course, I told him he was crazy."

I had many things to say, yet every choice seemed a betrayal. The distance between us became a yawning gulf.

She turned again to face me. "Are you going to find Mickey's killer? *Was* it Brent Charmichael?"

"I'm not sure yet. Will you help me?"

"I'll help you with that. I won't help you bring down Frank. He had nothing to do with that. I'm sure of it."

"But you know what they're into? You know the scope of it? You know that's why Mickey's dead?"

Her eyes shimmered with diamond-like reflections, then tears thickened just below the irises. "No," she whispered. "I don't know why Mickey is dead."

Her head tilted forward and her shoulders rose up with tension. One hand came up to her face and the slender fingers followed the line of her nose then padded delicately at her closed eyelids. I wanted to put a hand out to comfort her, but I didn't. I waited for her to throw me out.

Between sniffles, she managed to speak. "All these questions, Henry. What are you after? How is it connected to Mickey's death?"

"Are you sure you want to know?"

She lifted her head and stared at me. Without losing focus, she traced a fingertip beneath each eye, a practiced move, like an expert painter cutting the final trim. Her oval eyes narrowed and the pupils seemed to darken. "Try me."

I had a thousand questions. I figured I'd get in two, maybe three.

"Who's this guy Spence? 'New kid on the block,' you said."

"What about him?" She took on a formal stiffness, like a hostile witness under oath.

"What was it that Mickey didn't like about him?"

"All I know is, Mickey was thinking about taking up with Brent, and Spence aced him out. That's enough, isn't it?"

"He told you this? What was the conversation exactly? When did it take place?"

"It was after they shot up Clancy's. When you made your rude introduction? Remember that?" I waited in silence, knowing I'd have to take more of this to get anywhere. When I didn't react, she continued on her own. "Mickey knew it was Brent right away."

I wanted to ask her why she didn't tell me *then*, but I could feel my emotive reflex. I pressed down hard to keep it in check.

"He said it was all over," she continued. "No more *deals*, no more alliances, nothing was going to happen. I asked him if he had talked to Brent, if it was something he'd said that caused this. He said it was just the opposite. They had been talking about getting together, without the likes of Frank and Milo. He said it was going fine, they were working on the details. Then the holdup happened. Next time Mickey talked to him, Brent was… he said he was 'a different person.'" Her eyes dropped away. "He said Brent just dumped him. Told him he was getting backing from this guy Spence, some new *angle*… so he basically didn't need Mickey anymore. He didn't need the money, he didn't need him, and he didn't need…anything."

He didn't need *you,* I thought to myself.

"After that, Mickey accused him of holding up Clancy's. Brent denied it, of course, but…well, I guess it got pretty heated. Mickey was livid when he told me. I knew he had something in mind, some way to get even. I *tried* to talk him out of it, but he didn't want to hear. He said, 'You, of all people…'" She stopped, her face frozen. She had almost let it slip—about her and Brent.

"Anyway, it was no surprise to me that he set that fire. I was expecting worse." After a pause, she added, "I guess it got worse after all."

I waited a minute to see if she would go on. She stared into the tree branches, into the darkening sky. "So it sounds like Spence has nothing to do with Milo either, then, right?"

"No. He was Brent's ticket out from under Milo's thumb. And Mickey was angry because we were left out. Still stuck with Frank."

I noted another slip: we. It was Mickey *and* Claire that had been left behind. I figured this was what Rhonda Schomberg had been referring to. But I wondered how Rhonda had come to know. And if she knew, Tanya would know. So maybe the whole family knew.

"And you don't know anything else about who Spence is, or where I can find him?"

Claire shook her head. "You think he killed Brent?"

"It's certainly a possibility. But it's hard to guess why, if they were going into business together. Could be the partnership went sour quick. Could be anything. The thing would be to find him. Did Mickey say if he ever met him?"

"Yeah, I think he had, but he didn't say when or where. Just that he had this bad impression of him. He called him a 'new-rich…well, *asshole*.'" Claire smiled minutely. "I remember that because it made me laugh. He never swears around us."

"When was it exactly that Mickey talked to Brent the first time? Do you know?"

"Not, really," she said vaguely. "A month ago, maybe. He didn't say."

It was a careless lie, deliberate and self-protective.

"And did you say Frank or Tanya might know him? Spence, I mean."

"I said, I thought Frank knew *of* him."

"Did he know of Mickey's plans to go out on his own?"

"No. I don't know. He knows now. *I* didn't tell him." She was quickly angry again. "You'll have to ask Frank about that. *He's* still alive. You can talk to him yourself."

I let that go the way of the others. The evening light had faded to dark and in that dimness Claire's features had become indistinct, blurry, as though she had aged before my eyes. Fitting, because she *was* different now, different from who I thought I knew, someone with different interests and a different kind of intelligence, someone with an angle of her own, and secrets of her own. But even so, I didn't want to make her a target. A few words, left unsaid, sustained a link between us, and I wasn't going to say them.

"I know you have no reason to believe me but I have to tell you, I am here to find the killer. Frank's another story, but I don't think he murdered anyone."

"Do *you* think Brent killed Mickey?"

The same question—always back to Brent. She wanted him to be the killer. Or she wanted him not to be.

"Maybe, but if he did, he was put up to it. He didn't act alone."

"How do you know that?"

"Someone else drove the car. And someone else killed *him*. It was too soon after Mickey's death to be unrelated."

Her eyes stayed with mine in alert repose, but without the depth and openness I had seen there before.

"I'm close to finding out who it was," I added. "That is, if nobody stops me."

She huffed a dismissive sigh. "If you're worried about me telling Frank, I'm not going to. I knew this was coming anyway. They got carried away." Her eyes brightened suddenly. "I told *you* that, didn't I? At lunch that day. You must have had a good laugh over that."

"I wasn't laughing," I said lamely.

"No, of course not. That would have been too honest." She glared at me and I stared back, tempted to confront her with her own deceptions.

"Anyway, I don't care. I'm out of it. I can't put up with this any longer. Not without Mickey." Her voice wavered slightly and she looked away. When she spoke again, her tone was low, almost a whisper, but she looked me straight in the eye. "Whatever it is you're up to…just don't ask me to help."

I realized how much I had told her, how much I hadn't denied. I wanted to lay it all out, give her the details, offer up all the justifications Luis had given me. But I knew she was too much a part of it. Or had been, anyway. And she would remain part of the family regardless. The family money was a reality for her and Shanie, even without Mickey. Maybe more so without him. What's so bad about the way they make it? I remembered having my own misgivings about that. What makes bringing down the secretary of state so important, anyway?

"Murder makes it important," I said out loud, answering my own question. "I'm going to find out who did it, with or without your help. Can you live with that?"

"Do I have a choice?"

"You can tell Frank."

"Tell him what? You said he didn't do it." She spoke right in my face, anger seething close to the surface again. "What do you want from him, anyway? What are you after?" The anger in her eyes didn't fade.

"It's better for you if you don't know."

"Better for *me*! Sure. Fine. Do what you want, but leave *me* out of it. I don't care. I don't care about *any* of you. Don't worry about *me*, Henry. Worry about yourself. The longer you stay around, the worse it gets."

She stopped herself but held my eyes with a wildly intense look, held it there as if to demonstrate the strength of her will. "Do you know what I mean, Henry?"

I nodded slightly, saying nothing.

"That goes for around here too," she stated and her piercing gaze dropped away. Pinholes of light glimmered at the corners of her eyes, beautiful half-moon-shaped eyelids, smooth as marble, perfect lunettes framed by the distinctly drawn arches of her brow. Even in the dimness

I could see it. I took it in. I had the feeling I would never again be this close.

"Goodbye, Henry," she said, her face turning away.

For a long inappropriate moment I continued to look, tracing her profile, the lines of her jaw, examining the irregular shape of her lips, straining towards the details of her feminine beauty. She never looked up. Such sweet self-torture, I could have stayed there…for a while.

I stood up from the bench and swung my leg free. Claire's posture didn't change but I sensed a subtle movement, a shiver or a shrug, the smallest shrug that could have been. Maybe I dreamt it. I took two weighty steps on the flagstones and turned and looked back. She had one hand to her face now, resting her elbow on the table's edge, the fingers splayed as if to veil herself from me.

I turned and walked through the open sliding glass door and made my way through her house. They were nice rooms in that house, comfortable, homey, warm. A man could be happy there, if he were given the chance. If he earned the chance.

I went to the front door and opened it. A breeze wafted over me, a current from the outside world that hadn't touched us in the back garden. I turned in the doorway for one last look, and Claire wasn't there. Just the soft rounded furniture in that warmly lit room. I closed the door and went back into the world.

Chapter 33

By the time I got back to Willie Junior's, the glum meanderings of my mind had spiraled down to a trickle of dead-end conclusions and far-flung expletives loosely aimed at myself. A low humming tautness filled my chest—vague, puny, inconsequential emotions that I didn't have any interest in exploring. Once through the gate, Pimpy harassed me with his usual simpering playfulness, pawing and bouncing, oblivious to my mood. I stooped and gave him some pets. "Just you and me, pal," I said.

Willie appeared behind the screen door, hips cocked, arms folded over his large chest, like a recalcitrant housewife confronting the wayward cuckold.

"'Bout time," he groused. "Man, where you been?"

"I was at the funeral. I told you."

"I been waitin' here all night. What was *I* s'pose to be doin'?"

"You were supposed to be waiting here all night."

Willie gaped at me unabashed. "What the fuck the matter with *you?*"

I gave the dog a final pat then stood to face Willie. "It was a funeral, Willie, it wasn't a party. The man was dead, the place was filled with mourners—sad, depressed, everyone dressed in black. Get the picture?" Anything was better than telling the truth.

Willie's smooth features scrunched up in exaggerated puzzlement. Staring off above my head, he put a finger to his temple. "Let's see. This the man you told me put a gun to the back of some dude's head and sprayed the field with his brains, right?"

"We don't know that it was him," I said, pushing past him.

"An' all these sorry *mourners*... they the family of crooks who's running the scams at these bingo halls. Am I right? They the *principles* of our investigation, right?"

"No need to mock them, Willie." I went into the kitchenette and opened the refrigerator and stared into it. Willie followed.

"Was your little chickie up there?"

"Her name is Claire."

"Oh, Claire," he said, dreamily. "Claire, Claire, Claire."

"Cut it out, Willie. I don't need shit from you right now."

"Don't tell me you fallin' for another *femme fatale*. Man, you got a real soft spot for them desperate housewives."

I slammed the refrigerator door and turned to face him. "You got some *reason* for digging at me?"

Willie looked down at me with a fading grin, shifted his weight, still holding my gaze. To avoid the look I was getting, I turned and opened the refrigerator again and rummaged through the top shelf: a nearly empty carton of milk, stale bread wrapped in plastic, an open pack of bologna, beer, eggs, a jar of pickles, various bottles of hot sauce. My appetite was going nowhere.

"We still workin' this crowd or what?" Willie asked, persisting but no longer petulant.

I took a deep breath. "Yeah, we're still working them."

"We're goin' after my car tonight?"

"Yeah, yeah, we're goin' out there. I just wanted something to eat."

"Nothin' here. Let's get something on the way. Don't want nobody breakin' in without us, right? And Duncan said he'd get it tomorrow, if it's still in one piece."

"Duncan called?"

"Yeah. He wants you to call him first thing in the morning…if you're not back in lockup by then."

"Why would I be in lockup?"

Willie smiled openly. "Don't ask me. That's what *he* said. I'd've said, '5-0'd', or 'G-house', 'Slammer', maybe."

I didn't see the humor.

"Anyway, he said we'd go through the *proper channels* tomorrow."

"You didn't tell him we were going out there did you?'

"Yeah, right," he slurred. "And *you* didn't have to tell him I ditched work the other day, neither. Put me on the spot."

I closed the refrigerator empty handed. "He came to that on his own, Willie. Not exactly a wild guess."

"Whatever. Let's go."

"I gotta walk the dog first."

"Pimpy? Man, that's all I been doin' is walkin' that dog. He's all strung out from walkin' and runnin' and peein' on every tree from here to Five Points. I've been *on* him like a *hostage*, dude. Figured you'd come back for him. No use waitin' on you otherwise."

I rolled my eyes. "Okay. Let's do it. You got something dark to wear?" I said indicating his loud-orange *Broncos* jersey. "And bring some gloves, just in case."

"In case of what? You got a little B & E in mind?" He sounded upbeat about the prospect.

"We gotta be ready for anything," I said, turning and ascending the stairs.

From my bag, I took my Beretta and a full clip and the shoulder holster and put them together and put them on underneath my black leather jacket.

I let Willie drive the Lexus which seemed to soothe his irascible mood, if it didn't do much for mine. Out past the airport exit, the traffic thinned and he took it up well past a hundred without comment. Like flying on ice. When he slowed for a landing on the off-ramp to Tower Road, he let out a satisfied sigh. "Man, that is *sweet*."

We stopped for a bucket of fried chicken at the last fast-food outpost on East Colfax then drove on to K & K Automotive Reconditioning. It was getting on to midnight.

The front of the building was fairly well-lit. Security lights along the irregular roofline flooded the front parking area. There were several cars parked along there but it didn't mean anybody was home. I wanted to make sure.

"Let's drive up to the gate."

"What's that gonna do? I thought we were here on the sneak."

"We gotta know who's here before we can sneak around them."

We rolled along the side of the building to the grease-smeared metal door of the office. Its wire-mesh window was a dark empty square. An over-kill of floodlights illuminated the chain-link gate, the razor wire spikes glistening under their beams. What we could see of the yard was quiet and only indirectly lit. Several rows of cars were visible but the Mustang wasn't among them.

We drove the length of the building and into the empty field at the far end. Nothing stirred. No lights shone from within. I directed Willie back the way we came and we backed into a space near the driveway from where we could see the gate to the impound lot and all along the front of the building. Willie passed the bucket of chicken. I took a piece. The breading was by now soggy with grease, the meat stringy underneath, all of it sprinkled with too much pepper. It tasted great.

Willie said, "Let's go check it out. We can't see nothin' from here."

"We don't need to see anything else. We just want to watch for comings and goings."

That and another drumstick bought me five minutes.

"Man there ain't no one here. Let's just go see if we can spot the 'Stang. We gotta know where it's at if we're staking it out. What if they come in from the back?"

He had a point and there was no stopping him anyway.

"What about the dogs?"

"You're a dog lover. What's the problem?" He gave me a low chuckle as he opened his door. "Anyways, bring the chicken."

"What? What for?"

"Just bring it, will ya? And bring your gloves. Maybe they'll soften the dog bites."

"Willie, wait," I said, but he closed the door, strode off. I got out to follow.

There was a line of small trees, something like scrub oak, running along the top of a berm from the highway to the fence. We moved along there, keeping the trees between the building and us. The humming sound of an occasional car moved through the darkness behind us along the open highway. The air was still, and cooler here than in the city.

When we dropped down next to the fence, Willie pried at the metal slats that were woven through the wire links. He didn't get anywhere with it.

"Man, I can't see nothin'. Gimme a boost."

"What are you talking about?"

"Lift me up." He cupped his hands together forming a stirrup. "It won't break you to follow one a' *my* ideas for a change."

He needed a boost in morale as well. "Here. Here's your chicken," I said, not wanting to make it easy.

"Man, just set that down and boost me."

Knees bent, I linked my hands together. Willie stepped into them and clawed his way up the fence until his face was even with the razor wire. He was heavy. I could feel it in my back.

"Man, they's a lot a' cars out here. Oooo-wee. Hey, there's an old GTO. White boy car, right?"

"Do you see the Mustang, Willie? Don't be window shoppin' while I'm carrying you."

"*Hush.* Hold *still.*"

I stopped breathing and listened. Thumping sounds approached from . I couldn't tell where and I couldn't turn to look. Then the fence caved toward me, the links smacked against my shoulder, and a vicious barking exploded as if in my ear. I fell backwards into the weeds. Willie came down straddling me then fell onto my legs. I twisted to my hands and knees and scrambled away from the barking, every instinct telling me those dogs were coming through the fence.

Climbing up the mound, I dove over the top and rolled behind the trees. Then I turned and scanned what I could see of the building. Nothing happened while I watched, although the dogs kept on barking. I could see Willie crouched in the darkness at the bottom of the berm. "Willie!" I hissed. "Get out of there."

He made an inarticulate hushing sound. The barking dropped off to yelps, then whimpers, then stopped altogether. "C'mon back," he said.

I wanted out of there but it was plain he wasn't coming. I slid down the slope to find Willie shoving a peppery drumstick under the wire at the bottom of the fence. The dogs, three of them, sustained low growls in rhythm with their chewing. I could hear the chicken bones cracking between their jaws. One of them sneezed away a dose of the pepper-coated skin. Then a sharper growl emitted as if in defense of a discarded morsel.

"Let's get out of here, Willie."

"Hold on. I got them all mellowed out." He let out a low chuckle and it struck me that it sounded like a calmer version of the growling dogs. Whatever its effect, the dogs remained subdued. I stepped softly along the fence to the corner post and peered around at the building. All was quiet.

"I saw it," he said, "I saw the car."

"Where is it?"

"At the far end of the front row, up near the building. We could get up on the roof."

"What the hell for?"

"To keep an eye on the car, man. What we doin' here?"

"We're watching to see who shows up. They'll never make it to the car."

"Why the hell not?"

"'Cause we'll *stop* them before they do."

"Man, what kinda play is that?"

One of the dogs barked twice, sharply, inquiringly. He wanted another piece. "Feed your friend, there, Willie."

"Dammit," Willie said, digging into the bucket. He slid another knot of bread/chicken under the fence.

"Lift me up," I said. "I need to get a look."

"Lift *you* up?"

"Quit screwin' around, will ya. Give me a lift."

Mumbling protestations, he bent over, cupped his hands, and lifted me effortlessly. I could see the Mustang, just opposite a triple set of garage doors, as if in line for a reconditioning some time soon. There were no signs of life, no lights in the rear windows of the building. I dropped back down to the ground.

"Let's get outta here before we run out of chicken."

"That shit's gone, man. I figured we'd feed 'em one of *your* shoes next."

"Funny. Let's just leave them to the bones and get back to the car."

I made my way along the fence. "What about *my* car?" Willie pleaded.

"C'mon. I got a plan." Without looking back, I kept moving but listened to make sure he followed.

When we got back to the Lexus all was quiet except Willie. "Man, let's get up on the roof. We can keep a better eye on it from there."

"And we'll just swoop down on them like Batman, right? Did you bring the capes, Robin?

"Har, har. Okay, one of us'll stay down here. We need *radios*. I got my cell phone. I can call you."

"On what? The pay phone down the street?"

"Why you don't have a cell? Man, this operation's just badly *equipped*."

I smiled at Willie's animation. "Get in Willie. I'll tell you the master plan."

"She-it, man," Willie said, climbing in. "Let's hear this *master plan*."

"They're not gonna get to your car, Willie. We don't want them to. There's nothing in it that they want. I made that up, right?"

"I ain't stupid, Henry."

"My point is, we're not interested in some citizen's arrest for B & E on a junkyard. Whoever shows up got the word from someone at that dinner last night. It will be Charmichael's killers or someone working for them. We'll confront them see how it shakes out."

"It shakes out like they gonna *shoot* us *too*."

"We'll have the element of surprise." I zipped opened my jacket and flashed the butt of my Beretta. "And I got this."

"Hey man, now we talkin' *equipped*. You bring one for me?"

"The cops got my other gun. We'll have to make do. You can hit them with your cell phone."

Willie rolled out his chuckle. "Oh, man," he said, leaning forward towards the dash, "I think this'll be more *apropos*." From the small of his back, he brought forward a Smith & Wesson automatic, beautifully chromed-out and polished, and with carved grips. It was a pimp's gun, major bling, impressively menacing. It was huge, probably a .45, but it fit Willie's hand just right.

"Now, dammit, Willie. Do I have to lecture you on this? We're not here for a shootout."

"Yeah but why *you* packin'? 'Sides, we're dealin' with killers here, you just said. Man gotta protect hisself."

"Listen. Don't even *think* about using that thing for anything but cover. We shoot these guys, we're not gonna find out anything from them."

"We don't have to shoot to kill, bro'. Just wing 'em in the arm or leg."

John Wayne again. "You can't shoot that well, Willie, no one can. Besides, if you wound them they'll be suing you to kingdom come."

"Suing us? What you mean? We're officers of the court."

"Where'd you get that bullshit?"

"We're workin' for the *DA*, aren't we?"

"We're paid informants. That doesn't give us the right to use deadly force. We're not that kind law enforcement, Willie."

"If we get paid on the books, we're *employees* of the DA. Makes us officers of the court. I got that from Duncan."

"Don't let that legalese go to your head. You seen a paycheck?"

"As a matter of fact, I been wantin' to ask about that."

"I'm saving it for your legal defense fund. Take my word for it, you aren't an officer of the court."

"So what am I supposed to do? Let them *shoot* you?"

I smiled at that. "If it comes to that, which it won't, just lay down some cover fire. Shoot over their heads to distract them."

"Yeah, yeah. I know how to lay down cover."

"You do, huh? You learn that on CSI Five Points, or what?"

"Man, why you jivin' me? What we doin' here, anyway?"

"We're here to intercept some suspects in a criminal investigation. You can't just shoot the bad guys."

"Yeah, yeah, I get it. I ain't anxious to *shoot* nobody." He sighed resignedly. "Sure hope these guys know *their* legal limits as well as *you* do."

"Just follow my lead on this, okay? No guns unless we're threatened. And then only to scare them."

"Ah'ight, ah'ight. Chill out, bro. I'll follow your lead."

We sat in an uncomfortable silence while I pictured a scene from *Bad Boys*: tricked-out Hummers, AK's spraying bullets, pony-tailed bad guys dropping left and right, sirens wailing out of the frame. Duncan would be pissed if we survived.

"Charlton Heston would stand up for me," Willie mumbled, "And he a *white* boy."

"You kidding? Those NRA rednecks? They'd shoot the nigger first, ask questions later."

"All the more reason," Willie huffed.

I couldn't argue with that. We remained quiet for some time, both of us staring out at the empty pavement leading to the impound gate. One of the dogs moved along the fence, nose to the ground, feet shuffling along the bottom edge. He came into view through the space at the end of the gate and seemed to focus on us. Poking his snout through the gap, he sniffed the empty air then moved back into the yard.

Sleep nudged at my shallow thoughts, weighed down my eyelids.

"How's Maxine?" I asked, by way of fending it off.

"She's all right, I guess. Studies all the time. Doesn't have time for any fun."

"Fun like this?"

"Man, she don't even *believe* I'm out here with you. 'Stakeout?' she says. 'Yeah, right.' You gonna have to set her straight, man."

"You told her?"

"You better believe I don't spend overnight some place without her knowin' the details."

"What did you say, exactly?"

"That we was on a *stakeout*. Workin' for the *DA*."

"Nothing else?"

"Nothing else is her business. Ain't no reason to get her interested." He stared at me with a gleam in his eyes. "What about *your* woman?"

"My woman?"

"C'mon, man. *Claire*."

"She's not 'my woman'."

Willie gave that a slow chuckle. "So *that* what got you all tied up. She blow you off?"

"No. I mean, we're not involved so…."

"Yeah, well, *she* involved," Willie stated flatly.

Reaction stirred inside me but I knew what he meant and I didn't have the strength—or the grounds—to argue. I forced it down, kept quiet. Naturally, Willie didn't take the hint.

"Seems to me," he said, "with her brother gettin' killed an' all, we gotta look at her for doin' that Brent dude."

"I've been all over that. She's clear."

"She got an alibi? 'Cause she sure wasn't with *you*."

"If she killed Brent Charmichael, it would have been for revenge, right? There's no reason for her to have stolen his computer and disks."

"So you know what was on the disks, then?"

"Records, bookkeeping, stuff like that."

"'Cause you've seen it?"

I didn't want to concede the point but there it was staring me in the face. My anger waned, giving ground to a low-grade fear. I cleared my throat, sighed like I was exasperated, and stared out the window hoping Willie would let it slide.

"'Sides which," he continued, "you told me she worked with the books some, didn't you? With that old man Willard. "

"For the *Coyne* organization. Charmichael worked for *Milo*. There's no way she could be doing both. Hell, she's practically family."

"Yeah, that would be my point."

Ignoring him, I tried to think it through. Considering Claire's lie about the timing of Mickey's overtures to Charmichael, it was possible that things were going on between them well before Spence came into the picture. Claire had said they were working on the details. That implied a previous arrangement, a working agreement. Then Spence comes along, offers Charmichael a better deal, and Mickey gets cut out. That would explain Mickey's outrage. But if Mickey had been negotiating with Charmichael, it was likely Claire was included. She's his sister, after all. Who else would he trust? Reason enough for her to want the disks.

Dark thoughts for someone pining away. What bothered me more was that I hadn't previously considered it.

I remembered the lunch at Pagliacci's. Claire had made a reference to having seen some figures, having worked with Frank's father. She had casually confirmed the method of laundering the bingo money through BACCO into the dummy corporations. I wondered how well she would take that—and for how long—if she *wasn't* in on the skim. She could have been involved with Mickey's plan from the start. Hell, she could have hatched it. She could have proposed the idea to Mickey *and* Brent. She had her own past entanglements with Brent, after all, details of which I had been glossing over—and she had avoided sharing. She could have a *lot* to hide. And one way to hide her involvement now would be to sluff it off on her brother. He was dead. He couldn't be hurt. A little hard-hearted, maybe, but the revenge factor could have helped her over the hump.

And if that was true, her promise to me—not to tell Frank—was as empty as the wind.

"I just wanted to make sure you covered all the bases," Willie was saying.

"What's that?"

"About Claire. I mean, I *know* you, Henry. You have a tendency to root out a damsel in distress...even when there are no fire-breathing dragons for a million miles. I just wanted to make sure it didn't cloud your...*perspective*."

I noted, among other things, the jive intonation had dropped away. He sounded—exactly—like Duncan. I could feel the blood rising to my face.

In the semidarkness, he couldn't see it but I turned away just the same. "Yeah," I said, "In this case, there are no dragons."

Surprisingly, Willie picked up on my tone. "Yeah, well, anyway, sorry it didn't work out. Seemed like a nice woman."

"You haven't even met her," I said, rather more fervently than I intended. "Anyway, she's a bingo queen, like you say. Part of the investigation, like anyone else."

"Yeah, whatever." Willie slid down in his seat, shifting to get comfortable. "I wish we'd a' thought to bring some coffee," he said. "So we just gonna sit here all night?"

"As long as it takes. I've told you detective work isn't sexy. It's basically grunt work, boring stuff. Like this. You wanted to be a detective, you're getting some practice."

"Practice, she-it." I thought he'd carry on the banter but he dropped it. "I'd rather get some sleep."

"Take a doze. I'll wake you if anything moves."

Relieved, at first to be left with my own thoughts, it wasn't long before they turned on me, twisting the emotive knife of my foolishness. I recalled the perks Claire had listed, the free car, the schooling for Shanie, her house paid for by Mickey. With Mickey gone, she'd have to fall back on Frank. I imagined her going to Frank and Tanya, playing her cards, telling them what kind of threat was afoot with Spence infiltrating Milo's operation. The competition was going to get tough. She wanted to help. And, of course, they'd feel sorry for her. If things worked out, she'd be in line to succeed Mickey, have her own club instead of working the floor and the pickle bar. And the one thing that could put a kink in her plan would be a loose-lipped ex-boyfriend who still held a grudge. It was a worst case scenario, but in the face of my own blindness to it, I began to see it as the key to the whole puzzle.

But all this was hazy thinking. She wasn't the bingo queen. She had rebuffed an arrangement with Dennis. She could have run circles around that boy, set herself up like Tanya had done with Mickey. But she didn't want that. I tried to think back on her words, tried to picture her speaking, wondered if I had missed something big.

Sleep weighed down on me and, by now, I welcomed the relief. I let my thoughts drift into daydreams, though they kept circling back to Claire. I imagined her showing up out here, swaggering into our trap. I pictured her leathered out, Catwoman masked, TEC-9's extending from her hands. Taut and animal-like, she scaled the wire mesh fence like some super-villain lizard. I knew it was Claire. I yelled out her name.

She dropped to the ground, breathing hard, sexed-out in black. Peeling off the mask, her dark eyes glistened with fear and strength, like cornered prey ready to break. But then she smiled and shook out her hair, all feminine confidence. She looked fantastic. She needed my help, she said. I didn't fall for it. I confronted her with her lies, the whole charade, the way she had played me, betraying the betrayer. She told me I didn't have the guts to shoot. I realized I was holding a gun.

I pleaded with her, blamed her, tried to make her listen. She told me she'd done it for Mickey. Waving those TEC-9's like magic wands, she called me out, said I would have done the same. Then she turned coy again and told me about the money—huge amounts, we could split it, millions. I knew she was lying even while I found myself calculating my share. I wanted to believe. Her voice sucked me in. The gun grew heavy in my hand. I looked down on it and my arm seemed to lower of its own accord. I wasn't all there. I floated like a phantom, drifting towards her, the ground beneath me out of reach. I tried to speak, but my voice wouldn't come. Claire was smiling now, watching me as if watching the drug take effect.

There was a commotion, people approaching, shouts and noises I couldn't see. I couldn't turn my head. The strange milieu I floated in had thickened, started swirling. I tried to back away through the cloying current. My arms wouldn't move, I couldn't get my footing. The noise grew louder, pounding in my head. That's when I knew I was dreaming.

Struggling to awaken, I opened my eyes to a terrible brightness. I was awake but the pounding didn't stop. The windows had steamed up, images moved behind the fogged up panes. I wiped at the glass. A fist was hammering on it, then a face came into view, leering with mock surprise.

It was the man in black, the operator of the impound lot. His thick features held a wry, gritty grin framed in the circle I had wiped clean. He blinded me with his flashlight again, just for fun. Turning away, I swung my arm to wake Willie.

"Hey! What up. Don't be hittin' on me, man."

"We got visitors," I said, still groggy, my words rolling out through a mouthful of marbles. I lowered the window, staring at the man's protruding gut. He bent down again to peer in. The horizon glowed pale blue behind him, the sun hadn't come up yet.

"You boys been here long?" he asked, a gruff humor lining his tone.

"We're waiting for our lawyer," I said, attempting to sound offhanded, feeling like I fell short.

"Must be an early riser. We don't open till eight." He looked at his watch, a half-dollar-sized circle on a two-inch wide spiked leather wristband. "You got about an hour and a half. Why don't you go get some coffee? You look like you need it."

"Yeah, maybe we'll do that," I said cryptically, uncertain whether I should act tough or obsequious. Apparently, it came out more towards the latter.

"Wouldn' want you boys scarin' off my clientele," he said through his sarcastic smile. He straightened up and turned away and walked lazily across the lot. He looked back at intervals as if to make sure we weren't dozing back off. I started the car.

"Wha'd he say?" Willie asked, barely able to muster the energy to be insulted.

"He said we were a couple of amateurs for falling asleep on the job."

"Yeah, well…" and his words faded off before coming to life again. "Hey, what about the 'Stang."

"We can't do anything with him here. Let's just wait for Duncan."

"Wait. What if something happened?"

"If something happened, those dogs would've barked. I would've woken up."

"Yeah, sure," Willie said, chuckling. 'You'd'a woken up, crack de-*tec*-tive that you are."

I drove onto Colfax, still in a daze, wondering what I had missed while I was trying to solve the surreal dilemmas of my somnambulant imagination.

Willie was chuckling to himself. "Some *master plan*," he grumbled. "Worked like a dream."

Chapter 34

To avoid the I-70 rush hour logjam, we went stoplight to stoplight for the better part of an hour along Colfax, making languid small-talk just to keep ourselves awake. We stopped for breakfast at Pete's Kitchen, a Capital Hill hole-in-the-wall that the boomer brunch crowd had taken to, lately, making it impossible to get a table on weekends. Seven A.M. on a Tuesday morning was a different story: old codger insomniacs, homeless sobered winos with just enough for a cup a', several pile-driver types coming off the graveyard shift, and two cops—one black, one white—sitting at the counter with the proverbial coffee and donuts. Not a polo shirt in sight.

The cops were eyeing the winos when we came through the door, then they eyed us. We fit right in: a pair of cat burglars licking our wounds after a botched moonlight sortie. We looked like we had slept in our car. My clothes were wrinkled and smudged with dirt. Willie looked like a pimp, as is often the case, but one who's probably on the outs with his hos.

We took up stools at the counter and ordered the special. As soon as the waitress poured coffee, I took my cup back to the pay phone to call Duncan.

"Where are you?" he asked, a trace of wonder in his voice.

"Pete's Kitchen. We didn't get arrested, if that's what you mean."

"Congratulations. You still want me to get Willie's car out?"

"Yeah, yeah, the proper channels. When can you do that?"

"I'll take a long lunch. Ride out there with you guys. That's assuming there's no hang-ups with Aurora PD. I'll check with them, see what they want."

I told him to call us at Willie's where I was hoping we'd get some sleep. When I returned to my stool, Willie's coffee had kicked in and he was yapping it up with the white cop sitting one stool away. They were talking gun control—of course. I leaned back to see if the bulge showed from the .45 tucked in Willie's belt. It wasn't obvious.

"So, what you're sayin' is, there ain't no legal way to transport a piece within the city limits 'less you got a permit. An' you can't get one a' those without some reason related to your business."

"*Legal* business," the white cop emphasized. He was old for a street cop, probably over forty, though the softness of his features didn't go with twenty years on the force. "It doesn't qualify if you're a pimp or a dealer," he said with a clever smile. His partner laughed at that and Willie joined in as if he wasn't the butt of the joke.

"But what if you buy a gun? Legally, I mean. Like at some sporting goods store. How do you get it home?"

"You have to get someone with a permit to transport it for you."

"You can't carry it home in the *box*?"

"Not in the city limits."

Willie knew all this. We'd had this argument before. There was a glitch in the laws—the state and city statutes weren't consistent—and he never tired of pointing it out. I nudged his foot under the counter. He didn't respond.

"Man, that's bullshit. How you s'pose to protect yourself."

"If no one carried guns, you wouldn't have to."

"Too late for *that*. All these punks in *my* hood packin' on the way to *middle*-school."

The cop shook his head sadly.

"Hey, how's about if you were working for the DA?"

I kicked Willie's foot. He swiveled away towards his new friends.

"You thinking about getting a job there?" the cop said, with obvious skepticism.

"Man, I *got* a job. I'm working for Rollins, Jeffery, & Associates. I'm a legal *assistant* down there."

"Good for you. But lawyers can't carry guns either."

"But I was thinkin' 'bout workin' as an investigator for the DA. Like, you know, an *operative*."

The cop gave him a sidelong frown that said, 'good luck'.

"Those guys packin' all the time, ain't they?" Willie persisted.

"They're officers of the court. Law enforcement. Like us."

"How about if you were workin' undercover?"

I kicked at the back of his leg under the stool.

"Yo! What?" Willie swiveled back towards me with a grimace and a half-stifled grin.

I gave him my deepest scowl. "Finish your breakfast. We gotta go. I talked to Duncan."

"Wha'd he say?"

"He said we could get your car." I paused, hoping to keep Willie distracted. One of the cops signaled for their bill.

"So? What else?"

"We have to go back out there with him."

"When's that?"

"As soon as you finish eating."

The cops gathered their things to leave. Willie turned to them. "So what about it, working undercover?"

"Best thing would be if no one carried guns," the older one said again.

"Yeah, well, I could go with that if everyone else would. You guys too, huh?"

"That'll be the day. Take care now."

"You all be careful out there," Willie said with his Tiger Woods smile.

"You too."

They sidled along the line of stools, stopped and had a word with one of the winos. He showed them a fistful of coins. They let him be.

When the door closed behind them, I jumped on Willie. "Are you fucking *tryin'* to get us busted?"

"Man, I was just talkin'. That law don't make no sense."

"Write your congressman. In the meantime, don't toy with these guys. They're part of our investigation, remember? You're just baiting them…"

"Man, I keep tellin' you. The best cover is right up front—get in their faces."

"You've got a lot to learn about bein' subtle, Willie. Let's get out of here."

"Man, *I* got a lot to learn. *You* ain't teachin' me nothin' 'cept how to sleep in a car."

"Let's just go. You can sleep in your own bed."

"I thought you said we were going to get my 'Stang."

"Duncan will call when he gets it sorted out."

Surprisingly—or perhaps not, given my rant—we got back to Willie's in complete silence. He went straight upstairs as I put in a call to Luis. I didn't want to, but I hadn't called in last night. Failure to follow procedures. I expected the standard reaction but I didn't get it.

"Where are you?"

"Willie's place. I'm sorry I didn't call…"

"Where's his house again? I've been over there, but I forget."

"You're coming by?"

"I've got something I want to show you."

I guessed, this time, he couldn't talk on his phone. I gave him directions and ducked into the downstairs bathroom. By the time I was out of the shower, Luis was petting Pimpy on the front porch. I pushed open the screen. He ventured in to stand in the entrance way, no further.

"What you been up to?" he said in an overly casual tone.

"I spent some time with Mickey's family last night. Trying to get an angle on his involvement with this guy Spence."

"The younger sister, huh?" he said, shining eyes and the smallest of grins. "Wha'd she tell you?"

I contemplated stonewalling him because he was right, but I needed to fill in the blank spots or he'd sniff out more on his own.

"She didn't know him. Mickey told her that Brent Charmichael decided to team up with Spence instead of him."

"Him who?"

"Mickey."

"You mean Mickey was hooking up with Brent again? When did that come about?"

"It didn't or at least it didn't get very far. Mickey approached him about it several months ago. I told you Mickey was looking to get out from under Frank's thumb and that he and Charmichael had tried going out on their own before."

"The little venture that got queered by the Cline killing?"

I nodded. "They were thinking about making another go at it."

"Was the girl involved in that?"

"No," I said, telling half the truth. "It never really got off the ground. Charmichael gave Mickey the snub. He told him he didn't need him or his money. Apparently, this guy Spence is well-heeled—or has backing. You find anything out about him?"

Luis regarded me, his eyes still shining, his lips pushing up toward the wide nostrils of his nose. "Robert David Spencer, if it's the same guy. Goes by Bobby Dee, R.D., Spence, and a slew of other AKA's."

"Where'd you find him?"

"Connally found him. Knew the name right off. Said he'd heard it at an interdepartmental meeting recently. From Captain Kearns."

"Kearns? As in vice and narcotics?"

"That's right."

"Why'd you go to Connally?"

"Interdepartmental cooperation, Henry, ya know? You said you needed it quick. Those boys down at records, the more I want it, the slower they go. I figured Connally could cut through the tape if *he* wanted it. And in this case, he did."

"So he knew the name."

"Apparently narcotics has been workin' this guy as part of a syndicate. There's some kind of distribution network set up that he's part of. They've been tracing it backwards for a while."

"For meth?"

Luis frowned, glared at me for being right. "There was this major buy coming down, set up by Kearns' undercover people. Big enough quantities for a conspiracy rap. But then they stumbled onto a DEA mole. Kind of pissed off the Feds and they pulled jurisdiction on it. Major brouhaha, I guess, but the guy wasn't blown."

"So that'd be an example of interdepartmental cooperation?"

Luis frowned again. "There's always friction. It's part of the job—as you should know."

I let it pass with nothing more than a satisfying grunt.

"Anyway," Luis continued, "the Feds got this whole task force set up. Sure as hell don't want us pokin' around in it."

"What else did Connally say?"

"I'll let him tell it to you." He stood there stone-faced.

"What's that mean?"

"He should be here any minute."

"Connally? What the hell for?"

"Interdepartmental cooperation, Henry. This guy Spencer is big, has partners—backers, like you said. Connally's gonna want you to stay clear of it."

"What about our investigation?"

"We go back to bingo. That's where we're supposed to be."

"What about these two murders?"

"Connally's homicide, Henry. It's his show."

"But Luis, I'm close. I can smell it."

"I don't doubt it, but it's not our realm."

"What if it's the same realm?"

Luis sighed. "You'd like that, wouldn't you?"

"There's more to it than that, Luis. You said Spencer's big. Spencer has money. Spencer's running a meth operation. We got a history of meth arrests with the Flood brothers, and Brent Charmichael was using. They're all Milo's people. Brent was going out on his own. He didn't need Milo's backing anymore, like he didn't need Mickey. That's because he was hooked up with Spencer." Luis arched his brow with the obvious question. "We know he was running with the Flood brothers," I persisted. "They did the job at Clancy's together. So how come Alois Flood got sprung? Suddenly he has the scratch for a high-dollar mouthpiece. Where'd that come from?"

"So what, Henry? That's not our realm."

"It is if we're following the bingo money. We want to know where the extra cash flow is coming from, right? The money that BACCO spent to get Herrera elected? The money that Rhonda Schomberg made last year? That paid for Tanya's Mc-mansion? The increases on the quarterlies while attendance is down? That's our realm, isn't it?"

Luis didn't say anything, didn't move. He hadn't moved in a while. His dark eyes stayed with me but his thoughts went somewhere else. I think I saw it click for him. The shiny eyes narrowed and a sardonic grin toyed with the corners of his mouth. "You think Spencer was buying into bingo?"

I nodded and let him think about it. I thought about it too. It was the first time I saw this picture. It made me feel like I was right where I was supposed to be.

Chapter 35

Pimpy made a noise from his spot in the kitchen then he got up and went to the open door, tail wagging. Some watchdog. Tom Connally appeared in the doorway filling out the frame of the screen with his bulk, his face a professional mask, immune to Pimpy's antics. He didn't look happy to see me but I felt good enough to smile at him anyway. Luis stepped over and pushed open the door letting the dog out and the police captain in.

"You're making house calls these days?" I said, feeling almost giddy. "To what do we owe the honor?"

Connally exhaled, unamused. "The usual. Tryin' to keep you out of trouble."

Heavy feet pounded down the stairway behind me. "Man, we got a convention goin' on or what?" Willie said as his legs appeared in the stairwell. When his head cleared the top of the doorway, the sarcasm fell off his face. "Well, now. Look at you."

"Willie Randall Junior." Connally sighed. "How's your old man these days?"

"The Doctor's good, yeah, he's good. Law abiding, as usual." Willie cracked a cocky grin, but it wasn't enough to fill the room.

"And what about you?" Connally countered. "Stayin' out of trouble?" He knew Willie's record better than I did. And Willie knew he knew.

"Free, black, and twenty-seven," Willie jived. "Got a job with Rollins, Jeffery, & *Associates*. Not to mention my freelancing with Henry here."

My bright mood sank a notch or two. I gave Willie a hard look. He pretended not to notice.

"Freelancing, huh?" Connally glowered humorlessly. "We got some place we can talk?" he said, looking at me.

It wasn't the smart thing to do but I felt compelled to defend Willie's presence. It was his house, after all. "Willie's part of the investigation, Tom."

"Which investigation is that?"

Surprisingly, Luis piped in. "Willie's been helping out with infiltrating this bingo crowd. Workin' the games an' such. He's a registered paid informant."

"Registered!" Willie blurted, the word slipping out. I shot him another hard glance and our eyes locked for an instant. "Damn right," he said, nodding his head. "Registered."

Connally shifted his weight, jutted his chin to stretch the thick skin above his loosened tie. "Well, it's none of my business how you run your investigation," he said to Luis, "but I've got one that's strictly police business."

Meeting Connally's eyes with a dogged glower of his own, Luis said nothing. Two bulldogs, staring each other down, digging in for a growling standoff. Then Connally took a breath. He looked to Willie, then to me, then back to Luis' stoic pose. Maybe he counted to ten before speaking. "Come to think of it," he said, his gaze shifting back to Willie, "I guess I remember a time or two when you came up with some good info."

In some desperate attempt at telepathy, I willed Willie not to say anything clever.

"Damn right," he said again.

Connally took that in stride. "I'm not here about your investigation, gentlemen. Like I said, I have an investigation of my own." He focused on Luis again. "You understand how a capital crime might take precedence here, don't you?"

"Absolutely. I was just explaining the various aspects of that to Henry."

"Looks like I'm in for another scolding," I said, grinning at Willie. "You don't mind if I take this beating alone, do you, Willie? Maybe we could just sit around the breakfast nook, let you get back to bed."

"Yeah, that's all right," Willie said, in a rare demonstration of tact. "All this prob'ly too *subtle* for me anyway." His eyes sparkled at me and he chuckled for everyone's benefit as he turned to climb the stairs. I led the way into the kitchen.

"Chip off the old block," Connally mumbled.

I didn't bother to disagree. "Have a seat, gentlemen." I gestured toward the breakfast nook tucked in under the corner windows. Connally squeezed his way into a chair and Luis sat across from him. I found cups and poured us some coffee. Feeling confident, I leaned back against the counter, sipped my coffee, and waited.

"Luis bring you up to speed on this Spencer deal?"

I nodded. "Only a little. Tell me more"

Connally took me in with those hot Irish eyes, a steady look, almost calm, but intensity shown through. *He* had questions for *me*, not the other way around. But I figured it was give and take. Interdepartmental cooperation, and all that.

Shifting his gaze out the window, Connally fumbled inside his coat for a cigarette. He lit up, took a deep drag, and exhaled it like a sigh. Then he looked at me again. "Vice and narcotics has been on to him for a while. Methamphetamine. He's got someone manufactures it, he ships it, he deals it, but apparently he doesn't use. That doesn't give him the same kind of weak spot that most of these skells have. Strictly in it for the money. Course he's left a whole lot of burnouts in his wake but no one's given much up about him yet."

I nodded, sipped my coffee.

"DEA has been on to him too, but Kearns' people didn't know about that until recently. Shoulda been workin' it together, which they are now. But the Feds are real sensitive about that, if you know what I mean."

"I think I do."

"So you understand why I want you to back off."

I didn't nod to that. Connally waited.

"Luis said we should go back to our bingo investigation. Let you do the homicides and let Kearns and the DEA worry about Spencer."

"That's right," Connally said, and Luis nodded agreement.

"The thing is, they're tangled up in our bingo operations."

Connally sighed again but his face didn't turn any redder. "How do you figure? How'd you even come across him?"

"Some of the bingo people told me he was hooked up with Brent Charmichael."

"Bingo people who?"

"Someone in Mickey's family." Connally's eyes remained glued to mine. I did my best to meet them.

"The sister," he said, not bothering to make it a question.

I nodded, unhappy with myself. But it was give and take. I reminded myself that there were no fire-breathing dragons for a million miles. I told Connally what Claire said about Mickey and Brent going in together and how Spencer had showed up to ace Mickey out.

"She said 'Spencer'? Like that?"

"She said Spence, with initials she couldn't remember. R.D. was one of her guesses."

"She say anything about the meth connection?"

I shook my head. "She didn't know about it."

"Probably not the same guy."

I shot him a quizzical look, which he did his best to ignore. "What about the meth connection?" I asked.

"What connection? That Brent Charmichael used crank? There's a couple hundred thousand of them."

"Brent was a user, the Flood brothers were users, one of them went down for a rap. Brent was going in with a dealer named R.D. Spence. Brent turns up dead and you don't think there's a connection?"

"Your source didn't say he was a dealer. 'Sides, Spencer's underground. Behind the scenes."

"All the more reason for him to be moving into something new."

Connally didn't say anything. That had to mean he was curious.

"What does narcotics know about Spencer? How big is he?"

Connally shrugged and crossed his arms, his upper body folding in with resistance. He regarded me for a moment but then something in his eyes relaxed. "All right, Henry," he said, taking a drag from his cigarette. "I'll tell you this. They don't know how central he is to this ring. It's multi-state for sure. That's why DEA is in it. Several labs maybe, definitely more than one. And they think he's goin' mobile with them. It's the latest thing. They've busted a trailer home and found the aftermath in a few motel rooms but it hasn't caused a hitch in the supply. The dealers in Denver are still dealin' and the supply has increased if anything. That's where DEA has their plant, in with some of the street hawkers. But he's pretty much entry level. All they know is that it's coming in from out of state. Probably Wyoming. There's a good supply showing up recently in Cheyenne."

Bells went off. Cheyenne. Bennie Palmer. Bingo!

"There's also an operation in Salt Lake City that smells like the same MO but they think it's getting shipped into there too. And Reno has a problem. Might be related, might not."

"So they don't know where it's coming from, where it's being manufactured?"

"That's right. Could be a number of smaller labs but…apparently there's some consistency to the product. And the volume is…"

"So maybe a wholesale lab. Could be Cheyenne?"

"Could be lots of places. DEA isn't all that forthcoming about the details."

"What about the money?"

"What about it?"

"I mean, how big is it dollar-wise? And where's the money going?"

"Hell, they don't know that. It's all they can do to trace the dope. But there's so much of it goin' around, so many speed freaks getting it fronted…apparently they've occasionally tried to sell to each other. So they can't tell where to look for the source."

"What if we knew where the money was going?"

Connally's eyes rolled. "What are you getting at, Henry? Who cares about the money? It's going into his mattress. Off shore or whatever."

"Hear me out on this, will ya?"

Luis nodded. "He might have something, Tom."

Connally looked to Luis, then to me, then he settled back in his chair. He took a final hit off his cigarette and mashed it out. "Okay, Henry. Let's hear it."

"I was thinking about how they've been tracking down the operatives for these cocaine cartels out of Columbia and Mexico."

"It's not the same. This stuff's being produced *here*. There's no customs trail."

"But customs hasn't stopped the coke traffic either. It's coming from too many starting points, crossing at too many places. So they look for the money. When it gets big enough, it shows. They start tracing it back to the source. Some guy pays with green for a mansion or a yacht, they keep an eye on him, see where he travels. They got the tax people involved now and through them they get into bank accounts. You deposit more than ten thou in cash these days, right? You gotta have someone sign for it. They're following the money?"

"Okay, fine. They follow the money. Just like in the movies. You seen any big piles of money lately?"

"Yeah, Tom, I have."

Connally huffed, then the creases around his mouth and eyes lifted into a taunting grin. "Where? Bingo?"

Luis said, "We don't have all the details yet but the numbers are big. Pretty impressive even at the start but maybe doubled, tripled in the last year."

Connally's eyes slid towards Luis again, then came back to me. "Okay, let's hear the rest."

Luis was hearing me, so I addressed him instead. "It's always been a laundry, right? We knew that. It's just gotten bigger. Way bigger. The only thing we haven't found is the source of all this extra cash. It's not coming from bingo."

He thought it over, his eyes unmoving. Uncharacteristically, Connally waited on him. I did too. I took a cigarette from Connally's pack on the table, lit it, and blew smoke. Luis met my eyes and nodded. It was all I could expect by way of an endorsement, so I went with it.

"The thing about bingo, Tom, is that it's strictly a cash operation. And how do they deal with all that cash? Through puppet corporations. According to the regs and their filings they don't take anything for themselves except expenses and nominal salaries. They can't even own the halls. Even the games are run with mostly volunteers." Connally's look wasn't exactly encouraging but the taunting smile was gone. "So what do they do with it? They donate it. They pass it on to non-profit charity organizations. Much less IRS scrutiny in that realm. And the bingo regulators—the secretary of state—they can't follow it beyond the point of donation. They can't follow it once it's in the hands of these secondary corporations."

"Okay, so what happens to it?"

"It pays the salaries and expenses of the operators of these secondary organizations. They, in turn, donate the excess proceeds to other non-profits. And so on down the line. But the thing is, these secondary corporations are under fewer regulation. Only tax law binds them. They're free to donate to political organizations, neighborhood groups, schools and churches, whatever. They can even offer grants to individuals. *And* they're free to pay fat salaries to their administrators. Essentially, they can do whatever they want with it."

"Except for IRS, right?"

"Yeah, but *they* aren't law enforcement. They watch for red flags, pull an audit, launch some kind of paper war until they can show fraud. But these dummy corporations are built for handling that, putting them off the trail. A sharp accountant could keep it circulating for several years." I paused for affect. Luis nodded slowly. "It's happening now, Tom. We're in on the ground floor."

Connally's face was still but his eyes were alive with interest. "So what? Where does it end up? Who are these people in the secondary organizations?"

"It's the same people who operate the halls. Or their family members and close friends. People they can trust without formal agreements, without contracts, without the usual paper trail. It's based on trust, more or less, and the fact that nobody wants to kill the golden goose. My guess is, if we look deep enough, we'll find Spencer's name or one of his aliases on their rolls."

Connally chuckled. "Sounds like a pretty big leap."

But Luis was further down the path. "Hold on, Henry. If the real money's coming from Spencer, the people you got connected to him are all working for Milo, not the Coyne family. Some of Milo's filings have shown an increase, but not that much, and not all of them. That's why the increases coming out of Coyne's operations were a flag."

"Which ones are showing in Milo's operations? Brent Charmichael's club?"

Luis paused for an instant before nodding his head. "After the fire, I took a closer look at Broadway Bingo. Their most recent quarterlies showed some pretty big grosses, as good as any of Frank's clubs. He's making enough to be in on the scheme."

"That's the place that got torched, right?" Connally said. "I thought that was Milo Finnes' club."

Luis nodded. "Charmichael owns the building. Milo was the licensee."

Connally's eyes shone. Addressing Luis, I said, "What about Charmichael's house? Did you check on that?"

Luis nodded solemnly, with no trace of his usual reticence. "That was a good guess, Henry. He's owned that house for seven years. I checked with the county clerk. Last year he paid it off. He also bought up three lots adjacent and one across the street. Scrape-jobs, basically, but he bought them outright. No mortgages and no liens on any of them." He turned to Connally. "All these sites have new construction goin' up on them. Kind of low-brow spec houses."

"Yeah, I saw that," Connally affirmed. "So Charmichael's been comin' into some money."

"But Henry," Luis said, "this still doesn't connect to Coyne's operations. I mean, Frank didn't have anything to do with Charmichael."

"Not recently, not that we know of. Maybe Frank didn't want to play ball. So they went over his head."

"To whom?"

"Someone else in the Coyne family that's connected to the cash flow. Someone connected to Brent Charmichael or the Flood brothers. Or someone who has been. It could be old man Willard. He's the accountant. And *he* knew Charmichael from back when he and Mickey worked together for Frank."

"Or it could be Tanya," Luis said. "She's the one who had the fling with Charmichael."

"Wait a minute," Connally said. "Tanya Gilmore—as in Mickey's widow—had an affair with Brent Charmichael?"

We both nodded. "Willie sniffed that one out," I said.

Connally huffed again, but he didn't dwell on it. "And who's this guy Willard?"

"Willard Coyne. He's Frank's father. He's the one who set up the dummy corporations originally."

"He's Tanya's father too," I added, "Tanya is Frank's sister."

Connally shook his head, coughed out a chuckle of befuddlement. I could sympathize, but it was starting to look like something.

Luis was with me. "You're thinking maybe Mickey didn't want to play ball either?" he said. "Got wind of the deal with Charmichael and threatened to blow the lid off?"

"Makes more sense than killing him for all these petty rivalries."

"And you're sayin' they're launderin' money for Spencer?" Connally asked without a trace of doubt in his tone.

"I *know* they're laundering money for somebody." I looked to Luis. "Tell him about American Community Services."

Luis nodded. "It's a political action committee. Set up a little over two years ago. It donated a hundred K to Marcia Herrera's campaign, among others. Lobbyists, community groups, NRA."

"So how does that tie in?"

"Willard Coyne is on their board. So's his wife. And his daughter, Tanya."

"But they're not big enough to move that much, are they? I mean, how much money are you talkin' about here?"

Luis took up the argument in full force. "All in all, bingo last year did $300 million gross. That's what they report, anyway. Conservative estimates are that's about eighty percent of the take. They've got plenty of room to launder through these PACs and shell corporations."

"And they could make more room by holding back a bigger percentage of their own cash flow," I added. "That's what they're good at. They've been doing that for decades. That's why we're investigating them in the first place. They know how to launder."

"How much of this three hundred mill is covered by the Coyne family?"

"Five years ago, they peaked at about forty million gross on paper," Luis said. "If our estimates are accurate, that means they skimmed another six or eight mill." Connally's eyebrows went up. "Last year, the same licenses did almost sixty."

"How many licenses they got?" Connally asked, his mind working on all cylinders now.

"The Coyne family and a few other individuals we've been able to connect them with—they have forty licenses, give or take. A few of these are small potatoes—moveable games, special events, stuff like that. But the bigger ones, the ones that are attached to public halls, they're showing increases of forty to fifty percent." Luis looked to me and nodded. "These are the ones that do enough volume to hide added cash flow."

"And you don't think it's possible their business has increased that much?"

"Bingo incomes statewide had been on a steady decline since they legalized limited stakes gambling up in Central City back in '93. That put a huge dent in their gross revenues. Then, right after Herrera got elected, they went on the increase again."

"They were already in place to be hiding cash," I said. "But their volume went off so they started looking for another source of income. Drugs would be one obvious choice."

"But it doesn't sound right for the likes of Frank Coyne," Luis said. "I mean, he's a queer bird in a lot of ways, but drugs is not his style."

"Like I said, maybe he doesn't know. Or he doesn't know where it's coming from."

Luis gave me a questioning look but Connally didn't give him time to ask. "How many of these dummy corporations are there?" he asked.

"We know of about a dozen," Luis said. "There's definitely more but we haven't been able to trace them all. The secretary of state's office hasn't exactly been cooperative."

"Isn't that neat," Connally growled, a wise-guy smile crawling across his face. He was beginning to appreciate the picture.

"When Herrera took office," Luis said, "she fired all of her investigators within two weeks. Most of what we got to work with comes from those investigators—their personal files."

"And she got a hundred K from this PAC? So if she's stonewalling the corporate info, she's probably in on it. She could be gettin' all kinds of kickback." Connally's eyes came up to meet Luis' steady stare. "Why doesn't someone go after *her*?"

Luis was silent for a moment and I deferred to him. Eventually he said, "Somebody is."

Leaning forward, Connally regarded Luis patiently. Give and take, I thought to myself.

"It's a high-level investigation, Tom," Luis said. "I'm not sure how much you want to know about it. We're looking to bring it to CBI and from there it would go to a grand jury."

"CBI? You mean *your* office isn't enough to handle it?"

"We don't know who all might be involved. In my office, only Barnes knows about this."

Connally took a moment to think that over. "Barnes started it? He initiated the investigation?"

"No," Luis said, shifting his weight slightly, leaning forward in his seat. "It came down from the governor."

"Jesus," Connally said, shaking his head. "Sounds like politics to me."

I looked to Luis to see if he was going to give Connally the same lecture he had given me. He sat there like a Mexican Buddha, gazing down at his pudgy hands folded on the table. He turned his head and looked out the window.

Connally addressed me. "So you're thinkin' they took out Mickey because he was gonna blow the lid off? How do you know he wasn't involved?"

"We know he was left out. Charmichael snubbed him. Maybe Mickey didn't take to the drug angle either. And if Mickey knew the extent of it—and he was bound to find out sooner or later—that would be reason enough to threaten to blow the whole scheme open. Mickey didn't like Spencer. He got pissed as hell when he found out Charmichael was dealing with him. Burning down Charmichael's hall was to let them know that he meant business."

"What about Charmichael though? Why'd he get taken out? Sounds like he was the pivot man in the whole thing."

I cast my eyes toward Luis but he wasn't going to field it. He continued to stare out the window, appreciating the finer qualities of sunlight on the hedges. Between the two of us, I was the one to stick my neck out. That was my job, after all.

"Maybe he became a liability," I said calmly. "Maybe somebody was putting the heat on him, drawing too much attention to the operation. Maybe somebody was looking hard at him for an old murder case. Something like that."

Connally smiled, then he laughed shortly, pleased with the idea of having screwed with the bad guys. That didn't last long, but he took up the line of thinking. "Maybe that's how they put Charmichael up to doin' Mickey. Told him the heat would be off if Mickey took the fall for the Cline killing. I told you they were playin' it back and forth against each other."

"Then they took out Charmichael to cover their tracks."

"Yeah, but 'they' who?"

The question was addressed to me and I let it float out there long enough for Connally to get his teeth into it. If he wanted to know that, I was in the driver's seat. I didn't want to gloss over the point.

"I don't think we can eliminate Frank," I said, eventually, although I didn't believe it. "He's the one who can keep a secret. On the other hand, his father is the accountant. I haven't gotten that close to him yet but I know he still works the books. And Tanya's a possibility. They're both involved in American Community Services. She's a bit dainty for a pointblank sendoff, but she's definitely seeing the money and there is that old breakup with Charmichael. Maybe she's still pissed." Both men smiled minutely but didn't give it any time.

"How much is she involved in the operations?" Connally asked.

"She holds several of the licenses," Luis said. "And she's on the board with BACCO."

"What's this BACCO again?"

"Bingo Association of Colorado Charitable Organization." Luis said. "It's the umbrella corporation for all these licenses. It's who they donate to in the first round."

"You looked close at them, I suppose?"

"They run that one pretty clean. Frank gets a salary of forty thou a year from them. Tanya gets less than that. Aside from a few other administrative expenses, the rest goes to other non-profits. But they've got three other dummy corporations that redistribute to the second tier. American Community Services is the newest one of these. Herrera hasn't let anyone see those records since she took office. We've tried two or three different requests. It always comes up unavailable. Apparently she keeps that file in her desk. Same people involved though."

"Except Frank, right?" I said. "Didn't you say he wasn't in on American Community Services?"

Luis nodded, smiling. "You surprise me, Henry." Then, turning to Connally, he said, "It's just the three of them. Willard and his wife and Tanya."

"I don't think he has a taste for politics."

"Where was Tanya when Mickey got it?" Connally asked.

"At some society gig with the mayor's wife," I said. "I haven't been able to verify it yet. You think you could check on that, Luis?"

Frowning, he made a note to himself.

"What a mess," Connally said. "Sure confuses the hell out of a simple murder or two. And I don't think DEA is gonna be too excited about it either. Sounds like something for the criminal division of the IRS."

"That would take forever," Luis said, beating me to it.

"But we could gather a lot of info on our own," I said, trying to sound nonchalant. "Under the guise of a criminal investigation."

Connally chuckled. "You mean, use a murder investigation as cover to gather evidence of tax fraud?"

"Not exactly," I said, ignoring the sarcasm. "I was thinking the other way around."

Both men looked at me blankly.

"We could flush out the killer under the guise of investigating the money laundering. Like you said, Tom, the capital crime takes precedence. But I'm already in place. We could play them against each other with what we know about the money and who's moving it. Maybe let it leak that there's an investigation underway. They might try to buy us off with a tip, give somebody up for the killing."

"And you think that would be Spencer?"

"If he is newly involved with this bingo crowd, he wouldn't have any qualms about cleaning house. And *they* wouldn't have any qualms about giving him up."

"He's not around though. He's got outstanding warrants in Colorado. 'Course, it could've been any of his lieutenants or front men. Or even some amped-out speed freak who's into him for a fat tab." Connally frowned and rolled his fingers on the table top. "If it comes down like that," he said trenchantly, "we'll never pick our way through all the narcs."

He was as unhappy about giving his investigation over to them as I was about giving ours to him. But safe to say all of us wanted to move while the tracks were fresh. When you're this close, it breaks right away or it drags on for years behind a platoon of lawyers and accountants.

"Well, that's not the only place to look," I said, "and it's not the only way to get to him."

"How do you mean?"

"There *are* some bingo people who would kill to keep the game up. Harvey Cline is evidence of that."

"But his killers are dead," Connally said. "Mickey and Brent."

"You know that for sure?"

"That they were the killers? Yeah, pretty much."

"Even so, it set a precedent. If Mickey threatened to bring it all down or Brent became a liability, it's the bingo people who stood to get hurt in the short run."

"So you think it *could've* been someone in Coyne's operation?" He sounded irritated again.

"More likely they could have sanctioned it or helped set it up. Had to be someone close to Charmichael, close enough to get him home alone and put a gun against his chest."

"If that's what happened," Connally said.

"What's that supposed to mean?"

"It means you're guessin'," he said, suddenly riled. "It means you don't have anything solid to go on." He looked down to the table, spotted his cigarettes as if surprised to see them there, then reached over and grabbed them.

"You got something else to go on?"

"I got better things to do that follow dead-ends." Connally rooted through the pack of cigarettes, fished one out, and lit it. He blew smoke over his shoulder, then met my eyes with a cool detachment. "The lab guys are still working on it, but it looks like Charmichael could have offed himself after all."

"How'd they come to that?"

"There was some tattooing along the side of his face, gunpowder projectiles, like a gun went off near his head. That extra bullet? In the wall above the desk? He may have tried to shoot himself in the temple then couldn't quite bring himself to do it. Or maybe his hand moved as he pulled the trigger. The bullet missed but the discharge at that close range tattooed his skin in the area. On the second try he put it to his chest. Bigger target."

I looked at him thinking he was bullshitting me but I couldn't come up with a reason why he would. "That can't be. You said yourself he wasn't the type."

"Hell, that's just a guess on my part. Who knows why people commit suicide?"

A poignant question, considering our gathering. Both Luis and Connally knew the truth about my father's death. I passed over it, certain that Connally didn't intend the reference.

"What about the traces on his hands? You said there was something funny about them."

"Yeah, well, it's not conclusive. The smudges don't line up with the way he'd hold a gun normally but you don't hold a gun normally when you aim it at yourself. And there *were* smudges."

"Of course there were. He fired four shots at Mickey Gilmore a few hours earlier."

"Maybe so. Maybe that was spur of the moment, some kinda rage that he realized later he couldn't get away with. Or live with."

"What about the missing computer? All the disks being gone."

"He may have done that himself beforehand. Didn't want to leave anything behind that would incriminate anybody."

I scoffed at that. "C'mon, Tom. He'd have no qualms about leaving his associates holding the bag. Loyalty wasn't his strong suit. Burnt bridges everywhere."

"That's just a guess too, Henry. You never met the guy 'til he was dead."

"We know he turned coat on Frank and was about to turn coat on Milo. And what about his getaway plans? He had tickets to San Diego, remember? His bags were packed, for Christ's sakes."

"Maybe he changed his mind. Hey, I can't explain all the whys and wherefores, and neither can *you*. I'm just tellin' you what the lab boys found so far. We won't get the full report for a couple of days, maybe longer. But the gunpowder tattooing is there. I saw it." He tapped a finger to his head just above the cheekbone. "You saw it too, didn't ya? How do *you* explain it?"

I remembered the marks, remembered not knowing what to make of them. The three of us sat in silence, mulling over the question. Luis and I stared at Connally as if waiting for him to expose the joke. He sat there smoking, taking a turn at appreciating the hedges in the yard.

"I don't buy it," I said. "Somebody orchestrated that scene. I could smell it. Maybe the killer put the gun to his head after shooting him to make it look that way."

"Could be. The full forensics will be able to tell us that. If the tattooing occurred after he died, it wouldn't bleed the same way or the skin wouldn't react the same. Whatever they call it, they'll be able to tell."

"So the possibility exists," I said, aware of my twisted wishful thinking, "that he was murdered. *And* we still have the other person in the car with him."

Connally took in a long drag of smoke. "You got somebody in mind?"

I didn't want to share my one good lead but the trail was getting splintered.

"Benny Palmer," I said.

"Palmer? Who's he again? Coyne's supplier? Bingo stuff, right?"

Luis nodded. "What makes you think of him?"

"He's got a warehouse up in Cheyenne. You mentioned it yourself."

"Cheyenne Supply, he calls it, matter a' fact. Works from out of state to avoid Colorado regulators. So?"

I pointed to Connally. "You said DEA had Spencer working out of Cheyenne."

"That's not enough of a connection."

"But as it happens, Palmer is hooked up with Milo too. And, therefore, Charmichael. He's makin' deliveries to Milo's operations."

"You didn't tell me that," Luis cut in, interrupting Connally's reaction. His eyebrows dipped and his narrowed eyes narrowed further.

"I didn't know it was important until now."

"When did you find that out?"

"It was at that meeting, just before Mickey got killed. Mickey was on the ropes, trying to justify setting the fire. Palmer suggested they call for a truce with Milo's outfit before things got out of hand. Mickey jumped him for that. Accused Palmer of wanting to expand his business. Tossed it off in the middle of things to distract from his own disloyalties. He said 'a little birdie' had spotted one of Palmer's trucks at Milo's warehouse. I gathered it's here in Denver."

"And he copped to it?"

"More or less," I said. "He countered with a 'so what' kind of response and kept up the attack on Mickey. They passed over it in the moment. Not long after that the shooting started."

"Where was he later that night," Connally asked, "when Charmichael got it?"

"I don't know but I could find out."

"You think he could be good for it?"

"I don't think he's got the balls, frankly, but he's in pretty deep. He could have been desperate enough. Or could have set it up."

"You mean, 'cause he's in with this Milo guy? So what? Sounds like they were all in on it, except Mickey."

"I wouldn't go that far. But there's more to it. I figure Palmer for running meth down here from Cheyenne. Under the bingo supplies. The same trucks. That's what they were hiding from Mickey. Then he would get Brent or the Flood brothers to off-load and distribute it to the dealers. If they weren't dealing it themselves."

It was just a guess but neither man offered any objections. Both of them turned to look out the window, their eyes taking in the grounds and Leroy Street's house next door as if searching there for verification.

"Tell me again," Luis said to the window, "about when this came up. At that meeting at the Palace. What were the reactions?"

"To tell you the truth, I don't remember it that well. They were all pretty riled at Mickey. He and Frank were yelling back and forth. Mickey tossed it out to deflect the accusations. Frank tried to shrug it off. Chuck Burrows too. They may have just been sticking to the point. Palmer was definitely pissed off. Defensive. He said something like 'We all do what we have to.' But nothing ever came of it. Like I said, that's when the shooting started."

Connally's eyes swiveled in my direction. "Burrows, huh?" he said, then stared off as if picturing the man. "I got no love for him, personally," he grumbled, "but he's an ex-cop. That don't make him an angel, but it's hard to see him getting' involved with a bunch of speed jacks. I mean, he's seen what that shit does." He took a breath, as if reining in the vehemence that had crept into his tone. We knew what he meant: these people trashing their lives with energy and intention, driven by their meth addiction. Self-destruction, when it's that blatant and amped up, is difficult to watch, difficult to humanize. "Anyway," he added, "he wouldn't trust them, for one thing. I just don't see it."

"He may not be involved. Like Luis said, it doesn't sound right for Frank either. And I don't see it for Mickey. Maybe the drugs aren't making it into the Coyne operation. And that's why Palmer started supplying Milo—to get it to Charmichael. I haven't seen much of him since that came out. He was conspicuously absent from the big powwow Sunday night."

"What about the money laundering?" Connally said. I was pleased to see he was still interested.

"Could be Palmer does an end around with the cash, directly to Willard or Tanya."

"You got anything to show that Palmer has that direct a connection with them?" Luis asked.

"Not the details, but he's obviously around. And it could be somebody else. We don't know yet who works the transfer of funds to these dummy corporations, but whoever it is could be doing the creative bookkeeping, turning it around clean, and passing it back through Palmer to Spencer after a cut."

"But Palmer didn't do Mickey, 'cause he was there." Connally said.

"Could be one of *his* flunkies. He doesn't drive all those trucks himself."

"You got a line on anybody like that?"

"Not yet, but it won't take much."

Connally focused on me with the usual amount of misgiving in his eyes. I didn't fall to pieces and after a moment he dropped his gaze. The three of us sat in silence. I felt good. I had built a strong case.

Finally, Connally looked over at Luis. The two of them shared a look, then Luis shrugged. "I think it's worth looking into," he said.

Connally's eyes widened in an expression of mild dismay, but when he spoke, he wasn't displeased. "This'd be under the auspices of your bingo investigation?"

"For a while. We got more to do, anyway. And we don't have much time to do it."

Connally nodded slowly. After another long moment, his eyes met mine.

"Okay, let's see what comes of it."

"One thing, Tom," Luis said. "Nobody else can know about this. I mean nobody else in the department. Not yet."

"Yeah, I get that. Nobody's gonna hear it from me. And definitely not Joe Perkins, right? He get in touch with you yet?"

I shook my head. "I've been pretty hard to find."

"Not a bad approach," Connally said with an ambiguous lift of his eyebrows. With some trouble, he extricated himself from the chair, and he and Luis followed me out of the room. As we entered the living room, Connally talked to Luis about setting up some direct lines of communication. I heard the boards creak at the top of the stairs. Willie was not asleep.

Connally turned to me at the door. "Are you still comfortable outside? No cracks in your cover?"

I thought of my conversation with Claire and what she said about Frank not trusting me. "One of the family," I said.

He gave me an appraising look. "I would want to be kept informed as we go, ya know," he said, with a tone of disapprobation. "You get something shaky on Palmer's alibi, we could bring him in for questioning. You understand? I don't want you tryin' to force a confession out of him."

"That's definitely your department," I said, doing my best to sound earnest.

Connally glared, checking for sarcasm. "So you're staying in touch with Luis?"

"Right on schedule," I said, smiling at Luis. He tweaked the side of his mouth without letting Connally see it.

"It's important, Henry. This is dangerous stuff. I told you, no backup."

"I took you seriously on that, Tom. Don't worry. I am being careful." Saying that was coming pretty easy by now.

"But are you bein' smart?"

From just outside the doorway, holding the screen open, Luis said, "He's bein' *too* smart, if you ask me."

We all chuckled over that one but you wouldn't call it sharing the joke.

Chapter 36

Not five seconds after the screen door slammed, Willie clamored down the stairs, coming to a flatfooted stop at the bottom as if presenting himself for inspection. He was dressed for town: a burnished black leather sport coat over a synthetic satin shirt that reflected light in different hues of lavender; new-looking blue jeans with the cuffs rolled up; black and white high-top sneakers that looked like they might be his dress pair. Only one silver chain—not too gaudy in size—draped around the outside of his shirt collar. He was wearing teardrop purple shades with gradient lenses, dark enough to hide his eyes. He held his cell phone forward in one hand as if ready—and not afraid—to use it.

"Where's the party?" I said.

"Man, I is *fresh*. You dressin' *down*. What *you* know?"

He ran his free hand smoothly over the eighth-inch stubble of hair on his head, as if that would have some kind of effect. My three-day beard was more supple.

"I can't compete," I said.

"Damn right. You goin' like *that*?"

"Goin' where?"

"Duncan's on his way, man. Be here any minute."

"He called?"

"Man, I called *him*. Gotta get my ride back. *He's* ready."

"Okay, Willie. I'll go see what I can scrounge up that doesn't clash. How about you walk the dog."

"Man, that dog is spoiled."

"He'll shit in your yard if you don't," I said, taking the stairs two steps at a time.

I put on a clean shirt and my shoulder holster and wore my heavy jacket from the night before to hide the bulge. I wondered if Willie was packing, but decided not to ask. By the time I got downstairs, Duncan had arrived, and he and Willie were provoking Pimpy in the yard.

Duncan greeted me with a questioning look, running his eyes along Willie's six-foot five-inch frame. I shrugged.

"'Bout time," Willie groused.

We climbed into Duncan's mini-van, leaving the dog in the yard.

"When did you get this?" I said.

"You like it? The family car for the new millennium. Comes with a built-in child seat. Check it out." Duncan reached back next to Willie and pulled forward on a section of the seatback. A padded contraption unfolded into what looked like a miniature plastic roll-cage.

"Yeah, that cool, that cool," Willie said, rolling out one of his low chuckles.

"The time will come for you too, Willie. I've seen that gleam in Maxine's eyes."

"That gleam pointin' way off in the future, bro'."

"Front and back comfort zones, six-speaker stereo, child-proof power windows and seats, power moon-roof, thirty-five miles to a gallon in the city. It doesn't do well in high speed chases though, so you boys are out of luck."

"Man, I jus' hope nobody *sees* me in this thing," Willie said.

"Yeah," Duncan said, "Me too."

"How'd you do with the paper work?" I asked.

"No problem. Just have to go by Aurora PD on the way."

"*By* there? I'm still not cleared on those charges Harris snagged me for."

"I thought you said he didn't press charges."

"Not yet. Connally swore a writ to get me transferred before he had the chance. But…"

"Connally released you without clearing it with Aurora?"

"He didn't release me, exactly. He put me up on B & E charges and let Coyne's lawyer go my bail."

"Breaking and entering? What the hell's that about?"

"Part of my cover. You don't want to know."

Duncan thought that over. "So Aurora could still file against you?"

"They still want to, far as I know."

"So already you've got me transporting a fugitive."

"I'm not a fugitive, Duncan. I told you, Connally worked it to keep me undercover."

"But he didn't tell Harris. What's the thinking in that?"

"Man, those Aurora cops is *dirty,* man," Willie piped in. "They's all on the take with the *bingo Mafia.*"

"What's with you and the *slanguage,* Willie? This go with your outfit?"

"Man, we on the *street* now, Duncan. Gotta talk the *talk.*"

"Whatever," Duncan said. "Anyway, you're investigating the Aurora PD too?"

"We don't know that anybody's on the take out there," I said, shooting Willie a look. "But I'm still under deep cover and that's the way Luis and Connally want to keep it."

"Deep cover, huh? You talkin' the talk, too?"

"Tha's right," Willie said, "We is *deep* cover."

Duncan laughed and looked to see if I was serious. I kept my face forward to hide my smile from Willie.

"Anyways," Willie said, "I gotta make some calls."

While Willie got on his phone, Duncan continued questioning me. I told him what I could to appease his curiosity, steering clear of any of our leads into the world of methamphetamine. Duncan has an attitude about drugs these days, mostly, I suspect, from a desire to bury his own past in that regard, a past that I had shared with him before he turned so pearly white and respectable. It was hardly sordid by today's standards—a few finals week cram sessions assisted by the latest in campus pharmaceuticals, smoking dope on summer weekends after that grueling first year. He missed the late 80's for the most part—by choice and by marriage—although we'd had a few good late night conversations when the cognac started to get the better of us, and I had gram. But these days, it was apparent that he had ambitions and concerns about his future, grounded in a chain of accomplishments whose weakest link might be that he would have to say he never inhaled.

Willie hooked up with a brother named Jo-jo and the jive from the back seat was low and fast and mostly indecipherable. I didn't pay it any mind until I heard him mention Spence. I turned in my seat.

"Who're you talking to?"

His dark eyes flitted to me in mid-sentence, but he didn't miss a beat. "Ah, no man, it ain't the 'C' I's lookin' for. 'Sides that dude behind some wrong shit. Them base heads all over the shit 'fore it goes to the curb….Plus which, they usin' that *Menita*, cuz. You know that shit, don't ya? Tha's right, tha's what I seen….Yeah, that *was* from the brotha', ah'ight. Got down on a bag for a little freeze an' spent the whole fuckin' night on the *throne,* know that?" Willie, and apparently his friend, shared a hardy, extended laugh. "Yeah, man, I ain't shittin…" he added, and that caused more of the same. "'Sides, this dude on the line a *whiteboy*. I ain't takin' him down ta' D-town, an' he ain't coppin' from some damn cherry on the corner neither. We talkin' a full *bag* an' he wanna deal with the *man*, ah'ight? So's he can get a taste hisself….Nah, man, it ain't nineteen, he don' want it. He gonna cut the crystal 'fore he buys. Tha's why we lookin' for this Spence dude. Word is he got a factory connection."

"Is he buying *drugs?*" Duncan asked with no small amount of anxiety in his voice. "Is he doing a *drug deal* from my *car?*"

"No, no." I was somewhat appalled myself. "He's, uh, following a lead in our investigation."

"Following a *lead?*"

"Yo, cuz, I'm down on that too," Willie was saying. "Ain' my bag, neither. But this dude's *fat,* man, know what I'm sayin? We talkin' *crates.* We could all make out, ah'ight?"

"*Crates?*" Duncan said. "Crates of *what?*"

"Take it easy, Duncan." I turned fully in my seat to face Willie and gestured with my eyes towards the back of Duncan's head. "What are you doing? Get off the phone, will ya?"

He waved a big hand in my face. "Man, you got the juice, cuz. I *know* you do. You *always* hooked up. All you gotta do is put the word out. Everything cool, we can do this thing."

"He *is* talking drugs, Henry. I told you about this before. I'm not getting involved in another one of your phony buys."

"Willie," I said, "*Get-off-the-phone.*"

"Yeah, man, hold on a minute. I got a sit-chi-*a*-tion." Willie palmed the phone. "Man, what *is* your *problem?*"

"You're out of line, Willie. You're setting up a buy in your boss's car."

"Man, this ain't no buy. I'm trying to find this *Spence* dude."

"Never mind how you even know about him. This isn't the time or place." I nodded toward Duncan again, bulging my eyes.

"Oh, *man.* Jus' chill a minute, will ya?" Willie brought up the phone to speak. "Yeah, Jo-jo, I gotta go." He paused to listen. "Yeah, tha's right. Them bitches *all* like that, ain't they." His smiling eyes came up to meet mine, narrowing jocularly. "Jus' troll for this Spence cat, ah'ight? You snag somethin', you got my cell….Tha's right, posse out bro."

He pushed a button on the phone, watched for the disconnection. "Man, you dudes *gots* ta' *chill.*"

"Willie, you don't make drug deals from my car. If you're working for me, you don't deal drugs at all."

"Man, Duncan. He *asked* me to. *I* don't do that shit."

"That's right, Duncan, I did," I said, giving Willie my surliest eyeball. "He was putting the word out on a suspected meth dealer that might be tied in to Brent Charmichael."

"These guys are into speed?"

"More to the point, they're into the money from it. This dealer, a guy named Robert David Spencer, he's big. It's possible he's laundering money through the bingo operations. They're in place with all these shell corporations to put more cash through the wash than what they got coming from the halls."

Duncan looked over at me, incredulous. "You're kidding me. Are they *that* big?"

"$300 million a year," I said blandly, bored with repeating it.

"Jesus, who'd've thought?" Duncan said. "Bingo."

We pulled into the parking area of the Aurora Police Department. Duncan went in alone to push through the paperwork, leaving Willie and me hunched down in the car.

"So you listened in on my talk with Luis and Connally," I said.

"Man, it's my house. 'Sides I gotta stay up on this shit if I'm gonna help."

"I thought you didn't know anybody dealin' meth. White-trash high, you said, if I'm not mistaken."

"Man, tha's what Jo-jo gave me, too. All kinds of shit. Gonna ruin my rep!"

"I appreciate the sacrifice," I slurred. "You think they'll come up with something?"

"He got a brotha knows a brotha. Guy who's connected."

"Okay, can't hurt. But you gotta be a little more tactful in front of Duncan, ya know?"

"Man, I thought he was *hip* to this. Thought it was cool 'long as I was workin' with *you*."

"Yeah, well, I'm not exactly on his top-ten list when it comes to drug deals. He was along for the ride once when I found a dealer's body."

"Well, shit man. You coulda told me that."

"I'll smooth it over for you, but show a little tact, will ya?"

"Tact," he said. "Jesus. Now I gotta worry about *tact*?"

"You remember that chase coming out of Central City last time?"

"Oh, *yeah*, man. That was a *trip*, was'n' it?"

I nodded towards the building. Duncan was coming into view. "He remembers it differently," I said.

"Man, I told you he's a bust. We got *outa* there *clean*, didn't we? What was the name a' that *escape route* you took us down on? God Awful Highway?"

"Oh My God Road. And it was *your* driving that he remembers."

"Oh, no. *You* the one told me to take it. Eggin' me on…"

"My point is, that's the last time the three of us were on a case together. He made a point of mentioning it to me. Let's not give him any reasons to worry. Just keep it low-key till we get the Mustang. Duncan doesn't need the excitement." I turned in my seat. "Be tactful."

Willie huffed as Duncan opened the car door. He slid in holding a sheaf of papers in one hand. "All set." Then, noticing the silence, he said, "What? You guys talking about me?"

"Just reminiscing about the good old days."

"Well, let's get this over with. I gotta get back to the real world."

I sneaked a look at Willie. He drew his pinched thumb and forefinger across his lips, eye's shining, brows lifting. Entirely too much fun.

We pulled into K & K Automotive Reconditioning and parked just outside the open gate. The man in black stood bent at the hips, leaning on the top rail of fencing that marked off the office door. He looked like he looked every day, I'd guess. His hair looked dirtier, if that was possible, smoothed back in sculpted waves. Even behind the mirrored sunglasses, I could tell he took Willie in from head to toe. A deprecating smile crawled up one side of his pockmarked face but he didn't say anything as Willie approached and stood in front of him, fully a head taller.

"Come back to get your car, huh?"

"Tha's right," Willie said. "This here's my *lawyer*."

"Lawyer, huh? Well, good for you."

Without further niceties, he led the way into the office. The gum-chewing blond behind the counter was working hard on a mechanical calculator, punching buttons, making it ring. Looking up, her jaws stopped moving in recognition. Her nervous eyes shifted to follow the man in black as he made his way behind the counter. With his back to the room, he leafed through some pages on a clipboard. The blond watched us, watched him, watched us, then finally broke the silence.

"Can I help you?"

"Hi, I'm Duncan Pruett. I represent Mr. Randall here in the matter of getting a release on his nineteen-seventy-five Mustang."

Duncan's professional posturing was lost on her. The pale-blue eyes skipped from face to face, nervous as a cat in heat. "Okay, then. Which car is that?" She nudged at her sticky bangs with the back of her forefinger. They refused to cooperate.

"It's that beat up Mustang, came in on Saturday," the man in black grumbled.

"It ain't beat up, man," Willie said, picking up right where they had left off. "I'm re-*storing* it. It's a *classic*."

"So you said." He turned and cleared his throat with a growl and shoved the clipboard across to Duncan, keeping a heavy hand splayed over the top sheet. "You got the release forms from Aurora PD?"

"$218.30," Duncan said, sorting through his briefcase. "That the total?"

The man nodded. Duncan came up with several forms, displaying them on the counter, one at a time. It moved slowly. Willie pulled me aside.

"You got the cash for this, man?"

"Me? Why would I do that?"

"Ah, c'mon, man. You're jivin' me, right?"

I smiled. "Yeah, I'm jivin' you, Willie."

Duncan looked over the charges then slid the clipboard towards me. The man in black gloated. I counted out the money, laid it on the clipboard, and slid it back to him, ignoring his smirk. He shuffled through the papers, all thumbs, his hands too big for the stapler. I waited. Willie jingled the keys in his pocket, then stepped to the window that looked out over the junkyard. We watched as the man in black sorted the pages, putting them into their proper places; a cubbyhole here, a clipboard there, several of them under the register drawer. The man was as quick as a counter clerk at the DMV.

When his hands were empty, he faced the three of us on the other side of the counter. "Okay, yer all set," he said. "I'll take you on out to get yer car." He turned toward the door that led into the yard.

"Man, 'bout time, too," Willie mumbled.

With one hand on the doorknob, the man stopped and turned to face Willie. I could see Willie's face reflected in the mirrored lenses, dark orbs like the pupils of some steely-eyed insect. The man took his hand off the knob and fingered around the chest pocket of his shirt, prodding deliberately as if digging for something important, a key or a receipt, something essential to our endeavor. The stubby fingers came out with a pack of gum. He shook out a stick, pealed the wrapper off with some difficulty, then put the stick to his lips, biting off a quarter of it at a time.

"You got some problem with the pace a' my work?" He garbled his words around the still hard stick of gum. It was a slow day. He was pressed to fill the time. For some reason, I took pleasure in watching Willie feel his way around that quick mouth of his.

After a bit of a stare down, Willie took a different tact. "Oh, hell no," he said, almost apologetically. "It ain't that. I just been without wheels for a few days, ya know? Man gotta have his ride, right?"

Duncan stepped forward. "If there's nothing else required, my client would like to retrieve his car. I know he's got other appointments and he's probably concerned about my fees."

The man's face turned toward Duncan. "Yeah. I know. Yer his lawyer."

"Duncan Pruett. And I didn't catch your name. I want to be sure to pass on to the Aurora Police Department how cooperative you've been."

The mirrored glasses turned from Duncan to Willie and back again. "Ben," he said. "My name's Ben. Come get yer car, boy."

Willie's face went slack. The man named Ben turned and opened the door and stepped out into the yard, letting the door close behind him.

"Tactful, Willie," I said under my breath, gripping on his upper arm momentarily. "We just want your car."

Willie turned his head. "Tactful, huh?" We looked through the window of the doorway together. Ben was strolling into the junk yard looking like he was counting off his steps. "Yeah, I'm all about tact right now."

"We'll wait for you out front. Follow you home."

"Tact," Willie said, as if to himself, moving to open the door. Before it closed, I heard him say, "So what kinda ride *you* got, Ben?"

The gum-chewing blond poised behind the counter started to move her jaws again, working her lips to hide an entertained smirk. "'Bye, now," she said, all smiles.

We sat in the minivan for five minutes before Willie's Mustang came fishtailing through the open gate spewing dust and gravel in its wake. Just after him, the man in black loped into view, then stopped bow-legged at the gatepost and gave Willie a departing finger. Willie waved back, answering the gesture, and howled at us as he drove by. The Mustang hardly slowed before shooting out onto the highway.

"Still needs work on his tactfulness," Duncan offered.

"Yeah."

Before we could follow him, before Duncan had even started up the van, before I saw the two bullet holes in its truck lid, I recognized the beige and white Cadillac as it rolled into view from around the side of the building, like some implausible replay as a bad practical joke.

The master plan had worked.

Chapter 37

"That's *them*," I yelled, startling Duncan.

"Them who?"

"Charmichael's henchmen. They're the ones that pulled the holdup at Clancy's."

"Clancy's?" Duncan said, clearly baffled. "What the hell are *they* doing here?"

"They're following Willie. His car was bait."

"You set a trap? What are you talking about?"

"Just *follow* them, Duncan. Willie could be in some trouble here."

He put the car in gear and rolled forward but he didn't lose the thread. "Is this why you waited a day, Henry? To set this up?" From the edge of the driveway, I could see Willie at the crest of the rise. The Caddy lagged a good ways behind.

"There they go," I said, trying to deflect any further interrogation. "Don't lose them."

Duncan pulled out to follow. The engine whined painstakingly.

"Does Willie know he's bait for these thugs?"

"Yes. Well, not exactly."

"What the hell does that mean?"

"We set the trap for last night. We staked out the car, but they didn't show. Is this the fastest this thing will go?"

"I'm not getting into any kind of high-speed pursuit here, Henry. You understand that, don't you? You can wreck your own car and Willie's too, for that matter, but not mine."

"There's not going to be any chase, Duncan. They're just following him." I said it with more conviction than I felt and I could sense Duncan's suspicions.

The minivan had no power. One minute seemed like five before we got up to sixty at the top of the rise and caught sight of Willie in the distance. Traffic was thin so he was easy to spot, a quarter mile ahead. The Caddy was keeping a safe distance behind him. I was grinding my teeth at the pace of our progress and trying to think clearly through the options.

Duncan was no help. "You *know* these guys did that holdup?" he persisted. "Are they armed? Did *they* kill Charmichael?"

"Just shut up a minute, will ya? I gotta figure this out."

"Figure what out?" Duncan snapped. "They're *killers* and they're closing in on Willie. It's pretty clear to me that we need the cops."

"They're not *killers*, Duncan. They're just the hired muscle."

"You mean, they're only following orders? Willie's old man will be happy to hear *that* at the funeral."

"Duncan, *please*." Willie slowed as he approached the intersection with Tower Road. The Caddy stayed back, keeping a car between them. We were finally gaining ground.

"No way, man. I *know* you in this situation. I'm not going to let this escalate into some kind of Fast Five car chase scene. This is *not* going to be another Central City. Willie damn near killed us on that fucking mountain jeep trail."

"Oh My God," I said.

"What? What's the matter?"

"That's the name of it. Oh My God Road. Anyway, we got away, didn't we?" I said before I could stop myself.

"Got *away*? Henry, I'm an attorney. I don't go around seeing what I can get away with. It was too fucking close for me, dammit, and I'd say *your* luck's running out. You didn't exactly get away with..." He stopped abruptly and his foot came off the gas. I knew I was in trouble. "Are *these* the same *guys*?"

"What? Who?"

"The ones you were shooting it out with on Parker Road?"

"I...I don't know for sure."

"You don't know *for sure*?"

I had to laugh. It was a guilty, feeble laugh. "All right, Duncan. It's the same *car*. I didn't see who's driving, okay? But they're not who killed Mickey Gilmore. That was a different car."

With an incredulous look stretching his face, he leaned forward and craned his neck, trying to hold my eyes. "What?"

"Duncan, step on it. What do you wanna do? Let them chase Willie down?"

"I'm calling the police," he said, reaching behind the seat and shuffling through his briefcase. "That's what I'll do. 911."

When his hand came up with a cell phone, I could have kissed him.

"You've got a phone? Lemme call Willie."

"No way, man. You'll cook up some wild plan..."

"Okay, Duncan, *all right*! Just get us back in the city limits, all right? We bring Aurora cops in on this, I'll be back in the joint before you can say 'due process'. It will blow the investigation. *Ducan! Please!*"

He paused, staring intently through the windshield, the cell phone jammed between fingers still gripping the steering wheel. The engine whined as we gained on the Caddy. Willie had stopped at the traffic light. The Caddy had crawled up two cars behind. Duncan slowed up not 50 yards behind them.

"We need to warn him, anyway. Don't you think?"

"All right, call him. Tell him where to go. Then we're calling the cops." He handed me the phone.

Willie turned north on Tower and the Caddy followed, still keeping a distance. By the time we got to the intersection, the light had changed. An older pickup was stopped in front of us, not taking the turn on red.

"Go around him," I said.

"I'm not going around him. This isn't an emergency vehicle, for Christ's sake."

I punched in Willie's number. From our vantage point, we could no longer see either car. "Christ, Duncan, we're losing them."

Duncan glared at the red light, leaning forward slightly, his hands kneading the wheel. "Jesus *Christ*," he said, twisting around to look in all directions. Then he maneuvered the van around the pickup and cut across his bow onto Tower Road. "If I get a ticket for this..."

"Fine, fine, just catch up."

Tower Road was four lanes and had more traffic. There were several cars in both lanes ahead of us, too far away to identify.

Willie answered, "Yo, what up?"

"Willie, Enos Flood is on your tail."

"Henry? That you?"

"Willie, the master plan worked."

"*Master plan*?" Duncan huffed.

"Enos Flood's Caddy is following you. They had the place staked out. They picked you up when you drove out."

"Ah'right, the *master plan*! I gotta hand it to ya, Henry."

"You see them? It's that Caddy that we scoped out behind Holiday Bingo."

"Yeah, yeah, I think I see 'em. They're hangin' back a ways. What's our play? What's the next move?"

Yeah, that. "We need to lead them out of Aurora. Then we call in the cops. Denver cops. We can hook-up with Connally that way. But we have to get out of Aurora first."

"Ah, man, why you wanna do that? I thought we wanted to *get to* these dudes. Why don't we pull them over? You carryin' ain't ya?"

I glanced over at Duncan. He was intent on his driving. "Never mind that. I think this is the best way to play it. Duncan thinks so too."

"Man, I *told* you he's a bust."

"Listen up, Willie. You know where Smith Road is? It's just before the I-70 interchange. It runs west along the railroad tracks."

"Yeah, I think I'm coming up to it now. I see the crossing."

"Turn west, follow it until we get to the county line. I'd say it's about two miles. I'm gonna call Connally direct and get him to send cruisers. Don't try anything fancy, okay Willie? You being in the car was not part of the plan. I don't know what they'll do."

"Well, what good's it gonna do if the cops show up? I thought you wanted to squeeze these guys."

"The main thing is just to identify them and find out who sent them. Enos is probably driving...."

"Yeah, Enos...penis. He the one you smacked around, right? He's gonna be happy to see you again."

"The feeling's mutual. And there's a second person in the car but we didn't get close enough to see who it was. Could be Enos' brother. Could be the man we're looking for."

"Man, this case is gonna *crack*, bro. I can *feel* it. If only we could... "

"The situation calls for caution." I looked over at Duncan. "And some tact. Got it? We gotta use some tact."

Duncan coughed out a sarcastic laugh, shook his head. Willie was howling on the phone. "Yeah, I got your *tact*, man. Right *here*."

I could imagine the gesture. "We're still a ways behind you. Duncan's driving like his grandmother, so you want to slow up a bit, okay?"

"*Slow up*? Man, tell him to get *on* it. I need some *backup*, ah'ight?"

"Did you get onto Smith Road?"

"Yeah, yeah, they're two cars back. I think they're just layin' back to follow."

"That's what I'm hoping. We're comin' up on Smith Road now. We'll have you in sight in a minute. I have to get off to call Connally. We'll set up a location and I'll call you back."

"Okay, man. But tell Duncan I ain't workin' for him no more if he gets me *killed*." His low chuckle punctuated the statement.

"I'll pass that on. Keep a steady speed. We'll be there."

I hung up and punched in 911. "Willie said he's quitting if he gets shot before you get there."

Duncan looked over at me unamused. We made the turn onto Smith Road following a beat-up Toyota that looked like it was going as fast as it could at about thirty-five. Duncan floored the gas pedal and pulled out to pass. The minivan's exhaust hissed like an overwrought compressor. "He can't quit," Duncan said, "I'll fire him."

Smith Road this far out is a rural highway, two lanes of blacktop with dirt shoulders. It runs parallel to the main corridor of railroad tracks coming out of central Denver railyards. Only a few cross streets intersect it and what development there is along its southern edge is light industrial; warehouses, trucking firms, no residential. Further west, at the edge of the Denver city limits, the road runs directly in front of the grounds of Denver County Jail. I figured that was a good place to pull them over. No innocent bystanders and plenty of help in the area. What could happen?

The 911 operator wasn't much help. When I asked to be patched through to Captain Connally, she told me that's not how things worked and asked me where I was calling from. She called me 'sir'.

"Look, lady. I know you can do this, I…"

"What kind of emergency are you having, sir?"

"I've got a gun and I'm not afraid to use it," I yelled. "Does that qualify?"

That pretty much cut through her procedural reservations, though Duncan didn't like it.

"Christ, Henry."

The operator turned me over to her supervisor and I told him the same thing about the gun, "…unless you let me talk to Captain Connally." He said he'd get right on it, then tossed off commands in the air, intentionally loud enough for me to hear it. Not all that convincing. "What should I tell him?"

"Tell him this is Henry Burkhart and I'm in the midst of a pursuit of armed murder suspects. Is that enough?"

"Hold on." He took a minute but something got verified in that time span. He had us connected to police dispatch when he came back on the line and the dispatcher asked me what I wanted without question. They were surprisingly calm. While dispatch worked on finding Connally, the supervisor pumped me for our location.

"I'll tell Connally, no one else."

He assured me they were working on that, rattled off a few cautions, asked me how *he* could help.

"Is this Mr. Pruett?" he asked.

For an instant, I was taken aback. They had ID'ed the phone. "You guys work fast," I said, sneaking a sidelong glance at Duncan. "The latest technology."

"Can you tell me what the problem is, Mr. Pruett?"

"There they go," Duncan said.

We watched the Caddy a hundred yards ahead pulling out to pass. I couldn't see Willie's Mustang. A traffic light further on had just turned red. I hoped Willie had stopped for it.

"Punch it, Duncan."

"What was that, Mr. Pruett?" the voice on the phone said.

"This is Henry Burkhart." I spelled it for him. "You tell Connally I've got...*hostages*. Tell him I'm pulling over his suspects—*at gunpoint*—in front of Denver County Jail. Smith Road and Havana. Got that? Henry Burkhart. Smith Road and Havana."

I hung up the phone and punched in Willie's number.

"Hostages?" Duncan said. "Was that really necessary?"

"Yo, bro, 'S'up?" Willie answered the phone. "Those dudes closin' *in*."

"That's right. You saw them?"

"Yeah, they're back there. I'm stopped at some boulevard, maybe Peoria. They pulled in one car back. I think they're just scopin' me out."

"All right, we're comin' up on you, a few cars behind the Caddy. Now, listen. I told the cops we'd pull them over at Havana. It's right past the county jail."

"*County*? Now, what you wanna do that for? Man, there's gonna be cops all over us."

"That's the idea. Just lead them up the road but take it slow. We gotta give the cops a chance to get there."

"Man, why don't we jus' see what the fuck they want!"

"Willie, that ain't the *play*, okay? It's too dangerous."

"Ah'ight, ah'ight, I'll lead them on down the road. I'll go slow enough even Duncan can keep up."

But that's not the way it happened. When the light turned green, the car behind Willie turned right, leaving nothing between Willie's Mustang and the Caddy. Once they were through the intersection, I caught a glimpse of the Caddy swerving out from its lane. Duncan edged out to get a better look and I leaned over to see. Enos Flood was accelerating towards the Mustang.

"*Punch it*, Willie, they're coming down fast. They're making a move."

"Yeah, man, I see that…*oh, shit!*"

I heard the report of the gun. Two shots like firecrackers popping in the distance. "Willie! They're firing on you!"

"No *shit*, Sherlock! I'm outta here!"

"Duncan, pass these guys. Get up there. Willie's taking fire."

"Christ," Duncan hissed, as if intoning a prayer. He swerved into the on-coming lane and strained to pass two cars. We could see Willie in the distance and the Caddy just behind him, straddling the middle line. We weren't gaining any ground. Another shot sounded.

"Willie! You all right?"

He didn't respond. Swerving back and forth across both lanes, he put a little distance between himself and Enos Flood. We were a good hundred yards back. I had Duncan's phone pressed against my head, repeating Willie's name, when he suddenly shouted, "*Yo, man, get your asses up here!*"

"We're coming, Willie, but you're goin' too fast."

"Man, I *ain't* slowin' *down* for these jacks!"

"Look for a place to turn. A parking lot, a side street, some place where you could change directions and bring them back to us."

"Bring them *back* to us?" –Duncan.

"What about the cops?" –Willie.

"Just do it!" I shouted but I didn't think he heard.

The Mustang's brake lights flashed and Willie took a hard sliding left into the driveway of a warehouse parking lot. The lot was empty, the place looked abandoned. The Caddy made the same turn with considerably more trouble, skidding past the driveway and bouncing over a drainage ditch. Willie's car disappeared around the corner of the building. The Caddy spun out, righted itself, and labored sluggishly to follow. By the time Willie came around the near end of the building we were coming down fast. Apparently ignoring my instructions, he shot back onto the road heading west. The Caddy appeared in front of us lumbering towards the road.

"Wait for them, Duncan. Hit the brakes."

"*Wait* for them?"

"Keep them in front of, dammit," I yelled, but he was already applying the brakes.

The Caddy gained speed across the lot and barreled onto the highway ahead of us, nearly clipping an on-coming car. Enos was getting impatient.

"Punch it, Duncan. Stay on their bumper."

Our momentum brought us up close, but Duncan hesitated, and the Caddy pulled away.

"Willie! Willie! Pick up the *phone,* dammit!"

"Yeah, I'm here. You with the program now?"

"We're right behind him but he's too fast for us. You'll have to slow him down. You might draw some fire, so stay low. You slow him up, we'll ram him from behind."

"*Ram* him?" Duncan spat. "What are you *saying?*"

"You got a better idea? Okay, Willie, swerve in front of him and slow him up. Don't let him get next to you."

"You better *be* there, man!"

"Say it again for Duncan."

I held the phone toward Duncan's ear and I could hear Willie's desperate plea. "You gotta *be* there for me, boss-man!"

Duncan hissed loudly, his face intent on the scene ahead. I took it as a good sign. The Mustang swerved into the on-coming lane. The Caddy followed suit, leaning more heavily into the slaloming motion. We gained some ground.

"Okay, Duncan, you gotta do it. Get up on the inside, right on his bumper. When you have a chance, as he cuts back in front of us, ram the back corner. Drive *through* the impact. Drive his rear end around. You got it?"

"Henry! This is crazy!"

"It's a standard maneuver, Duncan. The police use it all the time."

"*I'm* not the police, Henry. They're *trained* for this!"

Two more shots sounded. *Pop! Pop!* I saw the puffs of smoke and an arm extended upward from the Caddy's right side window. Duncan saw it too. It looked like he just shot into the air to let us know they had guns. I had one too.

I took out my Beretta and cocked the slide, letting Duncan see it.

"What the *fuck*?"

"You gotta do it, Duncan. Willie's a sitting duck."

Ignoring Duncan's further pleadings, I crawled half way out the window, braced myself, and let off two rounds into the back of the Caddy. I was getting good at shooting that thing. Their brake lights came on for an instant and then they swerved left. Willie hit his brakes. They kissed bumpers. The Mustang shot forward and the Caddy rocked on its chassis, veering right. I saw a panicked face in the passenger window, a waving arm, and a gun.

"Do it, Duncan! Do it now!"

And he never let up on the gas.

We hit the back quarter-panel of the Cadillac just as it swerved across our bow. I heard the crunch and gripped hard to keep from getting tossed. The Caddy listed heavily going into a skid. I smelled the burning rubber. Then it heaved left, then right, then righted itself, cutting a clean diagonal across the centerline. Doing maybe forty, it dove into the ditch below the railroad tracks. It took out a barbed-wire fence, then met the embankment with a thud that I could feel in the air. Dust swirled around it as we rolled past.

I slid down into the seat as Duncan pulled onto the shoulder. He was panting through gritted teeth. Fifty yards ahead across the street, I saw the grounds of Denver County Jail. The nearest guard tower loomed high above the razor wire fencing like a modern-day squared-off turret. When we came to a stop, I jumped out of the van and took off toward the Cadillac. Willie had swung into a U-turn and came barreling past me, howling out the window.

"Ah' *right,* man. Ah' *right!*" He drove across the road cutting off an oncoming semi, its air horn belching loudly. I reached him just as he got out of the Mustang. He had a gun in his hand and a smile on his face. Breathing hard, I gripped his arm tightly, holding him back, but he didn't struggle against it. We stood there, fully tensed, watching the dust settle around the Caddy. Nothing moved. Its engine was dead, its front wheels were buried in weeds.

"You take that side," I commanded. "You see a gun, *shoot* the motherfucker!"

I was pumped.

We approached with exaggerated caution but there was nothing going on. I opened the driver's side door. Enos Flood was out cold, his head bloody against the wheel and his body slid down underneath it. His airbag hadn't inflated. Another body was slumped into the space beneath the glove box, barely visible under the ballooned airbag. He stirred slowly at first, then began flailing at the bag.

"He's got the gun, Willie," I said as he pulled open the passenger's door.

"No way. I ain't armed," the man yelled, panting hard. He struggled frantically, in some kind of claustrophobic panic attack, trying to pull himself out.

"Let me see your hands, *now!*" My adrenaline pounded and my arm holding the gun was shaking with the tension.

"Okay, okay, just don't shoot me!"

He raised his hands and, as he did so, he slumped back onto the floor.

"Where's your gun?"

He turned his head to look at me. His hair was cut jailhouse short and he was older than Enos, with rounder features, but there was no doubt he was the brother—Alois Flood.

"Hey, I don't *know*, man. I *dropped* it. Look, I was just firing over your heads."

"Yeah, right. Keep your hands right there or I swear I'll fucking shoot you."

He seemed to hear it. He didn't move. I made my way around the car. Willie and I each took an arm and dragged him out onto the dirt. "Face down and hands above your head," I said, trying to affect a policeman's authority. I put a knee in the middle of his back then holstered my gun and took off my belt. "Keep him covered, Willie." Twisting his arms down and behind him, I bound his wrists with my belt. It was an awkward knot, but there was no fight from him.

"I'm hurt, man, take it easy," Alois Flood whined. Then he said, "Hey, ain't you even got cuffs?"

I frisked him hurriedly. "Shut up or I'll smack you. Willie, keep your gun on him. If he moves, shoot him. If he makes any noise, shoot him. If he irritates you, fucking *shoot* him."

I was shouting it. Willie grinned broadly, staring at me with some disbelief. I bobbed my eyebrows. He got the message.

"Yes, sir. Whatever you say, sir." He cleared his throat to hide a laugh.

"I ain't gonna *irritate* nobody," Alois Flood muttered, as if to himself.

I circled back around to Enos scrunched and unmoving under the steering column. Duncan came up behind me speaking in a restrained frenzy. "What happened? Is he dead?"

Enos was out but he had a strong pulse. There was blood all over his face. "He's not dead and he's not dying." I found a handgun inside his jacket and the shotgun lay over the hump between the seats. I shoved the shotgun into Duncan's hands. "Stay here and watch him. If he moves, hit him with it."

"*What*? What are you talking about?"

"Just watch him. Did you put another call in to the cops?"

"Yeah, they're on their way. But Henry…"

"Just watch him. I'll be right back."

I circled back around the car ignoring Duncan's further pleas. Passing cars slowed, rubbernecking the scene. There was definitely something to see. A crowd was going to gather. Time was short.

Standing over Alois' prone body, I came down lightly with a knee into his back again and pushed his face into the dirt. Then I eased up and turned his face towards me. "You're a three time loser, Alois. You're gonna put in some real time this time."

"I want my lawyer, man."

"Yeah, you'll get your lawyer, all right, but it won't be Cator and Holmes."

He heard that. His panting slowed and he strained his neck to get a look at me. I rolled him over. I had his brother's gun in my hand.

"Spence is long gone, buddy. The Feds are on to him. If they haven't bagged him by now, he's out of state. He's not worrying about some small-fry con goin' down for a third rap."

He looked back at me clearly bewildered. "How…?"

"There's no time for this, *Al*. Think about it. You wanna buy yourself a walk or take your chances with a public defender?"

"What are you getting at, man? You mean *now?*"

I nodded. "Can you walk? You wannna walk away from here?"

"Yeah, I can walk. What do you want from me?"

"C'mon, get up. You've got thirty seconds before the cops show."

I dragged him to his feet and began walking him away from the car.

"What's next?" Willie asked, his face intense, his eyes lit with the thrill.

"Me and Al, we gotta talk. Keep an eye on the other one."

Duncan called my name, repeating it in increasingly desperate tones.

"I'll be right back, dammit! Give it a rest!"

I walked Alois away from the car and into the brush along the railroad embankment, talking into his ear. "You're small-time, Al, and you're on parole. You're goin' down hard for this one, no matter what kind of lawyer you get." I stopped him and turned him toward the way we came. "Take a look," I said, pointing towards the guard tower in the distance. Its inverted windows gave off a greenish reflection above the glistening razor wire coils. What dramatic effect! The perfect opening scene for the rest of his life bio-pic. "You goin' back in there or you wanna get outta here? You wanna let your brother take the rap this time? It's his turn, right? He got off on that last one 'cause you didn't snitch him out."

His eyes came away from the guard tower to focus on me. "Who the fuck are you, anyway?"

I grabbed his arm and led him further into the thickening overgrowth. "We don't have time for the social pleasantries, Al. You wanna cop to attempted murder or you wanna deal? Think fast. It's me or the cops."

We came to a clearing at the base of the embankment. He scanned the terrain as if sizing up escape routes. I spun him around, grabbing a handful of shirt. "What'll it be, Alois?"

His eyes were intense, dancing with panic. "You gonna cut me loose?"

"Right now, if you give me what I want. Who's behind you? Who put you up to this? You give me names, I'll give you a running start. I'll say you made a break for it and I didn't feel justified in shooting your ass."

"How do *I* know you won't shoot?" He looked afraid, but he was thinking.

"I could shoot you *now*, ya know? Take it or leave it. Time's running out."

He stood there mute, staring, panting heavily. Finally he spoke. "You want who?"

"Who put you up to this? Who's giving the orders?"

His face scrunched up with the effort to think things through.

"Was it Benny Palmer?" I said. "That where you get your orders?"

He took a few seconds before nodding his head.

"Who killed Brent Charmichael? Did Palmer do that?"

"Hey, I don't know nothin' about that. I got a alibi."

"Yeah, yeah, don't waste my time. I know about your gig at Lowry. That don't keep you from bein' an accessory."

He looked at me with something like awe. "Man, I tell ya, I didn't know nothin' before that came down. It was news to me when it happened."

"Did he talk about it afterwards? Did he say anything about it?"

"Nah, man. It wasn't Benny. Not the way he talked. Your guess as good as mine."

"But he's bringing in the dope from Cheyenne, right? He's bringing the crystal in those trucks?"

He hesitated briefly before nodding again, his eyes cast downward now. There's always some weird kind of hurt when a con turns snitch.

"Is he the one handling the money?"

"What money?"

"Who's handling Spence's money? We know it's comin' into the bingo games. Who's payin' Palmer?"

"I don't know, I tell ya. I only been out a couple a' months."

"Is it Milo Finnes?"

"Nah, he don't know nothin'. We been sneakin' around him the whole time."

"So someone in the Coyne crowd, right?"

"You mean Frank Coyne? Yeah, they're the money people, I guess. But I ain't never seen it."

"Then how do you know? You holding out on me?"

"It's *Palmer*, man. He works for Frank. Says so, anyway."

"And he put you up to this? Why were you after the Mustang?"

"Benny told us to shake it down, okay? He said they wanted something out of it. A disk of some kind. You know, a *computer* disk. From in the glove box."

"They who? Who was *he* taking orders from?"

"I don't *know*, man."

"Is it Frank Coyne? Tell me!"

"No. It's not Frank Coyne."

"How do you know?"

"It's some *broad*, man! A *woman*. That's all I know."

My line of thinking stopped. I took in Alois Flood's sweaty, dirt-smudged face. "It's a woman?"

"That's the way he said it. Palmer said *she* wanted this disk. Some kind a' *boss bitch* that Palmer dances in circles for. I don't know the names, man. I ain't in the *inner circle,* ya know?"

"Does Enos know?"

"I don't know, man. Ask *him*."

"Is Enos hooked up with Spence?"

"Hey, man, I ain't givin' up my brother. You got him, anyway. *You* get it out of him."

"But he's been frontin' you guys with crank, right? Spence, I mean."

"Yeah, sure. Nothin' much. We just been doin' a few deeds for the man. We get some tradeout…"

"And that's why he paid for Cator and Holms?"

"My brother swung that for me. Said we owed him for it."

"Who? Benny?"

He nodded. "That's the *only* reason I got involved. I swear." A siren whined in the distance. Flood turned to look for it then turned back to me. "Ah, c'mon man. You said you'd give me a chance. I can't go back to the joint."

Traversing the near horizon, red and blue pinpoints flickered along Havana Boulevard, moving towards Smith Road. One car so far but I heard other sirens. I loosened my grip and looked at Alois Flood. He stood crooked, favoring one leg. His clothes were twisted out of form, and his face was covered in dust, thick lines creasing his forehead. Worry, fear, fleeting remorse of some kind? His eyes pleaded, expectant and blinking twitchily. Just that moment, he was sorry. He wanted to run, his version of another chance, a chance to take it all back.

I knew it didn't mean anything. I had grifted him with promises that we both knew I couldn't keep, not within the law. He had lied to me the best he could, and told me just enough to see where it would get him. It wouldn't mean anything to go back on my word, give him up to the cops. He'd end up there anyway, sooner or later, caught again and again until he was too tired to run or too old to make trouble outside his own home.

I don't know why I let him go. Something in his face maybe. It lacked the meanness of his younger brother. It lacked the twisted intelligence. I tucked the gun into my waistband, turned him around, and unknotted the belt.

"Get the fuck outta here."

He faced me, rubbing his wrists. He gave me a searching look, yet bright-eyed, flush with emotion, out of place for his predicament. Then he blinked and turned and made his way through the weeds and scrambled up the scree toward the railroad tracks. He made it to the top and then he was gone.

I hacked my way through the dried weeds, then broke into a run as I saw the first cop car coming along Smith Road. I got back to the Caddy as they pulled over along the shoulder fifty yards beyond, rolling slower now. Willie and Duncan stood at the driver's side of the Cadillac twisting their heads back and forth between me and the approaching cruiser.

"He got away," I yelled. "He made a break for it and I pursued him, but he got away."

"*What?*" Duncan exclaimed.

"What you talkin' about?" Willie said, smiling shrewdly though.

"Duncan, put that shotgun down. You too, Willie. Ditch your gun. You don't want them to find it on you."

"Ah, man. We *undercover.* We the *good* guys."

"That buys you nothing right now, Willie. You're a black man with a gun! Ditch it! Drop it and kick it away. We'll tell them we found it in the car."

"*Man!* It's *my gun!*"

"*Willie,* I'll get it back, okay?"

The tires of the cop car skidded on the dirt shoulder just behind Duncan's van. Willie looked toward them and finally took my point. He dropped his gun and kicked it toward the car and scowled at me.

I approached the Caddy, leaned in, and lay Enos Flood's handgun on the floor, rubbing the butt to smear my prints.

Willie said, "What went down, man? You get something outta him?"

I frowned at him then turned my head to meet Duncan's calculating gaze.

"We made a deal. The story is, he made a break for it and he got away. Stick to it, or you'll see me in jail."

"Henry, you *fool*," Duncan said. "You can't *do* that!"

"I already did."

"Put your hands in the air," an ethereal voice commanded. "Step away from the car and put your hands in the air."

We all turned towards the voice. A solo cop with a bullhorn crouched behind the open door of his cruiser. He didn't aim it at us but I was pretty sure his hand, out of site below the window, held a gun. I raised my hands over my head. Duncan and Willie did the same.

"Stick with the story, boys," I whispered. "And nothing about being undercover until Connally gets here."

"Officer, I'm a lawyer," Duncan yelled out. "We're the ones that called you."

There was no response for a moment, no sound except the rumble from the engine of the police car. Through traffic behind the cop slowed to a crawl. Another cruiser approached, lights flashing, sirens wailing, flushing the onlookers off the road. It skidded to a stop just past Willie's Mustang. Two more uniforms popped open both doors and stood behind them. Hands unsnapped the holster straps.

The bullhorn voice intoned again. "You behind the car. Come around to this side."

Stepping lively, I did what I was told.

"All of you. Turn around. Walk backward toward the road. Keep your hands in the air."

We did as we were told. "What the fuck are you doing, Henry?" Duncan said, next to me.

"Just stick to the story. Don't worry about it."

"This is the *last time*," he growled.

"You always say that," I said. I couldn't resist. Willie chuckled. He couldn't resist.

"Lie down on the ground, keep your hands above your head."

We did as we were told.

Chapter 38

It took half an hour for Connally to arrive, during which time Duncan managed to convince the cops on the scene—about eight patrol cars, two unmarked, a couple EMTs—that we were the good guys. Or, anyway, he was. They put me in the back seat cage of a cruiser when they found out I had discharged my weapon. From there I watched Willie put on a show as the supposed victim. I heard his ebullient description of the events as a low-speed chase and attempted carjacking, that they had been after his "one of a kind" Mustang. "It's a *classic*, man," he declared, in the face of one doubtful crime-scene cop.

Duncan kept things at bay with a version of which I only heard snippets. It made me anxious to hear him drop Connally's name several times but there was nothing I could do about it from my cage. When the EMT's arrived, and then more cops to search for Alois Flood, containment of the scene loosened up, allowing Duncan and Willie to regroup outside my window.

"I told them you were a friend of Connally's," Duncan said, looking over his shoulder. "Told them your dad was a cop. One of these guys knows you. Recognizes your name, anyway. I think it's stabilized 'til he gets here."

"You didn't...?"

"I stuck with the story," Duncan said, frowning. "I'm pleading ignorance. But I won't do it at formal questioning."

Willie said, "I told them it was a *jacking*, man. I think they bought it."

Duncan gave him a look, then turned to me with a long sigh. "How are you going to handle Connally?"

"He's in on this, Duncan, don't worry. I talked to him yesterday. He ought to be able to get all this put on the shelf 'til they pump Enos Flood. Did he come around?"

"Barely conscious. Alcohol on his breath. They're talking about sending cops in the ambulance with him."

"How'd our story hold up about Alois Flood?"

Duncan's scowl deepened. "We're in deep shit if they catch him. Did you think about that?"

"He won't talk. We made a deal."

"Made a *deal?* With a fugitive felon. With the guy who was *shooting* at us. You made a deal."

"Maybe I didn't think it through."

"Yeah. Maybe." He turned away and hissed.

After a moment of silent groveling for Duncan's sake, Willie said, "So…wha'd you get outta him, anyway?"

Duncan, still fuming, cock his head to listen anyway.

"They were working for Spencer, all right. But Alois didn't know much beyond that. He's only been out of stir a couple of months."

"Then why the hell did you let him go?" Duncan demanded.

"I don't know, I wasn't thinking, all right? Maybe I bought a favor. It's too late now, anyway."

Duncan just stared. I said to Willie, "But he did give up Benny Palmer."

"I *knew* it," Willie said.

"Who's Benny Palmer?" Duncan asked.

"He runs a bingo supply for the Coyne operation."

"So Frank Coyne was behind this?"

"Not necessarily. He's been doin' business on the side with Milo Finnes too. And, according to Alois, he's transporting meth for Spencer, probably in the same trucks."

"This guy Spencer is Willie's drug dealer, then?"

"Hey, now," Willie chimed in, "He ain't *my* dealer. I don't deal with scum like that."

"You only work with the higher class pushers?"

"Nah, c'mon boss, I don't *do* that shit. What you riding me for?"

"Take it easy," I said in an emphatic whisper. "Both of you calm down." Duncan glowered.

"Well, shit," Willie said.

"Spencer's the majordomo behind a possible drug syndicate," I said. "Vice and Narcotics are on to him and DEA has a snitch planted in his organization."

"Great. The Feds. I can't *believe* this."

"So Palmer is our man," Willie said, overriding Duncan's tone. "We goin' after him?"

"Absolutely, if we ever get out of here."

"Look at my fucking car," Duncan commented, staring down the road, squinting into the low stream of sunlight.

"Sorry about that, Duncan. I didn't plan it this way." Duncan gave no sign that he heard me. "I know it's a drag but you saved Willie's life, you know." I eyed Willie and nodded in Duncan's direction.

"That's right, boss-man, you did good, ah'ight? You done *saved* my black ass. You the *man*, Duncan."

Duncan huffed out a short laugh, kicked a foot into the dirt. "Well, I had to do *something*," he said. Then he looked at me. "But *you're* gonna have to tell Sara about this."

With his wife, there was little ground for me to lose. "I'll do what I can," I told him.

He rolled his eyes then turned to look at the van again.

A plain-clothed detective and a uniform approached to break up our reveries. The uniform led Duncan and Willie away and the detective opened my door and leaned down to speak to me. He was a large man, sort of a farm boy demeanor. He had closely cropped light-colored hair and no eyebrows to speak of above close-set eyes. I didn't recognize him from anywhere.

"Henry Burkhart, right? You work for the DA's office?"

"Used to. I'm, ah, free-lance right now."

He introduced himself as Detective Kimbrow and said he was the crime scene commander. "How'd you come to be involved in this?"

"I was just along for the ride. Going to pick up a friend's car from the Aurora pound."

"You always carry a gun?"

"I have a permit."

"You didn't answer the question."

We exchanged manly looks. "I often carry a gun."

"Why'd you bring it along this time? Just picking up a car, right?"

"Is Captain Connally coming? I'd rather be telling this to him."

"Yeah, I heard you called for him. Who were you holding at gunpoint?"

I was thrown off. I thought he meant my little stroll with Alois Flood. "What now?"

"You told dispatch, 'hostages' at gunpoint. You were holding…"

"Oh, that," I said, chuckling with relief—completely inappropriately. "No, I…That was just to get your attention."

He pretended to smile at that. "So you're friends with the Captain, then?"

"He and my father were on the force together. Before you were out of academy, I'd guess."

The perfunctory smile faded. "That don't buy you anything. Why're you bein' such a hard ass?"

"I worked with cops for a long time. I don't deal with them now unless it's in the presence of a lawyer."

He looked at me with squinting eyes. I looked back at him, examining the rounded base of his forehead, searching for any sign of hair where his eyebrows should have been. The sound of a car pulling up on the dirt shoulder broke up our stare-down. It was an unmarked Crown Vic, glossy black, not quite a limo. Detective Kimbrow and I watched as the door swung open and Connally sprung out in one energetic motion.

"Here's your friend now. I guess we'll see what that gets you."

He closed the door on me and moved off to intercept Connally. Together they made a beeline towards the clump of cops and firemen surrounding the Cadillac. Kimbrow gestured in my direction and Connally glanced over but he didn't break stride. They came to a stop talking sideways to each other while watching Enos Flood finally get extracted from beneath the steering wheel. Once Enos was loaded into the ambulance, Connally made his way to my cruiser with a uniform cop in tow. Catching sight of this, Duncan and Willie also approached.

Connally opened my door and I got out.

"How're you guys doin'?" Connally asked, in a tone surprisingly devoid of reproach. "Anybody hurt?"

"Duncan's car took a beating," I said.

Connally knew Duncan from times past when he had vouched for me one way or another. They hadn't been on the same side for most of it but they had an understanding. Connally offered his hand and Duncan took it.

"Mine too," Willie piped up. "Got a couple new bullet holes."

"Makes you look mean in the 'hood, right?" Connally almost smiled. Then his eyes raked over Willie's outfit. "'Course it ain't gonna compete with your threads."

"Man, I'm fresh." Willie grinned, apparently happy to be treated as something other than a suspect.

"Officer Stead here will take your statements," Connally said, looking to Duncan and Willie. "He's with accident investigation. Be sure you go over all the damage to your cars in detail. That's for your insurance purposes. When he's done, you guys can go."

"What about Henry?" Duncan asked—bravely, I thought, especially considering his mood.

Connally briefly sized him up, then he looked at me. "Henry's gotta go through the shooting investigation. We haven't even taken his statement. I'll have to take him downtown. You got a problem with that, you can come with us." He met Duncan's eyes to see how he would take that. "Or are you suggesting you're acting as his attorney."

Duncan said nothing, weighing Connally's words. I motioned 'no' with a very slight movement of my head. "Not unless he needs one," Duncan stated.

"You need an attorney, Henry?" Connally asked.

"No, I'm fine. Duncan, I'll call you later."

Connally gestured towards his car. "Let's talk."

When we climbed, Connally rolled the windows up. I expected the shouting to start but that didn't happen. He was focused. He was on to something.

"So, Henry. That was fast."

"Things are happening," I said, vaguely, trying to read his mood.

"Yeah, I'll say. In fact, I'd guess somebody's *makin'* things happen." He looked at me with bright, cutting eyes and uplifted cheeks. "You drop that hook about the missing disk?"

I realized it wasn't much of a stretch for him. I smiled back but I still didn't trust the lightness in his tone. "I didn't intend it, Tom. It just came out."

He coughed out a laugh and his features exaggerated a doubtful look.

"Sunday night, right after you sprung me, that shyster Riggs took me to dinner at Tanya Gilmore's. The whole family was there. I got something of a grilling. When they asked me about the B & E charges, why I was in there, I couldn't think of a better story."

He shook his head. "Bullshit. You can always think of a better story. There's no stoppin' you when you get a bright idea."

"It was the perfect circumstance, Tom. Really."

With the amused expression fading, his eyes remained focused. "So wha'd you get out of it?"

Picturing Claire in my mind, I decided not to tell him it was a woman we were looking for. I had my reasons and I wanted time to think them through. I wanted to give him everything else but I couldn't tell him I let Alois Flood run free. I came up with a better story.

"Not that much, but I did get to Enos Flood before he lost consciousness. He told me Benny Palmer put them up to this."

"How'd you get that out of him? Twist his broken leg?"

"I may have insinuated the ambulance would get here sooner if he cooperated."

Connally gave that a snort. "Was Palmer at this dinner?"

"No, he wasn't, as a matter of fact."

"Who was? At the dinner, I mean."

I gave him the list. He took a moment to consider the names then he asked me to recount the events of the afternoon. I gave it to him straight except for the part about cutting Alois Flood loose. I told him he was sprinting by the time we got to the Caddy and that I gave chase, but never saw him past the railroad tracks.

"Was this before or after you talked to his brother?"

"I checked on Enos first but only long enough to see he wasn't armed. Then I went after Alois. But like I said, I lost him. When I came back Enos was still conscious." One lie leads to another.

"How'd you know it was Alois Flood?"

"Enos told me."

"Was Duncan there when you talked to him? Or Willie Junior?"

"No, they were still looking for Alois."

"Unarmed?"

He smelled something. I was beginning to sweat. He probably smelled that too.

"Duncan had a shotgun we found in the Caddy. Willie had his own gun. I, ah…I told him to drop it in the dirt when the cruiser boys showed up. I figured it would be easier that way."

Connally shook his head again. "Always outsmarting us, right, Henry?"

"Willie doesn't need the heat, Tom. You know how he'd get treated down there just for carrying concealed. *I* didn't even get asked if I had a permit."

"Do you?"

"I have one from when I worked for the DA."

"That'll help. We may have to bring it out that you're still with them."

"How soon?"

His bushy eyebrows arched but the eyes beneath them remained narrowed with interest. "You still think there's something to get out of it?"

"Nothing's blown yet if we keep my name out of this."

"Not possible. We'll have to pull a shoot team to review this. I don't know who's up but it'll be four guys from different precincts. No way I can put the quash on that." He paused and I kept my mouth shut. Looking down at his hands, he continued. "On the other hand, sometimes that takes a day or so to get everyone together. But you'll have to give a statement today. You could leave out any reference to Luis, maybe, until the full team convenes. That would put you in the shit eventually. But you don't mind that, do you?"

I ignored the jab. "Does the statement go public right away?"

"Depends on who's doin' the interview and what kind of favors they owe the press. We pretty much work in a glass bubble these days. We hold it back, that just gets the media hounds salivating. You'll be all over the news after that."

"Two days," I said. "Better than nothin'."

He frowned, as if I hadn't gotten his point. "You wanna dangle that hook some more?"

"It's already dangled, isn't it? No reason to reel it in now."

He chuckled suddenly. "You remember how we decided a couple of days ago that was too risky, right?"

I said nothing. It would just be digging a deeper hole.

Detective Kimbrow approached and knocked on the window. He and Connally exchanged thoughts about closing down the scene and instigating a wider search. A news van drove up, parking on the shoulder behind the line of cop cars. Connally looked at them, then looked at me. Then he told Kimbrow to keep everything under wraps for now. "No names, no suspects, nothing to do with live rounds. Nobody's shot, no body's bleeding. Tell them we think it was alcohol related. I'm takin' this one downtown," he said, thumbing in my direction. "Meet us there when you can."

It was a neat bit of misinformation and it told me Connally was still on board. But I wasn't sure it would do much good. A news chopper appeared low on the horizon just as we drove away.

"Shit," Connally said.

Once on the freeway, Connally got down to business. "You find out Palmer's whereabouts for Friday night?"

"Not yet but I've got somebody to ask."

"You feel like he's good for Charmichael?"

"He's in deep, no doubt about that. If he sicced the Flood brothers on us, he'd do the same to Charmichael, right?"

"But the Flood's are alibied for Charmichael's time of death."

"Enos is. You verify Alois' Lowry gig?"

"Air tight. Whole team of workers vouched for him. Plus their super."

"Must be some other thugs around."

"You seen 'em?"

"In Frank's crowd, you mean? Not really. Could be someone from Spencer's gang."

"'Cept Palmer ain't *in* Spencer's gang, is he? He's Frank Coyne's man, right?"

"We know he's hooked up with Spencer through the meth distribution."

"Do we? You get that from Flood too before he passed out?"

"It's not that big a guess, Tom," I said, mustering greater strength of conviction than the third-hand information I had.

"Why don't you think Palmer did it himself?"

"He lacks the killer instinct," I said, then I wished I hadn't.

"So you've verified that, then?"

I gave that a minute, as if to let it sink in. "He could have done it," I said, "if he was desperate enough. But someone else was in on it. He wasn't driving when Mickey got it and, like I said, he wasn't at the dinner where I laid out the bait."

"That don't mean much. Those people talk like it's breathing. Wha'd they have, thirty-six hours to pass it along the grapevine? That whole crowd of bingo junkies knows about it by now."

Bingo junkies. Connally thought that was funny. I smiled along with him but I didn't agree with his point. That dinner had the feel of the inner core. Everyone there was a bingo lifer and one of them had made the decision to kill. And if the others weren't in on it, they would go along when it came to protecting one of their own. On the other hand, I had to give Connally something if I wanted his support. And I was beginning to feel like I needed it.

"He's our best lead anyway. Maybe I should make contact with him. See if he wants to deal for the disk."

"You mean set up a meet?"

"Something like that. What do you think?" When he didn't say anything right away, I thought of a concession. "But I wouldn't want to go it alone. Not after today."

It's what he wanted to hear.

"We could set up a little sting, maybe," he said. "I think there's enough on him to justify a wire. Give you backup in case he tries anything." He glanced over at me, then looked back at the traffic. "You'd be willing to wear a wire?"

"Sure. Even if he's not our man, we'd get something out of it. Maybe approaching him would set the Coyne family in motion. Scare them out of the brush."

"That's what I was thinkin'. We'd have to be ready for that. You're gonna need help."

He knew I wouldn't like that. "You got someone we can trust?"

"I could give you Ross McQuitty. He's the one I put on Perkins' back. I told you he's clean."

"What about Perkins? Who'll watch him?"

Connally gave me a sidelong glance, nothing pretty about it. "He took a couple of comp days, coincidentally. I got a feeling he's tryin' to distance himself from this whole bingo shit-storm."

"Good for him."

"Maybe. We'll see. Anyway, I got a separate team assigned to the Charmichael killing. That frees up McQuitty for you."

"But I can't very well function as a mole with a cop on my back."

"You'll have to work around it, Henry," Connally said with added depth to his tone. "Or else we bring you in. There's not much life left to your cover anyhow."

"All right," I said. "When you put it that way…sounds like a good idea."

Connally chuckled. Pretty sure it was at me, not with me.

Chapter 39

When we got to the cop house, I spent a long thirty minutes in a windowless interview room pondering, among other things, how much time I'd been confined against my will in the last few days. I also thought about what Alois Flood told me and wondered if I could trust it. Even if it was a woman who gave Palmer orders, she could have been an intermediary. Ellen Coyne speaking on behalf of Frank. Or if it was Claire, since she hadn't been at the dinner, someone else had communicated with her. On the other hand, Tanya Gilmore was capable of acting on her own. She seemed the most likely suspect—and my personal favorite—given her grandiose, glittering life-style and her past involvement with Charmichael. Who dumped who in that tryst, I wondered? And when? I hadn't heard back from Luis on her alibi. Still, I couldn't see her killing her own husband, regardless their make-believe marriage. Nor Claire her own brother. So Charmichael did Mickey and either Tanya or Claire killed him. Or Frank had Ellen give the order. Maybe for revenge. Maybe to stop him from going over to Spencer. Maybe to keep him quiet. But who was driving when Charmichael did the deed? And how much did Rhonda Schomberg fit in to the whole family thing? She *was* at that dinner. By the time Connally showed up with Kimbrow on his heels, I had decided on a course of action. It didn't involve working with the police.

They grilled me again on the details of the car chase. Connally steered the questioning away from too much prodding, but he otherwise let Kimbrow do his work—without any mention of bingo. When it was wrapped up neatly enough, Kimbrow left and Connally led me down a carpeted hallway to his office.

"I had to tell Kimbrow you're a snitch," he said, over his shoulder.

"What for? What the hell…?"

"He wanted you locked up, okay? Today's chase, the B & E charges on Sunday. A shootout in Aurora before that. I'd've been suspicious of him if he hadn't."

"How'd he find out about Aurora?"

"Interdepartmental cooperation," Connally said through a snarly twist of his mouth.

"Does he know about the bingo connection?"

"Not from me. But I mentioned dealings with the secretary of state, and he's a smart cop."

When we entered his office, a man in street clothes was sitting in a chair flipping through papers in a manila folder. He was fairly young for a plain-clothed dick. He had a recently trimmed flattop of light brown hair and pugnacious features; a flat nose, protruding eyebrows, a square jaw and rounded cheekbones; a face that would hold up well taking punches in the ring. On the other hand, he looked smart enough to avoid a fight. His attentive eyes took me in with an expression that conveyed forethought.

"Ross," Connally said, taking up behind his desk, "this is Henry Burkhart. He's the one I was telling you about. Henry, Ross McQuitty."

We shook hands. McQuitty firmed his lips and gave me a man-to-man nod.

"I brought Ross up to speed about your cover—including Willie Jr.—and the time constraints involved. We got two days max. Now, here's what I'm gonna do," he said, like it was all his idea. "We get a wire and a remote for Henry, here. Then he makes contact with this perp, Benny Palmer, who supposedly knows something about the Charmichael killing. Henry's got some bait to set up a meet. But you can't do it on their turf," he said, his gaze taking aim at me. "Too hard to cover."

"I have the disk, supposedly. I can set the terms."

"Where you thinkin'?"

"How about Willie's house?"

Connally nodded as if he had already considered it. "You'd have to get Willie out of there though. No buts about it. He's a civilian and my guess is he's got more fancy firearms to go with his outfits. Hard enough keeping track of you. No way I'd wanna be responsible for his…*behavior.*"

I suppressed a smile. "I'm sure he'll agree to it."

Connally nodded, although a faint frown of distrust lingered on his lips. "We'll set it up there and we'll monitor the meet and see what we get. Whether he spills or not, we're gonna pick him up after. But like I told you, Ross, it'll have to be just you and me monitoring. At least until we collar him. That all right?"

McQuitty answered with a nod. No questions, no clarifications, no worries about backup. It was a little too smooth. I wondered what else was in their pre-rehearsed script.

"Now the thing is, Henry, Ross is gonna have to stick with you. I don't want you out of his sight. We'll keep up communications between us, leaving you free to mingle with your bingo pals, as long as you stay close. You understand that, Henry? You gotta stay close."

I nodded. "No problem."

"I'd like to put a tap on Willie's phone, too, but that involves getting techs in on it and approval from a judge. We don't have time for that, anyway. What else? You know how to contact Palmer?"

"Me and Ross can go by one of their clubs. I can get a number."

"What about the rest of the family?"

"The family? You mean the Coyne family?"

"Yeah, the Coyne family. And all the people at that dinner. We're expecting nibbles from them too, right? What were you gonna do with that?"

"To tell you the truth, I hadn't got that far."

Connally waited for me to catch up.

"I could contact the principles. Frank Coyne. His sister, Tanya. Set something up before the meeting with Palmer."

"What would you tell them?"

"I could say I want out, hold the disk out for the highest bidder. Maybe something would spill during the course of the bidding."

Connally thought that over. "You think it would go?"

I was sure of it. "It's worth a try," I said.

"I would want Ross to be there."

"He could be in the house, the next room. They're not going to open up in front of him."

"What if word gets to Palmer?"

"I don't see how that would discourage him. If he's in it with them, he'll pass it on. If not, my guess is he'll put in the highest bid. It's supposed to be Charmichael's records, after all. Palmer has a lot to lose if his relationship to Spencer is uncovered."

"You mean the hypothetical relationship."

"Yeah, that."

He pretended to think it over some more, then he looked to McQuitty. "You think you can stay with this?"

McQuitty's youthful features conveyed an expression of grave interest. "It depends on who's coming to deal. If we're just meeting with these bingo people, we could probably handle it." I didn't bother to disagree. "If the killer or killers show up, we ought to have backup on hand."

"But we don't know who the killers are." Connally asserted.

"It's not Frank or Tanya," I said, glossing over my own suspicions. "They're alibied up." I figured Connally was thinking about Chuck Burrows. A dirty ex-cop might be why he was showing interest. I didn't bring it up.

"You could do all this by phone, right? Using land lines. Set up a time. See who wants to shop? So we'd know who ahead of time."

I nodded. Lots of nodding going on.

"I'll be nearby via the secure mobiles with you, Ross," Connally continued. "I could have a couple patrol cars on radio alert in the area. Bring them in fast if things get sticky. Sound all right?"

McQuitty and I nodded. We were both just going along. I was itching to get out of there.

Connally said, "Okay, Henry, go to work. But Ross stays with you the whole time."

"I got that, Tom. You're beating a dead horse."

He gave me his standard doubtful glare but didn't bother to push it. He looked to McQuitty and McQuitty nodded obediently.

They left me alone to get the taping equipment. I waited two minutes before moving to the phone on Connally's desk. I called Five Aces Bingo. Frank wasn't there but was expected at about eight or nine, his usual time. It gave me an hour, two at the most.

When the door opened, McQuitty reappeared by himself, holding a tangle of wires in one outstretched hand. "Okay," he said, "we're clear to go. You wanna know how this stuff works?"

"Later," I said. "Right now, we gotta get out to Five Aces Bingo."

"What for?"

"We need that phone number for Palmer. You up for it?"

His eyes twinkled and he looked over his shoulder as if someone might be listening.

"You think things will heat up?"

I liked his attitude. "Probably. You play much bingo?"

"Can't say that I have."

"I'll give you the crash course," I said, smiling at my choice of words.

Chapter 40

We arrived at Five Aces just after seven. The lot was three-quarters full. We passed through the rows of cars trolling for Frank's Jag. It wasn't there.

"You wait here," I told McQuitty. "Any luck, I'll be out in ten."

"No can do, Henry. I'm comin' in."

"They'll make you for a cop in a minute."

"How so?"

"It's the haircut."

He laughed it off but stayed on point. "I'm sticking with you. Like Connally said."

"Yeah, but…I didn't think I'd have to wear you."

He shrugged. "We'll go in separately. I'll play a few games, try to get the hang of it."

I gave him my meanest scowl but he didn't cower under it. "All right, then. I have an idea. Although, you don't look like the actor-type to me."

He laughed that off too, an awkward chuckle. "Wha'd you have in mind?"

"A little diversion tactic. I can get in the office all right but I need some time alone in there. Otherwise I'll have to come up with another story. And I'm running out of stories. You think you're up to it?"

"What do you mean make a scene? Start a riot?"

"I don't think we have to go that far, but…" I told him how the games worked, one after another with a break in between to pay off the winner. I told him to mark out a row on his card and call a bingo before anyone else did.

"And what happens then?"

"They'll check your card, find out you cheated." I shrugged. "You argue the point, drag it out until I get there."

He said it sounded good. I didn't want to discourage him. Besides, what could happen?

"You'll have to wait for the beginning of the next game or it'll look too obvious. Which reminds me," I said, looking him over.

"What?"

"You're gonna be the only guy in there with a tweed sport coat and a gun."

"I have a Rockies jacket in the trunk. How will that do?"

"Broncos would be better but it'll do. And...you won't need the piece."

He gave me a studied look, as if wondering at my motives. Evidently he couldn't come up with anything treacherous. He shed the coat and the shoulder holster and put on the baseball jacket.

I went in first.

"N-41!" the caller called. "E-e-e-n-n-n-n...forty...*one!*"

It was almost nostalgic.

The register girl recognized me with a smile. She was all of eighteen. I smiled back and took up a position near the hallway. Ellen Coyne was working the far end of the room helping two volunteers set up the pickle bar. She looked busy enough to stay out of my way for a while, but the lights were on in the office. I could see it through the blinds. I stood there fingering the keys in my pocket, wondering if I should chance it. When McQuitty came in, I decided to stick to the plan. I watched him buy playing sheets and take a seat toward the front. He looked a little too well-groomed for that crowd but it does take all kinds.

A woman shouted, "Bingo!" and I turned to watch. A youngish mother of two with a flat black dye-job and a tank top that emphasized her failing attributes beamed and showed the winning card to her kids. They were too young to fully appreciate it. A floor-girl approached her, and Ellen joined them shortly. They read off the winning numbers to verify. I noticed McQuitty, two rows in front of them, carefully taking note. He met my eyes and gave me half a nod. He looked a little eager—overanxious. I didn't think that would hurt.

After the numbers checked out, Ellen made her way to the office. I stood in her path.

"Well, *Henry*," she said, through her matronly smile. "Nice to see you. Aren't you working tonight?"

"I just dropped by. I was looking for Frank."

"Yes, well, he's at Bingo Circle. Training the new people." She gave me a harried look then sidled past me. "I have to pay this winner."

Following her down the hall, I said, "Is he coming in tonight?"

"I don't think so. Those training sessions are kind of a handful." At the office door, she turned to give me a questioning look. "I thought you'd be with him."

When she opened the door, Dennis came into view behind the small desk. Seeing me, he looked flustered, as if caught sorting through his big brother's porno stash.

"Well, hello, Dennis," I said, emphasizing his name in a tone I hoped would convey a vague suspicion.

"Hey, Henry. Surprised to see you here."

"Why's that?"

Sensing the tension, Ellen interrupted the moment. "I need two hundred," she asserted, stepping around the desk.

Dennis rolled his chair back to let her get to the safe. With her back to me, they exchanged a look. Dennis' eyes flitted nervously. She took a thin packet of bills from the top shelf and left the room, tossing me a goosey glance. Dennis smiled self-consciously, swiveled in his chair, and then opened the blinds slightly, peering through to follow Ellen's progress. Eyeing the Rolodex on the edge of the desk, I drifted to the window and looked out.

"I hear you had some trouble today," Dennis said, without taking his eyes off the outer room. There was nothing out there but the back of a hundred and fifty tilted heads.

"Where'd you hear that?"

"Frank told me. Said there was some kind of shootout on Smith Road."

"Yeah, well, trouble seems to follow me these days. Where *is* Frank, anyway?"

"At the Circle. Training the new troops."

"New troops for what?"

"Bingo Palace. We're opening tomorrow night. Didn't you know?"

"The Palace is opening tomorrow? What's the rush?"

"We've had a whole flock of people out there wanting to check out the scene of the crime. Tons of calls too. Everybody wants to get in on it."

"What an opportunity."

"What's that?"

"So he's out there now, huh?"

"Yeah. He wants to talk to you," he said, airily.

"I've been tied up."

"I guess so. How'd you get away from the cops?" he asked, still keeping his eyes averted. He couldn't help himself. I figured he had an idea what Frank really wanted and he couldn't help rubbing it in.

"It wasn't my car. I wasn't driving. Cops figured it was an attempted car-jacking."

Dennis laughed harshly. "*Car*-jacking? That's rich. Did you get the disk?"

I said nothing and waited until he turned to look at me. "Are you in a position to speak for Frank?"

His eyes widened like his brother's and his mouth fell partway open. "No I…I was just asking…"

"'Cause I don't know who to trust anymore."

"What's that supposed to mean?"

"It means somebody *talked*, Dennis," I said, taking a step towards him. "Somebody at Tanya's dinner the other night. They put these thugs onto us at the impound lot. I'm *tired* of getting shot at."

Dennis stared at me, the appalled look frozen on his face.

"Did you talk to anyone, Dennis?"

"Me? No, I…" He blinked and his eyes fluttered, glancing at the door for help to appear.

"You talked to Claire, didn't you?"

Color rose into his face as his eyes came back to meet mine. "Claire's one of the family, Henry. She wouldn't…*do* anything like that."

"Like what?"

"You know. Tell anyone…"

"Who would?"

"*I* don't know."

I heard McQuitty call out, "Bingo, bingo," several times. I didn't think he had waited long enough.

"I suppose not," I said, turning to look out the window. Dennis swiveled in his chair and followed my gaze through the open blinds. One of the floor girls stood next to McQuitty holding his playing sheet. I caught her anxious expression as she looked around for help. McQuitty wasn't exactly hamming it up. Ellen Coyne approached from the pickle bar. After an exchange with the caller, Ellen shook her head. I could just make out the caller's amplified voice. "I'm sorry, sir," I heard him say and McQuitty mouthed something back. He grabbed the sheet from Ellen's hands and waved it in the air, jabbing at it with a finger. That's more like it. Ellen looked towards our window, then back to McQuitty. He stooped and craned his neck to bark in her face. He was getting into it.

"You've got trouble," I said.

"What the hell?" Dennis stood up, then hesitated.

"She needs help, Dennis."

He looked at me. I moved toward the door, opened it, then stopped to let him pass. He swallowed hard as he went out. He would need help too.

I closed the office door. Through the window, I watched Dennis approach the knot of people around McQuitty. A large man, wooly-faced and sun-burnt, looking like a biker on his night off, was trying to reason—after a fashion—with McQuitty. He wagged a thick finger in the space between them. McQuitty knocked it away then bobbed his head as if dodging a punch. Ellen gestured to Dennis, who was sidestepping through the rows. Other people were standing up. "Sir, please," the caller intoned through his microphone. "Everyone please sit down."

I pulled the cord to close the blinds then turned to the Rolodex. But then I couldn't resist the open safe. The manila folder that I had seen Frank and Ellen work out of was sitting on a middle shelf. The thumb-tab on it said, 'house'. I took it out and flipped through it. Loose accounting pages had numbers entered in pencil in daily columns next to a list of accounts; admissions, pull-tabs, game winners, pinball, gift shop. Many of them had two lines of entries. The dates went back several months. The leather-bound tally book was on the same shelf. I took it out and set it on the desk then peeked through the blinds.

McQuitty was in a shouting match with the biker who had a jean-clad woman half his size hanging on one arm, not exactly holding him back. Dennis stood with one foot between them trying to referee. He was losing ground. The people closest to them had backed away but most of the room was watching, standing and shuffling about. A few people moved towards the doors but couldn't bring themselves to leave, necks craning toward the action.

I turned back to the tally book. Comparing dates, I found the same numbers listed in the book and in the loose sheets but the latter had that second line of figures under every entry. The amounts on the second line were larger, significantly larger—than the ones above. Bingo! Checking the dates on the last few pages, I found the corresponding pages in the tally book and ripped them out and stuffed all of them under my shirt. I left the most current pages in the folder and put it and the tally book back where I found them. I closed the safe and spun the dial.

The shouting was getting louder, the threats more audible. Staring down at the Rolodex, it was time to go. I flipped the cards through the P's twice but didn't find Palmer. I was just about to give in to my inner panic when it came to me, the name of his business: Cheyenne Supply Company. Looking under the C's, I found the dog-eared card right away and ripped it out. Parting the blinds, I caught sight of the crowd, everyone standing now, and Ellen Coyne breaking away towards the office. I crossed to the door and opened it and waited. I heard Ellen Coyne's breathless, mumbling voice. I stepped through the doorway just as she rounded the corner, letting her bump into me.

"What's going on out there?" I said, grasping her shoulders as if to steady her.

"I'm calling the police. Some man, he's starting a fight. Dennis can't handle it." She tried to twist away but I firmed my grip.

"Hold on, Ellen. Let me deal with it. We don't want more cops coming out, do we?"

She looked up at me, breathing hard, trying to decide. I lightened my hold but guided her toward the window.

"You watch from here. If it gets out of hand, call them."

She wanted to think that over but shouts from the other room cut short her meditations. "Okay, but I'm going to stay by the phone."

"Perfect."

I strode into the big room then shouldered my way between the tightening circle of onlookers. McQuitty and the biker were exchanging pushes, adjusting their stances, growling out sub-verbal insults. The ratty blond with the jean jacket had joined in the debate with high-pitched commentary of her own. Dennis pleaded from one side, putting a hand on McQuitty's arm. McQuitty shook it off. I came up behind him and wrapped him in my arms.

"Okay, buddy, that's enough."

The biker freed his arm from his girlfriend's grasp, pushed Dennis aside, and swung a roundhouse left. I saw it coming and tried to turn away. The punch glanced off my wrist and found home on McQuitty's abdomen. It had something behind it. We went down in a heap, McQuitty landing on top. The biker jumped McQuitty as he rolled off. He took a couple of blows to the face before I could drive a foot into the biker's ribs. He fell to all fours and McQuitty knocked his arms out from under him, flattening him out. As he rose again, McQuitty was in position to nail him solid in the jaw. The punch and his own momentum sent the biker sideways like a halfback blocked out of bounds. He knocked over chairs and skidded a table into the row of gawkers on the other side. A wave of screams rose and fell around us.

McQuitty and I came to our feet and he started after the biker. "Okay, okay, that's enough," I said, holding him by the shoulders. With a powerful shrug he shook off my grip and wound up to throw a punch at me. I backed off just out of arm's length and put up my hands, open palmed. His dark eyes flashed, then relaxed, and he came out of his fighter's trance.

"We don't want a *riot* on our hands, do we?" I said.

Panting heavily, McQuitty looked around, saw the sprawled biker, barely moving, then looked back to me. "I guess not," he breathed. His smart-aleck grin pretty much broke character, as I took him by the arm and led him toward the entrance. "Why don't you go home and sleep it off, buddy." A few other voices echoed my feigned condescension.

Before we got to the door, I located Dennis at the edge of the crowd staring down at the prone biker. The girlfriend, hunching over him, whined dramatically.

"Dennis. Take care of that one. I'll be right back."

We made it into the parking lot and past the players who had exited as the fun died down. They watched us pass, still curiously voyeuristic.

"I'd say you made that a little too convincing," I murmured.

"And you said I wasn't the actor type."

"I stand corrected."

Once at his car, I told him to pick me up at the far end of the lot in five minutes.

"You'll be there, won't you?"

"After that," I said, nodding toward the hall, "I'm not going anywhere without you."

I went back into the hall. Dennis and Ellen leaned over the biker who was sitting in a chair with his head down. I caught Dennis' eye and motioned him over. We retreated into the office.

"Is he all right?"

"I guess so. He wants a piece of whoever hit him but I told him we threw the guy out. Is he gone?"

"I just watched him drive away. But I'd better leave too. I don't want our friend to remember who else hit him."

"Yeah, good idea. Hey, thanks for helping out."

"No problem. It was easier than it looked."

His eyes stayed with mine, but whatever was bothering him didn't come to the surface.

"Tell your brother we need to talk. I'll call him later."

I moved away but Dennis took my arm.

"Hey, Henry. About Claire."

"Yeah?"

"Well, I just don't want you thinkin'... She wouldn't do a thing like that."

"Yeah, I know. She's family."

Dennis nodded. "That's right. We all are."

"Well, the thing is, Dennis..." and I waited a few beats, "...I'm not."

I left him standing there with a guilty look on his face.

Around the corner of the building, I spotted McQuitty's unmarked sedan turning from Colfax into the side street. I headed across the lot.

"What's next?" he said, when I climbed in.

I was beginning to like this guy.

"Let's put some cheese in the trap and see who comes out to nibble."

Chapter 41

Willie was home when we arrived, sprawled out on the living room couch, Pimpy at his feet, in front of VH-1. The sound was off and he was talking on his cell.

"Baby, I gotta go," he said, eyeballing me in the doorway. "Yeah, it's Henry…yeah, I will…I gotta talk to him first." His eyes raked over Ross McQuitty coming in behind me. "Yeah, baby," Willie continued, "I *know* I gotta get it back. Let me *talk* to him first." He put a finger in the air like he was afraid we were going to leave. Then he stood up and tried to pace in the small carpeted area we were all standing in. I gave Pimpy a back scratching while we waited. "*Damn*, woman. Why you *on* me. I *know* what I gotta do." I gestured to McQuitty to follow me into the kitchen.

There were two messages on the answering machine. The first one was Maxine. Apparently, Willie was fielding that. The second came from Frank Coyne, two hours earlier.

"This is Frank. Give me a call as soon as you get this. Right away."

He left two numbers. I recognized one of them as Bingo Circle.

"That mean something?" McQuitty asked.

"Might mean he's surprised I survived that ambush."

"So you *do* think he had something to do with it?"

I wondered if that's what Connally had told him or if he was jumping to his own conclusions. "He's not my first choice," I said. "He'll have to wait."

"Why's that?"

"I wanna set it up with Palmer first. He's our main suspect, right?"

"Whatever you say."

I got a can of dog food from the refrigerator and handed it to McQuitty. "I'll make the call. You make friends with Pimpy."

"That's your dog's name?"

Ignoring him, I tried the number for Cheyenne Supply and got a recording. The second number on the card, a local number, yielded another recording, but this one was Palmer's voice. I told him I had something of Charmichael's that I knew he'd be interested in, "…but the Coyne's want it too. If I don't hear from you tonight, I'm going to Frank with it. It'll cost you one way or another." When I looked up, McQuitty was smiling hugely at me. "Too dramatic?" I said, and that drew all-out laughter.

Willie came in as I hung up the phone. "They got my *car* again, man. They got my car *and* my gun. What you gonna do about that?"

"Who's got your car?"

"The *pol*-ice, man. The fuckin' *Denver* cops this time. They're sayin' it's evidence."

I looked at McQuitty and waited for Willie to follow my gaze.

"Who's this?"

"This is the '*pol*-ice', Willie. Detective Ross McQuitty, meet Willie Randall Jr."

McQuitty set the dog bowl down and stuck out his hand, still smiling.

Willie stared into McQuitty's face then looked down at his outstretched hand as if it was some wart-covered alien claw. Finally he slapped the open palm and raised a half-hearted fist but didn't wait for McQuitty to fist-bump. "Okay, so what do *you* know about my car?"

"I don't know anything about it."

"Nothin' *'bout* it?" he exclaimed, dipping into the full-on jive tone. "Well, you *workin'* on it for me, or what?" He looked to me. "What he doin' here, Henry? I got the *man* in my living room every time I leave the damn door unlocked."

"You wanna relax a minute? I'll bring you up to speed. Besides, you're one of us now, remember?"

"One 'a *you*! Man, someone need a *history* lesson."

"Don't start, Willie. You know what I mean. We're all on the same side."

"Then how come they got my car?"

"For the same reason I spent the night in jail. We're undercover. And until we come in, we gotta play like we're the bad guys. Right? That's why I chose you, Willie, and that's why Captain Connally sent McQuitty here to work with us."

"So, Connally? You trust him now?"

"Of course I do," I said, "And you know why."

Willie took a minute to scowl, but he knew. He was there—and so was Connally—when I found out the truth about my father's death. It has never gone outside that circle of three. Even my mother doesn't know.

Willie huffed, looked away, but when he turned back and spoke, his voice had smoothed out. "That was Maxine," he said, holding out his cell phone in one large hand. "She's all pissed off. You're gonna have to talk to her, Henry."

"What the hell do *I* have to do with it?"

"You're gettin' me in trouble, man. *She* thinks so anyway. Gettin' me in trouble with *her*, that's for sure. You have to tell her we're working. Like, *actually* working, right?. All on the same side, right?"

I nodded acquiescence. Willie suddenly smiled. "Man, she's *all* pissed off at you."

Put her on the list, I thought. "Okay, Willie, I'll talk to her. But not tonight. We got maybe one more day to crack this thing. We're goin' after Benny Palmer."

Willie heard that. "Where's he at?"

"We're setting up a meet. Make a deal for the disk."

"Now you're talkin', man. Where's that goin' down?"

I arched my eyebrows. "Well…right here would be a good place."

"You gonna bring him *here*?"

"Subject to your approval, Willie. Ross here's gonna fix me up with a wire. I'll meet with Palmer, squeeze him a little, find out if he's the one who put the Flood brothers on us. Maybe he'll cop to doin' Charmichael. You and Ross will be nearby, waiting for the signal."

McQuitty took a breath to speak but I didn't give him the chance.

"Of course, it'll have to go down according to legal protocol. Connally's looking to arrest him anyway, so we're playing it the way he wants. We *are* on the same side." Stepping in front of McQuitty, I rotated my eyes in his direction, and back at Willie. "This calls for a little subtlety. Know what I mean?"

"Yeah, sure, man, whatever…. You and Captain Connally."

Glancing at McQuitty, I caught his knowing, sardonic expression. Everybody was wise.

"When's this *meet* happening?" Willie asked.

"As soon as we hear from him. I just put in the call."

"What about my car, man?"

"I can look into that for you," McQuitty said. "I'm sure we can take care of it."

"What about Duncan?" I asked. "Does he know about it?"

"Yeah, right," Willie said. "They got his car, too. He said *he's* workin' on it. "*Everybody's* workin' on it and *I* ain't got my *ride*."

"Did they give you some kind of receipt?" McQuitty asked.

"Yeah, they gave me this." Willie dug out a folded yellow page.

McQuitty perused it. "Let me make a call, see where they're at with this. Can I use your phone?" He indicated the old-school kitchen phone on the table.

"I'll need that one open to hear back from Palmer," I said.

McQuitty looked at Willie for a minute, then decided to admit that he had a cell phone. Connally would have his number.

I gave McQuitty a nod as the two of them retreated into the living room. Sitting at the table with my back to the doorway, I dug out Tanya's card from my wallet. I had an idea and I didn't spend much time weighing the pros and cons. I decided to play out my whole hand. I had good enough cards—and a few extra chips—to play more than one go-around before I'd have to start bluffing. I dialed the number.

Chapter 42

A man answered and said it was the Gilmore residence in an overly-polite tone that might have had an edge of annoyance to it. James, the resentful doorman. I gave him my name as if I didn't know him, and asked to speak to Mrs. Gilmore. He said she wasn't taking calls.

"I think she'll want to talk to me."

"Like I said, *Mis*-ter *Burk*-hart," he sneered it out, "she's not taking calls. I'll give her the message and we'll see if she wants to call you back someday."

He hung up the phone.

I dialed again, thinking maybe the butler did it. James picked up on the first ring. I asked for Mrs. Gilmore, nicely again.

"Look, Burkhart, she's not available. You keep calling here, we'll put in a complaint. Aren't you in enough trouble? Tanya's not taking *your* calls."

"Oh, it's Tanya now, is it? Getting friendly with the boss-lady these days?"

"A lot friendlier than you'll ever be. You keep harassing her, I'm gonna call the cops."

"Fine by me, lover-boy. Tanya would love more cops asking around."

"Maybe you'd like to settle this in person, asshole. Just the two of us, one-on-one."

"Nothing I'd like better, if you could find you way out from behind her skirts."

I heard a faint click on the line just as he was saying, "Look, you fuckin' jerk..."

"Hello? *Jimmy?* What was *that?*" It was Tanya Gilmore's not too silky voice. "Who was that on the phone?"

"Uh, yes, it's...Mr. Burkhart. I told him you were not available but..."

"I'll take it, Jimmy," she said with conspicuous coolness. "Please get off the line."

We waited for James—aka Jimmy now—to hang up. He took a long few seconds to do so.

"Henry, are you there?"

"Yes."

"Are you all right?"

"How do you mean?"

"Well, we heard about the...what was it, a car chase? They said there were shots fired."

"You hear about it from Frank?"

"Well, yes, but it was on the news. They had the news helicopter out there. I mean, live TV. That was you, wasn't it? It was out by that jail complex."

"They used my name in the newscast?"

She faltered. "I...I don't think so. I got a call from Frank. He told me to turn it on. He said it was you. We were all very concerned..."

"You don't have to worry, Tanya. I've got the disk."

There was a short silence and when she spoke again, the lightness in her voice was forced. "Well, that's good, Henry. But mostly we were concerned about you."

"So why didn't you call?"

"Well, I thought Frank...I don't know, Henry. I don't have your number, do I?"

"You could get it if you wanted."

"I'm sorry, I don't understand what you're getting at. If you're upset...I guess that's understandable."

"Cut the crap, Tanya. Let's get to the point."

Another silence followed, this one full and stagnant. "And what is the point, Henry?"

"The disk. If you want it now, you'll have to pay for it."

"I don't understand."

"I think you do but I'll lay it out for you. You had Mickey killed because he didn't like your little scheme with Spencer. Or if you didn't do it, you didn't mind that Brent got rid of him for you, before Mickey went public. Then Brent must have gone hinky on you too, so you got rid of him first hand. You thought you covered your tracks pretty well by taking his computer. But then this little disk turns up. And it falls into my hands. Fool that I am, I was perfectly happy to hand it over to you. Until you tried to have *me* killed. That was a mistake, Tanya. Now you have to pay for it. I'm getting out. And I want to be paid for my troubles. You follow me so far?"

Not surprisingly, there was a long pause. When she spoke, her anger was barely concealed by the flatness of her voice. "I'm afraid you're very upset. I'm sorry for you, Henry, but I'm not going to listen to this. I don't know how you could think such things."

"I know about your past relationship—your *personal* relationship—with Brent Charmichael. That makes it a little easier to 'think such things', wouldn't you say? And I know about your connection to Spencer's operation. I know that's where the real money's coming from."

"Now, you listen to me, Henry," she growled, "I didn't kill my husband. All these other matters have nothing to do with that. It means nothing to me without Mickey." Her voice cracked towards the end. I had to admit it sounded pretty good. But she didn't hang up. She should have, but she didn't.

"Come off it, Tanya. Mickey was in the way. I know that. He didn't like it when you hooked up with Spencer. I mean, drug money? That's dirty. Mickey didn't approve. But that's the bed you made and now you're gonna have to sleep in it. I'm sure you already have."

"What? What's that supposed to mean?"

"Well, it doesn't mean that Mickey cared who you slept with. But doing the man's laundry? That's another thing altogether."

"His laundry? What?"

"I *know* you know the term, Tanya? Money laundering. Spencer's money through the books at Five Aces and the other clubs. But Mickey wouldn't play ball at Clancy's, right?"

There was a telltale pause, then the cliché line: "I don't know what you're talking about."

I had to smile. "I think you do. And I think you know that's what's on the disk. I don't know how to open the damn thing but I bet someone at the secretary of state's office could figure it out. Or if you've got them in your pocket, I'll give it to the cops. Unless we make a deal—just you and me."

I knew I was on the mark. I'd mentioned Spencer three times and she hadn't acknowledged it—neither confirmed nor denied, as they say. She offered minor histrionics to buy some time to think, sniffling into the phone, sighing heavily. When she spoke again, she further advanced the obfuscations. "I don't know what you hope to get out of prying into my private affairs. Since when is it any of your business?"

"Since you tried to have me killed."

"I assure you, Henry, you're wrong about that. We *trusted* you. Frank said we could. We brought you into the family."

"No thanks, lady. Too many family members dying off."

"And you think *I* did it?"

"Either that or you're sleeping with the enemy."

She tisked into the phone then fell silent again. I was pretty much all in. I waited to see what it would get me. When she spoke, her tone was more controlled, down to business. "What do you want from me, Henry?"

Looking over my shoulder I could see McQuitty still on his phone and Willie seated next to him, talking in his other ear.

"A hundred thousand in cash," I said to Tanya, "or I take it to some other bidders."

"For that disk? We don't even know what's on it."

"Makes it kind of interesting, doesn't it? Kind of like a pull-tab."

"That's ridiculous. There's nothing on there worth that kind of money."

"Shall I take it to Frank, then? See if he's interested?"

"Do you think you can blackmail me?"

"Well, I'm giving it a try. If it doesn't work, I'll see what it's worth to Frank."

"Frank won't pay that either," she said, crisply. "It's not worth it. To me or him."

"So he's in on the deal with Spencer, then? Because whoever killed Mickey and Brent did it to bury their connection with them, past or present. Now my guess is some evidence of that connection is on this disk. If it's worth killing two men, it has to be worth a hundred thou, wouldn't you say?"

"I didn't kill Mickey!" she shouted. "I didn't kill *anybody*!"

"Sure, Tanya. I never really figured you did. You just lounged around your indoor pool while James gave you backrubs and alibis and you let the Flood brothers put them out of their misery."

Her labored breathing hissed into the phone.

"I never liked you, Henry," she almost crooned. "I knew it when I first saw you."

"Don't let it worry you, Mrs. Gilmore. I do business all the time with people I don't like."

When she spoke again, her voice returned to a forced version of its original smoothness.

"Let me tell you something, Mr. Burkhart. Can you listen for a moment?"

"Sure."

"I'm not paying you a hundred thousand dollars for that disk. I'm not paying you anything. Some people might frown upon the way I have conducted my *affairs*." She paused to let me take in the irony of her word choice. "Those people have looked down on me my whole life. It's nothing new and, frankly, I don't care anymore. I don't *have* to care. My father knows how I choose to live, my brother knows, and my husband knew all along. He was no better. We had an arrangement, we had a partnership. And I certainly don't give a damn what *you* think about it. It doesn't mean I killed him. There is nothing on that disk that implicates me in his death, because I didn't do it."

"And Brent Charmichael?"

"Brent Charmichael had his own problems, he always has, and they haven't involved me for quite some time. The fact that we were involved once is old news and it remains old news. There is nothing to connect us now—on that disk or anywhere else. He means nothing to me. He has meant nothing to me for a long, long time."

She stopped as if she might be finished but I didn't speak. It sounded like it might be true.

"You don't have to believe me, I'm sure you don't. But you, sir, are overplaying your hand. You're hustling a hustler, Henry Burkhart, and I know what cards you've played. You don't hold anything worth a hundred thousand dollars."

The criminal new rich, and especially Tanya's kind—getting their money from the run-off of the family racket—take a while to develop the skills needed to get their money's worth. They go after the bling and the brands and the new Cadillacs without thinking, because, finally, they can. And if they have new problems, they throw money at it the same way until it goes away. If she wasn't willing to pay, it probably meant I hadn't made it a big enough problem.

"Forget the bad publicity, Tanya. That's not what this is about. I want top dollar for it and if you won't pay I'll shop it around. What's it worth to you to keep the disk out of Benny Palmer's hands? He's hooked up with Milo Finnes now, right? Does that bother you at all?" I paused and she didn't come back with anything witty. "Maybe he'd give me a hundred K just to have the leverage…keep his little monopoly goin'."

She took enough time to make me think I had struck a chord. "He doesn't have that kind of money," she said finally. That encouraged me.

"Maybe you'd rather deal with him for it."

Eventually she said, "I'm not willing to pay anything for it until I see it. Until I see what's on it."

"That's better, Tanya," I said, feeling cocky again. "I guess I'm willing to negotiate. But it's not getting out of my sight until I see some cash. And I want it tonight."

"I can't get anything tonight. Surely we can discuss this tomorrow."

"Come off it, Tanya, There's cash everywhere. I stay around you'll send your goons after me. I'm leaving tonight, non-negotiable, and I want to get paid."

"All right, but I want to see it first. I want a print out."

"Quit stalling, Tanya. It's a pull-tab, like I said. You take your chances just like all the suckers in your clubs. Or else I take it to Benny Palmer."

"All right, all *right*!" she yelled. "I'll get you something. I'll *try*."

"You'll get it. And you'll meet me on *my* turf. Tonight." Glancing over my shoulder again, I gave her Willie's address. "Eleven o'clock. Come alone. Don't bring any boyfriends. If I see anyone else with you—your little houseboy, for instance—I'm going to shoot first this time. You know what I mean, right?"

"I want my car back," she said flatly.

I stifled a laugh. "Sure, that's fine. But then the price goes to one-fifty."

"You fucking bastard! I just told you I'm not going to pay that. I can't get that kind of money. You just said..." She stopped and mewled loudly into the phone—a cry of animal frustration.

"Relax, Mrs. Gilmore. Be nice and maybe we can do a little business. But be here by eleven or I'm going to Palmer."

I hung up, feeling almost giddy. But when that wore off—and it didn't take long—I wasn't sure what I was left with. She hadn't crumpled like I was half hoping she would, she didn't give anyone up, and she didn't seem worried about being tagged for Charmichael's murder. Threatening to go to Frank didn't phase her much either, which meant he *was* in on it. And if Spencer's name was no surprise to her, the fact that she didn't respond could mean either one of two opposite conclusions; she was totally involved but at arm's length, so posing for complete deniability; or she had no direct connection to him at all even if she knew about the arrangement. So it was Frank's problem or someone else in the family. She didn't wilt until I mentioned Benny Palmer. He was the threat, not the accomplice. And if Alois Flood had told the truth, if it had been a woman who put Palmer onto us, if it wasn't Tanya...

That left Claire.

I stared out the kitchen window, looking at the overgrown junipers that all but covered the neighbor's fence. I remembered Connally and Luis sitting here yesterday, staring out the window, thinking their own hard thoughts, trying to put it all together. But they hadn't thought about Claire. Because I hadn't told them. That was all on me.

Dennis had talked to her after that dinner Sunday night, must have told her about the disk. If she *was* still cozy with Willard Coyne, still helping him to cook the books, and if Charmichael was the go-between, and he threatened to split…she'd be the one to kill him. Unless what she said about wanting out was true. But then, if she was leaving with Mickey, and they planned to go out on their own with Brent, and Brent reneged and killed her brother…again, she'd be the one to kill him. Either way she'd be desperate to cover her tracks. She would have all kinds of reasons for wanting me out of the way.

I couldn't make myself believe it. I couldn't see her putting the number on me with the Flood brothers. No matter what her plans or motives, there were things she said and ways she looked at me that I couldn't believe were empty lies. I just couldn't see it. Sooner or later I'd have to look harder.

It would have to be later. Tanya was on her way and I didn't want McQuitty around to cramp my style. Tanya and I, after all, had established a certain rapport.

I moved toward the doorway but held up when I heard McQuitty talking. He was explaining to Willie the details of extracting his car from yet another bureaucratic quagmire. Willie wasn't taking it well. I turned and sat back down at the phone and punched in the number to Willie's cell phone.

"Yo, man, speak," Willie answered.

"It's me. Don't let on to McQuitty."

There was a short pause while he took that in. "Oooo-kay…What up, bro'? What happenin'?"

"I got a hold of Tanya. She's coming over here to deal. I can put the squeeze on her but not with McQuitty around. You'll have to get rid of him for me, take him out of here."

"Now, what? How'm I s'pose to do that?"

"I have a plan."

"You got a plan? 'Cause I'd love to hear another one a' your plans."

"Cool it, Willie. You're giving it away."

"Yeah, ah'ight. Whatever."

"Now, listen. When we get off the phone, tell McQuitty this was a call from one of your contacts. Tell him you got a friend posing as a player out at Bingo Circle. Frank Coyne is out there tonight and you can say Chuck Burrows was spotted there too. He's the ex-cop. Connally and McQuitty have a definite hard-on for him, so he'll be interested. You can tell it that way to both of us, for that matter. I'll come in there after I hang up. I'll beg off sayin' I have to wait here for Palmer's call. You followin' me?"

"Yeah, yeah. What about, you know…" He stopped abruptly.

"Careful, Willie."

"I mean…what you just said, bro?"

"You're wondering about Palmer?"

"Yeah, tha's it."

"No word yet. That might have to be tomorrow. Maybe we can convince McQuitty that Burrows might lead us to Palmer."

"Yeah, tha's good, tha's good."

"You with me? Got the story down?"

"Oh, yeah man. I got it. Now, where's this place again? Bingo Circle? Say, ah…" His tone dropped and, clearing his throat, he mumbled, "Heads up, bro'," and he went off into an indecipherable stream of jive.

I heard the floor squeak then saw McQuitty's shadow from the corner of my eye.

"No, baby, I can't, not tonight," I said in a subdued tone. "I told you, I'm still waiting to hear. Don't know how long." I turned in my chair and pretended to notice McQuitty for the first time. I gestured with a finger for him to wait. He nodded. Willie rolled out a deep chuckle that I heard stereophonically through the doorway and the phone. "Yeah, I'll call you tomorrow, I promise," I continued. "Can you take care of that other stuff for me till then?"

"Oh, yeah, baby," Willie was saying, "We gonna be on top a' that one."

McQuitty turned back toward the living room. I gave Willie directions to Bingo Circle. "You got it?"

"Yeah, man. We're comin' out there, ah'ight."

"Listen, Willie. Stay on the phone for a while after I hang up. Keep up the chatter. I'll come in and stand around with McQuitty like we're waiting for you."

"Yeah, bro, this is *good*. This is *real* good." He peeled off another elongated laugh.

I put the phone down and went to stand in the doorway. McQuitty stood near a floor lamp leaning into the light, leafing through a magazine. Willie was yucking it up on his cell, overdoing it as usual. I had to make an effort not to smile.

"Who's he talking to?"

"Beats me," McQuitty said, turning. "But it's not his girlfriend." He arched his eyebrows and gave me a benign smile.

"Yeah, sorry," I said, nodding toward the kitchen. "She's pretty bent about me working these night gigs. I am *deep* in the dog house."

"I know how that is."

Willie was saying, "Just sit tight, bro'. If they break up, you tail the Jag. That's Frank Coyne." I thought that was a nice touch. "Let us know if he moves, ah'ight. We'll be headin' out there right now. Posse out, dude."

He hung up the phone, smiling hugely, nothing subtle about it.

"Who was that?" I asked.

"Tha's my *man*, dude. Tha's the hound dog, my brother Clarence."

"Where's he at?"

"Bingo Circle, where I sent him. Said the whole *family* showed up out there."

"You mean the Coynes?"

"Yeah, Frank and them, and that ex-cop, too…ah, Burrows somebody, right?"

"Who's this now?" McQuitty got interested.

"Willie recruited a few friends to work the halls for us."

"Plus you promised to pay the brothas *extra*," Willie said, eying me keenly, "if they come up with anything good."

I couldn't hold back a chuckle. "So wha'd they come up with? Chuck Burrows is out there with Frank?"

"Tha's right. Some kinda major *meet* goin' down."

"What about Palmer?"

"Not sure. I mean he don't know him, right? But that don't mean he ain't there. Anyway, I told them we'd be right out there." Willie was entirely too happy about it.

"Well, I can't go. I've gotta wait for Palmer's call."

"Me and the rookie can go," Willie quipped.

McQuitty smiled good-naturedly.

"We can put a tail on them," Willie continued, "see if they lead us to Palmer."

McQuitty gave Willie an appraising look. If he knew Willie any better, this wouldn't work. As things stood, he was sucked in. "Tailing who? And what if something comes up here?"

"Nothing but answering machines so far. It's getting late. If Palmer is in Cheyenne, it'll take him three hours just to get here. I think we should shoot for setting it up tomorrow."

This time McQuitty gave me the appraising look.

"Hey, I'm in for the night," I said. "In fact, if I could get rid of you two, maybe I could make some time with my woman. Have her come over."

"Claire still talkin' to you, then?" Willie asked.

"More or less," I said, giving him a look that should have told him to zip it. I wasn't sure if McQuitty knew Claire was on the list.

"Hey, c'mon, rookie. Let's do it. Let's take two cars, so's we can track these dudes if they split up."

"You don't have your car," I said, shaking my head.

"I'll take yours, man. That Lexus you borrowed from that witch." His eyes sparkled wickedly. "And that way the rookie here can be sure you ain't goin' nowhere. That suit you, rookie?"

McQuitty took a breath and smiled disingenuously. "I'm not a rookie, Willie," he said, exasperated. "I was on the force in LA for seven years before coming here."

"Ah, I's jus' jivin' you, man. C'mon let's do this." He gave me a sideways glance, clearly pleased with himself. "What you say, boss? Sound like a master plan?"

He had me and he knew it. In his own convoluted way, Willie has the knack. His in-your-face, 'stand out to blend in' technique was apparently beyond suspicion. Who would do that?

"All right, Willie, all right. But you gotta be careful. It's not my car."

"Hey, man, I's cool. Be back in no time."

"You got your phone."

"Right here."

"And I have mine," McQuitty said.

"Give me the number. If anything comes up on my end, I'll call you. But it's probably too late, unless you guys find Palmer out at the Circle. If you do, maybe we can still set something up. You can be back here before he shows."

McQuitty thought it over, but I knew we had him too. His eyes showed wariness but he was tempted, maybe anxious for action. I took up a pen and a piece of paper. "I'll give you the address in case Willie tries to lose you."

He chuckled at that.

"Ah, c'mon, man," Willie said, "I ain't gonna ditch anybody. We on the same side, 'member?"

"There's no action here, Ross," I said.

He gave me a grin that reflected a certain camaraderie that I felt minutely guilty for taking advantage of. "All right," he said, "but give me this number too. I'll be checking in. Anything goes down here without me, I'm in deep shit. And I'm calling Connally from the car to check this out."

"Fine with me," I said, with lavish false confidence.

I saw them into the yard and gave Pimpy a few throws of the tennis shoe while they got into their cars and drove away. Pimpy was excited. When I heard the phone ring, I was too.

Chapter 43

"Hello, Henry."

The timing, I realized, was perfect.

"Hello, Claire. I was just thinking about you."

"I can only imagine." Her tone was friendly enough, maybe even a tad coquettish. But it didn't last. "I'm afraid there's been a misunderstanding. We have to talk."

"Sure."

"Now, I mean. And in person. Not on the phone."

"Well, I've got something going tonight."

"I'm sure you do but it will keep. I have to see you before you do something stupid."

Nothing sweet about that.

"I don't have a car," I said, "and I don't have the time."

"I talked to Frank. I know about the disk. You'll have to talk to me first." I wanted to think that over, but she didn't give me the chance. "Where's this place you live?" she asked making it sound like it was under a rock.

"Okay, Claire, if that's the way you want it."

Nothing but silence. I gave her directions to Willie's house, telling her to park on the street at the end of the alley, just in case.

"In case of what?"

"I told you I had plans," I said, not caring how it sounded.

"I can be there in fifteen minutes. Can we be alone?"

I had to smile at the way that could be taken, though there was no mistaking her meaning.

"I'd like nothing better," I offered silkily—contributing my own double entendre.

"Hmm," she huffed, and the line went dead. I put the phone down delicately, like it might be fragile, and I lowered myself into a chair as if the surge of emotion coursing through me might erupt with any sudden movement. I sat there waiting, listening, and doing my best wishful thinking. It didn't take. She was playing me. She could've been playing me all along, the whole time I had been worried about playing her. Beyond the embarrassment, I began to sense the danger. If Claire killed Brent Charmichael—for whatever reason, take your pick—she would have plenty of reasons to get rid of me. And if she didn't, I had better find that out before Tanya showed up. I knew what I had to do. There is no tactful way to accuse someone of murder.

I looked at my watch. It was nine fifteen. I needed a plan. I sat there staring out the window, seeing nothing, forming pictures in my mind of how it was going to be. None of the pictures held up very well but one of them—like in my dream—had Claire showing up with a gun in her hands, arms extended, aiming at me. I thought about the imaginary disk and decided I needed a decoy, something to give Tanya for her trouble. Or Claire. I could stash it outside, high up and out of sight. When I got what I wanted on the wire, I would lead her to it. And when she saw where it was, she would tell me to get it down. I would reach up behind it and grab the gun I had stashed there. Bang, bang.

It seemed a little extreme. Then I remembered more of the dream. I needed a gun.

Without a car, I couldn't get to my place for one of mine. That Willie would have an extra weapon or two was hardly farfetched but DPD had confiscated one of them yesterday and he probably took another one with him. I undertook a search anyway. Going through drawers and cabinets and cubbyholes here and there, I began to revise my plan as I ran out of places to look. I tried not to think about how handy Ross McQuitty would be if I hadn't sent him off. When I came across a pack of cigarettes, I gave up the search. Fumbling one out, I lit it and took a long drag. I had another idea.

I went into Willie's living room and walked my fingers through his CD collection. He had some vintage stuff in there: Willie Brown, Charley Patton, Coltrane. I kept going until I found the newer stuff, hip-hop and rap, gangsta' names that were mostly initials attached to more eloquent words like 'Fat', 'Dog', and 'Ice'. I took one out that had several glossy-skinned 'black chicks' reclining lasciviously at the feet of a brother the size and approximate color of Jabba the Hutt. Thick gold links wrapped around the tree-trunk of his neck like choke-chains on an overfed Doberman. This couldn't be any good, I thought to myself, stripping the liner notes from the case and flipping the disk silver side up.

Outside, along the front of the house, I looked for a place to hide it that would leave me an escape route. I could go for the disk—at the edge of the house or over the fence—toss it back to her from a distance and disappear around the corner while she scrambled to catch it. I figured she wouldn't come after me if she thought she had what she wanted. Maybe she wouldn't even shoot at me. It wasn't the perfect plan. The sensible thing would be to call McQuitty for backup.

I kept searching for the perfect spot.

Pimpy followed me around with the gnarled sneaker clenched in his teeth, nodding and feinting. Ignoring him, I made my way along the fence until I came up against the thick growth of junipers that lined the edge of the yard. The entangled branches along the waist-high fence made it impossible to get to the tree I had in mind. As I stood there considering the problem, Pimpy poked his head up from beneath the thickest part of the juniper branches, just a few feet in front of me. His big brown eyes blinked away dust as he looked at me imploringly, the shoe still hanging from his mouth, covered with drool and dirt. He had tunneled his way under the boughs all the way to the fence.

"Good dog, Pimpy. We'll have to send this one in to Lilian Jackson Braun. Show up those smart-ass cats."

Circling around into the yard, I called him out from under there and we played a little tug of war before I tossed the shoe for him to fetch. He went after it with his usual glee. Getting down on all fours, I looked under the sagging branches. I could just make out the weathered fence-boards six or eight feet in. Circling back around the bushes, I jumped the fence into the neighbor's yard and made my way to where the branches were thickest on Willie's side. The slats were bone dry and peeling paint. I pried one loose from the crosspiece, splitting it with a slight cracking sound. While I struggled with a second, more stubborn board, a light came on behind me on the neighbor's back porch. I punched out the board and squeezed through the opening. Under cover of the juniper branches, I placed the disk against a gnarled trunk and crawled through Pimpy's tunnel back into Willie's front yard. I came out on my hands and knees dappled with dried needles and strings of cobwebs. Pimpy greeted me eyeball-to-eyeball, dangling the shoe in my face.

Standing up to dust myself off, I heard an old man's raspy voice.

"Who' that?" the neighbor hollered, leaning out his half-opened door.

"Just playin' with my dog," I said affably.

"That Willie Junior?"

"No, sir, I'm a friend of his. I'm staying with him. Me and my dog…" I stopped myself before saying Pimpy's name.

"No need for you playin' in *my* yard is there?"

"Sorry about that. The shoe went over the fence."

Grumbling incoherently, he backed into his house, leaving the porch light on. I played a few rounds of fetch with Pimpy, then went into the house for a flashlight. I came back out to check the placement of the disk. It was there, round and shiny, next to the opening in the fence. If push came to shove, I had an escape route.

Returning to the kitchen, I went to work on the recording device that McQuitty had left. I fumbled around with it and a roll of duct tape until I had it secured in the small of my back. I went upstairs for a clean shirt and brushed the last of the juniper needles out of my hair. When I returned to the kitchen, I heard the tinkling of tags on Pimpy's collar. Looking out the kitchen window, I saw no sign of him. With the neighbor's light still glowing, the junipers cast long shadows across the empty lawn.

Pimpy didn't bark. Doggedly friendly, he seldom does. But I heard the tinkling of his tags again, like someone giving him a rough pet. Fingering the recorder at the small of by back, I flicked the switch and pressed firmly on the strip of tape that held the mike to my chest.

From the living room, I looked through the screen door. Claire stood just inside the gate bent over at the waist, kneading the dog's furry mane. She wore loose fitting blue jeans and a brown leather jacket. Her hair, falling forward in grassy waves, seemed longer than usual, obscuring her face. Pimpy's head jutted upward, his eyes half-closed and his ears relaxed, in that peculiar expression some dogs effect that looks more like a smile of satisfaction than anything else. Apparently they were hitting it off.

The hinges squeaked when I pushed open the screen.

"Hello, Claire."

She turned her face into the light. Contrary to what I expected—and thanks to the dog—her expression was warm, the corners of her eyelids creased with humor. "Who's this happy fella'?"

"Claire, meet Pimpy. Pimpy, Claire."

"Pimpy? What kind of name is that?" she said, with obvious disdain.

"I get that all the time. It's his name. I can't change it."

"Why not? It's embarrassing."

"Not to him," I said.

Claire frowned but her eyes didn't harden that much.

"You're a complicated man, Henry," she said, "in the strangest sorts of ways." She took two steps towards me. "Aren't you going to invite me in?"

I stood aside, holding open the screen door.

"This is your roommate's house, right?" she said, taking in the cramped living room with a look of mild dismay. She made no move to sit down.

"He's an old friend. I'm just staying here temporarily."

"And where do you go from here?"

I didn't say anything. I didn't want to play.

"Right, fine," she said. "All subterfuge and evasion. You talk in riddles then act like you expect me to understand. Who are you, anyway?"

I couldn't answer that one either. "This isn't the time, Claire. I think we had better stick to business."

"Business? Is that what you call it?" Her eyes narrowed into a penetrating glare, angry yet somehow bewitching. "I can't figure out your *business*, Henry. It seems to me you're into everybody else's. Why are you involved in any of this?" She waved an arm, gesturing at the second-hand furnishings, as if they represented the hodge-podge of my investigation.

I met her stare mutely.

"Okay then, don't tell me anything. But you can't do this to Frank."

"Do what?"

"One minute you admit you're out to get him and the next minute you're conspiring with him to blackmail his competition.

"Blackmail?"

"I don't know what you call it—blackmail, extortion, payoff—what's the technical term, Henry? Frank wants to use it against Milo Finnes, doesn't he? This disk, I mean. And the whole time you're telling *me* that all you want is to find Mickey's killer. But you won't even tell me anything straight about that!"

"I don't know who killed your brother but I *am* going to find out. My best guess is that Brent pulled the trigger. But if so, as I told you, he wasn't acting alone."

She watched me closely. "And what does that have to do with this disk?"

"You talked to Dennis?"

She frowned and tossed her head, making her hair drape over her shoulders. "I got his *version* of the story and it sounded preposterous. So I called Frank. He didn't want to say anything, so I told him you weren't being straight with me. I told him I had reasons to suspect…to suspect your motives."

I accused her with my eyes but it didn't get me much.

"I'm sorry, Henry, but there's just too much lying going on. Too many goddamn secrets. You, him, Dennis. Everybody's acting…*cagey*. And people are dying because of it." Her eyes burned into mine. "Well, aren't they?"

I nodded.

"What's on this disk, anyway? More dirty little secrets? More reasons to have people killed?"

Her indignation seemed genuine but I sensed a strand of more sinister logic, something calculated and reserved. She had secrets of her own. So far, she had been pretty good at hiding them but the edges were beginning to show. I decided to flush her out.

"Frank seems to think it's records of some sort, accounting records maybe, details of Brent Charmichael's dealings, how much and with whom."

"And is it?"

"I don't know. Nobody's opened it. But Charmichael was killed because of it. The killer took his computer and all the other disks and tapes."

"So he covered his tracks. But you found something, some evidence of his involvement?"

"Who said it was a man?"

She smiled, then laughed, her eyes glinting as they remained focused on mine. "Oh, I see. You think *I* killed Brent." She laughed again, shaking her head, a confident laugh, but it died off quickly. "Well, God knows I've had my reasons but it's nothing to do with what's on any disk."

I gave her my best suspicious glower but she pretended not to notice.

"If you have evidence of who killed Brent Charmichael—and who killed Mickey—you have to give it to the police, right? You can't use something like that to bargain your way into bed with Frank Coyne. That *is* what you're doing, isn't it?"

Her cheap shot made it easier for me to take mine.

"Brent Charmichael goes back a long way, doesn't he? He used to work with Frank. That means Willard Coyne, too. And Tanya, and Mickey, and you too, if I'm not mistaken. All one big happy family. But the family gets a little ingrown somewhere along the line. Incestuous, you called it, right? Brent slept around."

I paused and watched. It was subtle, but she blinked first.

"So he gets a little too close to Tanya and that livens things up. But it doesn't slow down Brent. Or Mickey either, for that matter. They go into business together with the man named Harvey Cline. Cline gets killed in the course of their little undertaking and they call the whole thing off. But not before they give each other alibis. Then Brent goes to work for Milo—betraying the family, you might say. What secrets he takes with him—about them, about you—he uses to barter his way up the ladder in Milo's organization. But after a while, that isn't enough. So he decides to go out on his own, flirting with Mickey again—and with you."

I waited to see her reaction and I got what I wanted. Her eyes went hot and brooding and a sigh of restraint escaped her lips. She breathed in as if to speak, but I cut her off.

"But it didn't work out, did it? And I can't figure out why not. There was enough money to go around, wasn't there? Maybe his cut was too big or maybe he wanted more than money. Or maybe you didn't like the company he was keeping. What was it, Claire? What was it that got Mickey killed?"

Her cheeks flushed. I found it rather sexy.

"You think *I* know who killed Mickey?"

"He was killed because he knew too much. He had something on Brent or he had something on the people that Brent was working with."

"And that's what's on this disk?"

"I figure there's a good deal more than that on there. I figure it shows that Brent went in with this guy Spencer instead and, as part of the deal, he brought in Benny Palmer. And I figure Palmer has been running more than bingo supplies down from Cheyenne."

She gave me a quizzical look, then another exasperated sigh. "Look..."

"I think if we had Brent's records, it would show a lot more cash coming in than the bingo halls could ever generate. If Brent was the go-between, he'd keep track of all that cash and how much they laundered through Frank's operation. And if we're lucky, his records show who was in on the wash, how much their cut was, and how much was spent to pay off the cops and the secretary of state. And I pretty much think that once a person knows all that, he'll know who killed Mickey."

Her fine dark eyebrows drew together and a look of dawning comprehension kept her eyes riveted to mine. Then they shifted to the doorway behind me.

There was a light rap on the doorframe, then Tanya Gilmore's silky voice. "Claire?"

She was early and she was dressed to kill, one way or the other. An off-the-shoulders cashmere top form-fitted her breasts well enough to display how expensive that boob-job must have been. And the hip-wrapping suede skirt was short enough for…anything. A trademark-dappled Louis Vuitton handbag hung by a strap over her right shoulder, just the right size for a hand gun. I didn't like it. I didn't like any of it.

"Join the party," I said, pushing open the screen. She wore no jewelry save a Lady's Rolex but she was made up for the occasion with artistically applied mascara, ruby red lipstick, and a generous layer of rouge. I could detect the scent of her perfume, cloyingly sweet, from four feet away. Pimpy must have liked it. He pranced over to Tanya and nosed her at the knees and up the visible thigh, searching for the source. Tanya sidestepped away, raising her hands out of reach and squeezing her thighs together. She looked from me to Claire and back again, plainly ill at ease. Pimpy wagged his pom-pom tail and panted happily, drooling in the vicinity of Tanya's glossy black mid-heel pumps.

Obviously she had a seduction in mind, probably along the lines of the black widow's technique. Maybe that's how she got close enough to Charmichael. If it worked on him, why not me. But Claire's presence clearly called foul on that play.

Apparently reaching the same conclusion, Tanya looked at Claire and folded her forearms across her chest as best she could. "Well, I didn't expect to find you here."

"Likewise, I'm sure," Claire responded, the catty tone unconcealed. Her eyes went the length of Tanya's getup. "Am I getting in the way of something?"

"I called her here," I said, "to discuss the disk."

"Sure," Claire said, ogling Tanya unabashedly. "Does Frank know about this?"

Tanya's glossy lips puckered into a pout. "Of course he does. He was there when Henry told us about it. *He's* the one who wanted to know what's on it. I was perfectly happy to have it destroyed."

"I mean, does he know…how you're playing it?"

Not pussyfooting around. A thought flickered across my mind that Claire was jealous. Tanya must have picked it up. "*He* called *me*," she said, a taut finger aiming at my chest. "I don't know why. Perhaps Frank should have handled this. I can't get any money, anyway, so you'll just have to wait." Her tone dipped when she added, "I couldn't reach him."

"You didn't try," I said.

Her eyes shifted away, feigning indifference.

"What money?" Claire asked. "Money for the disk?" She turned to accuse me. "You're selling the disk?"

"It's not what you think," I said without thinking.

"Of course it is," Tanya affirmed haughtily. "It's blackmail. You were going to sell it to the other side if I didn't come tonight."

"Other side?" Claire asked. "What other side?"

"So Palmer has thrown in with Spence, then," I said.

Tanya's eyes narrowed with anger. "You don't know anything," she told me.

"Spence again?" Claire entreated. "Who *is* this Spence person? And what does Benny Palmer have to do with it?"

Claire didn't know. That left Tanya.

"My guess is that Palmer is the go-between," I said, addressing Claire, "now that Brent's been taken out. The money went from Spence to Brent and from Brent to Tanya. Maybe Palmer was the courier. And from *you*," I said, nodding toward Tanya, "it went to old man Willard, right? He's the one who could launder it through the books at American Community Services and pass it out all nice and clean."

Tanya eyes widened with surprise, letting me know I had nailed it. She drew a breath as if to speak but Claire cut her off.

"What money?" she demanded. "What's this about laundering money?" She looked to me and then to Tanya. "That's what drug dealers do."

Tanya tightened her crossed arms and her face went rigid with restraint. Her eyes cut to the door as if about to make a run for it, but she didn't move.

"R. D. Spencer *is* a drug dealer," I said. "He produces methamphetamine and distributes it multi-state. He's big, he's very organized, and he's very deadly. And if Tanya didn't kill Brent Charmichael herself, then Spencer did it for her. Or he had his thugs do the dirty work. But whoever did it acted on orders from a woman, a woman who told him that Charmichael was gumming up the works."

"Tanya?" Claire asked, incredulous.

"How do you know any of this?" Tanya hissed at me.

"What was it?" I squared my shoulders to face her. "Was he takin' too big a cut? Did his habit make him too jumpy to work with? Once he got strung out, you couldn't trust him, right? And with Palmer doing the legwork, you didn't even need Brent any more. Or maybe he tried a little gambit of his own, threatening to go off with Mickey. Or to Frank, maybe."

Her eyes jumped at the mention of Frank's name. "That's insane. You don't know anything!"

"Yeah, that's it, isn't it? 'Cause Frank didn't know about it. You're bluffing about that, aren't you, Tanya? Frank didn't get a cut. It was just you and daddy. You and old man Willard."

"You leave him out of this!"

"And *he* sure as hell didn't want Frank to know. Maybe Willard felt left out of the game. Maybe he didn't like that his son was the bingo king, getting all the perks and publicity, having all the power. Maybe he was just plain envious."

"That's not true!" Tanya erupted. "*Frank* was the one who wouldn't share."

The cat was out of that bag. It came out big and mean and poised to defend itself. I let it wander around in the silence between us, so everyone could take a good long look.

"Frank?" Claire said, obviously confused.

Sensing the change in the atmosphere, Pimpy twisted to his feet and pattered into the kitchen. Everyone watched him go, as if thankful for the distraction. It gave me a moment to connect a few dots.

"So Frank was holding out," I said. "The proceeds from the halls were off. Central City took a bite and that's not what you're used to. So you cooked up this arrangement with Spencer. But Frank wouldn't go for it. Not that he had anything against laundering money. It's a family tradition, after all. But Frank was too prissy for the likes of R.D. Spencer, too country clean to get in deep with a drug dealer. So you pulled an end around and went to the old man. I'm surprised *he* went for it. Did you tell him where the money was coming from? Did he know that people were dying from it? Did you have Mickey killed when he threatened to tell him?"

Tanya was backing away, a look of panic distorting her painted features. "You, you…"

"You?" Claire said, turning to block Tanya's progress. "You killed Mickey?"

"I didn't kill *anybody*, you fucking bitch! It was *you* that made all this happen. You and that fucking *kid* of yours!"

And then they went at it. Claire lunged, taking a roundhouse swing. Tanya charged under it, hitting Claire in the chest with both hands. Entangled together, Claire clutching hands full of Tanya's ample perm, they went down in a swirl. Glancing off the couch, they tumbled to the floor with Tanya landing on top. They scratched and clawed in a whirlwind of awkward blows, grunting and mewling like netted banshees. But Tanya had some strength, got in a few good blows. The leather purse fell on the floor and I kicked it away, as I positioned myself over them.

I seized Tanya around the waist, lifted her, and pushed her across the room. It wasn't that easy. She found her feet and made a move to get past me. I grabbed an arm and swung her around on her own momentum, tossing her onto the couch. Grunting and panting, she sprung up on the bounce and made another charge toward Claire. With the heel of my hand, I straight-armed her on the bridge of the nose. I mean, you can't hit a woman but… She fell back stiffly, landing seated on the couch. Stunned and slack-jawed, she brought both hands to her face. A trickle of blood came from her nose.

I looked around for Claire. She had scooted away crab-like across the living room rug. She sat propped up against the doorjamb, arms enfolding her knees. The adrenaline from the girl-fight animated her features into an expression of amazement. She looked turned on—I couldn't help notice. Pimpy stood in the doorway just behind her, ears perked, eyes wide with interest.

I turned to face Tanya. Still panting heavily, her eyes glared with animal hatred just above her overlapping hands. "You can't always get what you want!" she hollered, in what I took to be some kind of psychotic outburst. "You can't always get what you *want*!"

I thought she had lost it completely. I shouldn't have smiled. Her fierce and desperate eyes cut to the door behind me, as if sizing up her chances to escape. But she didn't make the move.

"You *can't* always *get what you want*!" she shrieked.

And I realized—too late—it was code, the go-phrase. She had backup. I swung around.

Rhonda Schomberg stood in the doorway.

Chapter 44

Through the lenses of her strapped-on protective eyewear, Rhonda's eyes glistened with intensity and focus. Her hair was pulled back and held in place by a three-inch-wide sweatband. In a multi-tone beige full-length jumpsuit, hinting at camo, and brown high-top sneakers, she looked like the latest thing in feminist prepper attire for the upper-crust suburban set. There was no trace of the aloof composure, the amused refinement of the well-heeled lobbyist and socialite. It was almost funny, except for the big black gun extending from her gloved hands.

"I've heard enough," she said, perfectly deadpan.

"Rhonda?" Claire said, incredulous.

"Get up, Claire. Go stand by your boyfriend there."

Claire unfolded her limbs and I helped her to her feet. Pimpy emerged from behind us, tail wagging, brown eyes smiling, moving toward the door to greet the latest visitor.

Rhonda's gun swung in his direction.

"Pimpy!" I commanded.

His ears dropped and the fluffy tail went limp. Cowering in place, his uncertain gaze went to me, then to Rhonda, and back to me again. I patted my thigh and he came over.

"Keep that dog away from me," Rhonda said.

A strange sense of calm infused me as I realized who had done the killing. "So you're the one," I said. "You put the Flood brothers onto us today."

She affected a dry, sardonic grin. "If you want something done right…" she said, stepping further into the room and closing the door.

"Does that mean you did Mickey too?"

"Shut up, Burkhart." She kept her voice low but firm. "We've heard enough of your bullshit."

Still breathing hard, Tanya got up from the couch and sidled over to Rhonda's side, wiping at her nose. "Did you hear what he said? He's gonna tell Frank. He knows about—"

"You shut up too. You've said too much already. Jesus!"

Tanya's look of flushed panic faded some, an expression of rebuke taking its place as she turned her gaze to Rhonda. Jutting out her chin and looking suddenly petulant, she began preening herself neurotically, straightening her disheveled outfit and pressing back her tangled coif. Rhonda watched her with furtive glances, as if distracted by the movement. Tanya retrieved her purse from the floor and dug through it. I was thinking gun. Seemingly oblivious to the tensions of the moment, she brought out a tissue and a small mirror and set to work on the smudges of blood and her smeared makeup. Ronda took a breath.

"Where's the disk, Burkhart? And why don't you put your hands in the air. You too, Claire."

"What are you gonna do, shoot me?"

"Do you doubt that I'm capable of it?" She shifted the aim of the gun toward Claire. I raised my hands. Claire did likewise.

"Now, listen up you two." Her voice remained low—almost butch—and very controlled. "This doesn't have to be complicated. Give me the disk and nobody gets hurt. We were never here. And don't give me any shit about having mailed it to a secret friend who's going to send it to the FBI if he doesn't hear from you. Nobody leaves this room until I get the disk. And nobody leaves this room if I don't."

"But if you kill me, you won't get it."

"If I kill you, nobody else will either, and that's almost as good." Her tone turned mocking as she added, "Of course, I'd have to kill everyone in the room."

It was a bit melodramatic but it had the desired effect. Lowering her compact case, Tanya gave Rhonda a startled look, as if wondering whether she was included.

"What about the neighbors?" I said. "This isn't as isolated as Charmichael's bungalow."

"Quit stalling, Burkhart, or I'm going to let Tanya work on your girlfriend some more." Her gaze shifted to Claire.

The strange inner poise that had buoyed me for the moment drained off in a slow-motion swirl as the absurdity of my predicament came into focus: three women, all demonstratively loose cannons, each one hating me for different reasons. And there I was with a gun in my face, having sent my own allies chasing wild geese. Waves of fear rose up with the pounding in my chest as I realized we had gone too far. Like Rhonda said, Tanya had said too much. We all knew who did what and why and there was no way she was going to let us tell it.

Rhonda smiled a dry smile, sensing my trepidation. "Now where's the disk? Or do I have to twist her arm?" She motioned toward Claire again. "Bring her over here, Tanya."

Tanya seemed reticent. "What are you going to do?"

"Just *do* it. And keep away from him, in case I need a clear shot."

Tanya flinched at that, obviously wanting nothing to do with the blood and guts. But she did what she was told, crossing behind Rhonda and taking Claire by the arm. Claire struggled slightly but Tanya rose to the resistance.

"Stop it, Claire. You're just making it *worse*." Showing her strength, she shoved Claire down on the floor in front of Rhonda. The gun barrel followed her fall. I tensed for a move and Rhonda's eyes and the gun came up to aim at my face. I took a little halter step to regain my balance.

"Just *don't*, smart guy." Rhonda snarled. "I'm so *pissed* at you I could…"

I raised my arms a little higher. "All right. It's yours. But it's not here."

"Don't give me that pulp-fiction bullshit." Without taking her eyes off of me, she swung the gun backhand in a low arc, catching Claire on the forehead. Claire went flat with a whimper. Standing above her, Tanya's hands came up to her face in a gesture of surprise.

"I swear to God," I said, "It's just outside, around the front of the house."

Rhonda shook her head slowly. As Claire propped herself up on one elbow, Rhonda raised her gun arm upward.

"Rhonda, *don't!*" Tanya yelped.

The gun came around in Tanya's direction.

"God-*dammit*, Tanya!" Rhonda growled. "This isn't a *game*. You had your chance."

"Look, Rhonda," I said, "it's out there, I swear. I hid it after the car chase this afternoon. That makes sense, doesn't it? It's just out in the yard behind some bushes. Near the fence. I'll show you."

Glaring at me, Rhonda's mouth curled inward. Her gaze cut to Tanya and lingered there, as if confirming that she couldn't be counted on for much.

"All right. Tanya, tie his hands behind him." She brought a spool of thick twine from a deep outside pocket. She had come prepared. "I'll stay close to Claire. You try anything, Burkhart, I'll put a bullet through her heart. You understand me, don't you?"

I got the reference. Brent Charmichael—shot pointblank in the chest.

There was a grueling silence—awkward was not the word for it—while Tanya fumbled with the twine. It gave me time to think and it's times like that when I can really think.

Like any good lobbyist, Rhonda Schomberg had been pulling the strings behind the scene. With Tanya as her puppet, she had nurtured the connection between Brent and old man Willard and helped Tanya milk it for more than it was worth. But when the structure got shaky—because of Brent's habit or Spencer's involvement—she devised a way to cut and run. I figured she coaxed Brent into killing Mickey when he threatened to expose them. Then she killed Brent before he could run, eliminating any loose ends she didn't control. That left only Tanya, who was in too deep to object to her methods.

It sounded all right, up to a point, but it didn't do me much good in the moment.

I played back what I remembered of the two murder scenes, putting Rhonda behind the wheel of Brent Charmichael's blue Cadillac and afterwards in his home office. The fake suicide was an amateurish stunt but it hardly mattered once all the records connecting Brent with Tanya had disappeared. She had done that for Tanya's sake and, at the same time, put her in her place. And if the suicide didn't sell, it shifted the blame to the bingo rivalries. But I couldn't see Tanya sanctioning the murder of her husband. She was conniving, no doubt, and criminal and narcissistic, and there was no love lost between them, but she didn't have the stomach for violence. I couldn't see her having Brent killed either, unless Rhonda saw her through it, and unless Brent had killed Mickey. The timing on that was too good. If Rhonda needed a reason to get rid of Brent, she had to count on him killing Mickey, and that was too much of a coincidence. She would have had to get Mickey to torch Brent's club. But she hadn't done that—because I had. And Brent was about to run. If Rhonda knew that, she would have been driven to act.

That's when I saw how it happened, how it must have happened. And that's when I knew Tanya was our only chance out of there.

"You can still get out of this," I said to her, as she worked on tying my wrists. "I know you didn't kill anyone."

Her fumbling slowed for an instant. Then with a mean jerk, she pulled tight the knot of twine. She leaned in close to me and spat words into my ear.

"*I* told *you* I didn't kill anybody."

"That's right. Rhonda did the killing. She killed Brent because he killed Mickey. That's what she told you, isn't it? But she didn't tell you he was about to skip out."

"Shut up, Burkhart," Rhonda said. "We've heard enough." She held out another wad of twine to Tanya. "Tie her, too," she said, pointing to Claire on the floor.

"What are you afraid of? That you'll have to kill Tanya if she finds out? Because you're going to kill *us* once you have the disk. She told you that, didn't she, Tanya?"

"No one's going to kill anybody," Tanya said with a tremor in her voice, stooping to tie Claire. "Don't you see…Just give us the disk and we'll go."

"But killing has already happened. And we know about it. We know Rhonda killed Brent. *And* we know Rhonda killed Mickey."

Rhonda said, "Shut up, Burkhart…"

"Brent killed Mickey, goddammit!" Tanya erupted, overriding Rhonda's command. "And he *deserved* what he got."

"Was Rhonda with you at that luncheon, Tanya?" I asked, seeing the timing of that alibi as the only window of opportunity. "Was she there the whole time?"

Rhonda took two long strides and swung at me with the gun. I flinched but the barrel caught me just above the ear. I fell backwards onto the table next to the couch and tumbled to the floor. A lamp followed me down with a crash.

"That's enough goddammit. One more word and I start working on Claire. You understand me?"

It hurt to nod my head. Stealing a glance at Tanya, I saw her staring at me, her eyes wide with a shocked look, a look that was moving far away. I hoped I had put her on the right track.

Rhonda rummaged again into the pockets of her overalls. "Here, take this," she said to Tanya, holding out a revolver. "Get her to her feet."

Tanya hesitated, staring at the gun, her expression still distant.

"Tanya, dammit. It's taking too long."

Tanya took the gun, but her eyes, not meeting Rhonda's, conveyed doubt, questioning.

"Let's go," Rhonda ordered. "Get her on her feet."

Tanya reached down to help Claire, the gun held gingerly, unconvincingly.

I crawled to my knees then stood up. Rhonda turned me toward the door and prodded my neck with the barrel of her weapon. Its cold pressure sent shivers down my spine.

"No more talk," Rhonda said. "Where's the damned disk?"

I led the way through the door and into the long front yard knowing my plan wasn't going to work. With my hands tied, I couldn't throw the disc. And if I went through the fence, they would still have Claire. With a sense of panic knifing through my fears, my thoughts spun exponentially. I noticed the soft glow of a nightlight emitting through the curtains in a window of Leroy Street's house. Following the path of flagstone that edged the house, I hoped to rouse someone from within.

Rhonda kept one hand on my arm and the gun barrel between the shoulder blades. Behind her, I could hear Claire talking to Tanya in a tone too low to make out the words.

"Shut her up," Rhonda commanded. Pulling me up, she seethed words into my ear. "Don't try waking the neighbors, asshole. If you're dead nobody gets the disk. And you better believe I'll put Claire down with you."

I turned towards the junipers that lined the neighbor's fence. Up against its scraggly boughs, I came to a stop and gestured with one foot, pointing into the shadows beneath the sagging limbs. The light from the neighbor's back porch shone directly into my eyes.

"It's in there," I said weakly. "Underneath."

"Go get it."

"I can't get in there unless you untie me."

"Yeah, right. Down on the ground. Show me where it is."

I knelt and bent to look under the branches. It was easy enough to see from that position. "Right there," I said. "Take a look."

As I straightened up, she kicked me at the shoulder. I went over on my side into the bush and she shoved me onto my stomach.

"Don't move," she said, pulling out a small flashlight. "Tanya, if he moves, shoot him. Then shoot her."

I couldn't see Tanya's face but I didn't think she'd do it. Anyway, I had no choice. So when Rhonda squatted to her hands and knees, the gun hand on the ground, aiming the light with the other, I twisted towards her and raised my leg and came down hard with the heel of my shoe. I nailed the back of her hand. She let out a sharp cry as I caught her on the side of the face with my other foot. Frantically, I kept kicking, hoping to dislodge her glasses. She collapsed forward with a grunt but surprised me by kicking back, then scrambled beneath the branches. I kept on kicking until she had crawled out of reach. That's when headlights swept across the scene. It was Willie Junior in Tanya's Lexus, pulling in from the alley.

The headlights froze Tanya and Claire in their high beams like two stupefied fawns. Claire looked to me helplessly as Tanya tightened her grip and glared into the lights.

"Rhonda?" Tanya shouted.

"What the fuck?" Willie said, climbing out of the car.

I squirmed around on the ground, raking the dirt with my legs, feeling for Rhonda's gun. I could hear her panting just a few feet away. The branches rustled and jarred against her efforts but through the darkness and dust I couldn't see her.

"It's all right, Tanya," Rhonda gasped breathlessly. "Keep him covered. I see the disk."

"There's *people* here, Rhonda."

"Henry? That you?" Willie called.

"Yeah, Willie. Stay back." I gave up on the gun and swiveled around to face the woman and her hostage. "Take it easy, Tanya," I said, breathing too heavily to sound in control. "You didn't kill anybody. I know that. Don't make it worse for yourself."

"Rhonda! Where are you?" she pleaded, pointing the gun from Willie to me and back again. Willie stayed behind the car.

"Hold on!" Rhonda barked. "I see it."

"Rhonda shot Mickey, Tanya," I said, twisting awkwardly to my knees. "I saw it. Brent never fired the gun. The shots were fired from *inside* the car."

"Rhonda?" Tanya implored.

"He's lying!" Rhonda bawled from under the bushes. "Brent shot Mickey."

Tanya pointed the gun at me but she didn't shoot me.

"Listen to me," I said, raising my voice. "Rhonda shot Mickey. She was driving the car. I think you know that. She was missing from that luncheon, wasn't she? At just the right time?"

"That's not *true*!" Rhonda yelled. "Shoot him, Tanya! Fucking shoot him!"

"Brent didn't kill Mickey. I don't think he even knew that's what she had planned. Rhonda used him as cover, knowing his car would implicate him. Then she killed Brent so you'd only have her side of the story."

"Tanya, I've got it," Rhonda screamed, "I've got the disk. *Shoot* the lying bastard!"

"There *is* no disk," I blurted, then wondered if this was the best time to mention it. "There never was one, Tanya. It's a music CD. There's nothing on it."

"You're lying!" Rhonda wailed, grunting wildly.

Lights came on along the wraparound porch of Leroy Street's house.

"What the sam-hill's goin' on out here?" Leroy's raspy voice croaked from somewhere out of sight. Leroy appeared, rounding the corner, hunched over in a full-length nightshirt, his cane extended in front of him. "Goddamn, Willie," he groused, steadily tapping his way along, "you ain't got non a' those no-account 'brothas' a' yours…"

"Uncle Leroy, get back!" Willie hollered from behind the Lexus.

"…Causin' a ruckus all hours a' the night…"

The screen door opened from Willie's house and Pimpy bound into the yard. He went in one direction then the other, looking for a playful gesture. Tanya followed him with the gun.

"Pimpy, get back!" I yelled, inanely.

The gun swung toward me.

"That you, Henry Burkhart?" Leroy demanded, seemingly oblivious to the danger. Tanya swung around, eyes wild, taking aim at the approaching ghostly figure.

"Leroy, she's got a gun," I said. "We have a *situation* here!"

"Sit-chi-*a*-shun?" Leroy said, coming to a stop and circumscribing the scene with a slow, arching, unfocused gaze. "Boy, I'll say. You wake up Martha, you'll have a sit-chi-*a*-shun, all right."

Another car pulled up behind Willie's in the alley. It was McQuitty. As Tanya swung around to take aim at him, the branches nearest me rustled violently, then Rhonda Schomberg emerged with a thump.

Tanya wailed at the sight of her. "Rhonda?"

Laboring to her hands and knees, she was covered in dirt and leaves and bleeding from the head. Her glasses were gone but she had found the disk. And she had found the gun. Squinting and blinking away dust and darkness, she held the case open in one hand, close to her face.

"You son of a bitch," she stammered and she raised up and waved the gun in my direction. I dove away as she fired. There was a quick hot sensation along my upper arm. More shots were fired, four or five in rapid succession, and Pimpy barked and howled like a hunted wolf. I landed hard, forehead first, unable to break my fall. Everything went light, bright red, then black.

Chapter 45

Time stopped—a sort of hiccup—then began again as the darkness faded towards gray. Bright spots emerged in my field of vision, then vague dark shapes took forms that didn't mean anything at first, and then they did. For a few long seconds, I thought I saw everything in still-frames, then I realized no one was moving. I rolled up on one elbow, smelling the acrid cordite before I saw the smoke. A gray plume drifted languidly in the still air in front of Tanya's extended arm. Ross McQuitty crouched in a shooter's stance just behind the picket fence. A diffuse silvery cloud roiled into the light above him. I watched as he shifted his aim to Tanya and Claire. That meant something. I struggled to my knees.

"Put the gun down, lady!" McQuitty commanded.

"Don't shoot," I pleaded, my voice sounding hollow and remote.

Claire's expression of shock seemed strangely calm next to the savage panic on Tanya Gilmore's face. Her large chest heaving for air, she stood glowering, her eyes fixed on a point beyond her gun in front of the juniper hedge. Following her stare, I saw Rhonda Schomberg lying in a crumpled, dirty heap, splayfooted, bent awkwardly, lifeless. The CD lay next to her, the labeled side up. Elaborate red graphics spelled out "Big Daddy-D" for all of us to see.

"Put the gun down!" McQuitty repeated. "This is the police!"

Tanya's arm swung in the direction of his voice, her eyes squinting into the light. McQuitty and Willie ducked but Tanya didn't fire. She stood erect and shaking, little mewling noises coming from between her lips.

"Rhonda?" she said in a whisper. Her rapt gaze drifted back to the body almost thoughtfully. Then the shaking gave way to sobs. Her arm slackened and I could have taken her easily, if my hands weren't tied, if I wasn't dizzy, if I could get to my feet.

"You can't always get what you want," she mumbled, as if something was forcing it out of her. "You can't, you can't…"

The gun arm lowered further and she loosened her grip on Claire. I motioned with my head and Claire moved away in baby steps.

"Leroy! Leroy!" It was Martha Street, Leroy's wife. Her broad girth, draped in satiny layers, came lumbering around the corner of the house. "*Lord*, Leroy, are you all *right?*"

Tanya half-turned in her direction. Her eyes brimming with tears, she watched imploringly, as if Martha's concerns might be meant for her. Her gun arm rotated away unconsciously, pointing to the no man's land between herself and the dead woman. McQuitty had a clean shot. I managed to stand and I stepped into his line of fire.

"Sure, sure," Leroy said, turning to be taken into Martha's massive, protective embrace. "Things pretty much done for here," he said with his head turned enough to keep a not-blind eye on Tanya. "That lady had some trouble. It's all right now, though, ain't it? It's all over."

Tanya's gaze, sorrowful and distant, came back around. I stepped forward gingerly, tugging at my bonds, feeling utterly exposed.

"It's over, Tanya. There is no disk. It's a decoy. There's nothing on it. There's nothing to worry about."

She looked at me, her face a mottled wash of tears and smeared mascara. "You're the police?" she asked weakly.

"I…I'm working for the District Attorney," I said, eyeing the downward pointing gun.

The intensity of her stare seemed to fade. "I *knew* we couldn't trust you," she said, her tone more indignant than angry, like a schoolgirl who had the right answer but didn't get called on.

"That's a policeman over there," I said, nodding behind me. "He's asking you to put your gun down. You'll be okay. You didn't shoot anybody."

"I shot Rhonda," she said, squeaking out the words in a halting falsetto. Hunching over, sobs racked her body and the gun dropped as she brought her hands to her face.

I took one step and kicked it away.

"It's okay, Tanya. You did the right thing."

McQuitty came up in a sprint. Stowing his weapon, he grabbed Tanya's arms and twisted her around. She gave a little squeak but didn't resist. His eyes cut around the yard like he expected more crazed women to come crawling out of the bushes. Willie came up behind him, mumbling exclamations. Pimpy followed on his heels, tail wagging only tentatively. McQuitty spoke commands into his cell phone.

"Hey, Willie, untie me will ya?"

"Man! You see that! Shot her *down*, man. Hey, you all right? I think you been shot."

"Just untie me, will ya? And you'd better see to your uncle."

"Leroy?" Willie said, fumbling with the twine. "Man, that ol' man *deserve* to get shot, prancing around in that *nightgown*...look like death itself."

I jerked away from his grasp and turned on him. "Can you get these fucking ropes off without the running commentary?"

"Sure, sure, yeah. Hold still."

As he pried at the knots, I spotted Claire standing meekly and very still at the front of Willie's house just beyond the glow of light from the front door. She was looking down with a fixed, wide-eyed stare, as if waiting for the ground to part in front of her.

Other faces appeared in the periphery, neighbors roused from their beds by gunshots in the night, closer at hand than usual. A few older children of various colors and sizes lined the front fence and peeked around from behind the trees along the curb. Approaching sirens and flashing lights sent many of them scampering. The older folks stood their ground, turning to watch the police cruisers unload.

When my hands were free, I went to Claire. Taking her by the shoulders I got nothing but that zombie look. I turned her around and began untying her bonds. Pimpy came prancing toward us, tail wagging fully now, eyes bright, like he had a lot to say. He did a little dance, then darted off. Claire's gaze followed the dog for an instant. I was glad to see some motor reaction. Once I got the twine loose, I rubbed her wrists then gently combed her tangled hair back from her face. The bump on her forehead was the size of half an egg. Her eyes, wide and empty, did not meet mine. She was in shock. I looked around for help.

Colored light-beams danced over the scattered assembly now. McQuitty walked Tanya toward his car, still spewing orders into his phone. Willie stood with Leroy and Martha on the wraparound porch, all of them yammering away. At the far end of the yard, one uniformed cop dealt with the line of onlookers jockeying for a better view. Another leaned over Rhonda's body, reaching a finger to her carotid artery. Their radios squawked intermittently, static-laced voices piercing the night in monotones, calm, objective, disinterested.

"Come with me," I said to Claire.

She raised her arms forward like a mock sleepwalker. When I tried to guide her, she slumped against me with most of her weight. I pulled her to me and she put one arm on my shoulder for support. There was no mistaking it for affection. We sidled that way through Willie's front door and into the living room.

I eased her down onto the couch.

"Are you all right?" I asked, feeling the inadequacy of my words.

She blinked a few times and her lips moved through a series of vague contortions. Her eyes closed then opened and seemed to come into focus. "Some water?"

I went for a glass of water, then a washcloth and some ice. When I applied the cold cloth to her forehead, she winced at first, then winced again, then took the cloth from my hands.

"Let me. Let me."

I watched as she dabbed at the goose egg, her features pale and drawn. Then she lowered the cloth and looked at me, her blue eyes suddenly attentive.

"Is it true, then?" she asked, without much force.

"Is what true?"

"All of it. You. Them. Rhonda." A tone of insistence enlivened her voice. "*Did* Rhonda kill Mickey? Or is that just something you said…"

"Drink some more water."

"*Tell* me, Henry. I want to *know*."

The slackness of her features was gone and she was blinking almost continuously but her eyes stayed focused on mine. I sat next to her on the couch.

"What I said to Tanya was my best guess. When I found Brent's body, there were burn marks on the side of his face."

"Burns? Someone burned him?"

"No, I mean, powder burns from a gun. More like scratches but inflamed. Powder burns come from a contact wound. But there was no wound on his face. This was different. The gun went off close to him but not aimed at him."

Her eyes narrowed with the effort to understand, then widened impatiently.

"Rhonda was driving that Cadillac, Brent next to her. I think she was egging him on to take the shot but he didn't actually do it. He wouldn't shoot Mickey. So Rhonda saw it through, she had to. She reached over in front of him and fired at Mickey. The gun went off close enough to Brent's face to cause the burns. I heard Brent scream in pain. I didn't know what to make of it at the time. The cops thought the scratches might have come from a failed suicide attempt." I paused, thinking she wasn't following me. But after a few seconds, she prompted me on.

"But that's not what you think, is it."

"No. From what I could tell, he was not the type."

"No," she said. "He's not the type."

I tried giving her a questioning look but she ignored it, looking away. I decided not to press it.

"The forensics guys will be able to tell. If it's from when Rhonda shot Mickey, it'll show a certain amount of healing before he died."

Her eyes came up again. "But you said you saw the shots fired."

"I saw the profile of two heads. I saw the flash of the gun going off. If the passenger had fired the shots, I should have seen his arm come out the window. He couldn't have taken aim from inside. Only the driver could have done that."

"And you know it wasn't Brent driving?"

"He wouldn't have had the tattooing on his face, would he?"

She watched me thoughtfully, vertical creases forming upwards from between her eyes. Then she dropped her gaze and turned away with a sigh. Having pushed this far, she was content to drop it.

It struck me again that her guiding interest was Brent Charmichael—the roll he had played, and especially whether or not he had killed Mickey. Then I remembered what Tanya said to Claire just before the catfight. *"It was you that made all this happen. You and that fucking kid of yours!"*

I looked up to find Claire regarding me, as if she had been following the slow dawning of my thoughts.

"You thought I did it, didn't you?" It wasn't exactly a smile she spoke through but her eyes were showing some life.

"You had something to hide," I said.

The eyes hardened. "Did you think I would turn on my friends?"

"Mickey didn't tell you what he found out. I see that now. He was trying to protect you. Trying to protect Shanie."

She looked away. I thought of Shanie, tried to picture her, tried to compare her features to those of the man I had found lying in his own blood. I got nothing from that, so I asked.

"He's Shanie's father, isn't he? Charmichael, I mean."

Her eyes closed and she slowly nodded her head. "He didn't kill Mickey," she managed. "I knew he wouldn't do that."

I lowered my arm from the back of the couch but she moved away from my touch. Leaning forward, her hands came up to her face, covering her eyes. I went to the bathroom to get some Kleenex. When I returned, she was sitting back again, sniffling, wiping at her dampened face with the heel of her palms. She took the tissues without looking up.

"You have all the pieces to your puzzle now, Henry?"

It was a slap in the face, long overdue. I wanted to say I was sorry but I didn't feel it. In fact, I had more questions. I wanted to ask her if Mickey had threatened to blow the whistle in order to keep her from getting involved with Brent again. Because I figured that's what got him killed. But Claire probably wouldn't know. I decided it would be best if she never found out.

I turned and stepped to the door and stood looking out through the screen. Connally was coming through the front gate. As usual, he didn't look happy to see me.

Chapter 46

I never saw Frank Coyne after that. The shootout made the morning news and my allegiances were made obvious by several inaccurate attempts by 'live at the scene' reporters and in follow-up 'breaking news' segments to guess which branch of law enforcement I worked for. I got police protection 24/7 for a couple weeks, then it dwindled down to a patrol car cruise-by once or twice a day. If they found me outside, they'd stop and say hello and tell me to put my dog on a leash.

The Coyne family name stayed in the local headlines for some time. Only their various mouthpieces gave interviews, the usual pablum about their clients' complete innocence and future exoneration. Two reporters at the *Rocky* fanned the flames for several weeks with 'investigative' stories on the Coyne family operation. They put a conspiratorial spin on matters of public record that no one found interesting a few months ago: the impressive amounts of money taken in annually, the non-profit tax status (which they likened, unironically, to religious exemption), the multiple corporate veils, the low-rent leases and the surprising number of unpaid volunteers. The exposé angle deepened with an ever-expanding list of Coyne family associates, past and present, which included other cops and ex-cops well beyond Joe Perkins and Chuck Burrows, a few city councilmen, a state senator, the mayor's wife, and at least one high-level monsignor, not to mention the plethora of minor players who 'have had run-ins with the law'. Many of the articles were laced with cocky quotations from past interviews given by Frank Coyne who, at that time, thought he had the media tiger by the tail.

Rhonda Schomberg made the news too, of course, but her status soon faded, likely due to her inaccessibility for an interview—and perhaps that seldom acknowledged cultural ethic that restrains even the predatory press from defaming the dead. She did become a repeating footnote in the politically charged series of stories about Secretary of State Marcia Herrera. Local pundits got a lot of mileage out of the supposed betrayal of the public trust—by an elected official, no less—as if this was the first time an election was bought and paid for by special interests. As is often the case, popular opinion, especially when fueled by inflammatory headlines, carries more weight than election results—eventually. Once the public 'consciousness' was turned against her, the governor felt compelled (he called it 'obligated') in appointing a special prosecutor to audit the workings of her office. In an attempt to stave off the dogs, she announced her intention not to run for reelection. That just made her sound guilty. Two months later she resigned altogether and the governor put his own man in her place. Various indictments were handed down just after New Year's. The lawyers feasted.

Tanya Gilmore was out and about three days after the shooting and, according to the press, was under a doctor's care 24/7. The investigation into her involvement, once it got tangled up by a slew of lawyers with greater clout and savvy than Stanley Riggs—not to mention a battery of psychiatrists—has been long and drawn out. With the dead woman taking the rap for the two homicides, nobody except Connally showed much interest in making Tanya an accomplice. But he can be a tenacious son of a bitch, so we'll see what happens. She did get some sympathetic press for saving my life, something that might play well in a plea bargain down the road—if forensics findings don't come in to play. She got one shot off, hitting Rhonda in the shoulder. McQuitty fired five times, hitting her twice in the chest, once in the back as she fell. No doubt.

The Colorado Bureau of Investigation has been all over the Coyne family, with old man Willard at the top of their list. On the basis of the tally sheets I had 'liberated' from the ledger at Five Aces Bingo, they undertook to investigate 'the infiltration of the bingo industry by organized crime.' Frank hired a PR firm to run interference. Well before CBI made any headway, the state legislature presented several bills regarding the regulation of bingo in our fair state. Without Rhonda Schomberg around to grease the palms—or murder the opposition—there was rare bipartisan support.

Regarding Tanya's involvement with R. D. Spencer, the DEA took up where we left off, although they weren't particularly interested in keeping us informed. They did, however, brag about their successes, even if it was Connally who set it up for them. Connally had Benny Palmer picked up on the night of the shooting on the basis of what he got out of Tanya before she lawyered up. He kept him canned for the full seventy-two hours, giving the Feds time and impetus to get a warrant to search his digs in Cheyenne. When Benny was finally released, he bee-lined to his warehouse to clear the evidence, and the Feds were there to greet him—holding the bag, so to speak. Possession of a controlled substance, possession with intent, conspiracy, interstate distribution. They got the Wyoming state tax boys in on it too. Word was he did all he could to sell out Spencer, the Flood brothers, and half a dozen other mid-range peddlers, but he still looks to do hard time. So far no one has sprung for his two-million dollar bail.

What I did hear that made me smile came from the criminal division of the IRS. In the wake of all the public scrutiny, they set up a local task force of eight in a regional office to investigate the entire bingo and raffle industry and the filings of all related corporate and personal interests going back several years. Talk about dogged. And the first person they reached out to for background was James Reivers, the previous investigator for the secretary of state, whose firing had indirectly instigated our investigation. Not long after that, Reivers got reinstated under the new secretary of state—and he got eighteen months back pay. Eventually he even thanked me.

My career took a bounce in other ways. Detective Harris of the Aurora PD saw fit to drop all charges once Connally cleared Mickey's homicide for him—with my help. I do the speed limit out there, just the same. And Luis got me in good again with District Attorney Barnes. We had a meet, the three of us. Barnes didn't ask me anything he didn't already know.

He commended my work and told me the governor knew about it. Maybe they'd use me again sometime.

Yeah, sure.

But I did get paid. Willie too. He got five hundred dollars for playing bingo, etc. Flush with our success, he was all over me again to start that detective agency we'd talked about. *He'd* talked about, I reminded him. Randall & Burkhart, he persisted. Okay, okay, Burkhart & Randall. I told him to keep his day job for the time being and, with Duncan's permission, he has.

Contrary—in a way—to what you might expect from all the negative publicity, popular interest in bingo surged. It was all the rage to claim to be a longstanding fan of the game. It didn't take long for Frank Coyne to catch the drift. When the Bellevue Shopping Center finally re-opened, Bingo Palace had yet another grand opening and they packed them in for several weeks thereafter. Eddie Lyons, Claire's ex, was running it in my stead. He was an often-quoted source of color and insight, a natural front man with a likeable voice, little of substance to say, and a catchy, down-home way of saying it. The halls were busier than ever, he said. Good family fun. They were glad the industry was getting cleaned up. It was the out-of-staters that were ruining it for everyone.

After the news coverage died down, I called Claire. I left messages about once a week for two months, but she never returned my calls. Finally, I got the nerve to call her parents. Her mother answered the phone.

"Yes, of course I remember you. You're that nice young man who lied to everyone."

"Well, it's nice to be remembered," I said.

Surprisingly, she laughed. "I suppose you want to talk to Claire? Explain everything to her? Something like that?"

"Yeah, I guess."

"That's what Claire thought. You just don't get it, do you?"

She paused as if that wasn't a rhetorical question.

"Well, I..."

"What you don't see is what it means to her. To us."

I decided I was meant to listen.

"I'm sorry if I seem too blunt, Mr. Burkhart, but I don't think I owe you any courtesy in explaining our…feelings. Nor does Claire."

She waited for me to make my exit or take a stand.

"I'll take it however I can, Mrs. Gilmore," I said, shifting the phone from under my chin to the more stable grip of my right hand.

"Okay, then. I'll tell you so Claire doesn't have to. We know you're supposed to be the good guy, Mr. Burkhart. Fighting corruption, chasing the bad guys, bringing to justice all those hoodlums in this stupid *bingo mafia*."

I found it impossible to hold back. "I found Mickey's killer."

"Yes, we're aware of that. And in some ways we're grateful. But it's not that simple, is it?"

"No, of course not."

"Claire lost her brother, Mr. Burkhart, and she lost the father of her child. And Shanie lost her father. Even if she hardly knew him, now she never will. Do you think it matters to them who broke what laws, who stole the money, who didn't pay their taxes? I can tell you, we didn't like Brent Charmichael from the start, and we didn't ever like the Coyne family. We knew how they made their living. We knew it was tinged. *Shady*. Is that a good word for it? Shady?"

"As good as any."

"We did what we could to discourage them but our children were grown, they had their own lives. We all have to make our own mistakes, don't we? People do what they're going to do. And then you deal with it the best you can. You learn to accept it. I don't mean that comes easy." Her tone descended, her last words choked off. When she continued, her voice had lost some of its vehemence.

"Things happened here," she said, "with Mickey and with Brent. And with you. I don't blame you and neither does Claire. Those boys have always been trouble. Brent was weak…*flawed* somehow. Even Claire knew that eventually. And you…well, I guess you were just doing your job. But people got hurt, people who didn't deserve it. No one deserved to *die*. And it doesn't matter to us what the reasons were."

I waited, absorbing her words, feeling the hurt, and knowing it wasn't mine.

"I *am* sorry," I said, after a moment.

"Yes, thanks for saying that. Maybe you are. But you have to see that for us you are woven into all this…this…the *tragedy* of it. Forgive and forget? Simple words for a very long and trying process. How does one forget? How do you forget the one thing and not the other? And forgiveness? Well, I thought I was something of a Christian before all this happened but now, I don't know. Perhaps now I am becoming one. I'm not there yet, that's for sure. And neither is Claire."

She fell silent and the silence lingered between us, expanding on the momentum of her words, stretching to encompass the scale and meaning of such fugitive emotions.

I said, "I think I understand a little better, Mrs. Gilmore. I just want to say, I liked Mickey and I'm sorry about what happened. I won't bother you again. And you can tell Claire…" I hesitated, not knowing what I could say. "Just tell her we talked," I said finally.

"I'll do that, Mr. Burkhart." But she didn't hang up. And then she said, "And thank you for listening."

The End

Made in the USA
Columbia, SC
30 June 2019